From the Dark to the Dawn

From the Dark to the Dawn:

A Tale of Ancient Rome

Alicia A. Willis

Seasons of His-Story Publishing

"Alicia Willis transports readers back to the troubled clash between the crushing might of Imperial Rome and the vengeful determination of the Celtic occupants of ancient Britain. *From the Dark to the Dawn: A Tale of Ancient Rome* will delight readers of historical fiction."
-DOUGLAS BOND, author of *Hostage Lands*, *Hand of Vengeance,* and many other books of historical fiction and non-fiction.

"A well-crafted tale set in a fascinating epoch. Alicia Willis delves far deeper than the "guts and glory" stories that many write about Rome and gets you into the brains of her characters. Her meticulous research is obvious, and the story itself is God-glorifying, entertaining, heartwarming, and heart-wrenching. Well done!"
-JOHN J. HORN, author of the *Men of Grit* series.

"Alicia Willis sketches a stirring tale that delivers a powerful message of friendship, forgiveness, and God's grace. An authentic period piece, it leaves you with a greater awareness that God's ways are higher than our ways and we are on this earth for His purposes. Anyone with a bend toward historical fiction will thoroughly enjoy this book. Definitely a moving, worthwhile, and edifying read!"
-JOSIAH JOST, *actor/writer with Jostie Flicks.*

"*From the Dark to the Dawn* is a remarkable tale of Christianity in the midst of oppressive Ancient Rome. Alive with historical detail, action, and vivid descriptions, it presents the life-changing power of God's love and forgiveness in a way that will strengthen your faith, encourage, and inspire you."
-CAITLIN HEDGCOCK, author of the *Baker Family Adventures* series.

"*From the Dark to the Dawn* is a thrilling tale of friendship, persecution, and redemption. Alicia Willis skillfully portrays, with unfeigned accuracy, what it may have been like to be a Christian living under the rule of an oppressive Roman Emperor. The relationships she establishes between her characters are palpably real. Historically authentic and doctrinally precise, this book will have you swiftly turning pages as the author takes you through a time fraught with war, injustice, fear, and persecution, but also where God's sovereignty, grace, and mercy are fully evident. Another outstanding book!"
–JEANNE DRENNAN, freelance writer and author.

"*From the Dark to the Dawn* encouraged me in my own walk with God and touched my heart deeply. It is not easy to read, but hard to put down. Emotionally difficult, yet inspiring. It is a book the reaches down into the depths of pain and climbs to the heights of joy. It is a book that pulls the reader closer to the heart of God."
-SARAH HOLMAN, author.

"Alicia Willis' *From the Dark to the Dawn* is an incredibly well written book, built on the Biblical principal of forgiveness, shows us the power of a man willing to give God what little he has and forgive his tormentors. This book will surely go down in history sitting beside *Pilgrims Progress.* My only disappointment was reaching the end. This book wouldn't let me go! Every page demands you read the next. Alicia Willis expertly weaves a story of suspense, love, and action into an amazingly fun read that will keep you coming back. This is historical fiction at its finest. I highly recommend it to any young teen or adult looking for a good read!"
-MICHAEL CAMP, reader and representative of Victory Baptist Church.

In the dark turbulence of ancient Rome, a rebellious Iceni captive meets his match in his Roman master. When Christianity enters the picture, the clash of race and rank is intensified as Philip seeks to win his master to the Lord and survive the terrors of persecution under Nero. A tale of faith, persecution, redemption, and romance.

Seasons of His-Story Publishing

Other Titles by Alicia A. Willis

The Comrades of Honor Series:

To Birmingham Castle

In Search of Adventure

Rising to the Challenge

Novellas:

God of Her Fathers

Remembering the Alamo

To my sister Lydia.

Thank you for the enthusiasm you have always portrayed for this story. You are the best sister anyone could ever have. I love you!

And to Joshua Hoppman.

Thank you for your friendship! You have always been such a support to me in my writing endeavors.

God bless!

Contents

Introduction

I cannot say writing *From the Dark to the Dawn* was easy. Truth be told, completing the story was one of the greatest ordeals—and blessings—I have ever undergone. To me, this is so much more than a story of an ancient land. In some ways, it is a mirror of our own lives today.

We as a people, in whatever country we call our home, are very comparable to ancient Rome. There is no debate in saying we face many similarities in our problems. In Ecclesiastes, Solomon tells us there is nothing new under the sun. If we traveled back, I think our cultural and personal problems of today could find correlation in what our Christian brethren experienced in decadent Rome.

Only, we have it so much easier.

Yes, we face temptation. We experience the darkness of the world. It grieves us to see sin abound, even as it did in Rome. In our own way, we too abandon and murder children, participate in forms of slavery, and substitute the gladiatorial games with violent videos. It is in those aspects that we are similar.

But, solely by God's grace, our culture has not *yet* reached the pinnacle of corruption Rome saw in her time. When considering the extreme immorality that governed nearly every individual, I think we are blessed. We are not culturally obligated to commit fornication, to worship false gods of sensuality, revelry, and war. Our culture has not embraced the morally degrading practice of human slavery.

And I think few of us really know what it means to suffer persecution for Jesus.

Yes, we are scorned, our liberties curtailed, our standards mocked. But few of us have truly faced persecution. When was the last time you saw your pastor covered in oily pitch and burned at the stake? Your children thrown into an arena and fed to starving lions? When did you have to huddle in the dark when you met with your brethren and whisper the hymns to keep from being overheard?

For that matter, when was the last time we went to church? Our brethren risked their *lives* to meet; we complain about the length of a sermon or meeting for a midweek service. We are so blessed.

I learned so much in writing this book. Many of the prayers expressed through the characters you are about to meet were my own. So were some of the temptations. Perhaps not in the same way, but in many similarities. Through God's grace, I have learned the importance of serving Him because I love Him – not to be rewarded. I have learned *nothing* will separate me from His love. He has taught me about forgiveness, about trusting His strength when all hope seems gone.

And now I pass these things onto you.

This book is historical-fiction, not a sermon. But I think we can learn so much through a story, particularly one that really could have happened and is completely accurate in its portrayal of the era. Through the story of the characters, I hope you will be blessed and uplifted in your Christian walk.

Taking a brief digression, allow me to say that every effort has been made to ensure historical accuracy. Years were spent in research, and I had the fantastic assistance of some very wonderful historians and teachers. Among them were Guy de la Bedoyere, David Potter, and John Yates, to each of whom I express my thanks.

Additionally, allow me to say that the customs, views, and expressions used throughout the book are modes of the time period, some of which cannot be considered the personal or religious views of the author.

May God bless each of you as you experience the darkness of the world and the new dawn only He can bring about in the lives of a lost, hurting world. *Ad maioram De gloriam*, to the greater glory of God.

-Alicia A. Willis

Part I

The people that walked in darkness
have seen a great light: they that dwell in the land of
the shadow of death, upon them hath
the light shined.

~Isaiah 9:2

Chapter One

61 Anno Domini
British Isles

Philip crouched in the tall grass, his heels poised to spring. His pulse raced, pounding against his chest. The smell of smoke and death was gagging. All around him, carnage and the bodies of thousands of his tribesmen were haunting reminders of yesterday's battle.

Indistinct shouts sent chills running up and down his spine. The Roman legionaries ran like red ants through the plain and glades, plundering, capturing, killing. Massacre was still in their blood.

They would kill him if they found him. Or, worse still, they would enslave him.

Philip peered through the grass. The sun glistened off of thousands of pieces of armor and weapons, half-blinding him. Many of the weapons had been stolen from the Romans themselves. Now, their fallen glimmer was a mocking reminder of what they had lost.

They had failed. His people lay dead in the thousands.

Philip's heart lurched as a legionary ran in front of his hiding place. He stumbled over a longsword, evoking a short chuckle from his comrades. The sight, trivial as it was, was a small consolation. The longswords of the Iceni had been no match for the Roman *gladius*. Short and efficient, the Romans had killed thousands of them with it. But at least it had played a small part in humiliating one of them.

His mind felt numb. It relived the events of yesterday, torturing him. How could this have happened? Their queen had been so certain.

On the rise of dawn, Queen Boudicca's chariot had ridden past their lines. Her stern voice had echoed across the plain, a haunting pre-battle speech.

"I am avenging my lost freedom, my scourged body, the outraged chastity of my daughters," she had said. Her flashing eyes and flying red hair added fierce weight to her words. "Heaven is on the side of a righteous vengeance. You will see that it is in this battle you must conquer or die!"

It had been a prophetic speech.

At the first charge, thousands of Iceni were killed by the Roman's javelins. The scene repeated itself on the second charge. And, when their angry fighting spirit had been torn from them and total disarray wrecked their lines, General Suetonius had pushed his auxiliaries forward in small units. The entire Iceni army had been surrounded.

The butchery had quickly turned into a massacre.

Philip shut his eyes, trying to wash out the horrifying images replaying in his mind. They had been so sure of victory. The Druid priests had assured Boudicca the forest gods were on their side, that they were right to stand against the lust of Rome. They would rule the world.

And, for a short time, it seemed the gods favored them. The Roman settlements Camulodunium, Londinium, and Verulamium had already fallen. Why shouldn't all of Briton be reclaimed from the Romans?

Victory was so certain the Iceni had brought their women and children with them. After all, they had three times as many soldiers as Suetonius. The Roman army was so inferior that the general could not even stretch his line of legionaries to meet their massive Iceni line, even at one soldier deep.

Beric, his own father, had brought his wife and two daughters along. He had left them with the other women and children along the ring of wagons and animals. And, up until the very last minute, Philip had begged him to not leave him with the women.

"I am a warrior, father! Not a child. Let me fight alongside you. Let me prove my loyalty to our queen and you."

But Beric's mind had been firmly made. At thirteen years of age, Philip was no match for a tough Roman legionary. Philip recalled his firm voice, the slight brush of his hand upon his bare shoulder.

"No, my son. We have warriors enough. Stand and watch the defeat of Rome. The legions have nothing to gain but our enslavement. We are fighting for freedom, for justice. Let the fall of their eagles show you what a proud thing it is to be a Briton!"

Philip felt a returning smart of resentment in his throat. The eagles had not fallen. The frenzied Britons had been slaughtered. And if his father had let him fight, he would not have lived to witness the deaths of thousands of his countrymen. *I would not have seen my family die.*

When the Roman auxiliaries had closed in around the Iceni, their cavalry had not spared the wagon ring harboring the women and children. Enraged by the Briton's revolt against their mighty empire, they massacred them. The terrified screams of his mother and sisters were memories Philip knew he would never forget.

He himself had barely escaped the thrusting *gladius* of a young centurion. Dodging the armor-clad monsters riding all over the field, he had somehow escaped into a wooded hollow. There, the agonized screams and scent of smoke had encompassed his senses in a night of terror.

Now, his keen eyes flitted over the battlefield. The legionaries were everywhere. He did not dare move. The slightest movement in the grassy sea of dead would attract the attention of the Romans.

An abrupt shout jerked his body. His heart lurched, pounding wildly.

Only a few dozen paces away, a group of hiding Iceni warriors were discovered. Their turbulent shouts were a typical act of chilling battle psychology. It had always worked before to frighten the legionaries out of their senses.

Not anymore.

Philip watched the Iceni run for their lives. The Roman legionaries chased them with the vigor of huntsmen. Several raised their javelins, their arms powerful beneath the flexible armor.

Great gods! Philip's mind screamed out. Before his eyes, three Iceni fell prey to their hunters. Would the carnage never end? His heart throbbed, sickened. *Why have you deserted us? Your priests, your people were slaughtered. Our queen was shamed. Why? Our cause was just!*

A touch lighted on his shoulder.

Philip's hand fell on his dagger. He jerked around, nearly choked with fear. The embarrassing reality of his own foolishness immediately rolled over him. No legionary would touch him gently.

"Philip."

"Father!" Philip half-rose. Shock seized hold of his body. He had not dared to hope his strong chieftain father had survived the butchery of the battle. But, evidently, his father was alive and well.

"Be still." Beric raised a stern hand of warning. He crouched beside him in the thick grass. Beyond him, Philip could make out several of their clansmen hiding in scattered assemblage in the undergrowth. "We are being sought."

Philip's eyes roved over his father's muscular body. Stripped to the waist, his broad chest was cut and streaked with dried blood. Dirt and smoke stained his face. Blue battle-tattoos still covered him, painted in ornate geometric designs. Even his deep cerulean eyes were lined with circular patterns. The paint was thought to hold medicinal powers from the gods.

The thought was an aching pang. *When did we lose your favor?*

Philip knew he should remain silent. But the burning question had been on the tip of his tongue too long. "Our queen?"

7

Beric's mouth tightened, deepening the weary lines around his eyes. "Dead."

Philip's stomach lurched. All of their hopes and dreams had been centered on Boudicca. "How?" His voice cracked. "Was she taken prisoner?"

"No. The Roman dogs would have spared her to grace Suetonius's victory parade." Beric spat into the dust as he said the general's name. "She and her daughters took poison yesterday. Those with her followed her example."

The news was less than surprising to Philip. It was only honorable for Boudicca to end her life after such a loss. Any leader would have done the same. But, his stomach sickened even still. *The future of the Iceni is dead.*

Beric seemed to sense his thoughts. "The gods have deserted us. We live to serve Rome."

"No!" Philip ground his teeth, his hands clenching into angry fists. "I will never serve them–the swine! They are merciless, unfair. Is it the fault of the Iceni that their gods were stronger?"

Beric glanced sidelong at him. "Then you better take poison with your queen. It is only a matter of time before they find us. And then will kill or enslave us." His voice grew weary. "For myself, I no longer care. Either end is more merciful than living to see the demise of our people."

"Then we must live." Philip felt the blood tingle in his cheeks. His heart throbbed. He could feel the pain and anger rolling like fire through his veins. "We must live to revenge ourselves, our people! Our gods will restore their favor. You will see–"

A bloodcurdling yell cut him short.

"Great gods!" Beric leaped to his feet, ripping his sword from its sheath. A dozen Romans burst through the underbrush, their *gladii* protruding on the sides of their scarlet shields. The Iceni clansmen scrambled to their feet and brandished their weapons, but it was a halfhearted attempt.

Their fighting spirit was gone.

Philip's heard thudded. A glance in every direction revealed the hopelessness of their situation. They were completely surrounded.

He felt sick and faint. So this was the end. Resentment against the gods boiled up within him. Why had they allowed him to survive this long only to desert him? *Take me quickly*. His fingers groped to the hilt of his dagger, drawing it out. He would die fighting.

"Halt!" The Roman commander shouted a quick order. The legionaries paused in fighting stance, their muscular legs taut and ready to spring. Philip could feel the fiery gaze of a young soldier rest upon him. His nausea doubled, realizing he was the legionary's target.

The centurion's steely gaze seemed to encompass the Iceni. "Throw down your arms." His speech was a confusing blend of Latin and Iceni words, but his meaning was clear. "Our orders are to end all resistance. Surrender and save your lives."

The clansmen looked to Beric. Philip could see the muscles in his father's back grow rigid. The weight of the choice could be felt in the very atmosphere. Should they surrender or die?

The tension snapped. Beric threw his longsword into the grass. Yanking his knife from his belt, he allowed it to fall from his hands, landing with the clang of steel on steel at his feet.

The others followed his example. Satisfied, the centurion grunted an order. "Bind them."

Half of the legionaries threw their shields down and ran forward, leaving the rest of the soldiers to stand guard. Roughly, they herded the Iceni into a circle and began tying their hands behind their backs.

Philip alone gripped his dagger. How could he surrender peaceably to these Romans, these monsters who had killed so many of his people? His eyes fell on his father. Beric submitted quietly to his captors, but his lowered head spoke volumes. How quickly the smell of victory had turned into the shame of slavery.

Run! Adrenaline coursed through Philip's body. His father chose slavery. He did *not*. Better to run, to take the chance of instant death than surrender. He turned, his legs pumping beneath him.

A strong hand landed on his shoulder. "Throw down your arms!"

Philip twisted and kicked, his arms flailing. He heard the warrior cry scream from his throat, cracking his voice. He clenched his dagger, raising it, feeling the perspiration seep between his fingers.

It was knocked easily from his hand.

Philip struggled to break the grip of the legionary. He knew it was a futile attempt. The young man had muscles every bit as large as his father and was at least a decade younger. Still, it was not until the legionary slapped him that he stood still, panting.

The legionary held him by the arms. His laugh grated on Philip's ears. "They train them young. What a spirited little wretch!"

"Well, bind him and put him with the others." The centurion snapped at him. "We've got other Iceni to flush out, you know."

The legionary's grip tightened around Philip's wrists. Forcefully, he began dragging him through the thick undergrowth towards the others. "Come on, you barbaric dog."

Fierce rebellion swept through Philip. Everything about the legionary's mocking tone, his inexorable hold filled him with fury. Before he could think about what he was doing, he kicked his captor below the waist.

The legionary doubled over. "Great Pollux!" His muffled exclamation was rent with agony. Philip watched in satisfaction, the laughter of his tribesmen coloring his cheeks. *Take that, you Roman dog.*

Scarlet with pain and fury, the legionary straightened himself. Snatching his sword from its sheath, he raised it over Philip's head.

Philip's mind whirled, his body paralyzed by fear. It was one thing to die fighting, with battle adrenaline pumping through his veins. It was another to perish in cold blood. The blade glistened in the sunlight, then, paused at the centurion's shout.

"Enough, Owen! Suetonius wants strong young captives, not old men. This boy's spirit alone is worth keeping him alive for. Give him a lesson, if you wish, then put him with the others."

The Latin words were a blur to Philip's ears. It wasn't long before he understood the centurion's meaning, however. Owen, as he was called, had a gleam in his eyes that was all too recognizable. Still holding Philip by the arm, he stooped to pick up a fallen switch.

Its quick sting across his bare shoulders revealed all too well the satisfaction it gave his antagonist to inflict the pain.

Philip cringed. He clamped his mouth shut, feeling the blood boil in his face and neck. Just another sample of so-called Roman justice. Burning, pillaging, killing, beating. They crushed anyone who even thought of rebelling against their tyranny.

A second stroke burned his back, smarting.

Its fire was a quick spark to self-defense. Philip twisted, again screaming out the war cry. *Don't submit. Fight!* No matter what the pain, he would never dishonor his people by obeying these Roman brutes. *Suffer fighting!*

Somewhere, in the blood-red haze fogging his senses, he heard the laughter of the other legionaries. Obviously, watching his angry struggle was amusing. Stung to fury, he recoiled, clawing and biting. Owen's grip tightened, hitting him again and again.

Nausea settled in the pit of Philip's stomach. He felt the strength being sapped from his body with each stroke. Desperately, he struggled to keep fighting, but the smarting pain was too intense. His body went limp.

The blows stopped. Philip knew it was not the legionary's mercy which spared him, but the desire to keep him healthy. The inconvenience of a captive who was unable to walk was too burdensome.

Philip collapsed in the grass. Sick from pain and shame, he retched violently. Owen didn't pause to let him rest. Philip felt his

11

arms pulled behind him. A rough cord bit into his wrists, tying them together.

"Get up!"

Philip stumbled to his feet. Owen shoved him towards the others. Fighting to keep his balance, Philip blinked back the blur impeding his vision.

A swift glance revealed Beric watching him. His face was grave, his eyes quietly sorrowful. Again, the shame of their situation smote Philip. Not only were they captives, but the son of an Iceni chieftain had been publicly beaten. Would their disgrace never end?

Owen slapped him into line. Philip could sense his anger was still livid as he tied him with the others. Willing his glare to utter his own bitter resentment, he raised his eyes for one fiery instant, his lips forming an unspoken insult.

Roman cur!

Owen's smoldering gaze met his, and Philip saw his hand clench. He knew he fairly itched to slap him again. Thankfully, he obviously decided his young captive had had enough punishment for one day. He turned away.

Philip spat in his direction as soon as he turned. Behind his back, he doubled his hands into fists. He would not die, he decided. He would live to tell his story to generations of Iceni warriors. His strength would inspire children; his brutal power would be told around their fires.

He inched closer to his father. However low, he knew his words reached Beric's ears. "The gods be my witness, I will return. I will end this tyranny! And the story of Rome's destruction will be a tale for *centuries*."

Chapter Two

61 Anno Domini–Several Months Later
City of Rome

A cool, refreshing breeze rustled the clear waters of the sparkling fountain playing in the large *peristylium* of a vast *domus*, situated in the section of Rome set apart for the noble classes. The leaves and blooms of countless fragrant blossoms rustled upon the currents of air, carrying their delicate scent to every corner of the garden.

Eighteen year-old Marcus Virginius sat on an elaborately carved bench, an open scroll in his hand. Try as he might, he couldn't concentrate. The works of Plato were strangely meaningless.

Forget him. Marcus's throat tightened without warning. He looked down, clenching the scroll between his strong fingers. *You are now the heir.*

His mind flitted back to two weeks ago, when a military official had arrived at the Virginius domus. His father Rowland had greeted the man with stern resolve. Somehow, they had all sensed the purpose behind the official's visit.

And they had been correct.

Legionary Owen Virginius, the eldest son and heir, had been killed in Brittania. Few details were known, but it was reported he had been murdered in an uprising among the captives. The strangeness of it was that he alone had been singled out. The officer made some mention of Owen having beaten a captive. Apparently, the prisoner had been the son of a chieftain.

And the Iceni had had their revenge.

British curs. Marcus's heart swelled. He was a man, too old for tears. But nothing could stop the aching loss he felt.

Owen had been everything to him. He had been strong, masterful, a proud Roman and good soldier. Among their noble *patrician* friends, he had been called a son of sons. But it had only taken a single flash of British rebellion for Mars to claim his life.

Marcus laid his scroll on the bench beside him. It was better not to think of what had happened to Owen. Better to focus on the life that must go on, on the position that was now his as the oldest son of a wealthy patrician.

A slave approached. Silently, he laid fruit and wine out. Marcus waved his hand at him. The slave quickly bowed and retreated, his eyes lowered in humble subservience.

Marcus aimlessly plucked a grape, rolling it between his fingers. He knew his presence was intimidating to the slaves. His friends told him a single glance of his dark eyes could crush rebellion like a stroke of the rod. They said his presence itself was masterful, authoritative by nature.

Owen would have been proud. It had been he who had first taught him how to deal with slaves. As boys, Marcus had been soft, unable to watch scourging without cringing. Owen had taunted him into hardening himself. Now, the passing years had given him a charisma of authority the Caesars themselves would be glad to wield over their subjects.

Marcus stood up. The day was warm, stifling. He straightened his white toga, thinking back to the happy boyhood days when he had not been burdened with the garments of Roman manhood. *Blessed youth.*

The sound of a step behind him brought him to the present moment.

"Wasting your time in the gardens? Great Jupiter, I will never understand your indolence, Marcus."

Marcus stiffened. The haughty coldness of his father's voice jarred his senses. Controlling his rising irritation, he met Rowland's gaze with quiet deference. "Surely, it is not indolence to mourn the dead, father."

14

Rowland moved nearer. "Mourn the dead?"

His face softened momentarily, then again hardened. Marcus knew he controlled his true feelings under typical Roman callousness. The power of the gods must not be questioned, no matter what their decision concerning his eldest son. His scornful voice grew cutting.

"So you sit mourning the dead like a *woman*. Is that what defines you, Marcus? Your brother was strong, a warrior of Rome. He would have accepted the will of the gods, not whimper like a babe in arms."

Marcus lifted his chin. He could feel the simmering indignation flash in his eyes. "I have neither whimpered nor cried, father. And you know I do not question the judgment of Mars. It is only..." His voice caught unexpectedly. Fiercely, he fought his rising emotion. *Get a grip on yourself.* "I only regret his loss. I know I can never be the son he was to you."

Silence hung over the air.

Marcus inhaled deeply. Rowland's brusque mannerism irked him to no end, but he forced himself to lower his tones. There was sorrow enough without additional conflict. "Let us not speak of Owen, father. His name alone is painful. And, as you say, we will leave the mourning to the women."

Again, Rowland's hard face softened slightly. "Agreed, Marcus. I am too busy for talk as it is. Go to the Baths or out with your friends—anything more profitable than being shut up in the garden."

Marcus half-bowed. His father's pointed disregard for his own inclinations was grating, but he resolved to submit. "As you say. I will return soon."

Swiftly, he strode from the garden, crossing the veranda into the spacious atrium. The steward was speaking with a house slave, but he turned as Marcus approached, offering him a low bow.

"My lord Marcus."

Marcus paused before him. "You are precisely the man I wished to meet, Demetrius. I am going out and want you to meet me in the forum in an hour."

"Yes, my lord. Where will you be?"

"Perhaps by the auction block." Marcus shifted. His irritation was already melting under the steward's quiet respectfulness. *Little wonder he rose so quickly in the ranks of slavery.* "They say a fresh lot of British slaves have been brought in. I've a mind to see them. At any rate, I may need you."

"As you say, my honored lord."

Marcus waved aside the steward's respectful bow. He strode across the atrium to the entry. Pausing only to allow the slave who kept the heavy gilt door to swing it wide, he stepped out into the warm, humid sunshine.

Outside, just beyond the domus, the *Vicus Tuscus* bustled with activity. Marcus stepped into the busy street, brushing shoulders with one or more hastily-striding plebians. The air was full of mingled shouts and lively chatter, a din of Greek and Latin tongues.

Marcus felt the lively atmosphere steadily easing his strained nerves. It was a relief he gladly welcomed. His father was never an easy one to get along with, and Owen's death had doubled his stern austerity. Not, he told himself, that he could blame him. For himself, he wished he too could harden himself against the cutting pain of their loss.

But, he could not. As he passed a colossal statue, his heart gripped with a familiar pang. He turned away, but it was too late. *Mars.* The god of war that he and Owen had worshipped together since their early childhood. Owen had become a soldier first, pledging himself to the service of Rome and the worship of Mars.

And, where one would have thought him blessed, Mars had let Owen die.

Enough. Marcus rebuked himself, realizing the bent of his thoughts. *Mars is my patron. I will not question him.* Still, he had to wonder if his self-chidings would ever truly satisfy his grief-stricken desire to know why.

Partially to divert his thoughts, he quickened his pace. Perhaps the bustle of activity, the unrivaled splendor of the Imperial Forum would stir his Roman blood to its old vigor. His strong legs pumped beneath him, his sandals slapping against the cobblestoned street.

As it rose up before him, the forum was indeed an invigorating sight. The hum of busy shoppers filled the air. Market stall traders loudly shouted the worthiness of their goods; slave masters boasted on the traits of their human wares. Wild and colorful, the atmosphere was exactly what Marcus had hoped would revive him.

This is what Owen died for. For Rome's glory, her people, her Republic. Perhaps no soldier could have asked for a more glorious end.

"A melon, noble patrician? They are sweet and crisp, I assure you!"

Marcus gestured impatiently. Great gods, but these forum peddlers grated on his nerves. He strode carelessly from one booth to another, glancing over the wares. Nothing he saw tempted his appetite.

"A pastry, sir? They are filled with the best dates. Do you not desire–"

"Enough." Marcus snapped at him. He played with the corners of his money pouch with complacency he knew must be fairly maddening to the peddler. The pastries did look appealing, the first food that had attracted him. At last, he tossed the man a coin. "Give me one."

Bowing and scraping, the peddler gave him his purchase. "The gods be with you, my patron."

"And with you." Marcus took the pastry with dry apathy. Biting into it, he savored its delicate sweetness before sauntering on his way.

Not far away, in the center of the forum, Marcus could see the slave podium. An auctioneer was mounted atop it, his singsong voice carrying over the busy clatter of tongues. A large crowd of buyers, mostly men, were gathered around the podium, surveying the proceedings with apparent interest.

Their amusement attracted Marcus. In his current state of mind, diversion in any form was welcome.

He quickened into a brisker pace, joining the compact spectators around the ring. On the outskirts, he settled his shoulders and made a little cough. As he expected, the lower classes glanced his way. Seeing his toga and obvious rank, they immediately cleared a path for him. Casually nodding, Marcus strode through their midst and procured a position within good view of the scaffold.

From there, he surveyed the shackled slaves. They stood in a dejected line, awaiting their turn to be sold with dull apathy. Their number was overwhelming, but he knew the slave business well. Only the young, strong, or beautiful. All others could be sent to the arena, for all their worth.

The majority of the slaves were blonde-haired and blue-eyed. *Iceni brutes.* Marcus felt a tinge of anger. Still, his interest grew. The British barbarians were certainly well-built, to say nothing of their good looks. Few, if any, Romans could boast such dazzling hair colors and fair skin.

His eyes flitted along the line of captives, making mental notes of their qualifications. Near the center of the line, his eyes stopped. If he knew slaves, he had found the prize of the entire lot. The captive was a young Briton, quite possibly no more than thirteen years of age.

Marcus knit his brows. The boy was young, but his other qualities more than made up for that shortcoming. Like all of the Iceni, he was tall and strapping, taut muscles protruding from his biceps and legs. He was attired in a short kilt, clearly designed to show his muscular physique to better advantage. But strength was not his only selling points. He was also strikingly good-looking.

18

Thick, wavy blonde hair covered his head, complimenting his cerulean blue eyes.

On all sides, fellow buyers were pointing out the qualifications of the young captive. He had already attracted more than his share of attention. The bidding would be intense.

Marcus felt a tinge of competitiveness. Slave auctions could be fierce. And there was nothing he enjoyed more than a little serious competition, a war of wits and gold. The young Briton was worth buying if only to prove that he could.

Sidelong, he noticed a legionary also studying the boy. Partially to test the waters, he gestured in his direction. "There is a hearty brute if I ever saw one. By the gods! What a profit I could turn over with muscles like those."

"You mean the lad?" The legionary did not shift his gaze. "If so, you have a good eye for slaves, patrician. Provided you can put up with some obstinacy, these Iceni captives are said to make the best attendants."

"You mean to buy him?"

The legionary turned. A sardonic smile played about his lips. "Provided the gods do not favor you more, friend. I know the gold dances in your purse."

Marcus laughed good-naturedly. "I like to know my competition, friend."

"And you will have plenty of it." The legionary struck his chest with a broad hand. "I do not give up easily. And a third of the men here have their eye on the boy."

Marcus made no attempt to hide his amusement. *Infernal braggart.* The Praetorian legionaries were paid higher than standard soldiers, but with a yearly salary of three hundred and seventy-five *denarii*, the chances of one procuring a slave such as the young Briton was highly improbable.

As he watched, the Iceni captive was thrust onto the platform and the placard lifted from his neck. The auctioneer launched into his customary singsong torrent of praises.

"Noble Romans! I have here an Iceni prisoner, taken during the heroic campaign of our own gallant General Suetonius! Note his blonde hair, his blue eyes. Slaves like this are not to be had every day, gentlemen. We will start at one thousand *denarii*. Undo the knots in your purse strings and begin your bidding now!"

The finger of the legionary went up. "One thousand-ten."

Bide your time. Marcus crossed his arms upon his chest, striking an air of nonchalance. He would wait until the fools had expended their resources.

"One thousand-ten! Any higher?"

Sprinkled throughout the crowd, fingers rose. Paltry bids were placed, bringing the amount to two thousand *denarii*. Everyone seemed to want the boy, yet was unwilling to commence the serious bidding with a substantial amount.

Marcus stepped forward. The foolery had gone on long enough. "Three thousand."

The nonchalance seemed to snap. At once, serious bids echoed throughout the buyers. Marcus's bid had launched an immediate campaign.

"Three thousand, two hundred."

"Three thousand, five hundred!"

Marcus lifted his finger. "Four thousand." He glanced at the young captive, looking for his response.

Surprisingly, there was none. The boy was rigidly motionless, his features taut and white. His stoicism seemed to indicate he cared little about who won his body and soul in the bidding. Instead, he cast many sidelong glances at a Briton waiting below the podium two slaves behind him. They seemed to share a connection, a mutual attachment of sorts.

Marcus cast his eyes over the British man. Perhaps he was the boy's relation. Things of that sort happened often. Still, it was singular that a boy with such high chances of becoming the property of a wealthy patrician was more concerned about another slave than his own future.

The bidding stilled. The auctioneer rubbed his hands together. "Come, come, gentlemen! Surely this is not the end of the bidding for so distinguished a slave. Look at his broad shoulders, his strong legs! Do I hear a bid for over four thousand?"

"Four thousand, one hundred." A Greek merchant near Marcus lifted his finger.

"Four thousand, one hundred it is! Any higher!"

"Four thousand, *five* hundred." Marcus spoke coolly. He looked to the Greek, awaiting his response.

The merchant threw up his hands, gesturing good-naturedly. "The gods favor you, patrician. I shall bid no more." He stepped back into the murmuring crowd.

The auctioneer looked around. "You have heard the bid for this lot. Have we any higher?"

"For an untrained barbarian?" The legionary Marcus had spoken with earlier lifted his voice with haughty derision. He seemed a bitter sport. "The sum is madness. Let the young patrician have his Iceni brute. I doubt there is another man among us who will squander so much on him."

Marcus laughed openly. The soldier's poor temper was amusing. He bowed towards him, his voice mocking. "We won't discuss the state of my means, friend. If *your* means will not allow you to buy the boy, state as much."

The legionary's face twisted. Muttering some indistinct rant, he stepped away from the auction block. Marcus allowed his satisfaction to gleam after him.

Again, the auctioneer rubbed his hands. He peered at the silenced crowd. Abruptly, he struck the gong beside him. "Sold at four thousand, five hundred *denarii!*" Then, to Marcus himself, "You have bought a champion, sir, though barbarian blood does flow in his veins."

"Barbarian or champion, the slave is a dog. You may send the bill to me at the domus of Rowland Virginius tomorrow." Marcus gestured carelessly. "Bring him to me."

Two of the city soldiers guarding the slaves gripped the boy by the shoulders and pulled him from the podium. With his new slave kneeling at his feet, Marcus tossed each of the men a *dupondius*. "The gods favor you." Then, to the boy, "Get up."

Philip understood the order and gesture. Slowly, shakily, he rose. His new master beckoned to him, signifying he was to follow. Silently, he obeyed. The young man led him several paces away from the auction block, then turned.

"What is your name?"

Philip understood the words. The last few months of captivity had taught him much, including how to speak halting Latin. "I am named Philip."

Even as he answered, he felt a thrill of resentment. He could never forgive his mother for choosing a Greek name rather than one of his own people. At the time, his parents had thought signs of outer influence might appease the Romans. *A lot of good it did.*

"And you are Iceni?"

"Yes." Philip bit his lip under the young man's probing gaze. He longed to turn his gaze towards the auction block, where his father would be sold soon. Above all, he wished he could escape the mastery of the man he knew owned him.

"My name is Marcus Virginius. Of course, you will address me as your lord." Marcus paused a moment. "You understand me?"

"Yes, my lord." Philip hoped Marcus would understand his stammer over the words as part of the language barrier. In truth, it was gall in his mouth to address any man as his master.

"Good. Follow me."

Marcus turned, his pace strong, yet casual. Philip sensed he had much to learn about his particular mannerisms. Everything about him was self-assured and masterful, yet strangely nonchalant.

Before they had gone far, another man approached them. His low bow seemed to signify he knew Marcus as his master.

"My lord Marcus."

"Demetrius." Marcus waved a sweeping hand over Philip. "I acquired one of the new captives from Briton. Charming lad, isn't he? I think he will do well as my attendant."

"Yes." Philip could feel the shrewd eyes of Demetrius running up and down him. "He is striking. Still, I will admit I do not understand your reason for purchasing another slave, my lord. The domus is adequately supplied."

"You were ever practical, Demetrius. Yes, we have enough of the common rabble, but even you must admit I have no attendant that can be compared with this young warrior. He will make a perfect stir when I introduce him to my friends, barbaric dog though he is."

Philip felt the flaming color rise in his cheeks. He understood enough Latin to know what his lord had said. Why this Roman insistence of calling him a dog? Marcus's haughty demeanor only deepened the tingling smart. Already, he hated him. His fingers flew into a tight fist, choking back the furious exclamation he wanted to scream from the rooftops.

Marcus didn't appear to notice. He turned his back on him. Apparently, he didn't expect that his new property would dare do anything but follow him.

Stupid Roman presumption.

Philip cast a swift glance over his shoulder. The crowds were milling, a packed rabble. It would be easy to lose himself among them. It would be easier still to discover who purchased his father. He would lay in hiding for a few days, then, join him. They would be together. He would be free.

The simplicity of it all was too alluring to pass up.

Philip felt the hot blood coursing through his veins. *Now!* He dashed into the crowd, zigzagging his path. He almost slipped on the sandaled foot of a peddler, and his hands brushed against the dirty cobblestones. His heart thudded.

Somewhere behind him, he heard a hasty shout. "My lord, the slave!"

They had seen him.

Philip dashed towards an inviting alley. It seemed so near, yet so far away. If he could only make it to its dark recesses...

A strong hand fell on his shoulder, spinning him around. "Are you mad, boy?" Angry and authoritative, Marcus glowered at him.

Philip twisted under the inexorable grip, nearly choked with rising panic. His mind whirled. If he was taken now, there was no telling what his new master might do to him. *Fight him.* The thought blazed like mountain lightning into his brain. Before he fairly knew what he was doing, he struck Marcus wildly across the face.

Marcus stepped back, relinquishing his grip. He looked half-stunned. Instant, fiery color washed over his face. "Eternal gods! Vile *brute*! How dare you—"

Philip turned, cutting off the furious shout. He plunged forward. His legs pumped, adrenaline spurring him on. There was no time to consider what he had just done. Or the consequences.

Another, more violent hand yanked him back. Philip looked up into the furious face of Demetrius, simultaneously feeling his arms pinned behind him.

"Insolent cur!" The man spat the words. "How dare you strike your lawful master? And he is the eldest son of Rowland Virginius! Come, brute, you will pay well for this."

Philip's heart lurched. He attempted a fight, but Demetrius's iron grip and sturdy strength were more than his match. He felt himself dragged along, his bare feet scraping the cobblestones. A slow blur encompassed his vision, then melted, his eyes focusing on the imposing figure of his master.

Marcus was composed and apparently recovered from his vehement blow, but Philip read intense fury in every feature of his countenance. He stood still, his dark eyes flashing. It went beyond saying he was unaccustomed to such brazen rebellion.

Philip ceased struggling as they neared. His heart pulsed. Given time to think, the full realization of what he had just done settled over him. He shuddered. He had witnessed a slave being scourged to death for trying to escape during the journey to Rome. What could he expect Marcus would do to him?

Marcus turned, as if to confirm his thoughts. His look chilled him to the core of his being. "You are a fool." His eyes narrowed. "A perfect fool. But I imagine it won't be long before you learn common sense."

Philip felt a shudder run down his spine.

In his peripheral vision, he saw several members of the city guard run up. Apparently, they had seen what had happened. Swiftly, they cleared a circle in the mass of curious onlookers. One of them brandished a heavy rod. With silent deference, he bowed his head, offering Marcus the instrument of punishment.

Philip's knees went weak. *No. No!* His pulse pounded so hard he couldn't breathe. He had forgotten nothing of his experience under the merciless strokes of the Roman legionary. And he had seen men die under rods like the one before him.

The seconds seemed like hours. Marcus did not take the rod. His sternness seemed hindered by some strange indecision. Did he not mean to take his vengeance?

Philip sent a wild glance at the soldiers, then, flung himself on his knees. He felt their hands brush his shoulders in a quick attempt to stop him, but he jerked away. Pleading for mercy was his only chance.

"My lord, I beg you! Do not let them beat me. I did not run to disrespect you. I only wanted to join my father! Have mercy–"

He stopped abruptly, realizing too late he was speaking in his native Iceni. Desperation washed over him–his mind was befogged. He could remember nothing of the Latin he had learned. Miserably, he raised his eyes to Marcus's face.

25

"My lord—"

"Enough." Marcus lifted his hand. He stepped a little nearer, ominous.

Philip shrank back under his shadow, feeling the blood drain from his face. Swiftly, he touched his head to the ground. What he was not allowed to say in words he could demonstrate in actions.

"Lift up your head."

Philip started. Slowly, he obeyed, a prickling chill rushing over him. *Marcus spoke in the Iceni tongue.* His speech was slow, true, but his every word was fully comprehensible.

"To strike your master and flee from him is an offence worthy of death, boy. You have been among us Romans long enough to know I could crucify you. Still, I will show you mercy—though, if you were any less striking or if I had paid any less for you, I'd have you beaten as soundly as you deserve."

Philip resisted the shudder threatening to roll over his shoulders. Marcus was frighteningly quiet. His voice paused, then, continued above him, low and dark.

"Take heed, slave. I am not a weak man. If you *ever* again strike me or run away, I will have you scourged until you cannot stand! Do you understand me?"

Philip met his stony gaze. He felt sick and shocked all at once. Yet, much as he longed to ask Marcus how he had acquired the Iceni tongue, he felt far too aware of his own dire strait to question him. He averted his gaze.

"Yes, my lord."

Marcus gestured at the officer, reverting back to Latin. "Take that rod away. It is not my pleasure that he be punished."

The soldiers drew back, clear dissatisfaction on their faces. Marcus beckoned, and Philip felt himself being yanked to his feet. His knees trembled. The sudden rush of blood from his head made him feel dizzy. He lowered his head, inhaling deeply. *Don't faint.*

When he raised his head, the curious onlookers and soldiers had scattered away. Marcus stood gazing at him in disgust.

"By the gods, rouse yourself! Do you think I granted you mercy to look like a dying sheep? Remember the exorbitant fee I paid for your worthless skin and look like a slave ought!"

The wrathful sarcasm in his master's voice sent a tingle of blood to Philip's face, but he obeyed. Shaking, he straightened his shoulders, blinking to keep back the tears that rose involuntarily in his eyes. This day had been too hard.

Marcus took him by the arm, clearly frustrated. His powerful grip was painful. Philip tensed, afraid he was going to hit him.

"What are you crying for? By Aphrodite! I showed you mercy and for what? You have not even bothered to thank me." He turned to Demetrius, his teeth clenched. "These Britons are utter imbeciles."

"The boy is unworthy of your clemency." Demerius's voice was grim. "I fear you will have nothing but trouble with him."

Philip exhaled, controlling his bated breathing. Panic again pounded somewhere against his throat, but he no longer cared. His eyes drifted towards the auction block. He could hear the auctioneer's incessant drawl. In another few minutes, he would be separated from Beric.

Forever.

He felt his arm released. Looking back at Marcus, he realized he had been following the direction of his gaze. Marcus's brows were knit in something like contemplation. Abruptly, he shook his head, gesturing.

"Take this wretched little cur home, Demetrius, and attire him in something decent. I will follow shortly. And," he added, as Demetrius bowed, "I will expect you to have taught him something of common propriety."

Fighting his rising emotion, Philip submitted to Demetrius's beckon. His legs moved mechanically beneath him. Weary and dejected, they carried him away from the noisy forum.

Chapter Three

To Philip, the trek to his new home seemed never ending. He walked meekly at the side of Demetrius, his spirit crushed within him. Everything seemed a blur. Was it possible that all the events of the last hour had truly happened?

He didn't raise his head until Demetrius made a slight pause. When he did, it was to see the tall composite columns of a large marble mansion. Demetrius gestured, his voice a grunt.

"The domus of Rowland Virginius."

Philip's heart skipped a beat. The grandeur was over-whelming. Silent with awe, he followed the steward up the steps to the elegant portico.

At the door, Demetrius knocked. A tunic-clad slave answered, swinging the door open. The steward brushed swiftly past him, clearly impatient. Philip followed him, feeling as if he was being transported to some new world.

Inside, the feeling deepened.

Philip stopped short, coolness washing over his perspiring skin. His eyes drank in the sights around him. Tall fountains, carved with the intricate countenances of men and animals, played softly in the middle of the room. One of them overflowed into a pool at one end of the *atrium*. Leafy flora and vegetation fairly littered the open courtyard, visible from the doorway.

Clearly, the Romans credited their wealth to their gods. Mounted upon pedestals or standing alone, marble busts of the deities gave the domus of a sense of coupled reverence and art. It was as if he was in a shrine.

Philip felt overwhelmed. Even his position as a chieftain's son had not given him grandeur such as he saw here. For as long as he could remember, he could only recall the mud huts of his tribe, except perhaps for the buildings of Roman settlements Camulodunium or Londinium. And even they had not compared with what he saw in his master's home. His thoughts breathed themselves into words.

"My master is a man of means."

"Your master is a man of many things, boy, not the least of which is justice." Demetrius surveyed him glaringly. "Bear that in mind."

Philip stiffened. As expected, Demetrius was not finished.

"You are not in your barbaric British Isles any longer, slave. You will find that the masters of the universe do not tolerate disorderliness, as would some. What my lord Marcus sees in you, I cannot tell; yet, I know that he is not a man to overlook rebellion a second time. Unless you wish for very unpleasant things to befall you, I advise that you treat your master as becomes a proper slave."

Philip dropped his gaze. His knowledge of Latin was not broad enough to have understood all that the steward had said, but he was quite well-aware that nothing less than complete submission was expected of him. Demetrius's irritated tone and expression revealed his unfavorable opinion of him, and it somehow conjured up a new fear.

"Will my master deal harshly with me on his return?"

"That is for my lord himself to answer." Demetrius turned his back on him, clapping his hands.

A slave appeared in answer to the summons. Demetrius motioned to Philip. "See to it that this boy is bathed and attired in something decent. He must be ready to attend the lord Marcus upon his return."

Half an hour later, Philip stood freshly bathed and attired in his new garments. Much to his relief, he was only given a short tunic and a simple pair of sandals. He would not for the world strike the cumbered appearance he had seen in so many Romans.

Demetrius was on hand to give his opinion. He nodded his approval. "You will do. It is a pity a change of raiment cannot change the barbaric blood running in your veins. I foresee my lord Marcus having a time of amending your manners."

Philip bit his tongue to keep from answering. It seemed the insults would never end. Demetrius looked as if he would continue, but was checked by a strong knock at the door. He wheeled around and hastened across the polished floor.

Philip involuntarily shrank back a little. Demetrius's haste signified it could only be the Lord Marcus who sought admittance. He pulled his fingers into fists, allowing them to bite into the palms. What would happen to him now? Marcus had spared him public exposure and chastisement, but he might have changed his mind about private revenge. After all, his new master was by all appearances a resolute young man.

Marcus stepped briskly into the entry. He was not alone. A tall Briton accompanied him, gravely erect.

Philip caught his breath. "Father!" He sprang forward, his arms poised to throw around Beric's neck. How could this be? They had always expected to be separated. Yet, here he was, apparently to stay.

Demetrius hissed a sharp check. "Be still, you fool!"

Philip slid to a halt. He could feel the blood tingling in his cheeks. He had forgotten everything for a moment, including his own servitude. Slowly, awkwardly, he bowed in Marcus's direction.

Marcus cocked an eyebrow, unimpressed. "So you couldn't even teach him how to greet me, Demetrius. I see I shall have to take all matters about his training into my own hands. Come with me, boy."

Philip understood by the gesture he was to follow Marcus. Not daring to cast so much as a glance at Beric, he followed his master's saunter from the atrium into an adjoining room.

The walls of the room were covered with cubicles, each holding neat rows of scrolls. The pungent smell of ink and new parchment filled his nostrils. Apparently, this was the *bibliotheca*, or, library.

Marcus threw himself down on a couch at one end of the room. "Don't stand gawking there. Come here."

Philip hesitated. What form of homage was expected of him? He moved forward, dropping awkwardly on one knee before his master's couch. A swift upward glance revealed Marcus once again cocking a brow.

"Your disposition is confusing, Philip. You are humble enough now, but what a strange contrast it makes to your shocking behavior in the forum. Jove, I would think even a barbaric little fool such as you would know better than to strike your master."

Philip was again surprised to hear Marcus's voice flow easily over the Iceni words. His surroundings made it impossible to imagine he was at home, but there was comfort in hearing his own tongue.

"My lord–" He checked himself, ensuring his soft tones hinted no presumption. "How is it you know the language of the Iceni?"

"I know many things." Marcus was curt. He rose from his couch to pour out a goblet of wine. He brought it to his lips, tasting it. "But, if you must know, my brother was a legionary of the fourteenth twin legion in your country. When he was transported, I made every effort to learn the language."

Philip felt a twinge. So the mysterious brother was one of those who had killed his people. The gods *would* have ordered it so.

Marcus continued. "This will be the last time I will speak to you in Iceni. You must learn our language and ways. Let there be no confusion–you know what I mean. I am still astonished by the insolence you are capable of." Philip felt as if Marcus's dark eyes were boring into his very soul. "But I do not think you will behave so again."

The words, however quiet, were an incisive threat. Philip could feel it. The realization of his master's absolute power over him breathed like a cold whisper down his neck. Everything about his new lord was authoritative, inexorable. He expected to be obeyed and obeyed well. And, if not...

Marcus settled himself more comfortably. "I have purchased your father. Your childish desire to be with him is pitiful, but I'm in a generous mood." He again touched the goblet to his lips. "Don't be afraid to speak to me. Have you nothing to say?"

Philip swallowed. "I am grateful, master."

"As you should be. Your thanks is woefully overdue, Philip. Although, I don't know what else I might have expected from you." Marcus rubbed his forehead contemplatively. "But, whatever else, I know you are not a slave who will flatter me into good humor—thank the gods!"

A muscle tensed in Philip's neck. "I am not as uncivilized as you think."

"No." Marcus's lips curled. "You are only an Iceni captive, taken from your homeland because your people dared think they could conquer the masters of the universe." He leaned forward. "You are only the insolent cur who *struck* me."

Say nothing. Resentment boiled up in Philip's throat despite the common sense holding his tongue. So this was the gist of being a slave. To be taunted, ridiculed, all at the whim of a sarcastic master.

A master whose only purpose was to get his money's worth.

He felt Marcus's eyes taking in his features, and he bit his lip. Blue eyes and blonde hair were swiftly becoming a curse.

"You will create quite a stir when I present you to my friends. *Hercules!* Few of them have seen hair like yours."

Philip tasted blood from the force of his own teeth on his lips. His chest swelled, surging with anger. This was becoming too much. "Among my people, I was not valued for my looks. I was a warrior, not a clown to be admired by Roman pigs! I—"

"Enough!" Marcus's face was suddenly terrible to behold.

Philip took one upward glance into his dark, flashing eyes and shrank back onto his knees. Dimly, he realized he was shaking. He lowered his head, half to hide his crimson face, half to appease the furious young man before him.

Marcus kept his seat. From what he had seen of Roman lords, Philip knew it was to his credit. They had precious little self-control. He felt certain it was only the remembrance of the high price he had paid for his new slave that kept Marcus from chastising his brazen temper.

He saw Marcus's fingers close tightly around his goblet. "You Britons have the faces of gods, but you come with a high price–the wills of *adders*! Eternals gods, Philip. Take some advice and learn your place quickly. You are as handsome a slave as ever set foot in Rome, but that will not save you from my justice if you continue to set your spirit against mine."

I will end this tyranny. And it will be a tale for centuries!

The pledge he had sworn at the time of his capture flashed into Philip's mind. This Roman pig might own him now, but it would not always be so. He would one day be *free*. And, until then, he would never allow his hatred to die. Even at that moment, it seeped into every core of his body.

He could feel Marcus glowering at him. He sensed if his lord continued lecturing him, it would be impossible to control another wave of rage. But, fortunately, the door swung open. From his peripheral vision, Philip saw it was a middle-aged man. Tall and dark, he was undoubtedly Marcus's father. *The master of the domus.*

Marcus stood up, flourishing. "See the purchase I made today, father! I obtained two of these Briton slaves, one as my attendant and the other as a present for you. It was only the other day you complained of the lack of garden attendants. What do you think?"

"He is strong and good-looking." Philip's skin crawled under Rowland's traveling gaze. "If the other one is as muscular, I will be very pleased of your present. But I hope you have not taken too much upon you, Marcus. They say these Britons are too high-spirited and obstinate to make good house slaves."

"I will add my voice to whatever unhappy master made you that quote." Marcus's gaze narrowed, casting a notable glare upon Philip. "Already, this barbarous wretch has been more trouble than all the rest of our slaves put together."

Philip fidgeted, understanding enough Latin to know what they were talking about. Would Marcus tell his father what had happened in the forum? He doubted the master of the domus would approve of his son's clemency.

"You will know how to break him in, Marcus. He is only a boy. Give him the feel of your right arm and it will amend his manners once and for all."

"Yes." Marcus looked sidelong at him. His eyes were dark, meaningful. "But I trust I did not pay such an exorbitant sum for an *idiot*. He will not test me."

Rowland shrugged. "Hopefully not. But, come—the evening meal is prepared. Bring your new slave along. He might as well begin serving at once."

Marcus snapped his fingers at him. Swallowing back his resentment, Philip followed him and his father from the room. They had spoken about him as if he had been no more living than the marble busts of the gods. Was he no longer human now that he was a slave?

It was a short distance to the *triclinium*, or, room where the family took their meals. Philip stood against the strong columns, taking in the room. It was only beginning to grow dusk, but the oil lamps were already lit, casting their warm glow over the table. The table itself was low to the ground, surrounded by comfortable couches decked with cushions. It would seem the family reclined as they ate.

His insides tightened at the sight of the food. Much of the bountiful feast was unfamiliar, but the scent was invigorating. His knees shook. He had not eaten more than a mouthful of bread all day. Still, it appeared that he was obliged to push aside his hunger until his master dismissed him.

The family filed in and took their places. Beside Marcus and his father, there were two women, one of matronly age, the other a child. Evidently, they were the mother and daughter of the family.

Taking his cue from the other slaves, Philip moved close to his master's side. Marcus gestured at a pitcher of wine, and he poured out a goblet full with hands trembling from hunger. For what seemed an eternity, he cut meat and offered platters. At last, Marcus waved him back, satisfied.

Afraid he was going to collapse, Philip stumbled against a pillar, allowing the shadows to hide his face. To divert his thoughts from his stomach, he gazed at the family members around the table.

He had heard the lady addressed as Persis. She seemed gentle, to say nothing of charming. Philip brushed aside his prejudices, allowing himself to admit she was beautiful. Her long *stola* was elegant, and she wore her dark hair in the neatly-coiled fashion he had seen adopted by many other Roman ladies. All through the meal, she laughed and chatted, flattering Rowland into perfect good humor.

Philip's eyes traveled to the child seated at her mother's right. She was delicate, even more beautiful than her mother. Eventually, Marcus addressed her as Diantha. Philip's heart skipped a beat. He had never heard a more breathtaking name, even if it was Roman.

He peered through the shadows, then, jerked back. What was he thinking? He was openly gazing at the female relatives of his master. A nervous glance revealed Marcus had not noticed. His intentions were harmless, but still, one could never know what Romans did to slaves who gawked shamelessly at their women.

He settled back against the pillar. Somewhere, deep inside, he was throbbing. The two women were beautiful, but they could never compare with his own mother and sisters. They had turned the heads of more than a few Iceni men. And, unlike Roman women, they could hold their own. Philip recalled the hours his father had taken, training them to fight.

"You may go."

Philip blinked at the curt tone. Marcus lifted a dismissing hand. "Go to the *culina*. The cook will give you food."

Philip bent his head. His legs shook as they carried him from the room. Another few minutes, and he knew he would have collapsed.

Rome! He could have spit on the polished atrium floor. How he hated her! She had taken everything from him—his family, his way of living, his liberty. He could not even eat when he chose. His life was in his master's hands.

Acidity tinged his tongue. Strange how he could even taste the bitterness of captivity.

A strong, tall figure was standing by the fountain, his back turned. Philip stopped short. *Father!* The sight of Beric almost erased the hatred simmering through his body. Here was his reason for still living.

His sandaled foot swished the floor with his sudden stop, and Beric turned at the sound. His grave features lightened, and he held out his hand. Philip dashed forward. Forget the pangs in his stomach. Food could wait.

Their arms met in a long embrace. Philip held onto his father's muscular body as long as could, basking in the comforting warmth. He was no child, as Marcus had taunted. But he was not ashamed of his love for Beric, either.

At last he stepped back. "Thank the gods, father! We were prepared to be separated, but the forest gods have shown us this strange mercy."

"Yes." Beric was strangely grave. "And we have another reason for giving thanks, my son."

Philip dropped his eyes. Was his father rebuking him? "What do you mean?" he asked, though knowing what Beric implied.

"I mean it was a strange power that worked in the heart of your master, Philip. How else can you explain the reason for which he spared you from brutal scourging or worse?"

Philip felt a flush burn in his cheeks. His father had not approved. "You know why I fled, father. It was cruelty in itself that the Romans carried us from our homeland, but I could not have born being forever separated from you. You are all have. I swear, had Marcus not purchased you, I would have only run away again."

"And, doubtless, you would have been captured and scourged before you went a mile. But, there—my heart is too glad at our reunitement to have more to say. I will thank the gods with you, my son. We have been shown great mercy."

"Not so great a mercy." Philip released his father's arms. His frustration began to well up inside him once again. "It is beyond endurance that you—a chieftain and loyal servant of Queen Boudica—should be demeaned like this."

"The gods have given us this lot. I do not complain, Philip. Our only choice now is submission to our fate and the masters who bought us."

"How can I submit to the people who have changed my every hope and joy into misery!" Philip did not quench the fire he knew burned in his eyes. His father might desire submission to the gods, but he did not. "The Romans would have done better to have killed us. This slavery is a cruelty that cannot be endured."

"Have you forgotten we ourselves had slaves?" Beric's hands rested with fatherly compassion on Philip's shoulders. "Take heart, son. Whether free men or slaves, we are the same race, the same people we were before."

"But—"

"Circumstances may change, but we have not." Beric fixed Philip with a grave, almost stern look. "Remain a Briton at heart, Philip, but never forget your life is in the hands of another. Think of me, of your people. Do not bring disgrace or death upon yourself with your rebellion, for it will do nothing for either of us. To be a true Briton, you must prove yourself noble even in the heartless jaws of slavery."

Philip slowly took his father's hand in his own. He was not sure he agreed, but there was love in every word Beric uttered. In the old gesture of love and respect, he pressed the hand to his forehead.

"I will try to do as you wish, my father. I will *endeavor* to be compliant to my master, if only for your sake. But I will never forget my oath." Philip paused, meeting Beric's blue eyes. "Rome will regret what she has done. And I will not always be a slave."

Chapter Four

Philip absently walked through his master's chamber, seeing that it presented its usual well-kept appearance. A single glance showed that everything was in its proper place, as it had been upon his last inspection.

He turned to vacate the room, then, paused, the sight of the flapping drapes bordering the large casement catching his attention. Almost grateful for an occupation, he stepped across the polished floor and straightened the sheer hangings. As his hands dropped from the material, his eyes fell upon the gardens beyond the casement.

Slowly, he lapsed into motionlessness, letting his mind go.

It had been one long week—a week full of new tasks, a new language, and the wearying adjustments to a strange new life. With each passing day, he grew a little more accustomed to his new surroundings. Still, he felt as if he would never fully master the Roman customs and way of living.

He had to grant their positions were not altogether distasteful ones. Beric had been assigned the position of a lower-gardener and was almost constantly employed beneath the instruction and commands of the head-gardener. Philip saw him much, though not as constantly as he would have liked. His own position as the attendant of his master was not an arduous one, yet he was obliged to be constantly at hand—constantly ready to fulfill the slightest desire of Marcus.

Marcus.

Philip's chest constricted and he tightened his hands into slow fists. How he hated him, if only because he was his master. There was very little other reason to hate him, but the fact that Marcus controlled him, *owned* him, was enough.

The injustice of his feelings smote him a little.

Contrary to his expectations, Marcus had thus far proven a reasonable master. He was determined that his new slave would submit respectfully in all areas of service, but, beyond that, was generally a considerate and pleasant young man. In fact, Philip sensed that Marcus had no real desire to ill-use him.

Of course, *while* he was doing all that was required of him.

Philip stiffened and cringed simultaneously, calling to mind the events of yesterday. For the first time during his first week of service to his new master, Marcus had lost his temper with him. Having never before served another, Philip knew his services were, at best, awkward. And, to say the least, Marcus was accustomed to skilful attendance.

An angry shiver ran down Philip's spine and his cheeks tingled, smarting in remembrance. Marcus, goaded to utter frustration, had lifted his hand against him. And, in that single stroke, he had felt the brutal resolution that governed the wills of the masters of the universe. Oh, he had controlled himself. He had stood rigidly straight and taken the blow, his pride refusing to allow any sign of pain. But, inwardly, he had cursed the name of Marcus.

"Philip."

Philip whirled around, his face burning hot. Attempting to control his breathing, he pulled himself erect. Fleetingly, he dared to consider how long his master had been standing behind him and wondering if he knew his thoughts.

Marcus surveyed him with a slow smile of amusement. "How easily you Britons color! What are you guilty of, I wonder?"

Philip met the young man's sardonic gaze, attempting to muster the correct Latin words to explain his behavior. "I did not hear you behind me, master. I–"

Marcus waved his hand impatiently. "I am not interested in your excuses. I am going to the Baths and want your services. Acquire some fresh clothing, then, meet me on the portico."

Philip hastened to obey. He had often wondered what the Roman Baths looked like. Now, it seemed, was his chance to find out. Snatching up a fresh tunic and toga, he draped them over his arm and strode quickly from the chamber to the appointed meeting place.

Marcus's impatience to be gone was evident. He turned curtly at the sound of his slave's steps, his brow furrowed. "Stand erect–I want to look at you."

Philip obeyed, stiffening. Marcus nodded slowly.

"Yes, you will do. Many of my friends will be present at the Baths and have heard much of you British captives. Prepare to be presented before them."

Philip's heart lurched. So he was to be paraded as an oddity before his lord's rich acquaintances. He did not dare speak. Not that he cared to offer Marcus the respect of an answer anyway.

Marcus seemed to sense his feelings. An expression of displeasure flitted across his handsome face. The careless pleasantness that usually distinguished his countenance disappeared, and he leaned ominously close to Philip.

"Remember you are a slave."

Philip, caught between boiling pride and honest fear, resisted the instinct to step away from Marcus. He stood still, conscious of the young man's imposing superiority. Everything about Marcus was a dark threat, even to the musky scent of his perfumed toga. Here was the *Roman* side of his master. He had seen this side of him yesterday and now knew to dread it, however much he hated himself for giving place to fear.

Marcus seemed to see his cringing apprehension. His dark eyes softened. Clearly appeased by his slave's fear, he stepped back. "Come," he ordered shortly.

As he spoke, Marcus strode lightly down the steps of the portico. Out on the street Philip had heard called the *Vicus Tuscus*, he set up a leisurely pace. Philip followed, creating a respectful arm's distance between them.

Though accustomed to walking at a much faster pace, Philip scarcely noticed the painfully casual tread. This was the first time he had been out of the domus, and there was much to see.

Rome. Colossal temples, the world-famous cobblestoned streets, a constant clatter of Greek and Latin tongues. People representing all nationalities swarmed the streets, some in the toga of citizenship, others dressed in the tunic of slaves. So this was the glorious city that had spawned such magnificence and brought her people to the height of masters of the universe.

Could anyone doubt she was favored by the gods?

Philip struggled with the thought. His loyalty to his own people was fierce, but there was so much to admire here. He drank in the sight and sounds like one parched from the desert heat. He had never seen such vast eminence, such glory. Rome fairly basked in greatness.

Standing under the shadows of the towering Baths confirmed his feelings. *Great gods.* He felt dizzy, as if his head was being turned. The marble structure was more massive than he had dreamed. Its delicately-carved columns, arches, and statues were palatial, nothing like he had ever seen before.

Marcus snapped his fingers at him. Coming down to earth, Philip realized his lord had moved on to the entrance and was waiting for him. He jumped to join him.

Inside was even more breathtaking. Philip came to a slow stop. The courtyard was massive, aglow with warmth and light. His eyes drifted over the tinkling fountains and high-domed ceilings. Here, for one fleeting moment, he could forget he was a slave.

"You are not in your barbarous Brittania any longer, Philip." Marcus was surveying him with an amused smile. "Did you expect your paltry mud-huts to have a place in Rome? What you see here is nothing. It does not compare with the majority of our buildings— the Circus Maximus, for example."

"I have never seen anything so magnificent." Philip breathed the words, not realizing he spoke in Iceni. "Your gods are very powerful."

Marcus laughed. "Our gods are all-powerful, boy. Come—I came for more reasons than to see you gaping."

From the sunny courtyard, Marcus led the way from the *apodyterium*, or, changing room. There, he hastily disrobed and handed his toga to Philip. A quick observation revealed the rows of cubicles in the wall. Philip folded the garment and laid it in an empty shelf.

He scarcely had time to do so before Marcus stepped from the room into the adjoining *caldarium*, where he slipped into the hot water. Steam rose thickly from the pool, nearly cutting off all view of the water itself. The air was thick and warm, and mingled chatter and laughter arose from the other men and boys in the apartment.

Philip watched the antics of the bathers with keen interest, although prudently keeping watch for any signal from Marcus.

The young man, as with all of his peers, took his time, seeming to enjoy the daily bathing ritual as much as any of them. Yet, unlike many of the bathers, he applied the *strigil* himself and did not once summon Philip to his assistance.

Philip felt no end of relief. He had only just seen the strigil applied and didn't have the slightest idea of how he was to perform this service if called upon to do so. He watched Marcus keenly, noting the smooth, gliding way he brought the *strigil* over himself and scraped away the oil used as a cleanser.

At last Marcus was through. He gave one masterful snap of the fingers, and Philip silently brought the towel he had obtained in the *apodyterium* forward. Marcus draped it quickly about himself and wordlessly strode from the pool into the next apartment.

At the door, Philip paused, surveying the proceedings within the spacious interior. This apartment seemed to be the massage chamber, as he gathered by the numerous marble slabs occupying the room.

43

As in the *caldarium*, the air hummed with activity and conversation, although the general atmosphere was that of relaxation. Towel-girded men sat or lay atop the slabs, enjoying their daily massage. Their slaves skillfully rubbed scented oils into their broad backs and shoulders, many of them applying shell scrapers in the process.

Marcus sauntered briskly to an open slab and stretched himself full-length across it, motioning to a bottle of cream.

"Use that stuff there." Then, as Philip stood in confused immobility, "What's the matter with you? Take that bottle!"

Philip cringed at the tone and quickly took the urn. Gingerly, he poured the rich, strong-scented contents into his hand. Apparently, Marcus expected him to massage him. He glanced at the other slaves for his example, then, began to knead the oil onto Marcus's strong back.

"By the spear of Mars, lad!" Marcus raised his head with a gesture of impatience. "Have you no muscle? Rub harder."

Philip's lungs began to burn, and he realized he had been holding his breath. He could feel apprehension rising like a burning choke-hold in his throat. To what extent did Marcus expect him to rub? If he should do so too hard... From the corner of his eye, he watched the other slaves, endeavoring to do as they did.

"Enough!" Marcus raised his head with an angry gesture. "Jupiter, but must I instruct you in everything? Plaudio," and he motioned to one of the professional attendants, "you attend me. My Iceni *warrior* has the arm of a woman!"

The attendant obeyed. Philip stepped back, struggling to swallow the sarcastic rebuke. Feeling disgraced, he watched as the attendant heartily pounded and massaged his master's back. He could almost curse the fear that had kept him from exercising the same amount of vigor.

At last, Marcus signaled that he was satisfied. The attendant stepped back, and Marcus motioned for Philip to hand him his purse. Taking out a bronze *dupondius*, he tossed it into the man's out-stretched hand.

"My gratitude for your services."

"The pleasure is mine, sir." The attendant bowed and withdrew. His departure left Marcus to turn glowering eyes on Philip.

"Aid me to robe, slave, if you can do that much."

Philip bit his lip. Marcus's utter frustration with him was evident, invoking his usual feeling of hatred. *Slave*–Marcus seemed to sense how greatly he despised the word. Why else would he couple it with his irritated rebuke? He only wanted to hurt him, to rile his spirit just because it was his right to do so.

He forced himself to make no expression. So what if he was nearly choked with bitterness? Marcus would not have the pleasure of seeing him angry. Forcing himself to concentrate, he helped him dress.

When Marcus was attired, he strode out to the sunny courtyard. Philip followed at a sullen distance. The Baths had already lost their charm. Now, their glory was acidity in his mouth.

Glory built on the backs of slaves.

A group of young men were standing in a careless group just beyond the massage chamber. Attired in white togas and attended by their own slaves, it was not difficult to determine they were patricians of Marcus's rank and status. One stepped out, extending his hand.

"Hail, Marcus Virginius! What has kept you of late? Have you taken to private bathing or none at all?"

Marcus laughed. Already, Philip knew that not bathing was unthinkable for Romans. "I have been here, Caius, but have had little time for your idle gossip. But, enough there. I have brought something today that should make up for my absence."

"And that would be?"

Marcus snapped his fingers. The unspoken command was clear. Philip stepped forward, fighting himself. He had dreaded this moment. A murmur of surprise and admiration circulated, and the blood tingled in his cheeks.

"Why, he has the face of a god!" One of the young men laughed. Philip's skin crawled, feeling his hand pinch his biceps. "And he has the muscles of a gladiator! You have made an excellent choice, Marcus."

"Can you doubt it? I pride myself in knowing a good slave when I lay eyes on one. Of course, he cost a pretty sum, but these Britons do not go for mean prices."

"Perhaps I ought to consider purchasing such a slave." Caius pulled Philip towards him, scrutinizing the width of his shoulders. Philip's heart pounded, nearly choking him. Would Marcus stand there and do nothing? "These Britons have the build and looks to be pleasing enough. But, by the gods! How he colors! Does your slave *object* to us, Marcus?"

Philip sent a quick look of appeal in Marcus's direction. His young master only cocked a brow, his expression nothing short of inexorable. The laughing tone of his voice proved doubly maddening. "He has the temper of Mars. I have never before seen a slave with such a proud spirit."

The first speaker laughed, his boastful tenors grating. "I would soon knock the temper from him if he were mine, Virginius. Has Rome fallen so low that she allows arrogance to control her slaves?"

"A shrewd question, but I do not generally pride myself in disabling my slaves as you do, Vitellis. It is said your attendant is still unable to rise from his bed. The unfortunate plight of being too fond of strong wine and flogging the life out of your slaves, eh?"

"Whereas you, Marcus, have the more sickening plight of a woman's stomach." Marcus's teasing laughter was silenced by a grim new arrival. A tall young man joined the group. To Philip, his countenance was eagle-like, strangely handsome. He fixed his cold eyes with disdain on Marcus. "Has the story reached you, my

46

friends? It is said that this Briton dared to strike and flee from our noble companion. But it would seem Marcus did not have the fortitude to see him beaten."

Marcus's dark eyes flickered. "I paid too much for this slave to have his looks spoiled by a misguided blow at the hands of those clumsy officers. And, what is that to you, Thallus?"

A mocking expression curled Thallus's lips. "How easily you become offended, Marcus. Of course my motives are only of the sincerest concern for your well-being." His hand closed around Philip's wrist. "Let me examine this slave you are so concerned about."

Philip jerked his wrist from Thallus's fingers. He had stood too long listening to the sickeningly sarcastic, meaningless exchanges between these Romans. What were they, these lords of creation, who stood about in rich luxury and made menacing remarks to each other? *Haughty pigs, drunk with pleasure.* And he had no doubt this Thallus was the worst of the lot.

"Keep your hands off me."

A shout of sardonic laughter echoed through the courtyard. Thallus's countenance grew black, spreading like poison across his face. He seized Philip by the shoulder, his grip painful.

"British scum! Do you dare command *me*?"

Philip's mouth twitched. He could only think of one answer. In one swift move, he struck Thallus across the face. Reeling backwards, Thallus stumbled to the marble floor. He laid a hand over his mouth, bringing it away crimson with blood.

Philip stepped a little closer. "And do you dare challenge *me*, Roman?"

Another shout of delighted laughter rose in the circle. Their mockery was like a goad. Thallus sprang to his feet and flung himself on Philip.

"Cur! How dare you—"

Philip was ready for the onslaught. Long hours of training had taught him rage rarely accomplished anything where physical competition was involved. He swung at Thallus, again striking him full in the face.

Thallus made a choking sound. Philip hit him again, following the blow up with a kick that sent him swaying to a prostrate position on the floor. For one fleeting instant, he felt himself at home, a warrior among the chieftains. He tightened his hands into fierce fists.

"British dog, am I? Now you have seen what a Briton can do!"

Thallus raised himself on one elbow, blood running in little rivulets from his nostrils and lips. "And you will learn how Romans deal with this sort of rebellion, scum. Marcus, call in the rods! This British swine shall see who is master. I demand it."

"You will make no demand of me, Thallus." Marcus's laughter rang out, supporting by the low chuckles of the others. "I think we have all seen who is master of this situation. Surely you would not like to threaten your honor by resorting to the help of others!"

Thallus's eyes kindled, a quick oath escaping his lips. "By the gods! Do you mean to—"

"Do I deny your demand?" Marcus cut him off. "Yes. My slave has beaten one some five years his senior. Shall I disable, torture him for doing it? No. I am rather pleased to see you getting what you deserve for once, *friend*."

The fire in Thallus's eyes was terrible to see. Despite the adrenaline in his blood, Philip himself felt a prickle of apprehension. But, looking at Marcus for his reaction, he saw his master was far from intimidated. He turned his back coldly on the prostrate Thallus, warmth in his eyes.

"Well done, Philip. You are a grand tribute to your people. Mars, but I should have instated you as my body guard rather than my attendant."

"He will keep his hands off me in the future." Philip spoke low, realizing for the first time the extent of what he had done. He half-averted his gaze under his master's keen eyes, unable to discern what thoughts were present behind his amused expression.

"As will we all." Caius laughed, making Marcus an approving nod. "Speaking for us all, I can wager none of us will have much inclination to try your temper. I had heard that the Britons are a very warrior-like race, but I little expected to find their spirit instilled in one so young."

"He is the true son of his country." Marcus continued to rest an amused gaze upon Philip. "I saw as much when he was upon the slave podium."

"And, in purchasing him, you have become a Roman worthy of the Caesars, Marcus." Vitellis spoke good-naturedly, simultaneously aiding Thallus to his feet.

"He has become a Roman imbecile." Thallus straightened his toga with a slow hand, fixing Marcus with a cold, meaningful look. "Any slave with a temper like that would very likely murder his master in his bed—particularly one whose master is too craven to check his insolence."

Marcus's countenance was chillingly quiet. "My slave knows his lord, Thallus." His dark eyes roved until they met Philip's, their meaningful expression holding him in masterful captivity. "He would not lift his hand or will against me."

Philip again felt the strange power of Marcus's authority. A new tinge of apprehension smote him. If it had been his master instead of Thallus, could he have controlled his temper? Or would he have dared to hit him? *And face crucifixion.* The thought chilled him through, realizing he didn't know the answer.

There was a fleeting moment of awkward silence.

Marcus finally laughed. "I have spent enough time in your company, friends. Farewell, and may the gods keep you!"

The others uttered a swift chorus of farewells. Only Thallus kept his peace, continuing to fix Marcus with a menacing expression. Marcus met his chilling eyes, sardonically lifting his hand in farewell.

To Philip, leaving the Baths was a blur. He was still shocked by what had just transpired. New dread settled in the pit of his stomach. Marcus was amused here. Would he be so later?

Marcus could scarcely keep from laughing aloud. He weaved a course around milling pedestrians and street side peddlers, chuckling inwardly.

By Jupiter, what iron wills these Iceni captives possessed! It was small wonder the divine Nero had considered withdrawing his legions from Britain. If their men were as brazen as Philip, the Roman legionaries would have had good cause for fearing defeat.

Stupid boy. Marcus shook his head. Philip knew what he might have done to him, but he had lifted his hand against a Roman patrician anyway. *And of all the patricians to choose.* He knew Thallus would not forget the insult. Not that he cared, but he wondered if Philip realized his own foolishness. Marcus made a mental note to scold him later.

Yet, for the time, he wanted to enjoy the moment. Philip had made this particular visit to the Baths a very enjoyable one. And for that, he was gratified.

Chapter Five

Alone in the little bedchamber connected to the apartments of Marcus, Philip looked down into the dark street outside the domus. The flickering torches of pedestrians were like fireflies, dancing in the darkness. It was an interesting view, but nothing could divert his confusion.

What a brash fool he had been. He had once again dared to strike and humiliate a Roman nobleman! Why did he always let his temper get the better of him? There was no explaining what strange power had both granted him victory over Thallus and spared him from a torturous death.

Marcus had not yet offered him a single reproof. In the back of his mind, he had always expected to be punished, perhaps even whipped. To say the least, Marcus's mercy was confusing. Did he not resent the insult his slave had offered his companion?

Philip cast one final glance at the street. In the distance, the temple of Vesta was aglow with light. The smoke rising from her sacred flame was a jolting reminder. He should thank the gods.

He dropped to his knees and raised both hands towards the ceiling. "Thank you, Anextiomarus." Somehow, even so far away from his people and priests, the Iceni god of protection had not forgotten him. "Thank you for sparing my life."

He stood up. Hopefully Anextiomarus would continue to be with him. He sensed that everything was not over. Much as he dreaded a confrontation with Marcus, it was pretty sure to come.

The sound of clapping hands sounded from the next room.

Philip's heart rate kicked up a notch. His own fear irritated him, but he could not curtail it. He had no desire whatsoever to go into Marcus's presence.

Stoically, he set his jaw. If he had to go, he would do so as a warrior, portraying no fear. He threw his shoulders back and strode into the next room.

"You summoned me, my lord?"

Marcus looked up from pouring out a glass of wine. "Yes." He was casually attired, dressed only in his simple tunic. Clearly, he had no banquet or other social event to attend that evening. He cradled his cup in both hands, his eyes narrowing. "What's the matter with you? Does it *offend* you to be called into my presence?"

Philip realized how stiffly he was carrying himself. To a discerning man like Marcus, he must appear positively mutinous. He settled his face more naturally. "No, my lord. I meant no harm."

"Good." Marcus tapped his wine glass contemplatively. He seemed to have something on his mind. "Tell me, what idiocy made you strike Thallus today?"

Philip stiffened. The confrontation was here. He inhaled slowly, attempting to quiet his nerves. "He had no right to lay hands on me."

"But you did not strike the others."

Philip said nothing. Marcus looked keenly at him, gesturing.

"You have been among us long enough to know how to keep your own counsel. That is well. However, I command you to answer me freely. Why did you not strike the others?"

"They did not grate on my nerves as soundly as that haughty pig."

Marcus cocked a brow. "And what does your father think of all this?"

"I have not told him, my lord."

Marcus laughed unexpectedly. "What?" he asked, apparently amused. "You have not told him? Why, you utterly thrashed a *Roman*."

"Is that such an honorable feat?"

Marcus raised his brows. A flicker of disapprobation darkened his countenance. "You are a fool." He paused, gazing keenly at Philip. "Yet, it is not within my will to castigate your incessant insolence. Come, I want you to wrestle me."

52

Philip felt his lips twitch with amusement. "My lord just called me a fool. Yet, he must know I am not so much of one as to have forgotten his threat."

Marcus smiled in his turn. "I give you permission to strike me–if, that is, you think you can accomplish the feat. I am not ill-trained in the arts of war." Then, with a sarcastic expression of amusement, "Come, my Iceni warrior. Fly at me as you did Thallus."

Philip didn't wait for further urging. He flew across the marble floor, closing the few paces between them. *By your own word, Roman cur.*

Marcus stood ready for him, standing with wide, well-braced feet and the calm confidence of a soldier. Every aspect of his well-developed muscles was visible, from his rounded biceps to the sun-tanned calves protruding beneath his short, close-fitting tunic. He cut an intimidating figure, and the half-amused expression in his dark eyes seemed to portray that he knew it.

Philip brushed aside any thought of apprehension. His master was formidably strong, but that meant nothing. He had downed young men twice his age in the wild British Isles. There could be little difference in throwing a Roman, however soldierly that Roman stood and looked.

In a single instant, Philip flung his entire weight against Marcus's chest. He gripped his shoulders, digging his fingers into the flesh. Expertly evading the strong hands flailing to seize him, he struck Marcus a savage blow on the neck, then followed up the stunning impact by a violent jab and shove.

Marcus stumbled back, the breath battered out of him by the jab to his diaphragm. Philip offered him a swift sweep of the foot, catching his sinewy legs. His balance destroyed, Marcus fell back, his right shoulder catching his fall against the hard floor.

Assuming as much cool nonchalance as he considered prudent, Philip stepped over him. Fighting his instincts, he forewent the kick that would have ordinarily finished his opponent off.

Marcus's expression was nothing short of astonished. "Jupiter, but you are strong! I have grappled with many men, but I have never seen a style quite like yours."

Philip bit his lip. Had Marcus expected to find an untrained weakling in him? Forcing his respect, he offered Marcus his hand. Marcus accepted it, rising with painful stiffness to his feet.

"By the gods! I shall feel that for some time." He grimaced, touching his swelling neck. "I might have known. You are as rebellious as any one slave could be. No common slave would strike his lord so heavily."

"You commanded it of me, my lord. I struck you at your own challenge."

"Truth." Marcus's mouth twitched with a hint of a smile. "You took my dare with ready vigor–and I cannot blame you. Jove, what a thing it is to be beaten by a slave!"

"Another round?"

"Yes." Marcus removed the silver bands encircling his wrists and tossed them onto his couch. "There–I am ready for you."

Philip drew back, readying himself. His eyes met Marcus's, anticipating his every move. Marcus stepped nearer, and, simultaneously, they circled one another. Then, Marcus himself sprang forward.

Philip braced himself, feeling the powerful force of the young man's strength. With lightening-like speed, he blocked his falling hand and averted the blow, twisting to disentangle himself. Assuming his first strategy, he gripped Marcus by the shoulders and twisted him downwards.

Marcus dropped to one knee, but quickly recovered himself. Swiftly, he regained his feet, shaking Philip's hands loose. In one rapid move, he blocked Philip against the wall.

"Take care, slave–I see your strategy."

Philip's breathing quickened. He attempted to dart past him and recover a favorable position, but Marcus's hand held him like a vise. Twisting, he struggled to free himself, seeking an opportunity to regain his hold on Marcus and force him back.

It was a futile attempt. Marcus had seen his strategy and it was too late to adopt another. And, in the face of his lord's superior strength, Philip sensed his inability to recover himself. He twisted, giving another, harder struggle. Marcus's mastery was apparent, but no Roman would down him without a fight.

Marcus easily forced him downward, albeit, making no move to strike him. On his knees, Philip looked up, knowing himself beaten. He hid his embarrassment with as much nonchalance as he could muster.

"You have caught on easily, my lord."

"Yes." Marcus released him. His eyes revealed his admiration. "And, it is to my own discredit that I have. You are some four years my junior, but I only won because you chanced to show your tactic. You are to be applauded."

The slow color came into Philip's face. Here was a Roman who did not scorn to admit himself beaten or to have met his match. Gratified, he bowed his head. "You are kind, my lord."

Marcus turned to recover his bands, fastening them thought-fully around his stalwart wrists. "Tell me," he said at last, "have you heard of tomorrow's festivities?"

"Yes." To Philip, the question was a pointless one. What slave in Rowland Virginius's household was not aware of the festival of *Cerealia*, the week-long celebration of the wheat goddess? A lavish dinner party was being thrown to most of Rome's most distinguished patricians and their families to celebrate the commencement of the festival.

"Then you must know that we will be in need of entertainment. After we returned today, Saturius approached my father concerning you."

"Saturius?"

"Yes. Saturius Quinctia, the father of Thallus." Marcus paused. "It seems Thallus desires to pit his own slave against you. Of

55

course, he only wishes to mortify me, but my father has given his consent."

Philip's heart sank. So now he, the eldest son of a chieftain, was to be brought to the level of an entertainer before every member of the dinner party? A wave of regret washed over him, and he struggled to keep from cursing his own arrogant folly. How little he had expected the forest gods to turn his show of strength against him!

"My lord, I don't know the rules of wrestling. I'm certain the way I came at you was far from within the guidelines."

"I will teach you."

"What if I fail?"

Marcus looked at him. "You will *not* fail."

Philip struggled to accept the irony in Marcus's voice. Had the decision been so finalized? He allowed as much appeal to creep into his voice and face as he dared. "I am only thirteen years, my lord. Surely you must consider your own honor! You said yourself Thallus desires this to humiliate you."

"That is why I tested you myself." Marcus fixed Philip with an immovable expression. "You are strong as an ox and nimble of foot. I have no fears for you–and your only fear must be failing me."

The meaning in Marcus's tone was clear. Philip felt sick. He must win or suffer. The choice was unmistakably presented.

"What if…" His voice cracked, nearly choking. "What if I don't–"

"Are you arguing with me?" Marcus stepped forward. He was ominously quiet, somehow threateningly so. The muscles tightened in his arms, and Philip sensed there was nothing that would keep him back from demonstrating who was master. His eyes narrowed. "Answer me."

Philip shook his head, miserable. A wave of rebellion shot through his chest, nearly choking him. By the gods, why should he be so demeaned? Why must his life be in total accordance to the will of his master? To be paraded as an object of sport; to be brutally punished if he failed; to constantly seek the pleasure of a man who cared nothing for him!

The thoughts brought the flaming color to his face. He could feel Marcus's dark, keen eyes resting on him, sending a prickle down his spine. Glancing sidelong, he saw his hand gesture ever so slightly, chilling him with the terrifying reality that his master knew his thoughts.

"I don't think you know who your lord is, Philip." Marcus played with his wristbands. His easy ability to remove them hinted at the readiness to take physical action. "Perhaps–"

"No." Philip's heart pumped wildly. Bound by dread, he bowed. Though outwardly submissive, he inwardly cursed the mysterious intuition that empowered Marcus to read his innermost thoughts. "I will do anything you command, my lord."

The following evening was warm and humid. The house of Rowland Virginius stood aglow with light, flooding the dusky street just beyond with warmth.

Inside, Philip stood leaning against one of the pillars in the atrium. As the attendant of Marcus, he had no household duties to speak of and was entirely at his leisure to watch the last-minute preparations of the dinner party.

In one corner of the banqueting chamber, musicians gathered, preparing their lutes and harps. An elderly slave made one final inspection of the chamber itself, fluffing up the cushions upon which the guests were to recline with delicate care.

Philip's keen eyes fell upon a group of beautiful young slave women. Their duties would be to serve and entertain the patricians–a volatile task when bestowed upon men who knew little restraint.

His heart ached as he looked at one of them. Though dark haired, she reminded him of his sweet mother, a gentle, yet courageous woman who had served her family well. Inwardly, he thanked the gods that she had been killed. It would have been more than he could have borne to see her turned into an object of Roman sport and lasciviousness.

At once, the laughing chatter of the women became stilled. Philip looked up to see Marcus stride through the entry. He motioned slightly to the women and they moved on, the delicate bells upon their wrists and ankles filling the air with their tinkling resonance.

Philip himself stood still, waiting. Marcus approached him.

"Are you prepared for the match tonight?"

"As ready as I will ever be, my lord."

Philip felt undeniable tension building up within him, seeing Marcus's features. Contrary to his usual carefree expression, Marcus's dark eyes held a glint of grim resolve. A cold chill washed over him, dwelling for one fleeting instant upon what might befall him if he failed.

Marcus eyed him menacingly. "Watch yourself well tonight, boy. I have a wager of fifty *sestertia* with Thallus, to say nothing of the value of my pride. I have no intentions of losing face with that despicable cur."

Philip felt a glimmer of mischief lightening his mood. "You do not like him any more than I do."

"I have little reason to. But we will not discuss it. Wrestle his slave into perdition tonight, and all shall be well with you."

At that moment, the steward announced that the house of Saturius had arrived. They entered the atrium with careless pomp, accepting the services of the slaves who hastened to serve them with callous unconcern.

Philip glanced at Marcus. Without taking his eyes from the party, Marcus answered his unspoken question, his voice low.

"The master is Saturius, his wife Julia, and, of course, the son and heir is Thallus. The young woman is Delicia, so named for her beauty."

Philip caught the slightly sarcastic ring that penetrated Marcus's tone as he said the last name. *Small wonder.* "A she-goat would be a greater object of beauty than she," he observed brashly.

Marcus wheeled suddenly about. His voice was a quick hiss. "Hold your tongue, insolent cub! Don't you know she is to be my *wife?*"

Philip stepped away from Marcus's flashing eyes, startled. He raised his hands, afraid Marcus was going to hit him.

Marcus glared at him, but did not move. "Her father and mine think our union will be a profitable one, both socially and politically."

"And—and you are willing to have her to wife?" Philip cringed at his own boldness, but was far too overcome with astonishment to check the burning question.

"Of course. I consider her a rare gem of accomplishment and high social status. Such a wife will greatly serve me in my future as a military patrician." Marcus paused, obviously annoyed. "But, by the gods, Philip, what is this matter to you? Will you never learn your place?"

Philip could not contain the disgust he knew must be creeping steadily over his features, but the knowledge Marcus was not far from passionate wrath curtailed his tongue. "I did not mean to give offense, my lord."

"Offense seems to be your greatest accomplishment. Go aid the other slaves at the door, and thank the gods my wagers are fixed on you tonight!"

Philip moved quickly away, fully understanding he was being punished. He took up a basin of water and threw a towel over his shoulder. So Marcus chose wounding his pride over striking him—a kind gesture!

He ground his teeth, his cheeks tingling. "Such generous forbearance," he muttered under his breath. "How careful he is of me when fifty *sestertia* are at stake!"

He moved across the wide atrium, unavoidably meeting the eagle-like gaze of Thallus. Even still, the haughty young patrician snapped his fingers at him. Resentfully, Philip obeyed the unspoken command.

Kneeling, he removed Thallus's sandals. His chest tightened, but he forced himself to wash his feet in the basin and dry them. The distasteful task done, he arose and looked Thallus boldly in the eye, offering a look of disdain in return for the young man's domineering expression.

"Will that be all, my lord?"

"Yes."

Thallus spoke coldly, his eyes holding an ominous expression. It was clear he had forgiven nothing. Philip fixed him with a fearless expression, unblinking, standing his ground until Thallus turned away.

Quickly, Philip put down his basin, wishing at all events to leave the entry before another party of guests arrived. From the corner of his eye, he saw Marcus come forward to greet his guests. Coldly, the young man shook hands with Thallus, then, took Delicia stiffly by the shoulders and kissed her on both cheeks.

A rare gem of accomplishment and high social standing—pure twaddle!

Philip shook his head. He was beginning to understand why Marcus had not punished his audacity more severely. He may be a slave, but he was no fool when it came to women. Indeed, he could almost pity his master for his unfortunate alliance.

The atrium was rapidly filling with guests. Uncomfortable by the clamorous noise and bustle of so many bodies, Philip slipped from the atrium into the banqueting chamber.

He took up his place in a quiet corner. His heart was already beginning to pound, but he brushed away the discomfort. Better to forget everything until the time of testing arrived. He would focus on the guests.

It was not long before all of the expected guests arrived and the banquet proceeded.

The female slaves carried gilded trays from couch to couch, presenting their tempting spreads of olives, salad, and oysters. The center piece of the feast was a large roasted boar, stuffed with radishes and onions, and basted in a sauce made of pepper, honey, and vinegar. The guests ate heartily, unmindful of the fact that seven courses were prepared for them.

Philip watched the gluttonous eating of the guests with inner disgust. The indulgence of these Roman patricians seemed to have no bounds. A tinge of gratitude penetrated his revulsion. At least being the personal attendant of his master kept him from the service of these swine.

From his position, he was clearly able to observe the occupants of Marcus's table. With an interest in his master's personal life he could scarcely understand, he watched them, Delicia in particular.

The young lady's giddy laughter was clearly discernable, even above the noisy din of the banqueting chamber. Philip shook his head. Flirtatious, haughty, and willful—he could discern her character at a glance. *The willfulness will change.* She was unsuited to Marcus to the core, but he at least would be the master over his own household.

Despite his personal opinions about her appearance, it was apparent by the behavior of the young noblemen that Delicia was considered a very attractive young lady. Philip grimaced wryly. *Little wonder, when strong drink flows like water.* He studied Delicia still closer, coming to a deeper assurance of the validity his own first impression.

Her stola was gaudy, its sea-green hue cutting a striking, goddess-like appearance. Rogue and powder embellished her countenance until all appearance of beauty was hidden, saved only by the flirtatious smile that hovered constantly on her parted lips. Like many Roman women, she wore a wig of curled light-brown hair, streaked by the blonde highlights that had taken fashionable Rome by storm.

Philip again shook his head. What could Marcus possibly do with such a wife? *He is no deity, but by Hercules! She'll wear him thin before the sun has set upon the marriage date! I wonder—*

"Philip!"

Philip started, jolted to reality by Marcus's stern voice. It was obvious the young man had summoned him more than once. He had risen from his reclined position upon the cushions and stood beside his table, impatience furrowed on his brow.

Quickly, Philip went to him, crossing his arms on his breast. "You called, master?"

"Yes—twice. Go now and prepare for the match. The guests desire their entertainment."

Philip felt an unmistakable chill run down his spine. Marcus was terrifyingly quiet, his dark eyes holding some unknown threat. Delicia's charms had not made the slightest good impact upon his humor. If anything, he seemed more merciless than before.

Philip bent his head, the icy hand of dread clamping around heart. *If I fail…*

"Yes, my lord."

Chapter Six

Alone in the quiet atrium, Philip quickly pulled his tunic over his shoulders and tossed it unceremoniously over a marble bench beside the pool. Thus stripped, he fastened a thin kilt of blue silk around his loins. In a wrestling match, ensuring his ability to move freely was essential.

Having completed his attire, there was nothing to do save return to the banquet chamber. Philip exhaled slowly, attempting to ease his growing apprehension. The room was warm, yet, a prickle of goose-bumps ran up his arms.

Philip ran his hands over his arms, considering. He was a Briton and, as one, he would fight and conquer. And, if he failed… Marcus would soon see that he could not wring a cry from him. Whatever terrible fate Marcus might hold for him, he would face it with quiet courage.

The gods aid me. Be it eagles or forests spirits—be my strength!

Surely, one of his own deities would help him. But, if not, Rome's gods would honor him for doing his best for his master. Philip squared his shoulders and threw out his chest before striding back into the noisy banqueting chamber.

A quick glance revealed that Thallus was nowhere visible. Evidently, he had gone in search of his own slave. Philip turned his attention to his master's table. Marcus beckoned him over, waving his hand over his table companions.

"Behold, friends! Here is the slave who will represent my wagers in the match tonight."

Delicia leaned forward, her brow quizzical. "Is *that* the infamous slave who struck my brother at the Baths?" A short laugh escaped her throat. "And I was of the opinion he was a rugged barbarian! Surely you are not going to pit that child against my brother's slave, Marcus."

The corners of Marcus's mouth tightened. "I am."

"And you expect him to win?"

"I do. These Britons have warfare in their very blood. Philip is strong and knows what is expected of him."

Delicia shrugged her pretty shoulders. "I can almost pity him for possessing a master with so little good sense. You might as well hand Thallus your *sestertia* now, my love."

Philip saw Marcus's eyes flash, his jaw clenching into a firm line. The other young men around the table shared a knowing wink, apparently amused by Delicia's sarcasm.

An uneasy feeling settled in Philip's stomach. For the first time, he was beginning to realize that it was no ordinary slave who was going to be pitted against him. Delicia's behavior signified it, and he certainly would not put it above Thallus.

He glanced at Marcus and saw with a sinking feeling that his fears coupled his own. Marcus was looking restlessly around the chamber, his eyes glittering.

In another moment, Thallus reentered the room. Marcus was instantly on his feet, his tones dark with indignation.

"By Jove, Thallus! Do you call this an equal match?"

Philip's heart failed him as he looked at the silent slave at Thallus's side. *A Goth.* Rugged, grim-faced, and muscular, he cut a formidable figure. The sickening feeling in his stomach increased, hearing Thallus's smooth tones.

"Come, Marcus! They are nearly the same age. What more can you expect?"

"I expected that you would keep your word, Thallus." Marcus's voice was tense with anger. "Your slave is both taller and broader shouldered than mine."

"And what of it?" Thallus laughed sardonically. "I have wagers to win also, *friend.*"

Marcus's mouth opened, then clamped in a hard, grim line. He turned, so fiercely Philip was startled.

"Confound the man!" He spoke in a type of hiss, his teeth tightly clenched. "Do not disappoint me, slave. I will not lose face to him.

Lose this match and—Jupiter be my witness!—I will send you to the arena. Do you hear me?"

Philip looked into his flashing pupils and knew he meant every word he said. He felt his own eyes flash, a tingling prickle running down his spine and clenching his hands into fists. *The arena.* The stadium of pleasure for the watchers, the grounds of death for the participants. Was this how he would end his days? As a gladiator? Or worse, as prey to starving lions?

Marcus resumed his seat. Philip saw his eye meet Rowland's, signaling his readiness for the match.

Rowland rose from his seat and lifted his hand for silence. An instant hush fell over the noisy banqueting chamber, and the guests turned expectant eyes on their host.

"Friends, as you all know, a wrestling match has been drawn up between the slave of my son Marcus and the slave of the noble Thallus Quinctia. By your pleasure, the contest will now commence."

A round of applause circulated. Rowland resumed his seat, gesturing.

Philip exhaled slowly, conscious of the cold beads of sweat on his brow. Now was the time. *Give me strength!* He stepped onto a mat in the center of the room, eyeing his opponent.

The German stood with wide-spread feet, his countenance grim. Evidently, their common lot was not one that brought them mutual sympathy. No doubt Thallus had made even worse threats than Marcus.

Philip fought to curtail his quickened breathing. *Relax. Fight like a Briton.* He glanced around, waiting for the signal.

An impartial patrician had been chosen for the referee. Without further adieu, he stepped forward and dropped a white handkerchief. With the traditional signal to start, Philip launched himself forward, a distant cheer echoing dimly through the hot blood pounding in his ears.

His body met the rugged strength of his opponent. Flailing, his hands fought to find the German's shoulders. In a flash, his fingers found his collarbone, then tightened, gripping his sinewy neck. The German twisted, his hands finding a place on Philip's shoulders.

Philip dug his bare feet into the mat. Jove, but the German was strong! He threw his entire weight against his opponent, tightening his strangling grip on his throat[1]. Marcus had spent much time impressing this point of the rules upon him—and he dared not forget them.

The German twisted again, but was unable to break Philip's hold. Adrenaline pounding through his veins, Philip forced him downwards, leverage increasing his strength. Slowly, agonizingly, the German was bent downwards until his hip brushed the mat.

The referee shouted a command. Philip released his hold, springing backwards. The first point was won! According to the rules, he allowed the Goth a moment to recover himself. He exhaled slowly, his heart beating wildly against his chest.

One point—two more to go!

With a rush of savage strength, the German sprang against Philip. Philip was startled by his vehement lunge. He twisted, his heart thudding. *Hold your ground! Don't let him—*

The Goth's hands found his shoulders, encircling his neck. Philip twisted violently, struggling to withstand his choking hold.

No! No!

The grip tightened. Philip gasped, choking. The German, with one savage move, thrust him downward, bending him against the floor. Philip cringed, feeling the mat beneath his naked back.

"Down!"

---

[1] This particular wrestling style was known as Pale or Greek wrestling. Points were scored when one player touched the ground with his back, hip, or shoulders (or upon being tapped out due to a winning submissive hold or being forced out of the wrestling grounds). Deliberate hitting/kicking was not allowed, although choke and other submissive holds were acceptable. Three points were required to win the match.

The referee's voice sounded above the noisy din, echoing in Philip's ears. He looked up, seeing Marcus through the red haze shrouding his gaze. The young man's countenance was dark, threatening. *The auction block, the arena...*

Philip sprang to his feet, controlling the groan that sprang to his lips. Already, his legs ached. The German was strong—and every bit as desperate as he was. With vehement force, Philip threw himself against his opponent, gripping his perspiring arms.

His breathing hot and hard, he looked into the German's eyes.

Bitterness. Rage. And the warrior's desire to kill.

Philip had seen the look before. He was not a chieftain's son for nothing. He knew the fierceness that governed this German slave. And he knew how to conquer him.

Making one violent, unexpected twist, Philip threw the German off his footwork. A second lunge, a fierce rush of strength, and he forced his opponent on his knees.

A roaring shout sounded in Philip's ears. *One more. One more!*

Behind him, Philip heard Thallus, his tones furious. *"Memento virgam, servies²!"*

Philip's breathing quickened. So his opponent would be flogged if he failed. *Little surprise.* Thallus was pitiless to the core. But, then, so was Marcus. It was his opponent or him—one of them must win, the other suffer.

Philip paused to allow the German a moment to recuperate. Their gaze locked, he saw the German's desperation. This next round would decide much.

With a shout, the Goth sprang forward. Philip was ready for him. Their arms locked in each other's deathly vise, the beads of sweat glistening on their tense foreheads. Philip dug his feet into the floor, pushing, fighting.

Don't trip. Don't fall! Force him down! Force him—

---

² Latin for "Remember the rod, slave!"

With a choked grunt, the German spun and stumbled to his knees. In a flash, Philip sprang atop him, forcing him to his belly upon the floor. He had him now.

As if in the distance, Philip heard the roaring cheers of the dinner guests. The German's hands flailed wildly, attempting to grip Philip's arm. Philip's breathing quickened. He knew the strategy.

Don't let him roll you! Don't let your back hit the ground!

Philip's hands tightened on his opponent's neck, choking him. Would the choke never be complete? *Great gods, help me!* His hands gripped harder, a rivulet of sweat running down into his eyes.

Then, he saw the signal.

Weak, nearly unconscious, the German lifted his finger. He conceded defeat.

"Down!" The referee's voice sounded through the hot blood pounding in Philip's ear. "The victory goes to the slave of Marcus Virginius!"

Shaking, Philip rose to his feet. The banquet chamber seemed to whirl around him, and he heard a wild din of handclapping and cheers.

You have won. Accept your victory.

Philip pulled himself erect. His heart pounded with an uncontrollable cadence against his chest. Slowly, as his mind cleared, he became conscious of his admirers. The women tossed golden bangles and silver denarius at his feet, lavishly applauding and cheering him.

A final surge of adrenaline coursed through his body, and he turned to lay eyes on his opponent. Already, the German was being dragged from the room. The expression of Thallus was terrible, his cold, grim countenance revealing his merciless intentions.

Philip felt a twinge, but brushed it resolutely aside. Men did not weep for their enemies. And, in the heartless jaws of slavery, it was every man for himself.

Marcus arose from his seat, beckoning. Philip approached him, boldly meeting the young man's eye. He had won, proving himself and his heritage before his conquerors. Inwardly, he breathed a tirade.

So much for your threats, Roman scum! The forest gods are not dead. Nor have they finished with me—or you!

"You have done well." Marcus spoke quietly, but there was a flashing light in his eyes that revealed his inner satisfaction. "Keep the spoils of your victory. You have won the right, and I am pleased to bestow them on you."

Philip bent his head. "The gods favor my lord for his generosity." He made no effort to hide his sarcasm. He had saved Marcus from disgrace before Thallus—and how graciously Marcus condescended to praise him!

Marcus alone could see his irony. His mouth tightened, but he made no reproof. "You may go."

Philip half-bowed, a sardonic smile playing about his lips. Turning, he gathered the spoils of his victory, then, straightened himself erect. A second round of applause met his ears. He lifted his hand before bowing, then, strode proudly from the room.

Outside the banquet-chamber, he stopped. The full reality of all that had occurred struck him like a *pugio* in the chest, and he exhaled slowly.

His heart had not yet resumed its normal cadence. *One, two, three...* Again, he exhaled. How strange was the favor of the gods! They had chosen him over his opponent. How else could he explain why it was not he who lay groveling for mercy beneath the fury of a master?

Philip straightened his shoulders, brushing aside the thought. He was not the victim, but the victor. And the victor he would remain.

"Hand me my belt." Marcus's tone was surly. Groggy and red eyed, he cut far from his normally dashing, handsome figure after a long night of revelry and heavy drinking.

Philip handed Marcus the belt, inwardly disgusted. These Romans drank like pigs. He called to mind scenes of the night before, as he had helped his inebriated master to bed. Little had he known that his victory over the German would inspire such uncontrollable consumption.

Insufferable louts, all of them. It didn't matter that his own people drank deeply. The Roman fashion of gorging themselves on food and drink went too far for his fancy.

"Bring me *mulsum*." Marcus's voice cut sharply through Philip's thoughts. "You doddering blockhead, can't you see what I want?"

Philip stifled an inner sigh and wordlessly poured out the honeyed wine. He had never seen Marcus so testy. Obviously, the consequences of such late night reveling were not as enjoyable as their momentary pleasure. "Will there be anything else, my lord?"

"Yes." Marcus's tight voice softened abruptly. "Tell me, Philip, what did your father say of your victory?"

"He was well-pleased, my lord."

"And, like a good son, you desire to give pleasure to your father. Am I right?"

Philip felt a tinge of confusion. He peered closely at Marcus. He seemed to have recovered well enough from last night's drunkenness, despite the lasting appearances. "Of course, my lord."

Marcus moved a step closer. "And, as my loyal servant, you desire to please me also?"

Philip gazed a moment at him. Marcus's dark eyes were sardonic. Despite what consequences might follow, he decided to play on his lord's sarcasm. "I desire to keep from the arena or the cross, master."

Marcus laughed unexpectedly. "Well-said. Continue to keep that desire." He cradled his cup and stepped to the casement, then, after

70

a brief glance at the street, turned about. "It would seem that you will have further opportunity to please me."

"What do you mean?"

"I mean that a champion wrestler such as you cannot be kept hidden. Already, I have had offers from two of my friends, desiring that you wrestle their slaves. I think it a good idea."

Philip felt the hot blood rush to his face. For a moment, he could not speak for anger. When he did, it was in a torrent. "By the great gods! How can–"

"Enough." Marcus's bleary eyes flashed with sudden fury. "You will do as you are commanded."

Philip's heart swelled with passion. How was he to continually endure such torture? How could he live under threat and in such constant peril of his lord's wrath? The thought was too much to endure.

Marcus stepped forward, considering him. "Come, Philip, I know you do not despise the laurels of victory. And, as your victories are a credit to your master, you have every reason for doing your best."

Naturally. There is no motivation like avoiding torture.

Philip ground his teeth. The overwhelming desire to attack Marcus, to fly at him with swinging fists almost frightened him. It was madness, he knew. But, oh! How easy it would be knock the haughty young patrician off his feet and prostrate him before his own slave. How doubly easy it would be to deliver one swift kick and watch him grovel in pain.

"You are a fool." Marcus's scornful voice cut through the red haze of his thoughts. "You think to rebel when you know no idiot would dare to do so."

Philip cringed, a prickle running down his spine. How did Marcus always know his mind? Was it so obvious? *Great gods! Will you never aid me? The man even knows my thoughts!*

Marcus stepped still nearer, chillingly quiet. "I will forbear to threaten you, Philip. We both know there is no need."

Philip swallowed hard. Of course. He had heard every threat Marcus had to make and knew his resolution better than any other. As always, his choices were laid clearly before him. A curse ran through his mind, condemning the unlucky fate that had brought him to this hopeless point.

Slowly, his hands found their place on his chest, averting his smoldering eyes. He was bound to speak submissively. "I am here to serve you, my lord."

"Yes." Marcus's contemptuous gaze rested on him. "So serve me well—and *live*."

Philip felt as if he were choking, helpless in the midst of his rage. *Live*. Except for avoiding torture, there was not much to live for if one was a slave. His heart twisted. Surely, somewhere, there was something beyond this meaningless existence.

Wasn't there?

Chapter Seven

Philip scanned the garden, feasting his gaze on the lush foliage. Its tranquility was refreshing, calming him. His eyes stopped at the sparkling fountain, resting on the clear water. Restless, yet calming, the liquid seemed to mirror his innermost being.

Eight matches. Seven victories.

The last two months had been one long, stimulating daze of activity and adjustments. Time had flown so quickly, without the full comprehension of its presence. He felt as if the days and weeks had merged into one never-ending blur. Days had been replaced by wrestling matches, giving life one sole purpose:

Victory.

But he had been treated well. Much as he hated to admit it, he had to acknowledge Marcus had met his victories with indulgence and even friendliness. Even after his one failure, when he had dreaded severe retribution, Marcus had said little. His confidence in his slave's ability to recover his prowess was firm.

Perhaps that is why he had taken such pains to prove himself on the next round. If Marcus had treated him harshly, he would have died rather than continue gratifying him. But Marcus had been just. And he had won every round since.

Philip shifted on his bench. The fates were surely with him. Now, he accompanied Marcus everywhere, his duties more of a companion than an attendant. And, within his master's wealthy circles, he was overwhelmingly popular. Everyone said he was spirited and handsome, a credit to his own country and to Rome.

Just thinking of it, he felt warm. It was followed by a twinge. His father said his mannerism had changed. He said he was careless, his manner free and pompous.

How the lowly love to ape their masters.

Philip stiffened. Only yesterday, Beric had called him aside and issued the first rebuke since their capture. It was strange how his words still haunted him.

How long do you think you can continue like this, Philip? Victory has spoiled you. You are haughty, willful, always exerting your demands. Marcus humors you for the time being, but he will not always do so. He is your master. I fear for you, my son. It will not be long before he brings you to your place.

Philip shrugged, trying to ignore the cold fingers of uneasiness creeping up his neck. His father was overly-cautious, perhaps even overbearing. Marcus was proud of his handsome, talented slave. Why should matters change?

He stood up, flexing his muscles. He watched their ripple with satisfied eyes. Strength had brought him far. Oh, he was still a slave. But triumph had won him many admirers and, one day, he would be the master. Under public pressure, Marcus would surely be bound to someday free him.

Marcus is a Roman, Philip. His indulgence is only of gratification, not affection. He will promote you only as long as you are bettering his popularity. And, when you have satisfied his desires, you will find that you are still his slave.

Philip ground his teeth. By the gods, why must his father insist on troubling his mind with dark forebodings? For the first time, he was content. His position was one of ease and pleasure–and Beric would not filch those things from him!

"Pluto take you!"

Philip turned, startled. Marcus stood behind him, frustration high in his face. He stepped towards Philip, his voice cross. "By Hercules, Philip, I have called you four times now."

"My apologies, Marcus." Philip assumed an easy air. Since the development of his popularity, he had lapsed into a less formal mode of address with his lord. Marcus had not stopped him. "For what reason did you call me?"

"I am going to the Baths. You will accompany me."

"And are you going to visit Delicia afterwards?"

"No." Marcus stifled a yawn. "At this point, the prospect of being tied to *one* woman seems a dismal bore. Thank the gods our betrothal is not yet official." Then, as Demetrius appeared, "Well, and what do you want?"

"The lord Thallus is here to see you, sir. He is in the atrium."

The look that crossed Marcus's face was decidedly vexed. "Confound the man! His visits are becoming increasingly more regular." Then, to Philip, "Come; I must meet with him."

Philip followed Marcus from the garden. He suppressed a sigh. If there was anyone who disliked a visit from Thallus as much as Marcus, it was he. Time had made no great change in his character, and Thallus was cold and disagreeable. At times, he wondered why Thallus bothered to visit Marcus at all. Was it because they were to be brothers-in-law? Or did he have a more sinister reason in mind?

In the atrium, Thallus stood impatiently awaiting the arrival of his host. As Marcus appeared, he stepped forward, extending his hand.

"Good day, Marcus."

"And to you, Thallus." Marcus scarcely touched the out-stretched hand. He seemed unwilling to hide the fact that his guest's visit brought him little pleasure. "What brings you here?"

"Do I need a reason to visit my brother-to-be? But, I do have a reason of more importance for my visit."

"Continue."

"Your handsome slave." Thallus's gesture was strangely tangible. Philip felt a pit settle in his stomach. "My father is hosting a large party one week from today. I desire to set a slave of mine against yours in a match. What say you?"

"I object."

Thallus started a little, then laughed and colored. "Oh, come, Marcus! The match will be fair enough."

"It cannot be fair enough in my opinion." Marcus maintained a cool, unyielding demeanor. "Your word profited little in the last match I agreed to on your terms. Philip is a valuable slave, and I shall not pit him against your sorry Goths."

Thallus's face rapidly gathered blackness. "I do not believe it is for concern for your slave that causes you to refuse me, Marcus. If I did not know better, I should say it was *cowardice*."

Marcus colored with what Philip knew was suppressed anger. "I do not know what you insinuate, Thallus. Of what am I afraid?"

"Your precious Briton, I should say." Thallus laughed discordantly. "We all know that he is a very rebellious, hot-headed slave and that you, Marcus, are still foolishly disinclined towards breaking his spirit once and for all."

"I have no *need* of breaking his spirit. It has served me well. And, as I have often reminded you, Philip knows better than to set his will against mine."

"Yes, so you have often said." Thallus's narrowed eyes were more eagle-like than ever. "But you have never proved it, Marcus. Command him to kneel at your feet and pay you the homage a submissive servant should."

"Is that a challenge?" Marcus snapped at him.

"It is." Thallus laughed. His smooth voice dropped like oil from a broken jar. "Unless, of course, you do not wish to sully your honor with his rebellion. And you do know he will rebel, Marcus."

Marcus's grim countenance befitted a gladiator. His lips tightened, the wrathful color tingeing his swarthy countenance. He turned, his sandals squeaking at his abrupt movement. "Philip, come here."

Philip clenched his teeth as he stepped forward. Already, he was seething in resentment. The two young men had spoken as if he were not present. Was he not a living being, a *champion* of the banquet halls of Rome? Or was he no more alive than the statues adorning the room? The thought sent burning heat pulsating through his temples.

Marcus's gaze was stony. "You have heard the challenge. Kneel at my feet."

Scorn flickered over Philip's mind. How easily Marcus had been persuaded to humiliate his slave. But he would not be so easily swayed. *Masters of the universe—cowardly, haughty swine! So you succumb to see me grovel. But you will not see it, Roman.*

"Do you hear me, slave?" Marcus's furious voice rent through the red haze of his thoughts. "Obey!"

Philip stiffened, drawing himself erect. Now was the time. He was a champion, a son of Britain! Marcus was *nothing*. And no worthless cur would humiliate him before a son of Rome.

"No."

The defiance in his tones rang throughout the atrium. It was shrouded by death-like silence.

Marcus started visibly. Shock and passion flooded his demeanor for one full moment before he acted. Philip braced himself against the pain as Marcus's hand found his arm, its grip furiously intense.

"Are you daring to defy me, you lowly dog?" Dark and low, Marcus's voice signaled he was giving one final chance.

Philip chose to ignore the warning. "I am." Adrenaline pounded through his veins, filling him with a strange, wild strength. He heard his own voice, all restraint broken. It seemed as if all the hate he had harbored since his capture chose this moment to break forth. "Better to be a dog of Briton than a swine of this accursed nation, Roman scum!"

A stinging blow fell across his face. Half-stunned, he stepped back, trying to regain his balance. Somewhere, deep inside, something rent. He could feel all self-control tearing, replaced by a rage he had never known himself capable of.

Curse, curse you!

He heard his own voice, shouting. A red haze blinded him, leaving only Marcus's shadowy outline in its wake. He projected himself forward. His chest brushed Marcus's side, his hands flailing to find his throat, to strike him, to kill him!

A second blow sent him spinning. Pain contorting his face, Philip felt the floor beneath him. A tiny stream of blood trickled into his mouth. He spat, struggling to rise. *Get up! Don't kneel!*

An iron hand seized him, pulling him upwards. Struggling, Philip lifted himself, only to feel a violent fist punch into his diaphragm. He choked, coughing, struggling to breathe. A second blow landed deep in his stomach, expelling the little breath still left in his burning lungs.

"Curse you!"

Philip dimly heard Marcus's enraged voice. He crumpled. Darkness shrouded his vision, then, slowly, an orb of light flooded his eyes. The room came into focus, revealing Marcus's furious countenance.

Thallus's mocking laughter grated in Philip's ears. "I shall return later, Marcus! And, by that time, I shall expect your *spirited* slave to have learned his place."

Philip coughed violently, attempting to breathe. He watched Marcus escort Thallus to the door, saw their hands clasp in farewell.

The uncontrollable rage was gone. Its wild power had left him helpless, weak. Philip raised himself on one elbow, dimly seeing a splatter of blood on his tunic. Slow panic began to spread through his chest.

Great gods, help me! It was too late to redeem himself, too late to run. Was he now going to die? Philip drew a shaky, gasping breath. He had no hope that the brunt of his punishment was over. He knew Marcus far too well for that.

Don't let him kill me! For the sake of my father—

Marcus turned, his countenance terrible. Even at the distance between them, Philip could see his eyes blazed with murderous, merciless intent. He stepped to a small table beside the entry and picked up a small *flagellum*. The small whip had never looked so ominous. His fingers closed around the handle, deliberation governing his every act.

A shudder ran through Philip's body, momentarily paralyzing him. Was he to be beaten to death? Marcus strode towards him, loosening the metal bands encircling his wrists.

You are still his slave. His father's words washed over his mind. Philip struggled to his knees, lifting an imploring hand, willing the uplifted *flagellum* to stop. "*Marcus!* Please—"

The whip descended, slashing his arms. Philip cried out in agony. He buried his head in his arms, attempting to protect himself.

"Roman dog, am I?" Marcus's angry voice cut through the hot blood pounding in his ears. "And what are *you?* Nothing but a plague! You will regret what you have done, filth."

A searing pain shot through Philip's leg. He swallowed, fighting back the impulse to scream. The whip descended again, over his calves, his loins. A wave of faintness washed over him, nauseating him. He felt his knees slide out from under him on the cold marble floor. Still shielding his head, he rolled onto his stomach, cringing as the fiery lash stung his thighs.

His lungs burned uncontrollably. He wanted to cry, to scream. A heavy weight pressed harder and harder on his chest, choking him. Tears welled up in his eyes, but he couldn't breathe to sob. The salty moisture crept down his perspiring face, stinging his cuts.

Dimly, he heard the rustle of Marcus's clothing and the whistle of the *flagellum* being raised. He lay still, waiting for the lash to tear his back.

So this is the end.

The sound of a crash filled the room. Philip saw the shadow of the *flagellum* as it was hurled across the atrium, landing with vehement force against one of the marble busts at its end.

He raised his head. Bewildered, he watched Marcus stride angrily from the atrium, leaving the lash where it had fallen. A death-like silence followed his departure, leaving only the echo of his blows pounding in Philip's ears.

Shaking, Philip lifted himself, struggling to his knees. Searing pain throbbed throughout his body, escaping in a sobbing moan.

He looked down, seeing blood seep from the crimson welt stretched across his arms. A cold trickle ran over his calves, and, touching them, he brought his hand away scarlet with blood.

A cold shudder ran over him. He bent his head forward, fighting the impulse to lose consciousness. His mind reeled and he felt sick, but bewilderment aided his struggle for sensibility.

Why had Marcus stopped? Had seeing his slave lie prostrate and helpless before him been enough? Or was he about to return?

Philip struggled feverishly to his feet. He was not going to wait for Marcus to return and order his crucifixion. Tears swam in his eyes, but he dashed them impatiently aside. *A son of Briton cannot cry. You cannot!*

His body protesting every step, Philip stumbled to the entry. Marcus's cape and money pouch lay carelessly thrown over a settee, where, ordinarily, a slave would find and restore them to their proper place.

Take them.

Philip snatched up the cape and threw it over his shoulders, hiding his bleeding arms. He quivered from head to foot, scarcely able to think.

There was but one thought that reigned uppermost in his fevered mind: it was now freedom or death. There was no other option. He would no longer endure this curse of slavery. If he lived, it would be as his own master. And, if he died, it would be by his own hand, not writhing on some Roman cross.

Leave now!

Casting one final glance behind him, Philip tucked the pouch into his belt and stepped out into the humid air.

Chapter Eight

Dusk was falling. Philip pulled his cape more tightly around him, quickly scanning the pedestrians still upon the streets. They paid him little attention. *Be natural.* So long as he carried himself well, no one would suspect him of being anything but a slave intent on an errand.

Philip's heart thudded wildly. For one fleeting moment, his mind dwelt upon his father. *Forget him.* If he was caught, he would die anyway. It was best to forever estrange his heart from Beric and focus on one thing: liberty.

Run. Before Marcus discovers you are gone!

He darted quickly down the marble steps. Stepping onto the cobble-stoned *Vicus Tuscus,* he mingled with the passing pedestrians, then, when certain he would attract no attention, broke into a run.

His lugs pumped beneath him, aching. Philip inhaled deeply and tried to ignore the burning pain shooting up and down his calves. His mind spun, and he felt weak and dizzy. Where had his strength gone? Where was the fearless Briton, the champion wrestler of Roman banquet-halls?

His eyes scanned the road before him, seeking sanctuary. Where could he hide? And, above all, how could he hide his true identity? An ordinary slave could easily escape unnoticed, but there was little chance for a Briton, whose blonde hair and blue eyes stood him apart from all others.

His Latin was tolerable, but could he hope to mix with the common people? There was precious little slang spoken in the Virginius household, and although he had picked up a few phrases elsewhere, he had previously scorned to speak them.

Run, run!

Philip brushed shoulders with a hurrying patrician, jarring him. With a muffled oath, the man shoved him aside.

"Watch where you are going!"

Philip stumbled against a nearby wall and warily watched the man hurry on. He stood still, his breathing ragged. His diaphragm was sore, still protesting the fierceness of Marcus's blow.

Slowly, he straightened himself erect and forced himself to take a few staggering steps. He *must* keep going. If he should be caught... The thought sent a thrill of fear prickling down his spine. Spurred onward, his legs again raced beneath him.

Before long, the *Vicus Tuscus* led into the *Imperial Fora*, revealing a maze of streets, colossal buildings, and temples. Philip shuddered. It was here he had been sold to Marcus and attempted his first escape.

This time I will not fail.

He paused, gathering his cape around him. His choice of options was dazing, to say the least. Should he attempt to gain employment in one of the many shops? Or would it be safer to lose himself among the poorest class of Rome, perhaps in the *Subura*, or, slum district?

Considering the language problem, Philip brushed the thought aside of mixing with the low-lives. And, weariness was already overtaking him. He could not hope to find sanctuary before the need for rest became necessary.

The necessity seemed almost immediately at hand. Philip struggled to keep his bleary eyes open. His head ached wildly, and he could scarcely command his legs to walk. He forced himself to take a few more steps, then, collapsed beneath a pastry booth.

The owner had gone for the night, leaving the booth uninhabited. Surely, he would be safe here until morning. He would snatch a few hours of sleep and regain the strength Marcus had sapped from him. Then, his mind would be clear for further decisions.

Philip pulled himself more fully beneath the booth. Wearily, he settled himself into a comfortable position and spread his cape over himself.

For several minutes, he gazed up at the stars, their luminous twinkle growing brighter as the dusky sky darkened into blackness. Slowly, a soft mist welled up in his eyes.

How different the stars appeared here than they had at home. The remembrance of the rolling green hills and rugged forests of Britain rolled over his mind, a striking contrast to the marble and stone surrounding him.

They were hard. Cold.

Philip shuddered. Like Marcus. Rome was all the same. From her colossal buildings to her masters, she was merciless, unyielding. How had he ever come to underestimate his lord's authority? Beric had been painfully right.

Marcus. Philip clenched his fists, swallowing back a moan as pain shot through the lash-mark scoring his arms. Oh, mighty gods! Marcus must not find him. The thought of what would befall him was too much to endure.

He turned over, his lips moving in silent petition. *Guide me, oh great gods of my forefathers. Keep Marcus from finding me. I will make good on my vow. I will destroy Rome. Only, keep Marcus away...*

Philip awoke with a start, feeling the warmth of the bright morning sun streaming upon his face. He squinted upwards, then, scrambled to his feet, scarcely avoiding the surly kick of a merchant.

"Oaf!" The man shouted, shaking his fist at him. "This is not a public inn! Begone, before I lay hands on you!"

Philip thrust a hasty hand into Marcus's purse and held up a small coin. "My apologies, good sir. Allow me to make good on my trespass by purchasing a pastry."

The countenance of the merchant transformed with radical speed. Striking a brisk mannerism, he bent his head. "Ah, yes. Permit me just a moment, young sir."

Philip grinned to himself. If he was a patron, then, apparently, all was forgiven. Impatiently, he waited for the merchant to select the delicate sweetmeat. When it was handed over, he tossed the man his coin and strode away.

The taste of the pastry was sweet on his tongue. It quickly became gall, a cutting reminder. He had often eaten sweetmeats like this in the banqueting hall of Marcus's friends. And, until now, he had enjoyed them.

His steps slowed, thoughts of Marcus foremost in his mind. Where was he to go?

Already, the forum was bustling with activity. Most of the street-side merchants and shop owners had opened for business, and the air hummed with a din of Greek, Latin, and foreign tongues. Plebians, slaves, patricians, and soldiers mingled together, intent upon business and pleasure.

Philip warily eyed the latter. Knowing Marcus's pride, he was certain the slave-catchers had already been informed of his escape. Was it possible the forum soldiers had also been notified?

Instinctively, he pulled the hood of his cape over his blonde hair, partially shielding his bruised face. The sight of a battered British slave with no apparent business to attend to was almost certain to attract attention.

"Move back!"

Philip stepped back against a wall as a line of shackled slaves were herded past him. The slave master brandished his *flagellum*, shouting an order in some foreign tongue. The slaves shuffled by, sullen and silent, their gaze fixed moodily upon the cobblestones beneath their feet.

Philip's gaze rested on their naked backs, scored by the whip. A shudder ran through him. *Welcome to Rome.*

The sound of the *flagellum* striking a victim echoed in Philip's ears. He turned away, gripped by nausea. Upon the auction block, he had known slavery was a curse, but now his entire soul rose up in sorrow for those about to be sold.

Was this really what life was all about? Men owning other men, torturing them, stripping them of hope and spirit? Why had the fates decreed it thus? He felt sick, but some compulsion forced him to watch the slave master herd his helpless prey towards the auction block.

His heart lurched. *Marcus!*

Surrounded by several soldiers and a man who could only be a professional slave-catcher, Marcus stood on one of the lower steps of the temple of Janus. His dark eyes scanned the milling crowd, restless, searching.

Philip shrank back against a wall, inhaling sharply. How was it possible? Marcus—*here?* Hundreds of runaway slaves inhabited the city; why had he not obtained his happy freedom as easily as they? Why had fate brought him only a few paces away from the young man he never wanted to clap eyes on again?

Run. Now!

Philip leaned forward, breathing hard. His eyes darted over the milling crowd, taking a quick survey of Marcus.

At that precise moment, the slave-catcher lifted his eyes, and, even from that far distance, Philip felt his gaze rest upon him. The slave-catcher brushed Marcus's shoulder in quick awareness, pointing.

Marcus's eyes narrowed, following the direction of the man's finger. He ran down the temple steps, his exclamation audible even above the forum's noisy din. "He is here!"

They had seen him! Philip turned and dashed into the hordes of incoming shoppers. He fought his way through them, wild adrenaline coursing through his veins. *Run, run!*

Behind him, Philip heard a slow murmur, like a storm rolling over the Mediterranean Sea. The sound loudened into a shout, spreading through the crowd.

"Stop him! Runaway slave!"

Philip's heart pounded uncontrollably. His lungs constricted, burning so that he could scarcely breathe. He couldn't stop; there wasn't time!

A rough hand rested on his shoulder, gripping his shoulder.

"Stop, in the name of the Caesars!"

Philip half-turned. In one fluid move, he drove his elbow into his antagonist's diaphragm, following up the forceful jab with a swift punch to the stomach.

The plebian let him go, grunting. Philip dashed on before the man could recover himself, hearing the cry resume behind him.

"Stop him! Stop him!"

Philip looked frantically about. Where could he go? Where could he hope to hide? From small to great, the crowd was against him, spurred on by the relentless shouts of his pursuers.

He stumbled over a jutting piece of cobblestone, his foot catching against a basket. Figs rolled out into the street, and the fruit peddler swore angrily at him.

Philip regained his feet, breathing heavily. Ordinarily, such running would be nothing to him, but not now. Pain shot through the lash marks creasing his legs, strangely sickening him.

Nearly spent, he darted down a side-street, again stumbling. He staggered forward, brushing against the chest of a tall, fixed form.

"Steady there, lad."

The kind voice calmed the pounding in Philip's ears. He looked up into the quiet face of a middle-aged man. Desperate, a wave of urgency burst from his throat. "Give me sanctuary, sir! I am spent."

Silently, the man motioned to the open door of a bakery directly to his right.

Brushing past him, Philip darted inside. He stood, panting, just beyond the threshold. If only the crowds had not noted his turn, he would be safe.

The man stepped inside, closing the door upon its rustic hinges. Philip looked up at him, attempting to recover his breath. "May the gods bless you, good sir! You will be well-paid—I swear it."

"Sit down, boy." The man gestured to a low couch. "I will bring bread."

Philip collapsed gratefully on the couch, his legs throbbing. His wounds burned like fire, doubtless from overexertion. His benefactor had aided him none too soon. Another few moments, and he was certain he would have collapsed in the street.

The man returned to the room with a platter of bread and olives in one hand, a pitcher of wine in the other. He set the platter before Philip. His bearded face was kind.

"I am Daniel of Judea. I was once a resident of Jerusalem; now, I am a breadmaker of Rome. This is my humble shop and home, which I open freely to you. Now, tell me, my young friend, who are you?"

"I am Philip, once of Briton." Philip spoke slowly. It was useless to hide his identity—any man with eyes knew he was a Briton. Still, it was almost as if admitting his ancestry was to acknowledge himself a slave.

Daniel seemed to notice his hesitance, but he did not question him. Stepping across the room, he took up a pitcher of water and a towel. With an easy air, he returned and knelt before Philip, removing his sandals.

Philip started a little. This man was no slave! Why did he wash his feet? He felt a tinge of color creep into his cheeks, strangely humbled and relieved. Surely this man did not know who he was, or he would never perform so menial an action.

"You are very kind, sir. I thank you."

"I am pleased to be of service to you, young Philip." Daniel looked up from drying Philip's feet, his tones even. "You seemed to be in a great hurry a moment ago."

"Yes." Philip felt foolish. What else was he to say? He could not explain his haste without lying, and, at the moment, his overwrought mind would not allow him to think of a single plausible excuse.

As his mind slowly clearly, the searing pain in his legs increased. Philip bit his lip, withholding a groan. He saw Daniel glance at the lash marks, his face gravely quiet.

New fear gripped Philip's heart, escalating his pulse to its former pounding cadence. *If he suspects you, you're as good as lost! He cannot know the truth.*

"These Roman charioteers will let nothing stop them," he heard himself say lightly. "I passed one in the street this morning and he gave me the lash for not hurrying past him quickly enough. Nice work, isn't it?"

"It is indeed." A strange smile hovered over Daniel's mouth. "By all appearances, he buffeted you pretty sorely, my boy."

Philip colored a little. Of course, his face must be covered in bruises. The heavy clouts of Marcus would have not have left him without a mark. "I–I tripped in an alley earlier."

The foolishness of the lie struck Philip even before the words left his mouth. This man Daniel would be dense indeed to believe him.

"Were you on some task for your master then?"

Daniel spoke matter-of-factly, as if he believed Philip's explanation. Philip's heart sank, but he fiercely chided himself. *You're a Briton. It is only natural to assume you are a slave.*

"Yes. My lord sent me out this morning." Anxious to change the disagreeable subject, Philip pulled a *dupondius* from the pouch at his waist. "I wish to repay you for your kindness. Please accept this coin as a token of my gratitude."

Daniel rose to his feet, returning the pitcher and towel to their former places. "No, young Philip. Freely have I received favor, freely will I serve you."

Philip stared at him. "You will not accept it?"

"No."

"But, why?" Philip felt foolish, stammering the words. But, then, it was small wonder he was surprised. There was not another man

88

in Rome who would reject recompense, even if it were a far more trifling sum than he offered.

Daniel looked at him with a gentleness Philip had never before seen in a free-born man. "My faith bids me do unto you as I would also have done unto myself, my boy."

"Your *faith*?"

"Yes."

Philip felt a wave of frustrated confusion. What sort of *faith* kept a man from accepting his well-merited reward? "You mean your religion?" he said, more as if in a statement of the facts than a question.

"You could call it that." Daniel moved forward, seating himself beside Philip. "Yet, it is no ordinary religion, Philip." He paused, his countenance contemplative. "More than a meaningless religion, my worship involves a personal relationship with my God, the One I love."

The concept was too much for Philip. Love one's deity? Honor and devotion were understandable traits, but *love*? He eyed his host. This Daniel was growing more and more confusing.

Daniel seemed to sense his bewilderment. Gently, he laid a hand on Philip's knee. "I see you don't understand, Philip. But, then, how should you? I dare say you've never heard of such a notion until now."

"You never spoke more truly." Philip smiled half-sarcastically. "The idea of turning down gold for one's God is unheard of in Rome."

"Or in all parts of the world, we could say." Daniel chuckled lightly. "And, I think you will find my faith more interesting still. You are a slave. Would it interest you to learn that there are no distinctions of race and rank in the teachings of my beliefs?"

Philip laughed. "Then it is small wonder I have never heard of your *faith*, my good host. It cannot be a very popular notion." Then, sarcastically, "Does your faith have a name?"

"We are called Christians."

A slow look of understanding flitted across Philip's face, and he moved a little back from his host. "Great gods, I have heard of you."

Daniel smiled a little. "You look startled to meet one of us."

"I am. Is it not illegal under the divine emperor to claim that religion?"

"Yes."

Philip gazed curiously at Daniel. Here was a man after his own heart. He broke the law and was not afraid to own it. "Then why do you do it?"

"Those who have seen and accepted the truth are not ashamed to stand by it, Philip. And, as Christians, we do not fear what the emperor or any other man can do to us."

"Even death?" Philip felt a wave of incredulity.

"Yes, even death. In Christ, there is no fear of death, because we have hope of life eternal. This life is but temporary, a passing shadow that is soon gone. It is after death we go home to our Lord Jesus Christ and will live forever in His glorious presence."

Skeptical as he was, Philip felt a slow tinge of longing. Daniel spoke with such joy, with the fervor of passionate assurance. It was if he had *purpose* to his life–a purpose other than living out the ceaseless routines of daily life, spurred on only by the hatred of those who owned and hurt him.

Blessed hope. What he himself would not give to have such an assurance! To live eternally with this glorious God, forever freed from the hated presence and name of Marcus!

Still, he was unconvinced.

"It sounds beautiful enough, but I don't understand why you Christians should get to live eternally. I've heard you drink blood[3], as our Druid priests do. Is this what your God requires of you?"

---

[3] The Romans took the meaning of Christian Communion literally and thought that they actually drank human blood and ate human flesh. The opinion that they were cannibalistic was among the many reasons Christianity became outlawed.

90

"The old rumor." Daniel waved his hand. "No, there is no truth in that speculation, Philip. It is no more than a wild tale, invented that our Emperor Nero might better serve his own ends." He paused. "But, as to what our God requires of us, it is only that we accept His free grace and forgiveness."

A look of scorn settled on Philip's face. "No god accepts us without a sacrifice of sorts."

"True." Daniel looked steadily at him, his features kind. "That is why our God sent His only Son, Jesus Christ, to die for us and pay the blood-sacrifice. He did so rather than demand the price of our sin–death–, thus showing us His great mercy and love."

Mercy. Love. Grace.

The words were new ones when connected with a deity. Philip pondered the idea in his mind. What sort of a God sent His only Son to die for mortal man? *A beautiful fantasy*, he thought dryly. *Beautiful, captivating, and impossible.*

"A strange God you have," he said aloud. "He sends His only Son to make princes of you all, but refuses to give you comfort here in–what was it?–your *temporal* home. I still do not understand why you won't accept my *dupondius*. Is it wicked to enjoy the means of pleasure?"

"No." Daniel chuckled. "Comfort is not forbidden to us, and I know you do not believe your own sarcasm." His hand found a place on Philip's shoulder. "My faith bids me welcome the stranger and help the weary, that is all."

"So you *can* accept it." Philip pulled the coin again from his pouch. "Since it won't offend your God, take it and let us have done."

Daniel paused a moment. "Truth be told, I have still another reason for refusing it, Philip."

"Why?" Philip felt the hairs bristle on his neck and a tinge of angry color washed over his face. "Is it because I am a Briton?"

"No." Daniel arose and stepped to the window, momentarily looking out. He turned, his voice and eyes gentle. "I do not accept it because I do not think it is yours to give."

Philip stiffened. "I don't know what you mean."

"I mean that it is unlawful for a slave to take his master's money and give it to another."

Daniel's steady tones unnerved Philip. His keen, quiet eyes seemed to see through him, as if he knew all the dark secrets he harbored.

He knows!

A sickening feeling of helplessness washed over Philip, gripping his body. His heart began to pump wildly, thumping against his chest. Shaking, he rose to his feet. "You imply a great deal, my host."

"And there is something in your eyes that tells me much, Philip." Daniel stepped toward him, gently laying his hand on Philip's trembling shoulder. "I am no fool, my boy. You were not lashed by a charioteer, nor did a fall cause those many bruises."

"What if you are wrong?" Philip defiantly met Daniel's gaze, desperately attempting to still his shaking hands.

"I am not wrong."

Slowly, agonizingly, Philip's gaze dropped. What could he say? If Daniel suspected the truth, there was no changing his mind.

He is a Christian. I have that over him. He can't turn me in—his own life would be at stake.

Emboldened by the thought, Philip again looked up. "And if you are right?"

"Then I would counsel you to return to your master."

A sudden bitter laugh caught Philip's throat. "Return to my master? If you weren't a fool, you are now." He stretched out his arms towards Daniel, anger boiling in his face. "See what he has done to me? I am scarred for life! And now you would see me nailed to some cross?"

"No." The pressure of Daniel's hand deepened on his shoulder. "Your punishment might be severe, true, but I cannot counsel you otherwise."

"Why? Does *Christianity* require that slaves endure torture simply because it is the will of their master to bestow it on them?" Philip spoke in angry bitterness. He could feel his countenance working, caught between fear and emotion.

Daniel considered him. His eyes were understanding. "You have been ill-used and vexed–I can see it clearly, Philip. I don't doubt you have suffered many wrongs, but, Philip, think upon your own actions. Have you been a faultless slave?"

"And if I haven't?" Philip spat the words. What right did this Jewish breadmaker have to challenge him? "I thought you Christians believed in *justice*. Is it right that I suffer, that I am forever scored by the whip?"

"I don't know." Daniel's voice was mild. "I don't know what it was you did or under what circumstances your lord punished you. And, truly, I am not here to judge either you or him."

"No." Philip shook Daniel's hand off his arm, stepping angrily away. "You are not here to judge—only to counsel me to return to the man who will see me scourged and writhing on a cross! You are not a slave–you don't understand what it is I suffer!"

A measured look of reminiscing flitted across Daniel's face. Slowly, he pulled up his sleeve, revealing a deep, crimson scar. "I know what it is you suffer, Philip."

At the sight of the lash-mark, Philip felt some of the fire leave his chest. His tones quieted. "Who treated you so?"

"A Roman legionary." Daniel spoke steadily, quietly. "I was brought here from Judea as a slave ten years ago. Water was scarce during one point of our journey, and I fainted from exhaustion on the way. I was flogged to my feet."

Philip felt his passion subside. If Daniel had been a slave, then, they shared mutual ground. "How did you escape?"

"I didn't." Daniel pulled down his sleeve, hiding the scar. "I was sold and labored as a slave in a villa for many years. But, eventually, I won favor with my master and he released me."

Philip's gaze fluttered downward. "There is no favor to be won with my master."

"Perhaps."

"Don't you care?" Philip felt a wave of desperate frustration. "Does my fate meaning *nothing* to you?"

"I care more than you could ever know, my boy. The injustice of slavery is something that will always grieve me, partly because I have been where you stand, partly because I am a Christian. But, still, I can only counsel you to return and submit to your master. There is no other way, both by Roman law and in the laws of my faith."

"Then I reject them both."

"Can you?"

Philip was stunned by the question. Truly, could he? He could hide for a time from the law, but could he forever? And, having once heard of this mysterious and beautiful Christianity, could he erase it from his mind?

Daniel stepped towards him, momentarily dropping his eyes. He then lifted them to meet Philip's gaze. "Philip, there is nothing I would want more than to keep you safe here. It grieves me to think of all you might endure if you are caught. But, as you know, I cannot harbor you."

"No." His passion gone, new weariness overshadowed Philip. "I would not have you risk your life for me. I will go."

Turning, he strode to the couch he had earlier reclined on. Picking up his cape, he threw it again over his shoulders, pulling the hood over his blonde hair.

Daniel watched him, his eyes strangely overcast. He seemed truly sorry to turn him out. Philip hesitated, then, quietly took the few steps between them and held out his hand.

"I thank you, Master Daniel. You have been good to me—I will not deny it. May your God bless you for your kindness towards a helpless slave."

"And may He also bless you, Philip." Daniel's voice was low. "I trust you will one day come to trust in Him and accept His mercy as your own."

Mercy. Philip laughed bitterly. "You are a good man, Daniel—and a dreamer. Mercy is not a thing to be shown towards one like me."

He turned and strode towards the door. Without a backwards glance, he swung it wide. A quick cry of alarm escaped his lips.

"*No!*"

Chapter Nine

It was too late to duck back into the safety of the house, too late to run or hide. Marcus stood a few paces away, surrounded by his soldiers and the slave-catcher. And he had seen him.

Philip stepped out into the street. He would not endanger Daniel's reputation and liberty by being caught within his home. Whatever his crazy notions, the man had been kind to him.

A dizzying plethora of thoughts ran rampant through his mind. Should he fight back? Or should he surrender peaceably, hoping Marcus would spare his life?

He didn't have the time to decide.

A second later, and Philip felt the heavy hand of the slave-catcher slap him, felling him to the ground. He grazed his shoulder painfully against the jutting corner of the bread shop, nearly striking his head. His hood fell back, exposing his countenance to clear view.

Kill me now. By my gods, your gods, and the God of the Christians, don't crucify me!

A figure stepped over him, blocking out the brightly-streaming sun. Philip looked up into Marcus's cold face, feeling his anger in the very shadow stretched over his body.

"Yes, this is the slave." Marcus's tone radiated cold displeasure. "Bind him and let us go."

The soldiers bent over him, jerking him by the shoulders to his feet. Philip made no move to defend himself. Dull, spiritless apathy washed over him. If this was the end, he had no strength to prevent it.

Marcus watched silently. As his hands were bound behind him, Philip dared to look up, allowing himself one moment in which to glance into his master's eyes.

That fleeting look was enough. Marcus's eyes flashed with inner passion, his expression menacing, and his arms crossed ominously upon his stalwart chest.

Mercy.

Again, bitterness flooded Philip's soul. What clemency was to be found at the hands of Marcus? One look at him, and he knew Marcus meant to kill him. A verdict of death by slow torture was written clearly on his stone-like features.

Despite the direness of his situation, Philip smirked. Perhaps now was a good time to become a Christian. At least he wouldn't have to face eternity with Marcus.

For that matter, how had Marcus found him anyway? That wretched rabble must have seen him. And, like good citizens, their only concern was the well-being of an offended, misused master.

What generous consideration.

"Hurry up," Marcus snapped. "Let us be off."

The soldiers straightened themselves erect, pulling the cords that bound Philip. Wearily, he submitted to their pull. He felt sick with apprehension. He was about to die and he was afraid. He—the son of a British chieftain and a former Druid worshipper—was afraid of death! Surely the gods mocked him.

"Wait!"

Philip paused, as did the others. From the corner of his eye, he saw Daniel approaching. Had he seen everything?

Not that it mattered. *A lot of good your counsel did me, Christian.*

"What do you want?" Though curt, Marcus made an attempt to speak civilly.

"Are you this boy's master?" Daniel spoke mildly, his eyes steadily meeting the cold fire of Marcus's gaze.

"Yes. What of it?"

"Your pleasure seems very far gone from him."

An unexpected glimmer of amusement deepened on Marcus's face. "You speak with the assurance of an *augur.*" His sarcasm swelled. "Allow me to express my deepest admiration for your prowess, noble friend."

"My apologies, noble lord." Daniel's voice remained free of ill-will. "I only meant to inquire after his well-being."

Marcus surveyed him with dark curiosity. "And why should the well-being of a runaway slave be of such *great* importance?"

"He does not seem an ordinary slave."

Philip marveled at Daniel's quiet, composed mannerism. Marcus treated him with the scornful arrogance of one who knew himself superior and was in no mood for the opinions of his inferiors. Still, Daniel maintained a gentle, mild tone and mien, his eyes strangely pitying.

Marcus laughed shortly. "No, he is not an ordinary slave. He is far from it. Do not let his good looks deceive you, my baker friend. Suetonius ought to have been strung up when he conquered Britain—and this sorry wretch is the worst of that race."

"And you mean to scourge him, crucify him perhaps?"

"Why shouldn't I?" Marcus's voice again grew cutting in its impatience. "He is disobedient and a runaway. The gods must have their sport with him."

Philip felt an unmistakable shiver run down his spine. He had been called the pleasure of the gods before. Now, it seemed, they were to turn that pleasure into merciless sport. Only they knew what terrors Marcus meant to inflict before killing him.

"You serve hard gods." Daniel paused. "Granted you knew the One, the Almighty Jehovah God, you would know that clemency is better than vengeance."

A slow look of understanding flitted across Marcus's face. "A Jew, are you? I thought Claudius got rid of your kind long ago." His irritation increased. "But, what it does it matter? This slave is my own. No man shall interfere with my justice."

Daniel stepped a little nearer, his voice low. "Young man, be merciful, even as you would wish to be shown mercy. This slave has done you great wrong, but you also could not have conducted yourself flawlessly." Then, with an emphatic pause, "Forgiveness is greater."

Marcus stood motionless, his eyes locked into Daniel's clear, unmoving gaze. He seemed bound by a spell, unable to speak or look away. The words seemed to linger in the warm air, strangely haunting.

Forgiveness is greater.

Philip himself felt bound by the extraordinary power of the concept. For a fleeting second, the sickening feeling left his stomach, relieving his mind of its torturous apprehension.

Forgiveness. Was this what enabled Daniel to look and speak with such quiet assurance? Or was it only a part of a bigger concept, a greater power that flooded men with the peace and love Daniel portrayed in his every action?

Then the spell was broken.

With a shake, Marcus freed himself from penetrating hold of Daniel's gaze, irritation washing afresh over his cold features. "I bid you good day," he said shortly. Then, to the others, "Follow me to the house of Virginius."

Philip submitted to the rugged pull of the soldiers upon his bonds. As suddenly as it had left, the deep pit of nausea returned to his stomach, washing him in cold perspiration. Again bound by bitterness, he glanced up into Daniel's face, then, turned resolutely away.

The half-hour walk to the Virginius domus was both the longest and most fleeting trek Philip had ever taken. Every step brought him closer to his demise, filling his heart with unspeakable dread.

His own fear irritated him. His queen, Boudicca, had faced a scourging at the hands of Roman officials with haughty bravery. Her every action against Rome had been fearless—even her own self-inflicted death, which had been an act of courageous defiance in itself. And hundreds of his fellow-Britons had followed her in her demise, refusing to live under the merciless regime of Rome.

Why couldn't he be as one of them? Why did he fear death?

From his infancy, he had been taught the Druid idea that life was a curse and death was to be anticipated with joy. Pain was fleeting, and, with his happy release, he would be forever freed from the hated presence of Marcus. So why did he dread his end?

Philip's breathing quickened as the mansion of Virginius arose before him. The soldiers pulled him roughly up the steps, shoving him inside. Shoved from behind, he stumbled through the entry and down the few steps into the atrium.

Marcus stood in a stern, masterful stance, his arms crossed upon his chest. "Unbind him."

The soldiers quickly cut the cords binding his wrists, releasing his arms from their cramped position.

Philip let his arms fall to his sides. A sudden shove sent him flying forward, his hands flailing before him. His knees made contact with the hard marble floor, his palms resting atop the cold surface.

He had been in this position before. Kneeling, groveling before Marcus. *Great gods, let this be brief.*

The silence grew long.

Philip's middle tightened, his heart pounding against his chest. He could feel Marcus's stony gaze resting upon him, piercing him through. After an eternity, the sound of his voice cut through the wild hammering in Philip's ears, echoing coldly throughout the atrium.

"You are strangely calm. Are you not afraid?"

Philip did not raise himself to look up. The last thing he wanted to see was his master's fiery, merciless eyes—the eyes that had always been able to see through him and conquer his flashes of rebellion with such strange power.

"Answer me, slave!"

The anger in Marcus's voice sent waves of fear rolling down Philip's spine, chilling, infuriating him. *Just shut your mouth, Roman.*

"Have done toying with me, Marcus," he heard himself say aloud. "Wreak your pleasure on me and end my miserable existence." To his surprise, his voice faltered. "Then I will be at peace."

"Peace." Marcus spoke scornfully. "Nothing about you has ever reeked of *peace*, Philip."

Philip raised his eyes, feeling them water strangely. "Then my death will be the better for both of us."

A smarting lump gathered in his throat. He swallowed hard, trying to control the rising mist in his eyes. *Get a hold of yourself! By the gods, die like a man.*

But he couldn't.

Despite his own fierce chiding, he could not stop the well of tears. He was afraid to die, afraid to meet the unknown afterlife. And he didn't want to go there on the wings of pain, breathing his last with nail-pierced wrists and ankles.

Marcus took a step forward, his mocking laughter filling the atrium. "By Hercules! My brave Iceni warrior is in tears! You *are* afraid, Philip. I have at last made an impression on you."

Resentment simmered in Philip's chest, but he made no answer. What need was there to speak? A few moments more, and his shrieks would be the only utterance he would ever again make in this cursed Roman world.

"Take him to the *culina*." Marcus's impatient voice broke through the apathy of his thoughts.

The *culina*? Philip's mind whirled in uncertainty. Why should he be taken there? Was Marcus going to poison him, leaving him to die in the throngs of agony?

Philip felt himself jerked to his feet, his arms secured in the strong grips of the soldiers. He was shoved forward, forced to walk through the atrium to the lowlier parts of the house, past the slave quarters, and into the *culina*.

At the door, he stopped.

A poker rested atop the bright open flames of the grate, its end glowing scarlet. Philip cringed, perspiration standing out afresh on his pallid face. Was he to be branded, as was so common? But the

101

poker bore no branding iron, no F-shaped mark, as was the custom when branding runaway slaves.

Marcus spoke behind him, his orders sharp. "Take that ring and fasten it around his neck. Mind that the ends are securely welded."

It was then Philip saw the steel ring, inscribed with the chilling words: *I am a slave who has run away from his master.*

Marcus's sharp, stern voice continued. "He has shamed and dishonored me before others, now let him live a life of shame and dishonor before all those who see him."

Philip's breathing quickened. He, the son of a British chieftain, was to be disgraced for life? This was his punishment—the never-ending shame of public exposure and humiliation?

No! No!

Philip twisted violently, evading the grip of the soldiers. He threw himself down on his knees before Marcus, desperate enough to think nothing of supplication. "No, my lord! I would rather die than be so degraded. Kill me, only don't dishonor my father's name! I beg you, Marcus!"

"Be quiet." Anger rolled over Marcus's face. "I have decreed your sentence. Almighty gods, Philip! Thank fortune your miserable life is spared."

He turned to the soldiers. "For the love of Aphrodite! Do as I have commanded."

The soldiers forced Philip to the grate, tearing the cloak from his shoulders. Twisting, struggling, Philip turned, one final, desperate cry escaping his lips.

"Marcus! *No!*"

A flashing look of scorn in his dark eyes, Marcus turned and left the *culina*.

Left alone in the little room adjoining Marcus's chamber, Philip stood motionless for several long minutes after the soldiers had left

him. Slowly, his hands found their way to the steel collar fastened around his neck, tracing its inscription.

I am a slave who has run away from his master.

A sudden torrent of tears rose in his eyes. Impulsively, he threw himself forward, flinging himself face down on his couch. *Why? Why?*

The salty tears crept down his cheeks. He didn't understand. Questions ran rampant in his mind, bewildering him, causing his head to ache.

There was one question that stood out from among the others.

Why hadn't Marcus killed him? Why was he not even now writhing on a coarse wooden cross, bleeding, lashed by the whip? He didn't understand. Marcus had sworn to kill him. Up until half-an-hour ago, he had seemed ready and willing to crucify him. And he had told another as much.

Daniel.

Philip rolled over onto his side, looking with bleary eyes at the wall opposite him. It couldn't be that the mysterious words of a Jewish breadmaker had provoked this change in Marcus's mind. It simply wasn't possible. Roman masters didn't break their sworn oath at the word of an inferior, particularly when the master was Marcus.

The very thought of Marcus sent anger rushing in a boiling wave throughout Philip's body. How he hated him!

His fingers brushed the collar about his neck, the symbol of disgrace he was to wear until it became the will of his master to file it off. *If* it ever became his will.

Raising himself, Philip suddenly shook his fist at the door leading to his lord's chamber. "I'll kill you someday, Marcus." His voice was a coarse whisper, his throat broken by tears. "I'll kill you! You think you've won, that you've conquered me, but you haven't. You haven't!"

Forgiveness is greater.

Philip sat a little straighter, startled. How clearly the words had met his ear! But how was it possible? He glanced uneasily around. Then, abruptly, he shook himself, disgusted by his own superstition.

Vengeance was his desire, his life's one hope. No Christian would filch that from him. They would not play tricks on his mind, deceiving him with beautiful tales. After all, perhaps it was true. Perhaps the Christians *were* sorcerers.

Swinging his sandaled feet over the side of his couch, Philip arose. He cringed a little, feeling pain discharge through his legs. Holding out his arms, he surveyed them bitterly. The lash-mark had begun to heal, leaving a deep scar in its wake.

So there he had it.

Rome had made another lasting mark upon him. First the murder of his family, his imprisonment, and his slavery. And now he was scored by the lash and bore a degrading metal ring around his neck, marking him as a runaway and troublemaker.

Weary and heartsore, Philip stepped to the casement, gazing out on the bustling streets of Rome. The tears threatened to again spill down his cheeks, but he held them resolutely back. He was a man, not a child.

And it would take a truly great man to conquer the monstrosity of Rome.

Upon the balcony adjoined to the room opposite Philip, Marcus also stood gazing out over the city. His dark eyes drifted over the afternoon sky, fixing themselves upon a lone starling as it glided upon the soft currents of air.

Abruptly, his handsome face contorted, as if in pain. His eyes closed, hiding a strange, sudden glisten.

"Owen." The name fell breath-like from his lips. "I was so happy when you were alive. I am not the man I was before. Your death has changed me."

Marcus's features again contorted, and, abruptly, he dropped his head into his strong hands. His lips moved in low, muttered syllables.

"May the gods be praised you are in *Elysium*. You, at least, have escaped the passions that torture us mortals below."

Chapter Ten

Philip awoke the next morning with a sick feeling in the pit of his stomach. For a moment, he lay motionless, unable to understand his depression. Then, slowly, the full remembrance of all that had occurred came back to him.

Slowly, he arose from his couch and dressed himself. The metal collar made dressing awkward, and he winced every time he felt its cold clasp. Who knew when it was to be removed—or if ever?

His dressing complete, Philip drew a deep breath. It was time to face Marcus. He didn't know if his offered services would be accepted, but he did not dare keep away. He squared his shoulders before stepping though the doorway dividing his little chamber from Marcus's spacious apartments.

Marcus was already awake, standing near one of the open windows. He cradled a cup in his hands, sipping of the contents. A flicker of sternness crossed his face as he saw Philip, and he set the cup down hard upon a table.

"It's about time you were up."

Philip swallowed hard. "Then you desire my services, my lord?"

"Of course. You didn't think you were exempt from servitude because you are no longer in my pleasure, did you?"

Philip bit his lip, fighting back the impulse to make a sarcastic reply. *Say nothing.*

He moved noiselessly across the room, taking up Marcus's white toga. Folding it in half, he silently draped one end over Marcus's left arm, around his stalwart back, then beneath his right arm. Stepping in front of him, he stretched it neatly over his chest, then across his left shoulder and arm.

His toga in place, Marcus stepped past him and picked his signet ring off a table, slipping it onto his fourth finger.

Philip watched in silence. Abruptly, Marcus turned on him, his voice sharp.

"Don't just stand there. Get me my *pallium*."

Philip lingered a moment. Marcus had several capes, each of which was considered suitable to be worn over his toga. "Which one, my–"

A sudden, stinging blow fell heavily across his face. Philip stepped back, barely suppressing an exclamation of pain and anger. Marcus leaned close to him, his tones dark.

"Just *get* it."

Philip lifted his eyes, momentarily meeting the cold gaze fixed ominously upon him. He did not dare allow his resentment to show. Marcus's close presence hinted chilling intimidation in its every sense, sending the boiling heat of fear and wrath rushing like adrenaline through his veins.

So this was how it was to be. No tolerance, no favor. Just the stern commands of a master, the ever-abiding fear of his displeasure, and his own subservience.

Aware of the crimson color high in his face, Philip walked across the chamber and took up the cape. Averting his eyes in the outer appearance of submission, he returned, draping the garment around Marcus's shoulders.

Without another word, Marcus left the room. Philip stood where he had left him, following his departure with narrowed, simmering eyes.

Marcus humors you for the time being, but he will not always do so. He is the master...

Philip felt a wave of sudden shame. How had his father known? How had he known that Marcus's favor would not last? He had scorned Beric's wise insight at the time it was given, but now...

The overwhelming desire to see his father struck Philip like a dart in the chest. With urgency he did not understand, he strode rapidly from the room, treading lightly down the stairs, and into the wide, luxurious atrium. From there, he stepped out into the garden.

A quick glance revealed his father, pruning the shrubbery.

Suddenly hesitant, Philip stood. The sound of his steps attracted Beric's attention and he looked up. Slowly, he straightened himself erect, his eyes grave and something like sternness bordered on his countenance.

Philip felt a sudden pang. So he was in disgrace with his father as well.

But, there was little wonder in that. He had scorned Beric's counsel, run away without saying goodbye, and brought shame upon himself and his father's house. Beric could not be expected to be at all pleased with him.

It seemed the gods were determined to humble him. And, perhaps humility was his now his best course after all.

Averting his eyes, he advanced. Meekly, he took his father's hand in his own, pressing it silently to his forehead.

There was a long silence.

Philip's heart swelled. Until that moment, he had not realized how much he valued his father's good opinion. Life was not worth living without it. *Great gods of my fathers, let him forgive me.*

Slowly, hesitantly, he looked up, meeting the quiet gaze of Beric's cobalt eyes. Adopting the deference of a Briton in the presence of his chieftain, he waited, yearning to hear a single word of favor.

The attitude had its desired effect.

"When I heard that my son had run away from his master, I did not think I would ever again see him alive. The gods have dealt mercifully with us both, Philip."

Philip continued his downward gaze, fixing his eyes on a tiny patch of delicate violets. "Part of me would prefer to be dead."

"Yet you live."

"Yes." Philip bit his lip. "Were I more of a man, I would end my life, but my paltry courage is not equal to the deed." Then, looking up, "Do you despise my cowardice, father?"

"No." Beric's unexpected return was firmly steadfast. "I know death is anticipated with joy among our people, but I could not rejoice in my son's demise. You are the only blessing left to me. And, perhaps, after all, the will to live is a greater strength than suicide."

"The idea is a strange one, coming from you."

"I don't doubt it. You know my zeal for the ways of our people was unsurpassed. Still," and Beric paused, "slavery has opened my eyes to many things. The beauty of life is one of them."

There was a short moment of silence. Philip at last shook his head, contemplative.

"I have heard so many new ideas lately that my head fairly spins with them. Would you believe that one of those mystical Christians gave me sanctuary yesterday?"

A flicker of interest glimmered in Beric's eyes. "What was he like?"

"Like any ordinary man, but gentler than most. He told me of his religion, and I must confess it was the strangest concept I have ever heard. But, somehow, it was beautiful too."

Philip's voice died away. Beric looked closely at him.

"Would you forsake your gods, Philip?"

Philip did not answer for a long moment. He struggled with a rising feeling of helplessness and confusion he did not understand.

For the life of him, he did not know why he suddenly felt strangely drawn to the Christian faith. Had he not mocked it in his mind only the night before? And how was he to explain to his father, chieftain of the Britons, that his gods no longer satisfied him?

"Father, I cannot explain what it I feel. I am…confused."

"Confusion is not a thing to reject. It often signifies growth. But," and gravity bordered on Beric's tones, "if you mean to deny your gods, Philip, I trust you will do so with great care."

He turned back to his work, brushing Philip's shoulder in fatherly affection before picking up his tools.

Philip stood motionless for a long moment. Slowly, he turned, stepping back into the cool atrium.

His father obviously had little to say, but Philip was relieved he had made no rebuke. No doubt Beric had seen the bruises covering his face and sensed he had undergone enough punishment.

And, strangely, he had not grown angry when Philip did not avow his complete allegiance to the forest gods. *Strange*. Did Beric respect his son's opinions and choice? Or was he only tired of rearing his rebellious son?

Philip brushed aside his thoughts. It really did not matter which. He had no intention of forsaking his gods. He was a Briton and their worship was good enough for him.

Still, he would not mind thanking Daniel for all his kindness. He had always been allowed to walk in the streets, and, as Marcus had not revoked that liberty, he could see no reason why he should not visit the little bread-shop.

Before he could change his mind, Philip took quick action. Stepping quickly across the atrium, he mounted the steps leading up to the entry and slipped from the heavy gilt door.

Out upon the *Vicus Tuscus*, Philip felt for the first time the shame of the collar around his neck. The slow color crept up in his cheeks, seeing countless pedestrians glance at the words inscribed upon the ring. Marcus had chosen an appropriate revenge. And he was right—the gods did desire to humble him.

Having no desire to linger in the streets, Philip arrived at his destination in good time. He rapped upon the door he had entered at the day before, but received no answer. Stepping around the side of the building, he stepped through the main entry into the shop's dusky interior.

Daniel was occupied with several customers, but he glanced up at Philip's entrance. A look of warm, almost relieved recognition flitted across his face, and he nodded shortly at him.

Philip felt a rush of relief. So Daniel did not reject his coming.

Silently, he waited until the customers left the little shop, then, stepped up to the counter. From its opposite side, Daniel leaned across the smooth top, his voice warm.

"Good day, Philip."

"Good day, friend." Philip paused, suddenly overtaken by awkwardness. But Daniel continued on, eliminating the need to explain his coming.

"I am grateful to see you here. I prayed long for your safety."

Philip felt a wave of mingled gratitude and confusion. Why would this man pray for *him*? It felt unsettling and, of all things, comforting.

For the first time, he realized the truth. He was lonely. And Daniel's kindness triggered something his embittered heart had not felt since his capture. Something that hinted of peace and the feeling that *someone* cared for him, humiliated and worthless though he was.

A sudden mist overshadowed his gaze.

What is wrong with you? One day a wrestling champion, the next a sorry sap! Be a man.

Philip lifted his chin, blinking back the irritating mist. "You are too kind, Daniel. That is why I came to see you. I wished to thank you for the goodness you showed me yesterday."

"It was nothing, Philip. I was pleased to serve you." Daniel paused, his eyes resting on the metal collar. "So this was your punishment?"

Philip's cheeks burned. "Yes."

"I praise God your master was generous."

"*Generous* indeed." Philip spoke sarcastically, the old flash illuminating his eyes. "My master knows I prefer death to dishonor."

Daniel stood considering him. "Does he know you are here?"

"I do not know or care."

"Were I not a Christian, I would call you a fool."

Philip gazed at him. "Why do you not? I would like to see what this God of yours does to those who disobey Him. Would He strike you dead?"

Daniel's eyes grew absent, a look of distant musing upon his features. "Our God, Philip, is not like the gods of the Romans. He cannot be compared with the deities of all other nations. He is love, not this vindication you speak of."

Philip leaned on the counter. "And what is love?"

Daniel looked at him, a grave smile hovering above his lips. "Your sarcasm does not do you credit, my friend."

"I am in earnest, Daniel." Philip looked steadily at him. "I do not mock you. Your religion is a strange one and I would know more of it. What is love?"

Daniel moved around the marble counter, coming to stand beside Philip. Slowly, his hand found Philip's shoulder. When he spoke, it was contemplativeness that seemed to hallow his bearded countenance.

"You must sense there is a true love beyond the worship of Venus or you would not ask me so sincerely, Philip. And you are right." He paused. "Love in its fullest meaning is best described by what our God did for us. He sent His only Son, Jesus the Christ, to die on a Roman cross for our sake."

"But I don't understand why. Why should a god die for mortal man?"

"Because we are unholy. Nearly our every action is corrupted by sin, and no man who is a sinner can stand before our holy Jehovah. That is why He sent His Son to die, taking our punishment upon Himself."

Philip struggled to understand the strange concept. Daniel seemed to see his confusion. The pressure of his hand deepened on his shoulder.

"Take your master as an example. What sort of a man would he be if he had let you go unpunished yesterday?"

Philip felt a wave of angry color wash over his face. What kind of a question was that? Did he imply Marcus had been *right*?

Daniel clearly noticed his annoyance and hastened on. "No, hear me out, Philip. Whatever his faults, your master is just. He could not overlook your behavior. But, if I had offered to take your punishment upon myself, he could have let you go, knowing that justice was paid."

Daniel paused a moment. "It is the same way with Jehovah. As the Righteous Judge, He cannot overlook sin. Yet, He could grant us a way of escape by laying our punishment on another. And that is what, in His love, He did."

Though inwardly irritated Daniel had implied Marcus had been just, Philip brushed away the thought and dwelt on his explanation. But, still, the idea of a deity loving mortal man was too much for his mind.

"And what must one do to receive this sacrifice, Daniel?"

"Nothing. Only true acceptance, Philip." Daniel's look grew distant. "As I have heard a dear brother in our faith say, only believe on the Lord Jesus Christ and you shall be saved."

"Saved from your God's wrath, you mean?"

"Yes, that, and also saved *unto* a new life. You become a child of God and are granted fellowship with His Son."

"Fellowship with *God?*"

"Yes. More than that, His Spirit dwells within you."

Philip looked closely at Daniel. "You do not deceive me, I trust. Are you certain these things are true?"

"More than certain."

"And this is what enables you Christians to face death without fear?"

"Yes." Daniel looked steadily into Philip's half-troubled eyes. "God's Holy Spirit is our Comforter, Philip. When the time comes for death, He gives the peace we need–the peace that passes all human understanding."

Peace.

The word stood out to Philip like a beacon of hope for a storm-lashed ship. What he would not give for peace, for the joy and confidence these Christians possessed. Like him, they knew grief, but, somehow, their manner of meeting it was so different from his own.

His heart twisted. Impatiently, he struggled against the rising feeling of emotion in his breast. His thoughts were turbulent, more than he could handle. He heard his own voice, low.

"It is truly a religion for the hopeless."

"And are you not hopeless?"

Daniel's voice was gentle, but his words cut Philip to the quick. It hurt his pride to realize his own low position. Still, his honest mind would not allow him to lie.

Yes. You are hopeless—hopeless and miserable. There is nothing for you in the way you are going. Your life has no meaning worth speaking of.

But who could tell if the Christians truly could offer him any better hope?

Chapter Eleven

Philip left the bread shop, shutting the door quietly behind him.

Squaring his shoulders, he inhaled deeply of the warm air. An hour within the bread shop had left him slightly cramped and keen for an aroma other than that of freshly-baked loaves. Still, though the fresh scent of the clean air was refreshing, it seemed strangely heavy, as if the atmosphere was closing in around him.

As he strode away from the shop, he could not shake the feeling that the air was thick and leaden. He felt almost as if someone was following him, but, looking around, he could see no one of suspicion.

A cold chill washed over him.

Why did he feel so strange, so turbulent? He had felt this way once before, right before his first clash with the Romans. It was almost as if, somehow, there was a looming battle.

A battle here in safe Rome? *Ridiculous.*

But he could not shake the feeling. He could not put aside the thought that, somewhere, a war was raging and he was mysteriously a part of it. But why?

As he walked, Philip lifted his eyes, seeing smoke rising from the Temple of Vesta. Her sacred fire burned day and night, attended by the Vestal Virgins.

Vesta. The goddess of home, the hearth, and family.

Philip paused in contemplation, his eyes drifting over the lazily-rising smoke. He had seen Lady Persis offer Vesta reverent worship, throwing offerings into the hearth-fire to discern her wishes and omens of the future.

The oddity of it struck him as never before. The goddess of family was served by virgins. *Not a whole lot of family happening there.*

Philip abruptly started, realizing his own thoughts. He doubted the deity of the Roman gods. He mocked them in his mind. And, worse still, he doubted his own forest deities.

The Christians already had a hold on him.

Philip struggled with the rising turbulence in his chest. How was this possible? It had happened so suddenly. In one day, he had gone from worshipping his gods and that of his nation's conquering foes to suddenly doubting their power, their very existence.

His chest swelled. Something tugged at his heartstrings, something more powerful than he had ever felt before. He couldn't fight it.

The air grew thicker, the atmosphere heavier.

Philip looked around. The milling plebians, the patricians, the slaves—didn't they feel it too? Why did they look so intent upon their activities, as if nothing was happening?

He broke out into a cold sweat. Fear pounded at his heart, suffocating him.

On one side, he felt darkness, a luring power that urged him to enter any one of the many temples around him and offer a sacrifice of renewed allegiance to the Roman gods.

What were the Christians but sorcerers anyway? They had cast a spell on him. He had to escape it! Instinctively, he sensed if he went to the temple, this strange turbulence would leave him. He would be free.

Or would he? Was it possible this terrible, looming heaviness would increase?

He gives the peace we need—the peace that passes all understanding.

Something like the flicker of torchlight seemed to be piercing the darkness. He felt it. But what darkness? It was the middle of the day; the sun shone high overhead.

What was *wrong* with him? Why was he feeling, seeing things no one else was?

Philip stepped toward the temple of Vesta. If anyone could help him, she could. Surely she would condescend to look upon the distress of slave. He would offer a sacrifice, pledging himself to her worship.

His steps jerked to a stop. No. He could not go.

He *believed*.

There was no use in offering a sacrifice to a goddess he knew was nothing more than the figment of a people's imagination. Vesta was dead. And so was the entire Pantheon.

Light rushed through the darkness shrouding his mind, rending it like a veil. It was as a new dawn, overspreading the sky and banishing darkness forever. The tugging on his heartstrings grew more intense.

He believed.

Philip turned, breaking into a run. *Run and don't stop!*

The darkness was gone and the air was light and clean, but he was being followed. This strange, unseen battle wasn't finished. Someone, something was trying to keep him from returning to Daniel.

His heart pounded against his chest. His eyes roved restlessly, searching for the fastest path back to Daniel's home. He leaped over fruit baskets, ignoring the angry shouts and amused laughter of the forum's shoppers.

Run!

Daniel's humble bread shop rose before him. Panting, breathless, he threw himself against the door, flinging it wide.

Daniel looked up, startled. Then, his eyes warmed, understanding.

He knows.

"Daniel, I believe." Philip felt the words spill out before he could think. There was no time to wait. He *knew* it. There was something urgent about his situation. Something was trying to hold him back. And he didn't like it.

His voice broke a little. "Daniel, I want what you have. I want this Jesus the Christ. I…I need your help."

"Are you certain?" Daniel moved closer. His face, tanned by the eastern sun and lined around his eyes with hardship, was gravely quiet.

"Yes."

"Do you understand what our faith rests on?"

"Yes. I mean, no." Philip's breathing quickened. "I understand your God died to save us from His wrath. I don't comprehend much beyond that, but I know I want it, Daniel."

Daniel wiped his flour-covered hands on his short apron. Kindness shone out from his eyes, but Philip sensed a grave hesitance. "Philip, I will not choose my words carefully. It was only yesterday you told me you rejected Christianity. And I do not think you know what you will be giving up."

"But I–"

Daniel silenced him with a gesture. "You hate your master. As a slave from a conquered people, you also hate Rome. I have seen it, Philip. You want revenge, perhaps even the deaths of your tormentors. These things cannot be in Christianity."

He paused. "You know already that persecution haunts us. I do not think you fear it. I only warn you, no man who puts his hand to the plow may look back. You cannot put Christianity on and off like a tunic."

"Nor would I wish to, Daniel." Philip lifted his chin firmly. "I am not fickle." Desperation bordered on his tones. "Why do you dissuade me? Am I not worthy?"

"None of us are worthy, Philip."

"Then why do you hold me back?"

"I have no desire to hold you back." Daniel looked steadily at Philip. "I would only ask that you be sure. Hate holds you a prisoner, but you must be certain you truly wish to be freed. Only then can I help you."

Philip struggled within himself, pondering Daniel's words. Vainly, he fought against the certainty that this Jewish breadmaker was right.

Hate did hold him captive, constantly gnawing at his thoughts, his heart. It washed over him every time he served Marcus, whenever he saw the flashing red cape of a legionary, when he touched the lash mark scoring his arms. He was controlled by hate, even to the point of planning his vengeful future.

He thought back on yesterday. He had wanted to kill Marcus then. A great part of him still wanted to. That was part of what troubled him. Maybe he *was* fickle.

Hate had caused him to live, but not in the truest sense of the word. He lived unto anger and bitterness. That wasn't life. Being honest with himself, it was a living death.

And he wanted freedom from its hold.

Philip looked up at Daniel. His eyes misted over, an aching lump rising in his throat. He was ready. Forget his sworn oaths to overcome the Romans, to crush Marcus. He was ready to relinquish this terrible hate and give it all to this Jesus who loved him.

"Daniel, you know I believe. I don't quite know why, but I do. I can give up hate if this God of love will help me. I want this peace you have spoken of."

"All which God does, He does for good." Daniel's lips lingered over the Jewish proverb, his eyes absent. "He will help you and give you this peace if you ask Him."

"Then *help* me, Daniel. Yesterday, you said I must call on Him. How?"

"Pray." Daniel's work-lined hands rested on his shoulders, gripping them. "You've only to ask Him."

Philip's eyes drifted upward. How many times he had looked up at a lifeless statue, flattering it, bargaining with the gods to fulfill his request. Now, however, there were no entrails of an animal to decree his future, no sacrifice to make in return for his demands. There was only quietness and the overwhelming feeling that Someone was listening to him.

Strangely, he never remembered exactly what he said. Looking back, he recalled something about wishing to serve Jesus Christ, about wanting to be freed from hate and bitterness. And, most importantly, he remembered asking for peace.

His first true prayer was no masterpiece, but, as Philip finished, he felt an overwhelming sense of quiet fulfillment. The die had been cast. He was a servant of Jesus Christ. And, come what may, he would be a good one.

Daniel made a gesture if he would embrace him, but Philip was too overwhelmed to respond. His mind felt as if it was spinning, overwhelmed with a plethora of thoughts and questions. One in particular stood out to him.

"What must I do now?"

Daniel laughed unexpectedly, his chuckle rolling through the room. "You are a Briton to the core, Philip. Always eager, always impulsive."

"I want a purpose, Daniel." Philip's tones grew low. "In my country, I obeyed my chieftain, following his commands in peace and war. Now you must be that chieftain. Command me."

"Jesus Christ is your leader, Philip, not I," Daniel corrected him gently. "And his command was this: love the Lord thy God with all thy heart, soul, mind, and strength; and love thy neighbor as thyself."

Philip considered him. Slowly, he dropped his eyes, fingering the metal band around his neck. "That will not be easy."

"Because you understand who your neighbor is?"

"Yes."

"Take heart, my friend. The ones Jesus spoke those words to did not begin to understand. You do." Daniel paused. "The servant is not above his master, Philip. The first step towards your own peace is in honoring Marcus."

Philip cringed. "I am beginning to regret I asked you to command me." He paused, allowing his resolution to return in full force. "I have many questions unanswered, Daniel. There is much I don't understand about this Christianity. But this I do know: I will do all within my power to please the God who loved me enough to die for me."

"Then I think you will do well." Daniel seemed to choose his words carefully. "If you ever need encouragement or help, I am always here. Come to me often, and I will teach you the ways of Jesus Christ."

"I will come." Philip stepped forward, attempting to take Daniel's hands and press them to his forehead in his old tradition. His heart swelled with gratitude. Already, his heart was lighter than it had been in many weeks.

Daniel stopped him with a quiet word. "That is not how we Christians part, Philip."

He pressed his hands across his chest, then, made the sign of the cross. Slowly, hesitantly, Philip copied him.

With an approving nod, Daniel held open the wooden door. "Go quickly to your master, Philip. And," he eyed Philip shrewdly, "it would be best if you informed him of your departure next time."

Philip bent in a half-bow before stepping out. "*Servus sum*[4], my friend."

Swiftly, he stepped into the street. Pausing only to wave, he broke into a light run, expertly avoiding all collisions with the milling shoppers.

As he went, he realized that the air was no longer thick. He could breathe freely and the darkness that had haunted him a few minutes ago was gone.

It was confusing, but, at the moment, he didn't care to consider it. All he knew was the sense of freedom bordering on his heart. Dozens of questions flooded his mind, but he was *free*.

Yet, somehow, he still sensed that he was being followed. It was not an eerie following as before, but, even still, he cast a glance behind him. No one out of the ordinary was there. There were only the milling shoppers, the rich patricians, the tall columns and shrines of the Forum.

---

[4] Latin for "I am your servant", a common manner of address with Roman slaves.

Philip turned back to the cobblestoned street before him. There was nothing to fear. It was as if he was being followed by a different person. There was no darkness, no chilling apprehension, only the peaceful assurance he was safe.

It was almost as if he was being guided. Or, rather, as if he *had* a guide.

Deny it as he would, Philip's heart pounded as he ran lightly up the marble steps of the mansion of Virginius. He had been gone for well over two hours, and it was past the usual time for Marcus's daily bath.

The atrium was quiet and still as he entered. Only the sounds of his sandaled feet upon the marble floor and the distant trickling of the fountain playing in the garden met his ears. Clearly, his absence had not attracted a dangerous amount of attention.

Noiselessly, he stepped from the atrium to the *peristyle* edging the garden. A quick glance showed the garden was empty, save for one individual.

Marcus stood before the family shrine. The morning sacrifice had long since been made, but it was obvious he had made a second offering of wine upon its altar.

Philip watched from the edge of the *peristyle*, observing discreet silence. Common sense told him announcing his return in the midst of his master's reverent sacrifice would be woefully imprudent. As it was already, his hands trembled, wondering what Marcus would do and say to him.

Finished at the shrine, Marcus turned. Instant anger flashed across his face, seeing his slave. "Where have you been?"

Philip exhaled slowly. Humble respectfulness was easy with Daniel; it was quite another with the young man who seemed to always get under his skin. "I was out walking, my lord."

"Without my permission? I've been in need of your service for over an hour now. I wonder you dared to leave the domus."

Philip bit his lip, attempting to control his rising anger. Why was it Marcus's tones always sent the blood boiling throughout his body, enraging him?

Love thy neighbor as thyself.

"My apologies, master." Philip felt the blood rise in his cheeks, but he had done it. He had begged Marcus's pardon.

Marcus cocked an eyebrow. "I should have clapped that ring about your neck long ago. Fancy getting an apology from a Briton!"

Philip clamped his teeth together. His hands doubled into fists, closing until the nails bit into the palm. *Say nothing.*

"Don't just stand there." Marcus snapped at him. "You've wasted my time as it is. Get my things for the Baths."

Philip half-bent, not trusting himself to speak. When he had asked Daniel to command him, he had not thought to receive an order this difficult.

Apologize for running away.

Philip almost jumped. What sort of idiotic thought was that to have? He had just humbled himself into the very dust! Apologize again? Never.

Honoring Marcus is your first step towards peace.

Philip ground his teeth. It was impossible. He couldn't. It was all Marcus's fault anyway. Had Marcus not driven him half-mad with pain and vexation, he never would have run away in the first place.

Where had such a thought come from anyway? Surely–*surely*–it had not come from the God he now pledged to follow, Jesus Christ.

Philip felt a tinge. A soft whisper echoed in his heart, urging him to obey. The twinge intensified, hurting him. Instinctively, he felt it: he would be miserable until he obeyed this mysterious command.

"Why are you just standing there? By Aphrodite! Will you never learn to obey me?"

Philip felt Marcus's anger in his stride towards him. He cringed, half-starting back. Marcus's hand closed around his arm, holding him fast. Philip swallowed hard, his heart thudding.

"*Marcus.*"

Marcus paused, his hand upraised. Philip looked up at him, shaking. Attempting to control his faltering voice seemed hopeless.

"My lord, I–I wanted to beg your pardon for–for running away. It was wrong of me to–dishonor you. I pray you will–forgive me."

For one fleeting moment, a look of dumbfounded surprise hovered over Marcus's clear-cut features. His eyes softened, as if touched. Then, abruptly, he drew back his hand and struck him heavily across the face.

Philip's heart swelled. He pursed his lips tightly together to keep from uttering his mind. The hot tears arose in his eyes, watering from the smart of the stroke. Inflicting pain was becoming a talent for Marcus.

Marcus leaned close to him, dark and threatening. "I am no idiot, Philip. I know the ways of slaves. Are you such a fool you think your humble little apologies will keep me from punishing you?" His grip tightening with painful intensity upon Philip's arm. "Do not try that trick again."

With a forceful shove, Marcus released him.

Philip stepped back against one of the columns to keep his balance. Marcus gestured fiercely at him, and he needed no further urging to leave his presence.

Swiftly, his heart thudding against his chest, he ran into the atrium, then up the steps to Marcus's bedchamber. Inside, he leaned against the door, closing his eyes. The heavy blow had set his temples to pounding. His hands shook wildly, but, by a great effort, he controlled them.

He had obeyed. And perhaps, after all, it was because he had listened to the mysterious Voice he had not been punished more severely.

Philip exhaled slowly. He was angry, angry at Marcus for so misjudging him. But, somehow, he was also at peace. He had done right.

Slowly, he straightened himself and went to gather Marcus's fresh clothing. The pain was still very fresh in his face, but he brushed it aside. It no longer mattered.

He had won his first great victory for Christ.

Chapter Twelve

Darkness shrouded the *Vicus Tucus*, looming and mysterious. The moon shone high overhead, its radiant beams casting dusky black shadows from the colossal pillars and formation of the mansion of Virginius.

Though it was several hours after the setting of the sun, the air was warm and humid. In sunny Rome, it was difficult to recall the icy snow and frigid breezes of Britain.

A lone owl flew overhead, casting its winged shadow upon the cobblestoned street. A single hoot issued from its beak, echoing with strange volume against the mammoth structures.

Under the covering of his hood, Philip glanced up at the bird, watching it disappear into the dark shadows on the soft currents of night air. Three weeks ago, he would have been terrified by hearing its call, knowing the omen of imminent death attached with its eerie hoot. Now, however, he was unafraid.

Beside him, covered in his own heavy woolen cloak, Beric walked in guarded silence. Only his sandaled feet made sound, falling in regular rhythm upon the cobblestones that characterized Rome.

Philip glanced sidelong at him. A prayer was heavy on his heart for him. Slowly, his mind drifted back to the afternoon when, two days after his conversion, he had first broken the news to Beric he was a Christian.

It still surprised him that Beric had made little comment. He had expected a stern rebuke for forsaking his country's gods, but Beric had met his announcement with a quiet respect he had never expected in a once-devout British chieftain.

And, more surprising still, Beric had only that evening requested to be taken to the Christian meetings.

The meetings.

Philip felt the icy fingers of apprehension creep up his neck. He cast an uneasy glance behind him. At the time of his conversion, he had not truly realized how very dangerous Rome was for Christians, but now there was no mistaking the peril his new faith had brought upon himself.

The proof was all around him.

The emperor's dislike of Christianity was intensifying with every passing day. Only a week after his conversion, Philip had heard of a mass execution in the imperial arena. Twenty Christians had been killed under the swords of gladiators and even more had been thrown to starving lions.

But, terrible as this event had been, it was becoming commonplace. Too commonplace.

Last week, another brother had met his pitiless end. But, this time, Philip had known him. He had a countenance to put to the gruesome story.

Marcipor, a close friend of Daniel's and a fellow-slave, had been caught with a basket of bread and wine for communion. When confronted and challenged to offer a sacrifice to Jove, Marcipor had refused.

And, he had been covered in oily pitch and lit on fire in Nero's personal gardens as a result.

Melancholy bordered on Philip's heart. It was difficult to think of his pain. Worse still was the certain knowledge that Marcipor had not died alone. There had been dozens with him.

His mind drifted onto the words of Paul. The apostle's epistle to the Romans was well-circulated, and Daniel had verbally translated it from Greek to Latin for Philip's special benefit during one of the meetings. All of the words were powerful, but one phrase stood out in particular to him.

And not only so, but we glory in tribulation also: knowing that tribulation worketh patience; And patience, experience; and experience hope...

Philip shook his head ever so lightly. Glorying in tribulation was not easy to do. The apostle Paul himself knew this. He had been imprisoned in Rome for two years before just recently being released. Before his captivity, he had been shipwrecked, flogged, stoned. And, though he had left decadent Rome to continue his missionary work, it was almost certain he would experience further suffering for the sake of the gospel.

But, in the midst of all his stories of suffering, Paul preached hope. And he was right. Philip felt a smile tugging at his lips, melting his despondence. Wherever persecution found them, the Christians seemed to spring back stronger and more powerful than before.

"Are you certain you know where we are going?" Beric's hushed voice broke into Philip's plethora of thoughts.

"Yes." Philip forced himself to focus on the present moment. "We'll be there soon."

Almost as he spoke, his eyes fell on a familiar door. A tiny, almost invisible symbol marked one corner of the frame. It was the *Ichths*, or, sign of the fish. They were about to be among friends.

Philip tapped the door with his knuckle, scarcely making a sound. The door opened a crack, but no wider. "Peace be with you." He whispered the password. The last few weeks had taught him well. At once, the gap widened, allowing space for them to slip through.

Just inside, his eyes fell on the others. *My brethren.* Men, women, and children sat grouped together, some on the floor, others on low stools. Their tones were hushed, sincerely joyful to be together, yet too mindful of the danger to raise their voices.

Philip raised his hand in silent greeting. Peace washed over him, as it always did when he joined his fellow-believers. He stood another moment, looking at them. Herein was the beauty of his new faith. Slaves sat with masters, Greeks mingled with Jews. And Romans embraced their conquered inferiors.

"Peace be with you, Philip." A delicate young girl drew near him, balancing a pitcher of wine on her hip. Her maidenly form was slim and shapely, and she wore her faintly-curling dark hair pulled back high on her head in the attractive Greek fashion.

"May the grace of our God be with you, Moriah." Philip crossed his hands upon his breast as he spoke, subservient. He was always at a loss for words with the pretty adopted daughter of Daniel.

The girl was Roman by birth, but, when Daniel had first found her, abandoned on a street corner, he had given her a Jewish name. *Moriah*. Philip dimly recalled Daniel telling him it was the name of a sacred location in Jerusalem, a place now defiled by Roman authority.

"We are all assembled." Daniel's quiet voice fell over the group. "Let us begin with prayer."

Philip moved forward to find a place among the brethren, motioning for Beric to follow. He knelt, offering a slight nod to the believers who glanced up at him. Beric knelt beside him, his garment brushing Philip's shoulder.

"Almighty Jesus, we are gathered in Your Name to worship You. We thank You for Your goodness and love. We praise You for Your death on the cross, for giving us eternal life through Your blood…"

Philip let Daniel's voice fade out. Normally, he listened with devout fervor, weighing Daniel's prayers in his mind and learning from his examples how to pray. Tonight, however, his heart was too full. Silently, he began his own petition.

Almighty Jesus, I thank You for Your goodness. I can't begin to praise You like Daniel, but You know my heart. You've delivered me from so much. Please continue to deliver me. I haven't begun to love like You love, but I want to.

Philip paused a moment in his mind. Did he really mean that? A brief reflection revealed he did. Hard as it was to forgive others, to love individuals like Marcus, he wanted to. He could not bear being bound by hate again.

Help me to learn how to love, Jesus. And I pray you will let my father see the truth about Your grace. Let him come to know You as I have done.

The completion of Daniel's prayer cut into Philip's own petition. Prayer requests and news began to circulate around the room.

One man's father had been imprisoned; yet another had recently wed and requested prayer for his unsaved wife; and Moriah quietly requested prayer for courage in witnessing.

The requests taken, Daniel quietly told of his personal salvation account, coupling his story with a full explanation of how to accept the free gift of eternal life. Philip knew he did so for the sake of Beric, desiring to witness to him without seeming too pointed.

The story seemed new every time Philip heard it. He wished he could recite the account of Jesus' life, death, and resurrection as fluently as Daniel. It seemed every time he came to the meetings, he realized how much he had to learn.

Too soon, the story came to a close. Daniel glanced around the room, his eyes shining from his bewhiskered face with a kindly, searching gaze.

Philip glanced at Beric. He did not expect him to be at all impressed. After all, he was a brave-hearted Briton, devout to his country's gods and the oath to destroy Rome. He was not even certain why Beric had requested to come.

To his surprise, Beric's head was bent low in his chest. Philip was almost startled to see it. His strong, jaunt father always sat upright, his chin held proudly erect, his eyes looking out on the world with the expression of calm, cool leadership he had always possessed.

"If there is no immediate business at hand, I would like to ask a brother to close in prayer." Daniel half-turned, as if to choose a brother.

Abruptly, Beric lifted his head. His voice, clear and firm, broke the stillness of the room. "I believe."

Philip's mind whirled. This was impossible. Did Beric really mean what he was saying? Just as quickly, guilt seized him. Where had been his faith? His own conversion had been swift; why should he doubt his father's sincerity? His conscience pricked him.

With God all things are possible.

Dimly, he saw Daniel move forward, grasping Beric's hand. Their tired countenances suddenly lightened by joy, the brethren gathered around them, touching Beric, murmuring words in his ear.

Daniel motioned for Beric to kneel with him, his hand gripping his new brother's shoulder. Beric's hand covered his face, his tones unsteady.

And, for the first time, Philip heard the sound of his father's voice being lifted to the One Almighty God.

Sudden emotion threatened to overcome him. Philip moved forward, kneeling beside his praying father and laying his own hand on his bent shoulder. At that moment, rejoicing such as he had never before felt filled his heart. He closed his eyes, basking in the warmth of his joy.

Abruptly, the words of Paul's epistle flashed into his mind, startling him. *For thy sake we are killed all the day long; we are accounted as sheep for the slaughter.*

Philip gazed over the assembled brethren. A strange heaviness masked his joy, creeping into every corner of his heart.

Why did those words seem to ring in his ears?

"By Hercules! You move with the swiftness of a tortoise! Hand me that *pallium*."

Philip stifled a sigh. It seemed that since his conversion, Marcus had grown even more irritable. He found constant fault with him, the slightest trace of his former favor and indulgence having completely disappeared.

Daniel had said it was to be expected. He had said that temptation and vexation was certain to come in its strongest forms at the beginning, attempting to lure him away him away from his new faith.

But that was impossible. Philip knew in his heart he was a child of God. And no man, not even Marcus, could snatch him from his Lord's hands.

He handed Marcus the garment, half-hoping his quiet submission would calm Marcus's temper. "Here you are, my lord."

Marcus took the garment slowly, his eyes narrowed with piercing coolness. Philip felt a chill of uneasiness. He glanced up, meeting Marcus's gaze, then, subserviently dropped his eyes.

"You seem weary." Marcus's voice bordered on suspicion.

Philip looked up. How did Marcus always know? He and Beric had not returned home until quite late, remaining at the meeting place long after everyone else had left. He had only caught a few hours of rest before the rising of the sun had prodded him to his feet. "I am a little tired, my lord."

He turned away to pour out the wine. Marcus's voice continued behind him.

"Where were you last night?"

Philip stiffened. His hand shook a little as he set the pitcher down. Turning, he handed Marcus the wine, not daring to look him in the eye. "Your wine, my lord."

"*Avernus* take the wine! Answer me, you fool. Where were you last night?"

Philip slowly drew himself up. The moment he had dreaded had come. He could not lie— that much he was certain of. But there were lives, lives other than his own, to be thought of. "I—I beg your pardon?"

"Do not pretend you don't understand me, Philip." Marcus stepped threateningly nearer. His fingers brushed the fastening on his right wristband, ominous. As was so often his case, his behavior hinted his readiness to take physical action if Philip continued to put him off.

Philip felt a cold chill. He remembered all too clearly Marcus's powerful strength. A cringing remembrance of the *flagellum* swept through his mind. But, if he was to suffer, he wanted it to be for the sake of his Lord, not his own disobedience. He titled his chin. "I was out walking, my lord."

"I wonder you dared to leave without my permission."

Philip fought to maintain an even, quiet tone. "You have never forbidden me to go out, my lord."

"I did not know my slave was such an idiot as to roam the streets at midnight. But, as I own, you are from the barbarous tribe lands."

Philip said nothing, though his heart swelled resentfully at the cutting sarcasm. Marcus eyed him.

"Surely your *walk* had a destination."

Philip's heart sank and he struggled to keep a forthright demeanor. "Yes."

"And *where* was it?"

Philip's mind whirled. What could he say? Even if lying was permitted for Christians, Marcus would see through his deceit in a moment. "It was a home–here in the city."

Marcus colored in angry vexation. "By the gods, Philip! You will not keep your master in ignorance. I demand the full truth from you at once."

So it was the full story or nothing. Philip braced himself. He would tell only what he could without risk to the others. "I was at a meeting of the Christian brethren, my lord."

Marcus cocked an eyebrow, surprise flickering over his face. "The Christian *brethren*? What nonsense is this, Philip? You are no Christian."

Philip swallowed hard, his heart pounding against his chest. "You are wrong, my lord. I am one."

Silence permeated the room.

Philip's heart pounded wildly. What would Marcus do to him? He averted his gaze for many long minutes, then, slowly, raised his eyes.

Marcus's countenance was expressionless. Abruptly, he turned around, taking up his mug of wine and cradling it in his hands. "So this will explain my misery of the last few weeks. Like all Christians, you pray curses down on the head of your rightful master."

Philip started a little. Was this what Marcus thought of him? Had he really seen no change in him since his conversion?

A sudden pang struck him. How could Marcus have seen much of a change in him, after all? He resented him, his commands. And he feared him too much to really show him how hard he was trying.

"You wrong me, my lord. I have made no such petition in my prayers." Philip bit his tongue almost the moment he spoke. Defending himself was certainly no way to convince Marcus he had truly changed. Or, rather, he *was* changing.

Marcus turned, displeasure deep on his countenance. "You have told me I am wrong twice in the last few moments. Is that the way you Christians are instructed to address their masters?"

"No, my lord." Philip felt a wave of shame. It was little wonder Marcus considered him the impudent fool he had always been. "My apologies."

Marcus eyed him. "If these Christians have taught you how to beg my pardon, then perhaps they are not so remiss after all. But," and here his voice grew low and threatening, "I will not be responsible for your safety. I care little whether or not you belong to this sect. My only concern is that you serve me well. Yet, if you are caught and fed to starving lions, it is your own doing. Do not expect me to save you."

Marcus ended with a look that assured Philip he meant what he said. Setting his cup down, he turned and vacated the room.

Philip stood where he was, motionless. So that was all. Marcus had not stormed or threatened him. Perhaps persecution would not come from his quarter after all.

A slow smile quivered about his lips. Once again, his faith had failed, but God had not. God would never fail him.

Three evenings later, Philip donned his simple cloak and slipped through the atrium to the *vestibule*. His father had already left for the meeting. As the meeting was scheduled earlier in the evening, they had thought it best to not be seen going by twos.

A snatch of a whistle lighted on Philip's lips. He had many questions for Daniel and was eager to arrive at his destination. Though he wished he knew more than he did, the anticipation of having his constant questions answered was a true pleasure.

"Philip!"

Philip felt the whistle die on his lips. With a tinge of apprehension, he stepped toward the library. Marcus stood in the doorway, a scroll in his hand.

"Yes, sir?"

"Where were you going?"

"To the meetings, my lord." Philip took careful survey of Marcus's expressionless face. "I shall not be out as late as I was before."

Marcus tapped the end of the scroll absently into his palm. "See that you keep that promise."

"Yes, my lord." Philip half-bent. Turning, he strode quickly away, of no mind to tempt Marcus's changing moods.

Marcus watched him leave. It was not until the sound of the closing door struck his ears that he turned, reentering the library.

What strange whims his slave had, to be sure. One moment an untamable barbarian, the next a contented Christian. He would never begin to understand Philip's restless energy and impossible thinking.

Without warning, a stern voice cut into his thoughts. "Have you dispatched your slave on an errand, Marcus?"

Marcus turned to face Rowland. Assuming a carelessness he did not feel, he threw his parchment down upon a low table. "No, father, I have not. Why do you inquire?"

"Because I think it very strange you allow him so much liberty. By the gods, do you want to lose him again?"

135

Marcus laughed slightly. "I do not think that at all possible. That ring about his neck should more than guarantee his safe conduct."

"I am glad you are so confident." Rowland's voice was dry, and he picked up the scroll Marcus had carelessly cast aside. "Where was he going?"

"To a Christian meeting of sorts, I believe."

Rowland looked up in sudden astonishment. "Marcus, I trust you are joking."

"No."

Rowland's scroll closed with an echoing snap. Angrily, he tossed it down upon the table. "By the great gods! And you have dared to permit it?"

Suddenly conscious of his father's displeasure, Marcus straightened himself erect. "Yes," he said slowly. "I saw little reason to forbid it."

"Little reason! Are you so foolish that you are not aware that the Christians cause all the ill that befalls Rome?"

"I questioned Philip somewhat on that score. He assured me he makes no such prayers."

"And you believe him?" Rowland spat the words. "Marcus, I am ashamed of you. We will be cursed by all the gods in turn if you do not put an end to this folly. Where is your Roman pride that you allow your personal attendant to worship a dead Jew?"

Marcus felt the color rising in his cheeks. He was accustomed to being treated like a man, and Rowland's angry sarcasm stung him to the quick. "I am as true a Roman as any man could be father. You know that."

"Then pray show a little Roman sense, Marcus! As your father, I command that you put an end to this nonsense or I shall take matters into my own hands by sending that insolent little cur to the auction block."

Marcus bit his lip for a long moment. So now his father threatened his pride and masculinity by threatening to take his own possession from him. He made no attempt to hide the cold anger bordered on his voice.

"Cease to threaten me, father. If it is your desire that my slave be rid of this Christianity, then you need only state as much. Your wish shall be my will—without such derision."

Rowland narrowed his gaze. "So you say. I am decidedly disappointed in you, Marcus. That you should for a single moment tolerate this infamous sect within my household is a severe dishonor to me."

Marcus averted his gaze to hide their smoldering. "My apologies."

Rowland turned and stalked away. At the door, he turned, his voice sharp.

"You say you are a true Roman at heart, Marcus. You shall prove it by dispelling all trace of Christianity from your slave. And," his voice grew cutting, "you better do it quickly. No dog of a Briton will bring a curse upon my household."

With a piercing glare, Rowland left the library.

Marcus stood still. Like rolling waves, anger burned in his countenance. It was not so much his father's command that infuriated him, but his blatant ridicule. He, the now eldest son and right hand of his father, had been humiliated and spurned like a child.

And Philip had been the cause of it.

"Jove be my witness." Marcus's hands suddenly doubled into angry fists. "Christianity shall indeed be wrenched from this household."

Chapter Thirteen

Philip crept noiselessly up the steps of the Virginius domus. He cast a quick glance behind him. Thankfully, it did not seem they were being watched.

Behind him, Beric's clothing rustled against his own. His close presence was warm. In the darkness of night, with danger lurking beyond every shadow, it was reassuring to have his father with him.

Philip stepped into the *vestibule*. A single oil lamp flickered, casting eerie shadows against the wall. The domus was silent. Somehow, its hollow darkness reminded him of the caves of Britain.

He turned. Beric's face was dimly illuminated by the golden lamplight, expelling the remainder of his figure into a shadowy outline.

"Marcus will be expecting me." Philip barely lifted his voice above a whisper. "I hope he is not angry I was gone so late. I had more questions for Daniel than I realized."

"Daniel is a wise man." Beric's tones were as hushed as his own. "I am pleased you spoke with him. Many of your questions had been in my own mind."

"And I find myself with a full dozen more to ask him. I wish I had the half of his knowledge."

Beric chuckled, his muffled laughter lightening the shrouded darkness of the atrium. "I don't doubt you someday will, my son. You are too keen-spirited to undertake anything half-heartedly." His hand rested lightly on Philip's shoulder. "But I have seen in the last few weeks how you are curbing your free spirit to deal respectfully with Marcus. And for that, I commend you."

Philip felt a warm rush. His father was not one to give praise lightly. Bending, he touched Beric's hand to his forehead.

"Thank you, father. Your commendation is kind." He straightened, grinning ruefully. "It may be a little premature, though. I am ashamed to admit it, but the very sound of Marcus's name boils my blood. I don't think I'll ever possess a tame character where he is concerned."

"Then I advise you go quickly to him while you are still under the influence of Daniel's preaching." Beric squeezed Philip's shoulder. "Goodnight, my son."

"Goodnight." Philip offered a half-smiling salute before striding quickly across the atrium and mounting the stairway to the family's sleeping chambers.

At the door of Marcus's chamber, he stopped to take a deep breath.

He was still very lighthearted from the stimulating conversation he and Daniel had shared, to say nothing of the pleasant evening he had enjoyed with his new brethren. Despite a slight twinge of conscience, he was not eager to come down from the joyful heights the meeting had taken him to return to the irritations of his duties.

Give me grace, Lord. He inhaled deeply, stepping into the well-lit apartment.

Marcus stood at one of the casement. At the sound of Philip's entrance, he turned, irritation, as always, high in his countenance.

Philip half-bent, his heart sinking. Marcus looked dour indeed. Inwardly quaking, he crossed his hands on his breast. "All hail, my lord."

"You were gone long." Marcus's voice was dark in its curtness. "I do not consider this a fulfillment of your promise."

Philip exhaled slowly. Marcus was not going to make it easy for him. Should he explain that he had come sooner than the time before? Or say nothing?

Marcus didn't leave him either option. "Still, it no longer matters. You are no longer to go to those meetings, Philip. And, for that matter, you are to cease your practice of Christianity altogether."

Philip started. The abruptness of Marcus's command was shocking. Surely Marcus did not mean what he said! He had said only a few days ago he had no objection to his slave's newfound faith.

Slowly, he ventured to speak, trying to sort through his feelings of disbelief. "My lord, I do not understand–"

"Then allow me to make it plain to you." Marcus stepped a little nearer, coldly authoritative. "Christians bring about all the ill that befalls Rome, to say nothing of the disapproval our divine emperor has for the sect. I have seen my duty as a Roman and will not tolerate its practices in any slave of mine."

Philip's heart sank. If Marcus's words were resolute, the icy frigidness of his dark eyes was even more so. But, *surely*, this was all impossible. "You cannot mean that, master."

"I do. The sooner you are purged of this folly, the better."

"But it is *not* folly." Philip felt a well of desperation growing within him. What had triggered this sudden intolerance in Marcus? "We do not bring about ill to Rome, nor is our emperor's dislike for our faith at all just."

"Enough." Marcus's eyes blazed. "Take care how you speak of Nero. Men have died for less than what you just uttered."

Philip bit his lip and looked down. Of course. This was Rome. Never speak your mind, never doubt the authority or infallibility of an emperor.

Marcus drew a little closer, his voice cruel. "I wouldn't know why you would care anyway, Philip. You make a worthless Christian as it is. Are you not bidden to obey and respect your lawful master?"

Philip felt a twinge. He would never be able to convince Marcus he was trying to change, trying to follow the example of his true Master. He chose his words carefully. "We are commanded to obey our masters as long as we are not ordered to do something against the higher authority of Jesus the Christ."

Marcus laughed callously. "And I suppose you will tell me obeying my command in this goes against this Jesus. But, it is no matter. You will heed me, Philip."

Philip averted his gaze. "And if—"

"If you disobey? You will not disobey, Philip. You will not wish to live to see the consequences."

Philip looked up, hoping to see a glimmer of mercy in Marcus's dark eyes. There was none. The young man was as grimly resolute as any master could be.

"Well? Do you understand me?"

"Yes, my lord." Philip spoke softly. He understood perfectly.

Marcus motioned briskly. "Then go to your own quarters. I do not require your services tonight."

Wordlessly, Philip strode across the chamber to his own sleeping place. Shutting the door, he leaned against it for many long minutes. As usual, Marcus had made his choice a simple one.

Obey or suffer.

Slowly, he went to his couch and knelt beside it. Though he was still new to this business of proper Christian prayer, he wanted to be on his knees more than he ever had before.

"Jesus." He began slowly, contemplating what he was saying. "You know what my master has decreed. And I know I cannot obey him. Give me the strength to resist him, no matter what he might do to me."

He paused. His conscience twinged painfully, and he resolved to make a full confession. Now more than ever, he wanted perfect honesty between him and his Savior.

"I am afraid of him, Lord. But the worst of it is that I still hate him. I struggle to love him like You have commanded. If I am to disobey him, I want him to see that this is not like all of my other follies. I want him to see a change in me. Please let him see that change, even if it is through my suffering."

Philip could scarcely believe the words fell from his lips. He dreaded Marcus's displeasure and cruel strength more than he would have admitted to anyone, but, at this moment, he felt he was willing to suffer if it would bring Marcus to see what true Christianity was.

"He was right, Jesus. I am a very poor type of Christian. But, somehow, help me love him and show him what a Christian can be through Your grace."

Again, he paused. More than anything, he wanted to ask to be delivered from persecution. But the words would not come to his lips. Dozens of his fellow-believers died daily. Was it fair that he ask to be excluded?

A struggle raged violently in his heart. He *wanted* deliverance. Surely, it was not wrong to ask for it. *But is it right?*

Slowly, his head sank onto his couch. It was all or nothing. He was not going to be a half-way Christian. "And, Lord, let it not be my will, but Yours. May Yours be done."

Philip felt unusually rested when he awoke the next morning. Still, his first thought upon opening his eyes was that of Marcus's command. For a long moment, he gazed at the open casement. It was too easy to lay there and think of all the terrible things his master might do to him.

Get up. Don't mope. Focus on Christ's strength.

He bounded out of bed. As he dressed, he thought on every possible positive outcome. Perhaps sleep had even altered Marcus's hardened demeanor. He forced himself to keep that thought in mind as he moved into the next room.

It was a vain hope.

Marcus said little while Philip aided him to dress, but, when he at last broke the silence, his words were the last ones Philip wanted to hear. "You have not forgotten my command?"

"No, my lord." What else was there to say? Philip had not forgotten and it was apparent Marcus wasn't about to let him forget.

"That is well." An unusually pleasant expression played about Marcus's countenance. "I have been considering reinstating you as

142

a wrestler. Within a few weeks, if all goes well," and he made a meaningful sign, "I intend to see you again upon the wrestling mat."

If all went well? *If I recant…*

Marcus laughed unexpectedly. "Don't look so uncomfortable, Philip. I have no doubt of your prowess. And, perhaps, you may win back my favor."

Marcus's favor.

Philip's mind flashed back to those few weeks wherein he had enjoyed the benefits of Marcus's good-favor. He had known little fear or even anger. Good company, Roman diversions, and fair treatment had all been his. But now he knew the truth behind those fleeting pleasures. Like Marcus's favor, they were temporal and meaningless.

"See that you are prepared to escort me to the Baths at my regular hour." Marcus picked up his *pallium*. "I will return presently."

Philip half-bent in silent compliance. Marcus strode briskly from the room, the sound of the shutting door announcing his full departure.

Slowly, Philip picked up Marcus's tossed-aside tunic and absently folded it. He had much to think upon, much to consider. It was not long before it struck him that Beric's counsel might better serve his purpose. Quickly, he finished his few duties and slipped down to the gardens.

As usual, Beric was hard at work. He offered Philip a brief nod in greeting, keeping on with his work.

Philip watched him, framing his thoughts into words. "Father, is it known you are a Christian?"

"I have not spoken of the matter." Beric did not take his eyes from his swift-moving spade. "Unless you have told the Lord Marcus, only you and I share the knowledge."

"He does not know." Philip spoke slowly. "And I am grateful it is so."

Beric looked up. "Why?"

"Only because he has strictly forbidden me to ever again associate with my Christian brethren." Philip felt a sudden tinge of discouragement. It was if speaking of it brought him to the full acknowledgment Marcus was not going to change his mind. "I don't understand it, father. It was only a few days ago he said he did not care what my religion was."

"Knowing your master, I dare say he did not make this command lightly."

"Truth." Philip gazed over the garden, contemplative. "He has promised any trace of my disobedience will be severely dealt with. I wish I knew what he meant."

Beric turned back to his work, his countenance expressionless. "And will you obey him?"

"You know I will not." Despite the gravity of the subject, Philip's mouth twitched in a smile. Beric knew he was not one to look back. But, then, perhaps he knew how deeply he feared Marcus. "But I do not wish to be foolish, father. I may die for disobeying Marcus. And, while I am not ashamed to die for Jesus, I don't relish the thought either."

"What do you intend to do?"

"I don't know. That is why I have come to you."

Beric slowly straightened himself. "I am far newer to our faith than you, my Philip. You alone can decide what is best to do."

"Are you willing to see your only son sacrificed for his Maker?"

"Yes." Beric rested his hand on Philip's shoulder. "I have always been willing to see my son give his life for his beliefs. It is the way of our people, Philip." He paused, a glimmer of emotion breaking through the resolution in his blue eyes. "But, my son, I only ask you are not foolish. It would break my heart to see you slain."

Philip felt a flood of grateful emotion. It was not often Beric shared his innermost feelings, and it touched him beyond words to hear the expression of his father's deep love for him. He took Beric's hands in his own, pressing them to his forehead.

"I will do as you say, my father. I can bear all for the Christ Who gives me strength, but I will not take any unnecessary risk. I will not heedlessly endanger the life you alone hold so dear."

Throughout the remainder of that day, Philip debated his best course of action. Was it wise to go to the meeting that night? Marcus would be on the sharp lookout, watching for any trace of disobedience.

On the other hand, was it obedience to his Lord to forsake the assembly of his brethren? He felt certain it wasn't, but it cost him a hard struggle to place his faith in Christ's will.

At last, Philip set his mind to go. Instant peace flooded his mind and heart, and he knew he had made the right decision. A prayer flitted through his mind. *Thank you, Jesus. Give me the strength to continue following Your will.*

Scarcely half an hour after his decision, Marcus announced his own intention to visit Delicia that evening.

A feeling of warm hope washed over Philip with the announcement. It was more than possible Marcus would not return until he had already returned home himself, and he chided himself for his lack of faith. Surely this was God's hand of Providence, giving him a way of escape from persecution.

The thought warmed his heart all that day and continued with him even until night fell. Marcus left, and, scarcely waiting until he had traversed out of sight down the *Vicus Tuscus*, Philip slipped from the Virginius domus.

He went alone. As occasionally happened, Beric was unable to break away from his duties. Lightly, he jogged through the quiet streets until he came to the house assigned for the evening's meeting.

Inside the simple home, Philip was warmly greeted by the others. He was somewhat late and scarcely had time to make his greetings before Daniel commenced the meeting.

In his usual quiet manner, Daniel prayed, making mention of several brethren in bonds as he did so. He then seated himself, and a brother named Simeon arose to speak.

Philip listened attentively at first, but his mind soon wandered to thoughts of the speaker himself. An elderly man of some sixty years, Simeon had been a Jewish rabbi before his conversion to Christianity. Yet, unlike Daniel, he had not come to Rome as a slave, but to escape the religious and military turmoil in Israel.

When Simeon finished, Daniel again arose. "Before we depart, I would like to ask if there are any requests for prayer."

Philip glanced around. There was always a multitude of requests, but, tonight, his fellow believers were strangely silent. He felt a twinge. He had a request of his own, but he had never before made a public request for prayer. He had always deemed himself too young and inexperienced to speak before the others, even though he knew exactly what Daniel would say.

Let no one despise your youth, Philip. You are young and new to the faith, but you are one of us.

As if he could read his mind, Daniel turned to him. "You seem as if you wish to speak, Philip. If you have a request, share it with us."

Slowly, Philip rose to his feet. His hands felt clammy as he pressed them together. It would seem Daniel was beginning to read his thoughts as easily as Marcus could. "I do have a prayer request that is very close to my heart, Daniel, but I fear it may be of little interest to anyone else."

"What is meaningful to you is meaningful to us, my boy." Simeon spoke before Daniel could answer, his voice rebuking. "Let us have your thoughts."

Philip was silent a moment, framing his thoughts into words. Simeon was a particularly gruff, zealous member of the brethren and it was especially difficult to speak before him.

His heart pumped with nervousness, and it was all he could do to speak. When he did, his voice shook despite his best efforts to control it. "I believe it is well-known that I am the servant of the noble Marcus Virginius. Last night, he forbade me to ever again associate with those of this way. He has promised to deal severely with me if I disobey... and, of course, I am disobeying even now."

He swallowed before continuing, remembering to breathe. *Calm down.* Still, he sensed part of his nervousness had nothing to do with being in front of the brethren, but because of the gravity of his situation.

"My master does not make threats lightly. I do not ask that you pray I am delivered from this trial when so many of our brethren are suffering, but I do plead with the Lord to give me whatever mercy He sees fit. If you would pray the same, I would be blessed."

There. He had done it. He had actually spoken before the entire assembly, despite his youth and all the other objections he had so often aroused in his mind.

Shaking ever so slightly, Philip resumed his seat, half-averting his eyes. He felt Daniel look kindly on him.

"We will pray for you, my young brother. It is not wrong to ask for deliverance, but we all can commend the submission you clearly manifest. Take comfort—we are all behind your cause."

Philip managed to nod. His heart slowly resumed its natural beat, warming with gratitude. He was glad he had spoken, if only to obtain Daniel's understanding.

The closing prayer was spoken and the meeting disassembled. Some of the members paused to speak to Philip, assuring him they would pray for his safety. Again, Philip's heart warmed. This was what had drawn him to Christianity—the concern of ordinary people for others.

He lingered behind the others. With the last member gone, he approached Daniel, crossing his hands on his breast in his old fashion of greeting.

Daniel laid his hand on his shoulder, the first to speak. "I am glad you spoke in the meeting tonight, Philip. It is well the others know to pray for you."

"I scarcely knew what to say, Daniel." Philip attempted a laugh. "I do not know why I was so nervous."

Daniel smiled, but gravity lingered over his bearded countenance. "It is a grave trial the Lord has seen fit to send upon you, Philip. I suppose you have a fair idea of what your master will do if he catches you in disobedience."

"I do not like to think about it, Daniel. I–I dare not."

"I understand." The pressure of Daniel's hand increased upon his shoulder. "And I am grateful you have not esteemed the security of this life as more important than loyalty to Christ."

"I could not, Daniel." Philip's voice grew low. "He saved me from a very miserable existence. Though a very poor sort of Christian, I could not shirk my loyalty to Him."

Daniel surveyed him contemplatively. "And why do you speak so of yourself? I have seldom seen one give himself up so entirely to Christ as you have."

"It is your great kindness that causes you to speak so, Daniel. I know I am an unworthy Christian. Even Marcus has told me so."

"And you believe him?"

"I must. Despite all my attempts to change, he has seen nothing good in me."

"Then I must think he spoke in unkindness. Philip, you must know you are a constant encouragement to me. You are no lukewarm believer, but one sold to the faith and determined to live for Christ. And I have seen many changes in you."

Philip felt a warm glow of gratitude. Marcus's callous comment had left him more than a little discouraged, and he had struggled with feeling his efforts had been in vain. "You will never know how that strengthens me, Daniel."

"I am glad." Daniel paused a moment. "Philip, do not let bitterness fill your heart for Marcus. His sin in opposing your faith is great, but I counsel you to continue in steadfast prayer for him."

Philip attempted lightheartedness. "Your counsel always comes at the most appropriate times. My prayers have been mostly for myself these days." Then, growing serious, "But I will not forget, Daniel. I–I am not ashamed to say I fear Marcus, but I am trying to love him as I ought."

"And that may be why you struggle." Daniel spoke gently. "Love cannot be forced. It is much more than that."

A wave of discouraged irritation washed over Philip. It spilled over into his voice. "I suppose I shall never learn to love properly. But if Christ looks at the heart, my attempts must mean something."

"Truth." Daniel's quiet voice was a striking contrast to his slightly heated one. "And, I, for one, desire to be found obeying my Savior because I want to, not because it is my duty."

Shame tinged Philip's heart, realizing how callous he had sounded. He softened. "Then you think I only attempt to love Marcus because it is my duty?"

"I do not accuse you, Philip."

"But what do you think?"

Daniel rested a hand on Philip's shoulder. "I think that suffering can destroy the strongest sense of duty, my friend. And, if true love is not etched in your heart now, it will certainly give way to hate when tested."

Philip looked downwards, fingering the metal collar around his neck. "And I am certain to be tested." His voice was low. "But I do not know how to give what is not in my heart."

Daniel squeezed his shoulder. "Pray for it, Philip. Pray for the love that is selfless, that keeps no record of wrongs."

The words haunted Philip all during his long, silent trek home. And, in his heart of hearts, he knew what Daniel had tried to tell him in his own kind, subtle way was true.

Pain had given him fear for Marcus, cruelty had given him hate, and his new faith tried to balance the remembrance of past wrongs with dutiful respect and something he tried to call love.

Glancing up, Philip's mind drifted to awe, taking in the bright gleams of the twinkling stars. They were a boundless cluster of light, shining out upon the darkness of Rome and guiding his way. Abruptly, he bit his lip. That was what he wanted–to be a light, shining out on dark hearts and guiding them home.

And he knew he couldn't be that light until he broke the hold of unforgiveness.

He *wanted* to show Marcus all Christianity was and could be. *But how?* Daniel said to pray, but was that truly all he needed to do? Was there something more, something that would break this hold of past pain and bitterness?

Be not overcome of evil, but overcome evil with good.

Philip stopped short. The clarity of the words had nearly been audible. Involuntarily, he glanced behind him. No one was there.

But it was enough.

Philip again looked up, allowing the starlight to rest on his face. Slow, sure peace flooded his heart. He had been given his answer. In repaying evil with good, he would learn to love Marcus the way he ought, the way he wanted to.

His steps quickened. The Virginius Mansion appeared before him, and he mounted the steps. He took each step firmly, creating a resounding slap on his sandals on the marble. Something about the sound was strengthening, however dimly it reminded him of blows.

Don't even think of about it. His back was sore with tension, but he brushed it aside and slipped inside the *vestibule.*

The lamps were lit, casting their beams over the shadowed interior of the domus. The fountains played in the garden, the sound of their dancing water echoing into the atrium.

Philip straightened his shoulders. His heart pounded like a war drum, but he refused to dwell on it. Fear would not control him. Swiftly, before he could think to stop himself, he stepped lightly up the stairs and entered Marcus's chamber.

It was empty.

A rush of relief nearly overwhelmed him. Attempting to resume his normal breathing, Philip leaned against the door, closing his eyes.

God had spared him from suffering, at least for tonight. If Marcus was still making his visit to the household of Saturius, he would not return until well-past midnight. And he would be too drunk to question his slave's activities during his absence.

Be not overcome of evil, but overcome evil with good.

Philip's eyes opened. The words had given him peace before. Why did they suddenly haunt him, striking fear into his heart?

In the darkness of the room, dread slowly enveloped him. Dark realization ebbed its way into his very soul, chilling him. He felt as if God was warning him, preparing him for something he had no power to resist.

You cannot replace evil with good if you are not faced with it.

Philip tried to put away the thought. But he could not. The weight of a terrible *something* he could not understand pressed harder and harder against his chest.

He went to his own room and lay down on his couch. As his eyes adjusted to the darkness, the haunting feeling doubled in intensity. God was trying to prepare him. He could feel it, perceiving it in every sense of his body. There was something difficult in God's will for him.

And he was not surrendered.

His eyes closed.

Lord Jesus, I want Your will to be done, not mine. But, please, do not try me. Please deliver me. Please, Lord. Don't test my desire to please You through suffering. Help me to love Marcus without being hurt.

Even as he prayed, Philip sensed the bittersweet truth. God, in His great love, had a great purpose for him. That purpose would shape and mold him into what he needed to be, both for his sake and for Marcus.

And that path, somewhere along it, would include suffering.

Chapter Fourteen

With the fall of dusk, Philip slipped from the Virginius domus. Everything about him was tense with nervousness. Marcus was home tonight and the likelihood of him discovering his slave's absence was very great.

Philip tried to brush his dread aside. If God could shut the mouths of lions, as Daniel had told him, He could deliver a British slave.

But his apprehension refused to die. All during the meeting, his thoughts remained on his strange intuition that something was going to befall him. It had haunted him all last night and all that day, growing from suspicion into a difficult certainty. He couldn't escape it.

With the close of the meeting, Philip slipped quickly up to Daniel, whispering a hasty word in his ear. "Pray for me."

He turned away before Daniel could stop him, his heart thudding. He could not bring himself to linger as he always did, speaking with the others or waiting to have private conversation with Daniel.

The terrible torture of apprehension was too great.

Swiftly, he jogged homeward. Somewhere, in the back of his mind, he entertained the faint hope that his swiftness might save him. Perhaps Marcus would not have noticed his absence.

But, despite his best efforts, the hope was a faint one.

The Virginius Mansion arose up before him. Dread arose in his heart, nearly suffocating him. He felt his pumping legs involuntarily slow, coming nearly to a standstill beneath him. He exhaled slowly, attempting to bring his thudding pulse to normality.

Hold me, Father. Only You can save me.

Bound by habit, he mounted the steps. One, two. The echo of his own footsteps was like the resonance of blows falling in regular rhythm.

God save me. Be with me!

Inside, the atrium was still and noiseless. Philip could hear his own heart thudding against his chest. He stepped cautiously forward, his sandaled feet swishing against the ornate floor.

"Where have you been?"

The stern voice sent a chill rushing down Philip's spine. Slowly, he turned, crossing his hands respectfully upon his breast. Whatever else happened, he must remember to give Marcus the deference Christ would wish him to show.

"All hail, master."

Marcus took a threatening step near him, emerging from the shadows into the light of the flickering lamps. "Withhold your pretty airs and speeches, slave, and answer me. Where have you been?"

The moment was nigh. Philip swallowed hard, meeting Marcus's angry gaze. *Show no fear. You are in His hands.*

"I was at one of the Christian meetings, my lord."

Marcus's eyes narrowed. His countenance was menacing. "I thought so, but refused to believe you could be so foolish. By Hercules, why did you disobey me?"

For a moment, Philip felt genuine pity flood his chest. Marcus was so controlled by anger, so lost within his own lust and cruelty. *He does not know.* He knew nothing of the peace of knowing there was a God who loved him.

A surreal calm settled over him. Before he could truly think, Philip knew he had his answer. "I had to go, Marcus. I had to learn more of my Savior."

"As you will need a savior, slave." Marcus's eyes were a dark flicker. They held a mysterious fierceness Philip had only seen in wild animals. "I swore to crush any rebellion in you, and I shall keep my word."

The strange, cold quietness of Marcus's voice sent a chill down Philip's back. He was accustomed to violent fury, but this was a new anger he had never before seen in his lord. Marcus was dark and merciless, controlled by some unseen force that was greater than his own cruelty.

Philip closed his eyes, breathing hard. For the first time, he recognized spiritual oppression when he saw it. *God, save me! He is not himself. He does not know what he is doing.*

Marcus clapped his hands sharply together. The sound brought the steward bowing into the atrium.

"You called, my lord?"

"Have the men in with the rods."

Demetrius left the room, saluting in silent obedience.

Philip looked at Marcus. He could feel the color waning from his cheeks, his body tense. So this was his punishment? To be brutally flogged, perhaps by Marcus himself? A fleeting downwards glance revealed his hands were shaking. He had not felt this much fear since his capture.

Marcus read his thoughts. "Yes, Philip." His entire body seemed sculpted in cruel resolve. He was one of a strong line of merciless conquerors. And he could be as ruthless as the best of them. "I will teach you once and for all that I am to be obeyed."

Demetrius abruptly reappeared with three of the men servants, one of whom held a thick rod in his hand.

At the sight, Philip's forehead broke out in a cold sweat. He cast a swift glance at Marcus, willing his silent plea to soften his heart. Surely, his stalwart young master did not mean to kill him. *Lord, help me.*

Marcus continued to look coldly at him, his eyes locking Philip in his hold even when he spoke. "Strip him to the waist."

Philip went cold. He felt his tunic pulled roughly down over his shoulders, leaving his back and arms bare.

A tremor passed through him, paralyzing his movements. He raised his eyes, watching Marcus step to the man who held the rod and take it from his hand.

"Now hold him down."

Philip's arms were grasped in a brutal hold. One of the men gave him a violent jerk, flinging him to his knees. In that moment, deathlike fear seized him. His thoughts whirled, realizing the truth behind his own terror. He was more afraid for Marcus than for himself.

The men knelt beside him, gripping his arms. Knowing in another second he would be forced down on his face, Philip struggled against them, raising one hand in appeal to Marcus.

"Marcus, I beg you! Let me speak."

"I will listen to one thing only, Philip." Marcus's voice was rigidly cold. "Give me your sworn oath you will denounce this dead Jewish carpenter, and I will forgive your disobedience this once. That alone will I hear."

"I cannot do that, Marcus."

The quiet resolution in his own voice sent unnatural peace again washing over Philip's heart. His heart pounded, and he knew his own inner terror of Marcus. Yet, he was calm, an assurance of pity overwhelming him.

Marcus did not know what he was doing.

Dimly, Philip began to realize the phenomenal forgiveness his Lord Jesus had for his enemies and so many of his Christian brethren had for their tormentors. It was power not of himself, but of Another.

His voice shook. "My lord, it is not for myself I speak to you, but for your sake. You do not know what you are doing."

"You think not?" Marcus's callous laughter filled the atrium. "Your master knows well what he is doing, cur." His eyes narrowed. "And I take pleasure in it."

"There is nothing you can do to me except what my Savior allows. You cannot truly hurt me, Marcus. You will only harden your own heart by this sin."

"Enough!" Marcus's face flamed, contempt livid upon his features. "What is your dead Jew beside the mighty pantheon of Rome? Do you think I fear you, your *God*?" His furious voice intensified, the rage deepening on his face. "You are *nothing*! Your God is nothing! And you shall learn whether or not the gods of your master are more powerful than this Christus you think you serve."

Philip's throat constricted. *Forgive him, Lord.* The words echoed in his ears, their blasphemy a curse to the Almighty God he loved.

Marcus gestured wrathfully to the men. "Hold him taut! We shall *see* if his God can halt my hand!"

Philip felt the cold floor beneath his stomach, the brutal grips of the two men who stretched themselves on either side of him to hold him down. He felt the motion of Marcus, stepping over him. His breathing quickened, his heart pulsating painfully in his chest. Tightly, he closed his eyes.

Finish well, Philip. Finish well!

The first blow fell. Philip heard the whistling sound of the rod's fall before it touched his body. Burning, stunning pain followed its descent, and Philip heard the sound of his own muffled cry echo throughout the room.

His hands doubled into tight fists, the warm perspiration seeping through his fingers.

A second blow fell. Philip swallowed hard, forcing his scream down instead of out. His mind whirled, but one thought stood out among the plethora of others.

You shall have tribulation, but I have overcome...

The curved rod tore into Philip's back. He cried out, his forehead resting in agony against the floor. He heard Marcus's upraised arm, heard the rustle of the garments upon his descending arm.

I have overcome for your sake.

"Idiot!" Marcus's frustrated, furious voice rent the whirling confusion of Philip's pain-ridden mind. "Say that you will obey me and I will stop."

Philip clamped his mouth into a firm line. *God help me! Help me!*

His silence enraged Marcus all the more. Philip felt his fury in the vengeful force of his blow, scoring the entire breadth of his shoulders. Another blow fell, and then another. Philip felt a warm trickle down his shoulders, over his back.

Before him, the ornate patterns of the floor lost their color and blended into one grey, whirling sphere. His stomach lurched; nausea threatened to overcome him. He could not think; he could not breathe to scream.

Slowly, the whirling room faded into a black mist. He sensed the blows descending on his back and shoulders, but he could no longer feel them. Confusion shot through his mind. Why could he no longer feel the pain?

Why? *What...* Something touched his hand, the hand held outstretched by the merciless grip of the men lying beside him. The voice in his mind became audible.

I have overcome for your sake.

The blows still fell, and Philip felt the world sinking into a deep, endless void of black. Was it death? But the voice was there, holding him up, keeping him from sinking further.

Nothing shall separate you from me.

There was someone with him. Philip could feel it, sense it. Darkness was trying to hold him down; he could feel the oppressive presence that had followed him before he gave his life to Christ. But it was fading; darkness was fading to light.

A final touch lighted on his perspiration-drenched hand.

Philip's eyes closed; he had no strength to keep them open. Slowly, with the dim knowledge Marcus had stopped, his mind reeled into peaceful insensibility.

There, pain ceased, but the assurance he was not alone did not.

When Philip awoke, it was to the sound of his own moaning cry. Racking pain shot through his back and shoulders, sickening him.

Why this terrible pain? What had happened? Thoughts ran rampant, ending with the image of a hard countenance.

Marcus.

His blurry eyes opened, and he felt the salty tears drying on his cheeks. The room came slowly into focus. Beric's grave, white face came into view, leaning over him. A brief glance revealed he was in his own room, lying on his couch.

Philip looked down. He was still naked to the waist. Blood drenched the tunic still lying loosely around his hips, ragged tears revealing where Marcus had struck his lower back.

A moan rose to his lips. His hands clenched into agonized fists, attempting to withhold the cries threatening to break from his throat.

It was then Philip sensed a warm tingle on his hand. Looking down, he saw nothing, but a fleeting remembrance crossed his mind.

The touch. The voice.

Philip's eyes closed and he leaned heavily back upon his cushions. He felt Beric lay his hand on his bleeding shoulder, his voice faltering.

"Philip, my son—"

Philip's eyes opened. He felt his mind slipping again into unconsciousness, but his heart burned with a sensation he himself could not understand. "Father, forgive him. He did not know what he was doing."

It was impossible for Beric to know whether Philip spoke to his earthly father or to his heavenly, but, in his heart, Philip knew whom he addressed.

It was to both.

Marcus poured out a glass of wine with a shaking hand. Lifting the mug, he cradled it in his hands, hating himself for the way they trembled.

"Curse him." His low voice intensified, and he set the mug down hard upon a table. "Curse him! The wretched swine!"

He stood motionless, breathing hard. His heart beat wildly, pounding against his taut chest. Slowly, he sank down onto a low couch, burying his face in his hands.

Great gods, why did this mystical fear envelop him? What had possessed him to stop flogging his slave before he had surrendered?

He had never been so enraged before, so intent upon breaking a slave's will. He had felt someone, *something*, at his shoulder, urging him to press on, to beat Philip until he swore to obey. And, while he could not recognize its identity, its presence did not disturb him. The truth be told, he was grateful for the dark pitilessness it had bestowed upon him. It had enabled him to keep on, to keep flogging his slave when another man might have stopped.

It was something far worse which unnerved him.

Marcus shuddered. His hand closed around his wine glass, lifting it to his lips. Shaking, he downed its contents at a single swallow and immediately poured out another draught.

For the countless time, he poured the wine down his throat. He waited. Frustration boiled up inside of him, and he threw the mug against the wall.

His mind refused to numb.

Again, Marcus dropped his aching head into his hands. An icy chill sped down his spine, and he hastily lifted his head. Nothing was there.

But there had been.

He had felt a strong presence, holding back the rage that controlled him and the mystical darkness which had spurred him on. His mind flew back over the events of the last half-hour.

Philip had ceased to cry out. He lay motionless, making no resistance to the brutal blows. That in itself was an act of unfathomable courage. Marcus had seen many slaves flogged and knew that before him had lain a boy possessing phenomenal bravery.

Philip's very courage had enraged him. He had lifted his arm to strike him for a countless time when, suddenly, his limbs refused to move.

Something had held him back.

Another cold shudder ran down Marcus's back. He had been paralyzed. He recalled seeing the men glance at him, wondering at the shock he knew governed his features. And still, that terrible, strong something had held him, refusing to allow him another blow. But that was not the worst.

That mystical force had been with Philip.

While that strange power had withstood him, it had seemed to be strengthening Philip. Peace fairly hovered over the wretched boy. It was as if he knew no pain, as if he could not sense his master's fury.

Marcus shook his head. Great gods, but these Christians were casting a spell on him! They were sorcerers. That must be his answer. Philip had tried to stop him, but his mystical powers had not worked in time.

Surely that is what happened! Surely—

Marcus stopped himself. Had he dared to almost think it? Jove! No Jewish carpenter was greater than the pantheon of Roman gods! How could he, a Roman, even entertain the thought?

Marcus arose. Stooping, he picked up his mug and refilled it. Lifting it, he made a solemn vow before touching the mug to his lips. "Great Jove, be my witness! No dead Jew is greater than you. I shall prove it. Philip will surrender—his sorcery will have no power over me!"

The flow of wine down his throat burned like fire.

Marcus clenched his fists. "Take care, Philip! Rome is god. And no other deity shall withstand me."

Chapter Fifteen

"Are you quite certain you are able to go out tonight, Philip?"

Philip looked up from fastening his cloak around his bandaged shoulders. He felt weary and, judging from Beric's concerned gaze, he knew his countenance was decidedly pale.

Yet, there was little wonder in all of that. He had suffered a long week of pain and discomfort before he had been able to leave his couch. And, though a day after he had first left his bed, he could scarcely stand upright.

"I think so, father." Philip paused, seeing the hesitance in Beric's face. "What is it?"

Beric half-averted his gaze. "Another flogging would kill you, Philip."

"If it is the Lord's will." Philip attempted to speak lightly. He didn't want to think about the pain, the terrible uncertainty of what Marcus might do if he caught him disobeying again. "I have been gone from the meetings for a week now. I can stay away no longer."

There was a moment of silence, broken at last by Philip.

"Will you not go with me, father?"

"Yes." Beric looked up. "I shall follow you in a half-hour. I have a few duties to attend to first."

"Then I shall be off." Philip forced a cheerful salute. Then, low, "Do not be afraid for me. No one shall pluck me from His hands."

Philip felt the assurance of his own words as he spoke. A week ago, he should not have been able to speak with such calm confidence. Now, however, he knew. He knew the peace that passeth all understanding.

As he walked through the atrium, Philip considered the brutality he had suffered. It seemed so long ago, yet, somehow so near. He thought back on the touch he had felt, of the voice that had given him such strength.

A smile played about the corners of his mouth.

The flogging had been merciless: the cruelest pain he had ever endured. But, for all that, it was sweet to know how close he had been brought to his Savior through the suffering.

He placed his foot on the step leading into the *vestibule*. Instantly, a voice sounded behind him.

"And where do you think you are going?"

Philip turned. His heart sank, and he struggled to speak calmly. "To worship my Lord with my brethren in the faith."

"You are scarcely able to walk." Marcus drew near, contemptuous. "Have you learned *nothing*? By the gods, it is evident you were not flogged long enough to make a suitable impression."

Philip looked quietly at him. "You made an impression on me, my lord."

Marcus suddenly slapped him. "I'll have none of your cheek! What do you mean by disrespecting me?"

Philip struggled to control himself, to control the anger that had arisen with the smarting pain of the slap. "I did not mean it as insolence, my lord."

"So you say. For a Christian, you are the most disrespectful, obstinate cur I have ever seen!"

Philip dropped his eyes. What was there to say? Marcus was determined to think ill of him.

Marcus continued to look contemptibly on him. "So you are disobeying me again. Have you no respect for me?"

"Yes. And I am willing to be obedient to you in all things. If..." Philip's voice trailed. "If only you will not bid me do wrong, Marcus."

Marcus laughed. "Since when do you care about right and wrong? And, even if you do, it is for your master to decide what course of action you are to take. Take assurance–you will be far happier doing the things I would have you to do."

Philip understood him perfectly. Marcus lived as any other young man did. He lived to pleasure, to what satisfied him. What was more natural than he should desire to corrupt his slave's faith than by tempting him with his own sins?

Choosing his words carefully, he met his gaze. "Things such as revelry and lust? Fornication, perhaps?"

"The more appropriate terms would be amusement and pleasure, my young fool."

"And you offer these things to me?"

"Yes, if you obey me." Marcus's frustration was lightened by the touch of a smile, playing alluringly around his lips. "Your Christianity has only brought you sorrow and pain, Philip. Recant it, and I will see that you are given pleasures such as you have never before known."

"What if I do not want them?" Philip maintained a quiet, steadfast mien. "What if I value my purity and faith in Christ more than these *pleasures* you offer me?"

Marcus again laughed. "Spoken like a naïve boy. When you have tasted the fruit of delights as I have, you will know which to choose."

Philip's heart burned with mingled indignation and pity. How low and hardened Marcus had become to offer him such things. When he had first known him, Marcus had seemed an upright young man, though Roman in his ways. Now, however, his heart was calloused.

And it was only growing harder.

"Marcus, Christianity is not something that can be taken off at will, like a tunic. You offer me cheap substitutes, but, even if I partook of them, I would only grieve my Savior. I would still be His child. No one, not even you, can take my faith from me."

The brow of Marcus darkened rapidly while Philip spoke. Fiercely, he stepped a little away from Philip, as if recoiling from a serpent. "Reject my well-meant offers if you will. If you want to be an idiot, it does not matter to me. But you will still submit your will to mine, Philip."

"You cannot make me." Philip's voice was low. "Nothing can take me from my God."

"We shall see." Marcus spat contemptibly. "Consider yourself fortunate I am determined to break your spirit and not your life. Were it otherwise, I would kill you where you stand."

Philip said nothing. He wanted to overcome Marcus's evil with good, as the Lord had been teaching him. But now did not seem the time to speak of Christian love and forgiveness.

"You are too weak to bear the punishment you deserve." Marcus gestured fiercely to the stairs. "Go to your quarters and do not dare leave them."

Philip silently obeyed, making a slight gesture of respect as he did so.

Marcus watched him go with boiling frustration. What a thorough idiot that boy was! He had even succumbed to bribery and still Philip refused to surrender his foolish will. Did he not know his master was certain to conquer him? Was he truly so ignorant of the things he had been offered to find no allurement to their pleasures?

"Stupid boy," Marcus muttered under his breath. He crossed the atrium, then, halted, hearing low voices at the top of the stairs.

"Marcus will not allow me to go out, father. Still, there is no reason why you should remain here."

"I will go, my son." Beric's voice was low. "Yet, it is a sore disappointment I must go alone."

Marcus stood motionless. The voices continued, but he did not listen. He had heard enough. *Beric is one of them.*

Perhaps that would explain Philip's frustrating obstinacy. Guidance and encouragement by a well-respected parent were certainly factors that would lend great determination to Philip's stubbornness.

Marcus strode into the library, contemplative. Though he had purchased him, Beric was not entirely his slave. He had been given as a gift to Rowland, and it was for Rowland to decide what to do with him.

"Marcus."

Marcus started a little. Rowland himself sat on a low couch before him, a pile of scrolls at his side. Recovering himself, he nodded politely.

"My apologies. I did not know you were here."

"Seat yourself, Marcus." Rowland motioned to a stool. "I want words with you."

Marcus obeyed, certain of his father's topic. Rowland considered him with sharp eyes before diving into the subject which vexed him.

"Demetrius tells me you at last flogged your obstinate slave."

"Yes."

"And has the lad yielded to your orders?"

"No." Too restless to sit, Marcus arose and paced the floor before his father. "I have scolded, threatened, and punished him, but he remains steadfast. I even tried bribery, but it availed nothing."

"Then are you ready to send him to the auction block?"

"No." Marcus rubbed his aching temples. He had been out far into the night, resulting in a headache of gigantic proportions. And dealing with the issue of his stupid slave certainly brought no relief. "Despite his rebellion, he is a valuable slave. I have plans to reinstate him as a wrestler, but I cannot do it until I have broken his will."

Rowland's eyes followed him. "I suppose you have removed from his path all those who would encourage him in his folly?"

Marcus stopped short. "Until a few minutes ago, I was certain I had, father. But it would seem Beric is a Christian also."

"There is little surprise there. Christianity spreads like wildfire." Rowland fingered his scroll contemplatively. "But neither slave will persist in their obstinacy much longer."

"What do you intend to do?"

"The only thing that can be done. Beric must be questioned. And, if he is found to be a Christian, he shall recant or die."

Marcus cocked a brow. "Sounds simple, but these Christians seem to be very obstinate in this matter of recanting, father."

A glint appeared in Rowland's eye. "Then, if he dies, it will be a proper lesson to Philip. All things considered, it is better to lose the elder slave than the younger. Beric is not worth half of Philip's value."

Marcus considered Rowland's words. Perhaps he was right. At any rate, his father had fresh vigor, a thing he himself was quickly losing. He had battled this obstinacy long enough.

"As you say then, father." He heard his own voice give casual agreement. Strangely, something pricked his heart, confusing him. Why was he compelled to have caution? He cared nothing for Philip. But he followed his instincts, allowing one tinge of mercy to penetrate his callousness.

"But let us wait until the morning to question Beric. It may be that Philip will reconsider and pledge to obey me before then."

The bright morning sunlight streamed through the tall casements looking out over the *Vicus Tuscus* in Marcus's chamber, casting patterned shadows upon the polished floor.

Philip moved casually about the room. Deftly, he straightened his lord's couch and folded his cast-aside toga. Marcus had seemed in a hurry that morning and had donned no more than his daily tunic and belt.

His shoulders twinged uncomfortably as he folded the toga. The work of healing had been slow, and he was constantly plagued by pain and weariness. He had arisen from his sick-bed sooner than he should have, but fear of Marcus's displeasure had driven him to his tasks.

Still, the recollection of the Presence he had felt while being flogged was a great sustainment. Had it been Jesus Himself who had been with him? Philip could not begin to know. But what little he knew was enough.

He had not been alone.

You are with me, Lord. Philip lifted his eyes for one fleeting moment to the ceiling before laying Marcus's toga in its proper place. *You will always be with me.*

The sudden sound of a disturbance caught his attention. He could hear a bustle and murmuring down in the atrium, as if the household slaves were gathering for some unknown event.

Philip stiffened. Marcus would be furious if he had summoned the household slaves and his personal attendant was not among them. As quickly as he could manage, he left the room.

At the foot of the stairs, he stopped. Horror sunk deep into his chest, so strong he felt dizzy. Like he thought, the household slaves were gathered together.

And in their center was Beric.

He was stripped to the waist and tightly bound. There was something in his face Philip could not discern, but he knew it as an expression he had never seen before. Grave, yet peaceful, he looked both a warrior and a child.

Marcus and Rowland stood on either side of him, both grimly resolute. Marcus's dark eyes were roving, searching for someone. Chilled, Philip felt his eyes rest upon him and saw him lift his hand in a fierce beckon.

"Come here, Philip."

Philip stumbled forward, fear pounding at his chest. What was happening? Why was Beric bound? Surely, *surely*, he was not going to be harmed.

Jesus, what is happening here? Help me; help my father! I don't understand.

"It has come to our attention that this surly wretch is a follower of the man called Christus." Rowland's deep voice was dark, his eyes roving over the assembly of slaves in ominous forewarning.

169

"Christianity is a crime worthy of death by edict of our emperor and so shall it be within my household."

He turned with a threatening gesture to Beric. "Slave, I give you one final chance to recant your foolish beliefs. Do so and save yourself from death by flogging."

Philip's heart thudded. He looked wildly at Marcus, unable to believe his ears. *Death by flogging... No, Jesus. No!* Marcus steadfastly refused to look at him, his cold gaze fixed upon Beric.

"Noble lord, there is nothing I would refuse to do for you." Beric spoke steadily. He bore himself erect, his shoulders squared. It was if he was again a chieftain, a warrior who esteemed his beliefs more than life itself. "But this one thing I may not do. I am a follower of Christ, and, as such, I will live and die."

"You are sentenced out of your own mouth." Rowland turned with a wrathful spat to the household guards. "Flog him to death."

No! No!

Numb with shock and horror, Philip flung himself forward, unable to think about what he was doing. He burst through the circle of slaves, throwing his arms around Beric's naked chest. "No!"

"Move that boy." Rowland snapped the order, motioning to the guards. "Be quick about it; I am losing my patience."

Philip tightened his grip on Beric's stalwart frame. The guards surrounded him, attempting to drag him away. He clung tighter, burying his face against his father's chest. "No! You cannot!"

"Philip!" Marcus's angry voice sounded in his ear. "Obey or you will be scourged with him."

Philip felt his grip loosening, weakened by the fierce pull of the guards. Beric leaned over him, his voice low.

"Nothing will separate you from God's love, Philip." His voice broke. "I love you, my son."

Fighting and struggling, Philip felt himself ripped away and flung violently onto his knees. Raising himself, he was in time to see

Beric being forced down on his face. His soul screamed out in helplessness. *God, help him! Help him!*

The sound of the first blow echoed in his ears. Resonating, the sound of his own agonized cry rent the air, hurting his throat. He struggled to his feet. "No! Stop!" He pivoted forward, adrenaline cutting off common sense.

Marcus caught him by the arms, spinning him around. "That's *enough*, Philip." His hiss was fierce. "Be still."

Philip was nearly blinded by a torrent of tears. Agonized, he threw himself on his knees. His heart throbbed. Slowly, surely, his oxygen was being cut off. Flailing, he found Marcus's hands and grasped them in his own.

"My lord, I beg you! Stop them! Marcus, *please.*"

"This is what shall be done to Christians in this household, Philip." Marcus's coldness was terrifying. Except for the night he had been flogged, Philip had never seen him so hardened. "His obstinacy has sentenced him."

The sound of blows melded with the hot blood pounding in Philip's ears. Wildly, he cast his eyes on his prostrate father. Dimly, he saw a rod descend, tearing the back of Beric.

Another agonized scream rose to his lips. He struggled to rise, to throw himself forward. It was then he realized he could not move. He was paralyzed, frozen by horror and disbelief.

"*Marcus!*"

His cry did not flicker a single muscle in Marcus's face. The face of the young man remained coldly resolute, as chiseled as the marble countenance of Mars.

Again, Philip saw the rod ascend, saw the blood that streamed over Beric's scored back and shoulders. Wildly, his eyes roved to Beric's face. *White.* As white as the foaming waves curling over the coastline of the icy North Sea.

He felt his world sinking, whirling into a dark, deep void. *Stay awake. Plead for him. Oh, God, where are You?* Reality began to fade; he was too dizzy to think straight. He fought against the blackness, struggling to keep conscious.

It was a vain attempt.

The sound of blows grew muffled. Blessed, dark quietness enshrouded him, cutting off the sound of his own cries and the horrible agony sickening his heart.

When Philip awoke, he found himself alone in a little chamber adjoining the library. Slowly, he raised himself, swinging his legs over the side of the settee he lay upon.

On the opposite side of the room, a motionless figure lay shrouded in a cloth, resting unceremoniously upon the floor.

Philip's heart lurched. Slowly at first, then breaking into a run, he crossed the room and threw himself at the side of the still figure. His hands shook wildly. *No, Lord. No...* Dashing away the hot tears blinding his vision, he forced himself to draw back the cloth.

Beric's face, even in death, was calm and resolute.

Somewhere deep inside Philip, a sobbing cry welled up within him. It broke forth, its sound the echoing, moaning sob of a broken heart. It was quickly followed by another.

Shaking, rent by sobs, Philip dropped his head onto Beric's chest. His hands stretched across the still body, holding him fast.

"No." The low sound of his sobbed-out denial was a whisper. His voice intensified, nearly inaudible by his weeping. "No. My father. My *father!*"

His fingers groped across the body, seeking Beric's hand. When at last he found it, icy coldness had already stiffened its joints.

The touch was too much for him. Something like a scream rose in his throat, but he choked it back. His entire frame shook uncontrollably, and he felt as if he was being turned inside out.

Half-raising his head, he looked downwards and saw the conjugated blood drenching Beric's body. Welts, bruises, and deep, bloody lines scored his body, marring all but his face. His face alone bore the peacefulness of a Christian martyr–a warrior at rest.

Why? Why? Philip clung to Beric, the tears running down his face in hot rivulets. His eyes closed, his hands gripping his father in angst-ridden torture. *Let me die. Don't leave me here all alone! Please take me, Jesus.*

"The men are here to take the body." Marcus's voice sounded behind him, strangely quiet.

Philip made no movement. Perspiration running through his fingers, he clenched his father's body tighter, his tears running onto the still chest beneath his face. *You shall not separate us. Jesus, where are you? Where are you!*

"Philip."

Philip felt Marcus's hands rest on his shoulders, gripping him by his garments. Rent with sobbing, he shook his head, resisting him. Marcus's very touch sent a shudder through his body. *Let me go. God, get that devil's hands off of me!*

Marcus's pull grew stronger. Philip felt a hand overtop his own, breaking his grip. Weeping, he stumbled to his feet, pulling fiercely away from Marcus. "No! Let me be. My *father!*"

Marcus held him fast, quiet and inexorable. Helpless in the firm grip, Philip could only watch as the male slaves bore his father's body from the room. He stood, shaking with tears, tensing against the clamp-like fingers burrowing into his arms.

With Beric's body gone, Marcus's grip loosened. Philip jerked fiercely away from him, stumbling to his knees besides the settee. Broken, weeping, he cradled his hands over his heart, dropping his head onto his knees.

He sensed it as Marcus left the room, shutting the door upon him.

And he was alone.

The minutes slipped into hours. Philip remained upon his knees, his shoulders shaking, the low sobs breaking from his aching throat.

Slowly, the sun made its descent. Evening fell, casting its gloomy darkness upon the little chamber.

Still, Philip knelt. Even with his eyes closed, he felt the trickling moonlight spill over him. Its cold illumination was shrouded in death, in the terrible pain aching in every core of his body. His tears ceased, too worn out to sob any longer. For one full minute, he listened to the perfect, haunting stillness.

Like death.

He raised his head, lifting his tear-wet face to the ghostly orbs of light streaming in from the casement. Before he could stop himself, he heard his own husky whisper echo back at him.

"Is this the way You treat Your followers? Is this Your reward for my faithfulness?"

The tears welled up in his eyes, spilling down over his white cheeks. His voice broke, ending in sobs that tore his heart. "*Why?* What sin have I committed that You would do this to me? Is it not enough that my entire family is dead, that I am a *slave*? Was it not enough that I was flogged for Your sake?"

His sobs intensified, racking his entire frame. Again, he dropped his head into his shaking hands. "Why?" His cry echoed across the room. "Why? Tell me why!"

Silence permeated the chamber, broken only by the sounds of his violent sobs.

Overwhelmed by his sense of loneliness, Philip lifted his head. His swollen eyes rested slowly on the place he had last seen his father's body. Only a reddish-brown mark remained, sealing the Virginius domus with the blood-sign of a martyr.

Nothing shall separate you from me, Philip.

"Is that my only comfort?" Philip cried out, his voice resonating in the darkness. "Is *that* the only promise You can give me? That I shall have Your love when You have taken everything else from me?"

My grace is sufficient for thee: for my strength is made perfect in weakness.

174

"Is that what You want?" Philip's sobs burst forth afresh. He cradled his hands on his chest, rocking himself. "For me to be weak? To take everything from me just so You can show me Your perfect strength?"

And we know that all things work together for good to them that love God.

"This has no goodness! What purpose can there be in my sorrow?" Philip rose to his feet. He could feel the suffering etched on his broken face. "Where were You when I needed You? *Where?*"

Silence filled his heart. Slowly, agonizingly, he again sank to his knees. A shame so fierce it nearly overpowered his grief rent his soul, tearing at him.

"Forgive me." The words fell in a broken whisper from his lips. "I am weak, Jesus. Be with me."

His sobs again threatened to break forth, but he held them in check. He lifted his streaming eyes to the ceiling. "I cannot bear this burden alone, Jesus. You are all I have. Please don't leave me all alone! Please be with me. I *cannot* bear this on my own strength. I will let Your strength be perfected in me, if only you will help me."

By some inner compulsion he couldn't explain, Philip felt his tightly-clenched hands open. Slowly, he stretched them out before him, raising them in mute worship.

"I let him go, Father. Only be with me!"

In that moment, a surreal peace flooded his heart. It was indescribable, mingling with his pain like a healing salve. He bent his head, his hands outraised. The tears continued to pour down his cheeks, but, slowly, new assurance filled the aching void in his soul.

Nay, in all these things, you are more than a conqueror through him that loved you. And nothing shall separate you from my love.

Chapter Sixteen

Gloomy darkness shrouded every corner of Marcus's chamber. Only the moonlight cast its faint beams into the room, glinting off of the gilt wine glass lying unceremoniously upon his couch.

The sight was like the numbing of relief of intoxicating drinks itself, alluring him to their fleeting forgetfulness.

Marcus strode quickly across the room. Shaking, he snatched up the cup and poured strong wine into its deep basin, spilling some of the ruby liquid over the side of the pitcher. Great gods, he had to forget this day. Inhaling heavily, he lifted the mug with both hands to his lips. Feeling the fate of a man parched in the wild deserts, he fervently swallowed the contents, draining the cup to its last drop.

His hands trembled. With a resounding crash, the glass fell from his hands, striking the hard floor and dashing into a thousand glistening pieces.

The echoing sound startled him. Abruptly, he turned and his elbow brushed the side of the pitcher. It too toppled, sending scarlet liquid pouring down over the table and onto the ornate floor.

Marcus bent to retrieve it. Instant nausea washed over him, tangibly stealing the color from his cheeks. Slowly, he straightened himself, unwilling to touch the wine. Its scarlet color was the hue of death itself.

The color of Beric's innocent blood.

Marcus shuddered. Barely pausing to undress, he threw himself on his couch, pulling a light covering over him.

For hours, he tossed. Sleep deserted his eyelids. Every sound was torture, every whisper of the breeze stealing through his casements was as a thousand spirits. Superstitious fear haunted him, and every passing second deepened his dread of seeing the ghost of Beric.

The wine intensified the excitement of his fevered brain, failing to bring the anesthetized relief he longed for. Great gods, but why this torture? Why could he not sleep?

With agonized slowness, his eyelids grew heavy. Drowsiness fell over him, sending him into the throngs of light slumber.

Its unconsciousness was more exhausting than being awake.

In his dreams, the white, agonized face of Philip haunted him. Marcus heard his cries, heard his frantic pleas for Beric's deliverance. And, somehow, he saw himself.

Cold. Hard. And pitiless.

Stop them! Marcus. Marcus!

He felt a grasping hand on his own, a desperate voice in his ear. And the final words of a doomed father, his love surpassing any thought of his own sufferings.

Again, the silhouette of Philip rose before his eyes. He tried to push him away, to silence the racking sobs reverberating in his ears.

My father! Marcus. Marcus!

Chilled by the sound of his own name, Marcus sat upright, panting. For several minutes, he peered into the darkness, perspiration standing out in little rivulets on his forehead.

It had only been a dream.

Or had it?

Marcus lay down, pulling his coverlet over his shaking body. It had not been a dream. It was real, relived in his fevered mind. Everything he had seen he had done. And he would never be able to forget, to wipe the agony he had witnessed from his memory.

Sleep again visited his eyes, but it was a restless slumber. He tossed on his couch until the faint grey light of the dawn stole into his chamber. Somehow, its presence did not bring the welcome relief he longed for.

He was groggy as he rose from his couch. He stumbled as he crossed the room, intent upon procuring fresh clothing. Normally, Philip would perform this service, but the boy had not appeared to fulfill his duties.

177

It was just as well. He had no desire to lay eyes upon him, upon the countenance that was sure to haunt him with reproach.

Marcus dressed and wearily fastened his wristbands. He glanced across the room. The wine he had spilt the night before still lay in a little pool beside his couch. Somehow, the light of day only intensified its color, more reminiscent of blood than before.

He clapped his hands. He would have a slave clean up the mess, removing its torturous parallels. Perhaps he could then forget. *Pluto guide me! Take the wretched soul of that slave and let me forget.*

The sound of footsteps caused him to turn. To his shock, Philip stood directly behind him. Marcus stood motionless. Much against his will, his eyes refused to budge, taking in every feature of Philip's face.

The boy was as pale as if he had been scourged himself. The blue eyes that had won him so much admiration were swollen with weeping, the exhaustion of his grief evident in every feature of his appearance.

Marcus felt a wave of anger. Here was the last person he wanted to see. But of course Philip would wish to remind him, to haunt him with the atrocities of what he had done.

"Clean up that wine." The command fell from his lips far more harshly than he meant it to. He immediately felt the injustice of his callousness. Philip's sorrow was natural. And he had certainly committed no offense by answering his master's call.

Silently, Philip obeyed. He knelt beside the wine, mopping up its scarlet pool. Without being told, he swept up the broken glass and restored the pitcher to its proper place. Finished, he rose to his feet and stood in silent subservience.

Marcus gazed piercingly at him. Now was the time to gain Philip's pledge of obedience, to finish the task of conquering his spirited stubbornness. And, upon receiving his oath, he would allow himself to lay aside his superiority. Perhaps lavishing comfort and indulgences upon Philip would lift the terrible burden bordering on his heart and mind.

"Philip."

With submission he couldn't help but marvel at, his slave lifted his eyes and looked at him. Marcus held him with his gaze, allowing his words to make his impression.

"Philip, if you doubted my resolution in this matter before, you are assured of it now. I am certain you would not like to meet the same fate as your father."

The boy's chin trembled. His blue eyes filled with tears and he averted his gaze, allowing the quiet drops to splash onto the marble floor.

Marcus continued, maintaining a quiet voice. Certainly, Philip was at a point where he was more certain to be conquered through gentleness than severity. "Give me your pledge that you will leave off the practice of Christianity. I shall then say no more."

Philip looked up, his eyes watery. "I cannot do that, Marcus," he said, his voice a broken whisper.

A sudden wave of anger penetrated Marcus's heart. He had been prepared to deal kindly with his foolish slave. Was the stupid, *stupid* boy still intent upon defying him? "And why not?"

"I am a Christian. Nothing shall separate me from my Jesus."

"So you say." Marcus's pent-up frustration burst forth, furious. "You continually speak of this perpetual union with your precious *Savior*. Where has He been, pray?"

He stepped forward, purposefully intimidating Philip with his close presence. His anger continued to boil over. "Where was your *Jesus* when I flogged you? Did He save you, end the pain you felt? Where was He when your father died? *Where!*"

"He has been with me." Philip's voice, though low, was steadfast. "He has never left me."

"A merciful God He is then!" Marcus spat the words, contempt livid on his face. "What loving Savior would watch his servant suffer and do *nothing*? Why didn't he deliver you?"

"He has." The tears rolled down Philip's face unashamed. "He delivered me from my sin, from the hate that once controlled me.

He has delivered me from fear. And, those things, Marcus, are the greatest deliverance of all."

Marcus stood motionless. His tongue seemed to cleave to the roof of his mouth. He could not speak, nor did he know what he would say if he could.

The greatest deliverance of them all.

It was a deliverance he wanted more than he would confess even to himself.

Philip continued to stand before him, his shoulders shaking with his unuttered sobs. His head bowed on his chest, the tears spilling down his white cheeks.

Marcus's heart twisted. *Wretched cur!* Why did Philip weep so unashamed? Why was every tear a torture to his heart, each falling drop a blow to his senses? And—oh, by the gods! Philip was a slave. Why did he care what he had done to him?

"Cease your tears, wretch." Marcus snapped the words, finding relief for his overwrought feelings in his lashed-out anger. "You are now fourteen years—a man among my people and your own."

Philip's voice shook. "The greatest Man, the Savior I love, wept for his friends. I am no greater than He."

Marcus clenched his fists until the fingers bit into the palm. Constant talk of this Jesus made him want to throttle Philip and have the whole wretched ordeal over with. The fierceness of his own shout echoed through the room, startling even himself. "Will you *never* give up this folly?"

Rather than terrify, it seemed to arouse new spirit in Philip. He raised his head, his eyes glistening with rekindled resolve.

"Never, Marcus."

Marcus's face burned. He scarcely knew himself for anger. How dare this lowly slave defy him, throwing the kindness he would have offered back in his face?

His hand itched to slap him. He began to raise it, then, abruptly, stopped short. Fiercely, he struggled against the truth. It was to no avail. He could not hurt Philip. That terrible Presence was at his side, holding back his hand.

Chilling fear washed over his heart, trickling down his back. He could not move. Philip's eyes remained locked in his own, waiting, cringing back from the blow he could not deliver.

With a rustling jolt, Marcus's arm came down to his side. He felt the color wane from his face. His heart pounded wildly, captured by mingled anger and fear. "Get out of my sight!"

Clear bewilderment lighted on Philip's face. He half-bent and backed away, evidently more than a little desirous to leave.

Marcus felt his frustration boiling up within him. It irked him to see his slave leave unscathed by the punishment he deserved. He suddenly found his voice. "Stay!" Then, as Philip turned, "I suppose you are ready to be sent to the arena?"

A visible shudder passed over Philip's frame. "I do not want to go there." His voice was low. "But it may be the will of my Lord that I meet Him sooner than I expect. And for that, I could not be sorry."

He again turned away.

Marcus stood still for a long moment, fairly boiling with frustration. Slowly, he began to pace. What was to be done? Philip was determined to defy him.

Perhaps the most frustrating factor was that he could do nothing. In his heart of hearts, he feared the Presence that had twice stayed his merciless hand. Its power was undeniable.

But where did it come from?

Philip had had no time to make some mystical petition this time. What if—oh, great gods! What if his God was real?

It is impossible. Marcus struggled against the sentiment that threatened to grow into a conviction. *This Christus was crucified. And the eagles in their realms forbid that the God of a slave should have more power the gods of mighty Rome!*

Marcus pressed a hand to his aching brow. He was tired of this whole miserable drama. Wearily, he leaned against a pillar, closing his eyes.

It was then he heard the low murmur of a voice, issuing from Philip's chamber. Marcus knit his brows. The foolish idiot was praying. Well, he would put a swift end to that!

Swiftly, he strode to the door separating his chamber from Philip's. The door stood half-ajar, and he lifted his hand to strike it fully open. By a sudden compulsion, his hand remained aloft, curiosity curtailing his anger.

How exactly did these Christians pray?

Looking through the crack, he saw Philip, kneeling beside his couch. His hands covered his face, and Marcus heard the low, sobbed-out petitions falling in broken intervals from his lips.

"Help me forgive him, Jesus. Help me forget what he has done to me and-and the one I loved best."

Marcus's hand dropped slowly to his side. Surely, Philip did not speak of forgiving *him*. No slave in his right mind would petition his god for the ability to forgive the master who had so mercilessly hurt him.

Philip's sobs intensified. "I cannot bear this, Father. You promised to uphold me; I beg You not to forsake Your promise. Give me strength to endure this trial. And, if-if I am to be sent to arena, help me to remember Your love even there."

The slow conviction sank into Marcus's heart. What Philip believed, whether true or not, meant more to him than life itself. Clearly, his threat of the arena had done little good.

He half-turned away, unwilling to hear more. But, against his will, Philip's final petition halted him.

"Jesus, I cannot undo the things Marcus has done to me. I am suffering and would gladly stop this pain if I could. But, please," and his voice faltered, "use these things for Your better glory. Use them to bring Marcus to You."

The blood drained from Marcus's face. His throat tightened, racked by a sudden burning ache. He could not have understood Philip correctly. Did he really petition his God to make him a Christian?

I must put an end to this! The thought spun in Marcus's mind. His slave dared to pray that he, a son of mighty Rome, would become a Christian. The petition was a dishonor in itself–to think that he could unite with a religion so despised by his fatherland, so demeaning in its acceptance of both slave and free men.

But, he could not move. He felt strangely touched. In all of his eighteen years, he had never before heard someone pray so earnestly for him, let alone a slave.

Marcus turned slowly away. Something tingled at the back of his eyes, sending a fine mist streaming over their dark pupils. And, for the life of him, he could not curtail the foreign moisture.

He did not know if he would if he was able.

Philip never knew how he survived the three endless weeks after Beric's death. Time flitted away on dark, dreary wings, blurring his days into one long, torturous existence.

His brethren were his greatest solace. Daniel in particular took him to his arms and comforted him, weeping with him. The loss of Beric was a sore blow to all those who had known him, and Philip found himself surrounded by heartfelt sympathy.

And, Providentially, it was a comfort he was often afforded. Three times a week, he slipped from the Virginius Mansion to meet with his fellow believers.

He was never stopped.

Strangely, Marcus seemed to turn a blind eye to his constant disobedience. Philip was certain he knew of his frequent night escapades, but Marcus never said a word to him. He seemed indifferent or–stranger still–afraid.

Philip often wondered what it was that had softened Marcus's heart towards him. He could not begin to understand it.

And for good reason.

The young man was excessively callous during the weeks following Beric's death. He drank himself into a stupor nearly every evening–stupors that often awoke into fits of violent rage. He was often away from the domus, spending many hours in the company of other young noblemen.

Gossip concerning the things he did while away was frequently circulated among the household slaves. Philip made every endeavor not to listen. But it was impossible to avoid the truth about the lasciviousness that was apparently mastering Marcus.

To most, it was thought that Marcus was simply sowing a few wild oats before he settled down to begin his career.

Philip, however, sensed differently. Was it possible that a battle was raging, a battle of the Holy Spirit against the forces of evil? Was Marcus attempting to flee the pangs of his own conscience, knowing the truth but unwilling to accept it?

Partly to fuel his own desire for complete forgiveness, partly because he truly cared, Philip prayed fervently for him. Seeds did not give life without death, he knew. It was time for the death of Beric to awaken into the full, life-changing transformation of Marcus.

One evening, Philip prepared as usual to go out. Absently, he fastened his cloak around his shoulders. It was a relief to him to do so. After all the time that had passed, the metal collar around his neck still brought a wave of color to his cheeks.

"Are you going out?"

Philip started. He had thought Marcus on his couch, sleeping off his wine. A tremor passed through his body, a single thought burning itself into his brain.

He had made a full recovery. He was strong. Strong enough to be flogged.

Outwardly, he maintained a calm demeanor, breathing a silent prayer. *You are in His hands.* "Yes, my lord."

"Where you are going?"

Philip flinched a little. "To the Christian meetings."

Marcus stood motionless. He beheld him with an expression Philip could not understand, new in its mildness.

The silence grew long.

Philip felt a new fear. What terrible punishment was Marcus conjuring up for him? Was he about to make good on his threat of the arena?

When Marcus broke the silence, his voice was very quiet. "Would you mind if I accompanied you, Philip?"

Shock spun through Philip's mind, nearly sending him off his feet. Was it possible? After all his prayers, was Marcus truly considering Christianity?

Almost instantly, his joy melded into dread. Marcus was callous, merciless to the core. His intentions might harbor some sinister plot, planning the demise of the best blood Rome had to offer.

"Why do you wish to go?" The curtness of Philip's query startled even himself. *Dear God, don't let him be angry with me.*

Marcus seemed puzzled for a moment. Slowly, the light of understanding broke over his face. "I mean them no harm, Philip."

"You must promise me that." Philip quaked at his own boldness, but he was resolute. No harm must come to his brethren because of his own foolish trust. "I must have your sworn oath, Marcus."

"Do you dare tell your master what he must do?" The wrath in Marcus's voice was unmistakable. The vexed color rose high in his forehead. "I can make you take me there, Philip."

Philip said nothing. He stood motionless, half-averting his eyes. At last, as the silence again grew long, he looked up.

Marcus met his gaze. As if tired by the whole affair, he made an impatient gesture. "Very well, you insolent cub. I swear upon my honor I mean no harm to your friends. No one shall be arrested or hurt by my accompanying you." Then, with doubled impatience, "There, does that satisfy you?"

Philip felt a twinge, sorry that his necessary disrespect had displeased Marcus. "Yes, my lord." He spoke softly, hoping his humility would appease Marcus. "I beg your pardon; I did not mean to anger you."

Marcus looked at him with narrowed, displeased eyes. "Let us be off."

Swallowing hard, Philip led the way, opening the door for Marcus. For a brief instant, he closed his eyes.

Do not let him be deceiving me, Father. Protect my brethren. If Marcus means us harm, let it come on me, not them.

"Hurry up!" Behind him, Marcus gave him a jarring shove. "Pick up your feet, cur."

Philip quickened his pace, controlling the momentary irritation that swelled in his chest. Swiftly, he ran down the steps and led the way down the *Vicus Tuscus.*

The sky was a mixture of deep grey and cobalt color, the horizon rent by the few streaks of light streaming from the fast-fading sun.

Pedestrians hurried through the street, intent upon reaching their homes before the danger of darkness fell upon them. Carriages of goods rattled past them, pushed by weary produce peddlers. Occasionally, a chariot rolled down the street, its owner flicking the team with the end of the whip held carelessly in his tanned hand.

Skillfully, Philip led the way through the streets, always conscious of the strong presence behind him. He forced himself not to consider what Marcus might do if it was in his heart to be cruel. *Oh, Lord God, please don't let this be foolishness on my part. Please, Jesus.* Instant consolation quieted him. Somehow, he knew he was doing right.

At last, he stopped before a small house on the *Vicus Jugarius.* The street was eerie in its darkness and the house itself looked deserted. He raised his hand to rap upon the door, but Marcus's low voice halted him.

"Are you certain this is the right house? By the gods, this is a place for spirits and vagrants."

"Fear not, Marcus; I have been here many times." Philip cringed as he saw Marcus's eyes narrow. As he rapped on the door, he chided himself for his own frankness.

Just give him every excuse to beat you when he gets you home, will you?

The door swung open, allowing room enough for Philip to slip through. Quickly, he stepped inside, motioning for Marcus to follow. "Peace be with you," he whispered before leading the way to the inner chamber where he knew the others were assembled.

The soft light of oil lamps illuminated the room. The low hush of voices quieted as Philip stepped inside. Glancing from his peripheral vision, he saw Marcus linger in the shadows.

"Peace be with you, friends."

"And peace be with you, my young brother." Simeon rose to his feet. "I greet you in the name of our Lord Jesus Christ."

Nervous apprehension pounded at Philip's heart. Half-gesturing, he motioned Marcus forward into the light.

An immediate gasp fell over the whole of the company. Marcus's toga and signs of rank clearly introduced himself. Philip knew beyond a shadow of a doubt he had no need of presenting Marcus as his master.

They knew.

Simeon, the first to recover himself, rested eagle-like eyes on Philip's countenance. "What is this, Philip? Is this young man the one we think?"

Philip's heart sank at Simeon's stern tone. With difficulty, he controlled his voice to speak quietly. "My brethren, I present my master, the noble Marcus Virginius."

Again, several indistinct exclamations circulated, mingled with murmurs that bespoke nothing short of horror. Several members of the brethren drew back from him, exchanging knowing glances of distrust and apprehension.

Philip looked at Marcus, seeing him stiffen. Yet, behind his proud Roman aloofness, he was quiet, as if he did not blame their feelings.

Simeon's countenance darkened, his stern tones increasing in severity. "You have done very foolishly, Philip. Is this not the man who scourged you for your faith, who turned a blind eye to your father's suffering? How could you bring such peril upon us?"

Philip felt mingled desperation and uncertainty. He was certain he had done right. A foreign timidity descended upon him, caught between Simeon's stern rebuke and Marcus's masterful eye. He attempted a faltering explanation.

"He swore on his honor to bring no harm upon us, Simeon. And, whatever ill my lord has done me, I believe him too noble to break his word. I—"

"He who would persecute one believer would persecute them all." Simeon cut him off, his sharp Jewish countenance fervent with zealous rebuke. "You have done foolishly."

"Do not chide him, my brother." Daniel arose. Philip felt his quiet, kindly eyes rest upon him, easing his distress. "You have forgotten our brother Paul and the persecution he wrought among the believers before coming to the gospel. Philip has brought his lord; therefore, let him be made welcome."

Simeon was silent. Daniel turned to Marcus, welcome clearly written on his features.

"I give you welcome, Marcus Virginius."

"Thank you." Marcus spoke quietly, and Philip was certain he recognized Daniel. For a fleeting instant, Philip wondered what Marcus's thoughts were towards the man who had aided his runaway slave.

Daniel was ready to commence the meeting, however, giving Philip no further time to wonder. Wordlessly, he motioned a low stool to Marcus, then, knelt on the floor beside him.

The meeting proceeded as usual, but it was difficult for Philip to keep his mind on the service. His thoughts remained active, fixed almost entirely on the young man beside him.

What did Marcus think of all of this? Did he find their simple worship and prayers strange? Was he touched? Or–and Philip shuddered inwardly–did what he see make him more determined to break his slave's will?

When the simple message and reading of Paul's epistle was complete, Daniel asked for prayer requests. Moriah was the first to speak.

"I ask prayer for a woman I have been witnessing Christ to. She seems very close to the truth, and I trust she will come to accept it very soon."

Glancing sidelong, Philip saw Marcus lift his head a little more erect, his attention caught by the sweet, clear tones. His dark eyes rested on Moriah, drifting over her delicate features and down to the folded hands in her lap.

Moriah seemed aware of Marcus's interest. She shifted uncomfortably, drawing her veil a little more over herself.

Philip felt a twinge of indignation. What right did Marcus have to look at her with such obvious attraction? To be sure, Moriah was as pretty as one could desire. Her very presence perfumed the air about her with grace and purity. But, she was a Christian maiden. And nothing could contrast her purity more than the lascivious lifestyle he was fully aware his master lived.

Philip endeavored to quiet his feelings. Perhaps it was only the novelty of a woman speaking before an assemblage comprised of both men and women that had excited Marcus's curiosity. Or perhaps he was intrigued by so beautiful a maiden giving herself over to the chastity of Christianity.

Don't judge him for motives you cannot know.

With that thought, Philip set his mind towards concentrating on the meeting. A few more prayer requests were spoken, then, Daniel prayed over the assemblage. The time and place for the next meeting was set, and then the service was concluded.

Philip looked at Marcus. He did not signify any immediate desire to depart, and, with a low "Excuse me", Philip hurriedly crossed the room.

Daniel was waiting for him. With his usual pleasant smile, he laid his hand on Philip's shoulder. "How does it go with you, Philip?"

"I am well, Daniel." Philip cast a glance across the room. Marcus sat where he had left him, his eyes fixed upon two or three of the brethren as they stood talking. "I only wish I knew what the future will bring."

"It is best not to know." Daniel caught the direction of his look. His voice grew low. "Is your master close to the truth?"

"I do not know." Philip drew a deep breath. "I pray constantly for him, but he seems very hardened to all things referring to the gospel."

"Why did he come tonight?"

"I do not know that either. Truth be told, I am afraid, Daniel. I do not trust his motives. He swore to bring no harm upon any of you, but-but that does not exclude me from punishment if he has a mind to hurt me."

Daniel was silent a moment. "He is a very handsome, pleasant-looking young man. One would not think from looking at him that he is the hardened individual we know him to be."

"Truth." Philip again looked across the room. Most of the believers had departed, and Marcus met his eye with clear desire to be gone. "I cannot linger here, Daniel. Please, pray for me."

"I will, Philip." Daniel paused. "And for Marcus."

"Yes." Philip felt a wave of shame. Why had he not requested prayer for Marcus? His soul was safe. It was Marcus who, in the end, would suffer if he did not accept the truth. "Goodnight, Daniel."

Quickly pressing Daniel's hands to his forehead, Philip turned and returned swiftly to Marcus's side. "You are ready to depart, my lord?"

"Yes." Marcus's tone was curt, and Philip's heart sank. With the growing fear he would be punished upon their return, he led the way to the door.

In the entry, Moriah stood awaiting Daniel. Philip offered her a silent salute as he passed. Marcus, however, slowed in his walk, resting his dark eyes on her face.

"Good evening, maiden."

Moriah met his intent gaze. A flicker of feminine spirit flitted across her countenance, and Philip was surprised by the firm boldness of her tone.

"Good evening, my lord."

Amusement played about the corners of Marcus's mouth. Clearly, he was not accustomed to having a woman answer him so curtly. But, there was little surprise in that. Philip had seen him melt an entire roomful of Roman noblewomen with a single turn of his flashing smile.

Half-bowing, Marcus continued on. Moriah did not give him a second glance, but Philip saw the bright color burning in her cheeks as he shut the door.

Chapter Seventeen

The walk home was a silent one.

Marcus had noted their course and led the return trek at a swift pace. Philip followed close behind him, dread growing within his heart. He could not begin to discern Marcus's thoughts. Was he angry? Or had his first experience of a Christian meeting touched his heart?

At last, they mounted the steps of the Virginius domus and entered the quiet *vestibule*.

Philip felt a familiar pang as he stood in the atrium. How many times he and Beric had stood there, speaking of the meeting they had just attended and the truths they had learned. Everything ached within him, longing for Beric. *Help me forgive, Lord. Help me see Marcus the way You do.*

"Come with me to my chamber." Marcus's voice was curt, and he did not wait for Philip's reply.

Still, Philip felt a tinge of relief. Perhaps he was not going to be punished after all. Marcus would never think of flogging him in his personal chambers.

In his room, Marcus threw himself down on his couch. Philip drew near and attempted to take his toga. Marcus, however, gave him an impatient push.

"Sit down."

Slowly, Philip obeyed, sitting on a low stool at Marcus's feet. It was then he noticed how pale Marcus was. The young man looked intently at him, his eyes searching.

"I have gone to your meetings and still I do not understand what it is you Christians believe. I know you worship some Jewish carpenter hailed as Christ, but that is all."

Philip considered his words carefully, attempting to discern Marcus's desire correctly. "Do you wish to know more, my lord?"

"Why do you think I seated you here?" Marcus's voice bordered on impatience. "Tell me everything."

Philip's eyes gazed searchingly into Marcus's. Was it possible this was the moment he had prayed for? *Help him understand, Lord. Somehow, touch his heart.*

As clearly as he could, Philip told the story of the Christian faith. He told how Jesus was the Son of God; born of a virgin; of his perfect life and ministry; of the cruel death he suffered on a Roman cross. And, in conclusion, he spoke of the Father's will to save sinners by slaying His only Son; of how whosoever who desired could accept the free gift of everlasting life; and of the eternal home Jesus was preparing for those who believed in Him.

Marcus listened quietly as he spoke, making no interruption. No trace of emotion or animation crossed his expressionless face during the narrative. His interest seemed the aspiration of one merely concerned with personal knowledge, not the workings of the Holy Spirit.

When he had finished, Philip waited in silence for Marcus to speak. His heart swelled in silent prayer for him, only too aware of the doubts and fears that plagued the heart of an unbeliever when faced with the truth.

Marcus's voice was cold when he spoke. "This story is altogether the most fanciful one I have ever heard. The mere notion of God sending His only Son to die for mortal man is ridiculous in itself. And I can safely assure you no crucified carpenter rose from the dead after three days in a stinking sepulcher."

Philip said nothing. How was he to answer? Such things were unheard of in the world. No deity of his knowledge had ever been said to become a man, let alone die for mortal flesh.

Yet it is true, Father. I thank You it is true.

Marcus motioned impatiently to his goblet. Philip slowly filled it with the sparkling, intoxicating wine. His heart ached as he watched Marcus take it in his hands, sipping slowly of the contents. Would he never realize that numbing his mind was not the answer to his struggles? That a drunken stupor could not rid him of heartache?

Marcus finally set the goblet aside. He stood up, unwrapping the folds of his linen toga. It was then Philip saw his hands trembled strangely.

"You cannot expect me to believe such an idiotic tale. There is little wonder ignorant slaves like you flock to accept Christianity. Perhaps you need the crutch of *love* and *sacrifice*, but I do not."

The haughty mockery in Marcus's voice was clearly bordered by something else. Philip looked intently at him. Could it be fear?

Marcus was evidently frustrated by his silence. Forcefully, he thrust his toga into Philip's hands, the color tinting his tanned cheeks. "By the gods! I tell you I do not believe this despicable story. And how dare you–a lowly, foolish slave–think I need this Jesus? I am my own master!"

Philip remained silent. Marcus was beside himself, governed by a force beside his anger. His hands shook and his wrathful color quickly gave place to an unfamiliar, taut whiteness.

The slow truth washed over Philip. Marcus was afraid, just as he had suspected. But afraid of what? Was it possible the strange dark force that had tried to prevent him from accepting Christ was also haunting Marcus?

Save him, Lord. Deliver him from his fears and bring him to You.

Marcus drew nearer. His stance was stiff and apprehensive, like a warrior preparing to defend himself from a sudden blow. His dark eyes flashed, his bronzed chin quivering.

"Don't flatter yourself by your silence, Philip! I can see your thoughts. You can hide nothing from me. You do think I need this Jesus, don't you? *Don't you?*"

Philip raised his eyes, his throat aching. Marcus's callous strength had often been to his own suffering, but, somehow, it hurt him far worse to see him in his weakness. He swallowed hard, knowing he must speak the truth.

"Yes, master."

Marcus leaned close to him, and Philip felt his hot, labored breathing upon his neck. "Well, I don't. I need nothing, let alone the religion of a *slave*! I–"

Marcus cut himself short. He turned abruptly away, but it was too late.

Philip's mind whirled. Had he truly seen those dark, flashing eyes glisten, melting into a soft mist? It was not possible.

Marcus stood with his back turned to Philip for many long moments.

Philip stood motionless, uncertain of what to do. Should he go to Marcus? But, if he did, what was he to do? He did not dare touch him. And he certainly could not speak. In this state of mind, who knew what Marcus would do to him?

He was spared from making a decision. Just when he was about to speak, Marcus broke the silence, his voice low.

"Go to your own chamber."

Slowly, with an aching heart and bewildered mind, Philip obeyed.

Philip slept little that night. In the next chamber, he could hear Marcus tossing upon his couch and knew that he also was awake.

Be with him, Father.

Philip felt an immediate twinge. Marcus's soul wrestled between heaven and hell, and he lay comfortably on his couch. It didn't seem right.

Before he fairly knew what was occurring, Philip felt an overpowering command to pray. Urgency overswept him, pounding in his heart. With lightning speed, he thrust aside his coverings.

Another moment found him on his knees. But it was not enough.

Philip felt a strong sensation, pulling him downwards. With arms stretched outwards, he prostrated himself on his face, extending himself before the King of creation. A fervor of petition flooded his heart, issuing into a ceaseless intercession he had never before experienced.

And, in the hours that passed, he knew it was only the boundless grace of his Savior that gave him the ability to pray with such passion for the young man who had killed his father.

The faint light of the dawn found Philip still stretched out upon the floor, his lips moving in silent supplication. It was not until the full beams of golden sunlight flooded the room that he rose to his feet, revealing tell-tale moisture on the marble floor.

But the battle was not won.

Philip felt the oppression in the very atmosphere of Marcus's chamber. The Spirit within him sensed the forces of evil, waging war over his master's soul.

Marcus was very pale and weary in appearance. While Philip felt only renewal by his long night's vigil, it was clear the struggle Marcus was enduring had entirely exhausted his strength.

And his good-temper.

Philip struggled hard to keep his self-control all during the difficult task of aiding Marcus to dress. He had never before suffered as many harsh words and heavy slaps as he did that morning. Marcus's spirits were sorely strained, and his only relief seemed to be in battering his slave about.

It was a relief to Philip when he left the room. He felt weary, his spirits decidedly more dejected than when he had risen from prayer. Aching, he moved listlessly around the room, seeking forgetfulness in work.

With his labors done, Philip waited for Marcus to summon him. The time for his daily bath was close at hand.

Marcus did not call.

The hours slipped away, and Philip neither heard nor saw anything of his master. When questioning the other slaves, it was said he had gone out; though, to where, no one seemed to know.

Concern bordered on Philip's heart. Where had Marcus gone? And why had he not called his slave to accompany him, as he always did? Even when in his deepest disgrace, he had always been required to serve Marcus. It did not seem possible that his master had left him behind as a punishment of sorts, although he admitted the prospect was more of a reward than anything else.

Afternoon slipped into the dusky shadows of evening.

At last Philip went out onto the balcony adjoining Marcus's chamber, gazing down the busy *Vicus Tuscus*. Pedestrians, chariots, and peddlers ambled past, but he could see no sign of Marcus. It was not until the last golden streams of light disappeared from the sky that Philip went in.

Absently, he lit the oil lamps, watching their soft beams cast warmth over the room. Humidity hovered in the air, creating an atmosphere of drowsy serenity.

Philip felt the overpowering desire for sleep stealing over him, but he staunchly refused to lie down. He must await Marcus's return. Resolutely, he attempted to silence the mystifying fear suspended over his heart.

Where was Marcus? Surely, he was safe. But, then… Philip felt a sudden pang. Suicide was widely accepted in Rome for those left with no hope.

Oh, God, don't let him have taken the coward's way out. Please—

The door swung wide. Marcus stepped into the room, his steps weary.

Philip started to his feet, nearly overcome with relief. "My lord! I—"

He stopped short. There was something different about Marcus, something new in his countenance. He was very weary and pale, as when he had left, but a new serenity seemed to hover over his countenance.

197

"I have not eaten at all today." Marcus came forward and seated himself wearily on his couch. "Hand me that fruit."

Philip obeyed, confusion filling his mind. Why did he sense something different about Marcus? Certainly, his appearance had not changed and his mannerism was very much like it always had been.

Marcus glanced up at him as he helped himself from the bowl of fruit Philip held before him. A flicker of something Philip could not understand crossed his face, and he averted his eyes.

With Marcus settled comfortably with fruit in his hands and a goblet of *mulsum* beside him, Philip knelt beside him. Draping a towel over his shoulder, he began to remove Marcus's dusty sandals.

Unexpectedly, Marcus lifted a remonstrating hand. The sudden color washed over his face, tightening his features. "No-no. Do not wash my feet, Philip."

Philip rose, confused. What ailed Marcus? He always washed his feet after his return. "My lord–" He paused, respectful hesitance checking him. "I beg your pardon, but are you quite well?"

Marcus looked up at him. His manly face contracted despite his apparent efforts for composure. His chin quivered, and Philip saw his tanned throat swell and tighten. Great emotion settled over him, flaunting all resistance.

"Philip..."

Marcus paused. He seemed unable to go on, again overcome by that mysterious emotion.

Philip's heart swelled. His proud, strong master had always been the exemplar of Roman self-control when it concerned emotion. Something extraordinary must have occurred for him to even momentarily humble himself before his disdained slave.

"Yes, my lord?"

"You were right." Marcus's tones were low and husky. He sat collecting his composure a moment, and his voice regained some of its usual firm timbres. "I went to the home of Daniel today."

Philip's eyes roved Marcus's countenance with fervent searching. "Yes?"

"And I spoke with him for hours. I asked him every question that ever entered my heart, and he explained it all. He told me what it is to be a Christian, to serve Jesus as His child."

Marcus paused. Again, his throat constricted. Abruptly, he arose and went to the casement, standing with his back to Philip for many moments.

Philip stood motionless. His heart thumped wildly, beating against his chest. What was Marcus trying to say?

"I have been tormented by many fears of late." Marcus turned, looking Philip steadily in the eye. "I know you have seen it." He paused. "But I think you shall see them no more."

Philip's mind whirled. Jesus alone was the conqueror of fear, the Giver of the perfect love which casts away dread and doubt. Without Him, there was no peace. "You don't mean—"

"Yes." Marcus drew himself erect, his shoulders squared. New resolve washed over him, highlighting his working features. "Come what may, be it life or death, I am with you."

"You are in earnest?" Philip took a step forward. His knees trembled, caught between disbelief and joy. "You do not mock me?"

"Yes. I have sworn it on my honor as a Roman. I am resolved that Christ alone is my hope, the strength of my life." Marcus's voice shook as he spoke. Unexpectedly, his hand clutched the folds of his toga about his heart. "Philip, I felt Him. I felt His call. I have heard it for weeks now, but could not bring myself to accept Him. I think you knew it."

"I was praying for you." Philip's voice was very low. The joyful reality seeped into every core of his being. Marcus knew! He knew the truth, believed in the existence of the Savior who loved him.

Thank you, Lord. Thank you!

His heart had been settling into a natural cadence, but it suddenly swelled and pounded against his chest. He felt tears washing over his eyes, blurring his vision.

Marcus believed!

Recollection of the fervent prayers he had made on Marcus's behalf flitted through his mind. What if he had not obeyed the heavenly injunctions to pray, to beg God for Marcus's soul?

He saw himself, his hands outstretched before his Savior. The doubts, fears, anger, and pain he had suffered rushed into his mind, overcoming him. He had not truly believed. But God had been faithful. He had turned Philip's weakness into strength, holding fast to His promises.

You were faithful!

Philip thrust himself forward. At that moment, Marcus was not his master, but a brother. All of the things he had done, all that he might do was suddenly lost in a blur of joyful exuberance and blinding tears.

And he embraced Marcus.

In that moment, Philip knew he had fully forgiven Marcus. He had not been sure before. Now, however, peace settled over him, healing the aching void in his heart. The past was gone, veiling the suffering he had endured.

Marcus embraced him back.

Philip's heart swelled. The hands that had held the *flagellum*, that had brandished the rod over him, now enfolded him. Nothing stood between them, not Marcus's haughty spirit or his own bitterness.

Only God could have wrought such a miracle.

Great are you, Lord! Great are Your mercies!

Philip felt a warm drop of liquid on his hand. It was not his own. Looking up, he saw Marcus's misty eyes resting on his scarred arms.

The lash-mark.

With every passing day, it reminded Philip of Marcus's fierce strength, of the mastery he had over him. The memory of that terrible day continually wrought fear in his heart, subjecting him to his lord's will. And the scar was but one of dozens. Philip knew the marks on his back and shoulders would last a lifetime.

"Christ forgive me, Philip." Marcus's voice shook. "I know He has the grace to pardon me, but I cannot expect you to. The wrongs I have done you—"

"Say no more, Marcus." Philip fought back the rising mist in his eyes. "The scroll of your past is sealed. You are a new creature in Christ."

"I flogged you. It was at *my* hands; I wanted to crush your faith myself. And your father, Philip—I cannot bring him back."

"It is finished. All things are new, Marcus." The aching lump deepened in Philip's throat. Only God, he knew, gave him the ability to speak forgiveness to Marcus.

Thank you, Lord.

Marcus could not speak. Philip saw him try, but no words issued from his lips. Instead, he offered Philip his hand. His dark eyes searched Philip's, supplicating.

Philip grasped his outstretched hand. He understood Marcus's wordless appeal, knew the emotion that prevented his speaking. "I forgive you, Marcus."

Uttering the words was like unleashing the floodgates of heaven's joy. Philip's heart sang. The hand that had comforted him in pain was with him again, touching him. He felt it.

And that hand would continue to be with him. Vast and mysterious, God's plan would not leave him helpless. It would continue to guide him, answering his prayers.

Even as the prayer of two saints—one on earth and one in heaven—had been answered concerning Marcus.

Chapter Eighteen

Alone in the library, Marcus's eyes drifted slowly over the scroll held loosely within his hands. His temples ached dully, and he lifted his wrist to rub his forehead. But, there was little wonder his head ached.

Marcus smiled dryly, considering the events of the last few days. The sheer amount of knowledge he had acquired during the four days since his conversion was staggering. He had not learned so much about any one subject since his young boyhood.

And that was without a strict teacher pressing him to learn.

Only last night, he had been baptized into the Christian faith. By his request, it had been Daniel who had spoken the blessing over him and lowered him in the name of the Holy Trinity into the Tiber.

Marcus's throat ached. Philip's emotion at his baptism had warmed his heart, but it could not alleviate the pain he felt. Try as he might, he would never be able to forget the things he had done.

You are new. Christ has forgiven you.

Marcus shook his head a little. Christ's spilled blood might cover his own blood-red hands, but it could never erase the memory of Beric's sufferings. The sight of the cruel rods falling on the martyr's broad back and Philip's agonized cries would haunt him continually.

He shut his eyes, attempting to wash away the remembrance. It was merely replaced by the sight of Philip, lying prostrate before him. He recalled the strange force that had stayed his hand, keeping him from completing the full measure of stripes he had meant to inflict on Philip.

He now knew where that power had come from. And he thanked Christ for it.

What a merciful God he served! How easily Jehovah could have killed him while he was torturing His servant. But, that would not have been the nature of the God of second chances.

"My lord?"

Marcus opened his eyes. "Yes."

Philip stepped into the library, crossing his hands on his breast. "I am ready to depart for the meetings, my lord. Is it your pleasure to come also?"

"Not tonight, Philip. My head aches, and I fear I would be poor company."

"Do you wish me to remain behind?"

"No." An amused smile played about Marcus's lips. "You have never let anything keep you from the meetings. There is no need to start now."

"As you say." Marcus saw Philip's face relax and knew how difficult his offer had been to make. The boy fairly lived and breathed the meetings. "I'll return soon, my lord."

"Hasten. The others distrust me enough as it is without my delaying you."

Philip hesitated. "I cannot believe they all distrust you, my lord."

"Perhaps not, but that does not mask the truth. I have heard enough to know they all think me an imposter. You and Daniel seem to be the only ones who have truly forgiven me. But what does it matter? I cannot blame them."

"If what you say is true, they are wrong, my lord. I was the one who suffered and Christ gave me the power to forgive. They should do the same."

Marcus laughed slightly. "People do not forget wrongs easily, even Christians. But it is just. Now, go, before you give them further reason to hate me."

"Yes, sir." Philip bowed and left the room.

Marcus watched him cross the atrium and leave through the *vestibule*. He dropped his eyes to his scroll, again rubbing his forehead.

The sound of a sharp voice did little to soothe the pounding ache in his temples.

"You allow your slave too much liberty, Marcus. I have told you so before."

Marcus rose slowly to his feet, standing before Rowland. Irritation gnawed at his heart, but he controlled himself to speak quietly. "Good evening, father."

Rowland ignored the polite greeting. "Where was the boy going?"

Marcus felt a sudden thrust. He had put this moment off. He knew that it had to come eventually, but words could not depict the dread he felt at breaking the news to his father. "He was going to the Christian meetings."

Rowland's face darkened with radical speed. "You are a constant wonder to me, Marcus! Have you not broken his obstinate will yet? How dare you defy me by allowing this folly?"

Marcus remained silent. Rowland's countenance grew livid.

"I am ashamed of you, Marcus. Since you are not man enough to control your own slave, it sorely disappoints me that I must keep my word and take this matter into my own hands. Tomorrow, that little cur goes to the auction block."

"No, father." Marcus spoke quietly, but he set his jaw with cool decision. "Philip is my slave. No man may sell him."

"Then what are you going to force me to do? Beat the two of you combined?"

Marcus set his chin with firm resolution. His father's sarcastic anger irritated him to no end, but he was determined to stand by Philip and his own new faith.

Be a man. Tell him straight.

"It may be that you shall have to keep that threat, father. As it is, I will not see Philip punished for going to these meetings. And, in all honesty, you must know I wish I was with him."

For once, entire bewilderment flickered across Rowland's blackened countenance. Marcus took a step nearer, his tones icy in their poignancy.

"You do well to look so confused, but it is the truth. I, who have so fiercely withstood Philip's faith, am a Christian. And I am not ashamed to own it."

Silence permeated the room.

Rowland's hands slowly doubled into angry fists. A wave of color washed over his face, then, sped away, leaving only white-hot rage. "May that be so, Marcus. I at least possess the shame any true-blooded Roman should have when faced with such an atrocity. By the spear of Mars! That I—Rowland Virginius—should have sired a miserable traitor!"

"I am no traitor." Marcus's face flamed. "My allegiance to Rome is as great as it always has been."

"Shut your mouth! Do not call yourself a faithful son of Rome when you are a *Christian*."

Marcus cringed. His fingers bit into the palms, squeezing back all he was thinking. The hate and rage boiling in his father's face was intimidating, even to him. But he refused to be cowed, to stand in slave-like meekness when Rowland challenged him. He was a man. And he had made his choice.

Rowland's furious tones loudened, his voice a spat. "Bring back that wretched Briton. I will wring his neck for this!"

"No." Marcus spoke through tightly-clenched teeth. "God only knows how I tried to conquer Philip's faith. He cannot be faulted because I saw the truth."

Rowland's eyes narrowed, piercing through him. He stepped closer, and Marcus felt the threatening presence he himself had so often intimidated Philip with. "Marcus, I give you one chance. Recant this foolish obstinacy and beg my pardon for defying me. Nothing more will be said."

"And if I refuse?"

"Then prepare to be cast from my will and this home forever. I will disown you, Marcus—the gods curse you!"

Marcus felt the color fading from his cheeks. He had known Rowland's wrath, but had not thought he would cut his only living son from his inheritance. He would be brought to the level of a beggar.

His heart pumped wildly. So he must forever bid farewell to the home of his youth, to everything he had known and loved.

"I will not do that, father. I am a loyal son of Rome and your eldest child. Those things have not changed. But I will not deny Christ. He is first in my life, and I have pledged to live and die in His service."

Rowland's countenance grew cold. "So be it. You have forever cut all bindings to me, Marcus. Collect your belongings and be gone; remain another moment in my sight, and I swear I will have you scourged!"

Marcus did not cast another glance upon his father's livid face. Speedily, he withdrew and made his way to his chamber.

With hasty hands, he gathered his money and what few articles he thought necessary. Clasping his *pallium* around his shoulders, he left the room.

In the atrium, Lady Persis stood weeping. Young Diantha stood beside her, the quiet tears trickling down her face. Rowland towered over them both, giving Marcus a withering glance as he came down the staircase.

"Get from my sight, miserable cur! You have prevailed upon my goodness for too long already."

Marcus said nothing. Silently, he strode past his mother and sister, pausing a moment to rest his hand on Diantha's curling dark hair.

"God be with you, little sister," he said, low, leaning over her.

Rowland clapped his hands, summoning the slaves. Knowing his threat of scourging had not been a vain one, Marcus straightened himself and strode across the atrium. At the door, he paused.

He was leaving the domus forever.

It was with a rapidly beating heart he stepped onto the *Vicus Tuscus* and mingled with the dozens of pedestrians. As he strode along, the numbing powers of shock gave away to grim reality. It had all happened so quickly. Within a half-hour, he had been reduced to pennilessness.

Looking down, Marcus saw that his hands shook. The confrontation with Rowland had been worse than he had anticipated. A burning ache seized his manly throat. Like Philip, he was forever separated from his father.

Only Beric had loved his son to the end. Rowland did not.

Marcus pulled his cloak more tightly around his shoulders. The lump grew in his throat, swelling with his aching heart. Fleetingly, he glanced up into dusky sky, streaked by the last strains of sunlight.

Guide me, Father. I am not ashamed to admit this hurts me.

A haunting, diabolical voice immediately sounded back at him, taunting him. *It is just! You who slew Beric, who tortured Philip. It is just!*

Marcus shook himself. Yes, it was just. Still, his soul screamed out, fighting the haunting presence. *I know it is just I be punished. But, oh, God, you promised forgiveness. Am I not a new creature in You? Am I not forgiven?*

The whirling mist of doubts and fears only plagued Marcus's mind more relentlessly. He tried to shake them off, but they screamed in his mind.

It is just! Murderer, thief. It is just. Just!

At the door of Daniel's home, Marcus paused to collect his scattered emotions. He seemed to grow more shaken with each passing moment. His serene coolness had given way to throbbing pain, aching in his heart and dissembling his usual fearless demeanor.

How could Rowland have done this? Did he not love his only living son? Their differences had always been great. And, until now,

Rowland had always permitted their varying opinions to stand respected.

Was coming to peace truly such an unpardonable sin?

The longer he lingered, the more Marcus felt certain he could not regain the mastery of his emotions. Inhaling deeply, he knocked for admittance. A brother opened the door, and Marcus slipped inside.

The inner chamber was aglow with oil lamps, lighting the serene countenances of the worshippers. Daniel stood in their midst, taking prayer requests.

Lingering in the shadows, Marcus surveyed the room until his eyes rested on Philip's face. The boy was seated on the outskirts of the brethren, intent upon what was taking place.

Marcus half-stepped forward, then, stopped. Moriah was seated beside Philip. The only remaining space was beside her, and Marcus knew his close presence would discomfort her.

The thought sent a pang to his heart. Like so many of the brethren, Moriah seemed to distrust and dislike him. She avoided him continually, and, whenever her sparkling hazel eyes happened to rest upon him, their pupils overshadowed with cool mistrust.

It was a mistrust Marcus could not fault. She was no fool. She knew what sort of a lascivious life he had lived, of his drunken reveling, of the harm he had brought upon two of the brethren she loved. And, by contrast, she was a beautiful, chaste young woman who had lived a pure life of service to Christ.

Marcus chose to stand.

Daniel glanced around the circle, ready to bring the prayer requests to a close. "Is there any final request to be made?"

Marcus felt a twinge, urging him to speak.

For a fleeting instant, he fought against it. He was a new believer. If he shared his heart, the others would criticize his motives. After all, he was the man who had tortured one of their beloved members. How dare he—a persecutor of Christians—speak before them all?

But his heart was too heavy for silence.

"May I be permitted a few words, Daniel?"

Daniel turned, surprise hovering over his bearded countenance. "We did not expect you tonight, Marcus Virginius. May peace be with you."

Marcus nodded. The aching pain in his throat had grown.

Daniel motioned him forward. "Come into the light and say what you will, my brother."

Marcus stepped forward. His strong hands closed into light fists, perspiration wetting his fingers. He swallowed, collecting his thoughts.

Speak your heart. They will not despise you for your weakness.

"My brethren." He stopped. His voice was shaking, husky.

Be with me, Father.

"My brethren, I have a request for prayer. I have been called to make my first sacrifice for Christ, and, while it is insignificant when many of our brothers are giving their lives, it is very close to my heart."

Marcus again swallowed. His peripheral gaze caught Philip, leaning forward with questioning concern on his face. How ironic it was that his slave cared for his wellbeing more than his own family.

"Tonight, I acknowledged my faith in Jesus to my father. I-I now find myself without a home or inheritance. If you would, my brethren, pray I may endure this loss with courage. I-thank you."

Marcus found himself suddenly unable to speak. He seated himself in a shadowed corner. Low murmurs of sympathy and acknowledgment met his ears, penetrating his aching heart with warm encouragement.

They care.

"We will pray for you, Marcus." Daniel's low voice was gentler than Marcus ever recalled hearing it. "And you will be homeless no longer. Until you are able to make your own way, you and yours will share my home."

Marcus could not speak. His eyes met Daniel's, allowing them to express his thanks. Slowly, his eyes drifted downwards, resting them upon Moriah's face. What did she think of him sharing her home?

Soft and unblinking, her hazel eyes met his for a fraction of a second. Pulling her veil taut around her pretty shoulders, Moriah turned away from him.

Long after the others had gone, Marcus stood at the casement in Daniel's home. The dark street beyond the bakery was quiet and still. Still, he looked out, his eyes overcast and somber.

You have provided for now, Father. But what future will I have? I am a patrician. My place is in the senate, in the law courts of Rome. How shall I obtain my career without an inheritance, without money?

Without warning, Marcus felt a presence behind him. Turning, he saw Philip behind him, waiting subserviently for his master to notice him. "Well?"

"Do I disturb you, my lord?"

"No." Marcus leaned against the casement frame, loosening his cloak. "What do you want?"

"It is late, my lord. Do you not wish to retire?"

Marcus rubbed a hand across his forehead. "I have not thought of the time. My mind is too occupied for rest, I fear."

Philip seemed to hesitate. Marcus gestured to him. "You may speak."

"I only desire to say I sympathize for you during this time of trial, Marcus. You feel your father's callousness keenly, I think."

"I do." Marcus looked past Philip. It felt awkward, discussing his problems with his slave. Still, he sensed the burning need to communicate with someone. Someone who cared. "I am his only son. And, while we've never been very close, I do respect and love him."

There was a moment of silence.

Philip raised his eyes with the same expression of hesitant respect. "He is watching, Marcus. He will not leave you destitute."

Marcus smiled a little bitterly. "Your wish to comfort me is admirable, Philip, but I think you are mistaken. Jehovah sent this trial as a punishment."

"I do not understand."

Marcus settled himself more comfortably, hoping to give a casual appearance he did not feel. "He is the Divine Judge, is He not? And no holy God would watch His devout servants be killed and flogged without punishing the author of that suffering."

"Jehovah is not vindictive." Philip's tone was indignant. "You are His child, Marcus. The things you have done are removed as far as the east is from the west. I have told you so before."

Marcus surveyed him contemplatively. Christian though he was, Philip's spirit could still rile with fervent heat. It was amusing in a way.

And presumptuous.

"Don't argue with me, Philip. Christian or heathen, I am still your master."

Marcus saw the burning color flood Philip's cheeks, crimsoning his British-white skin from chin to forehead. He averted his gaze, reverting to subservience.

"My apologies, my lord."

"I didn't mean you were to be formal." Marcus's voice softened. For the first time, it hurt him to see a slave cringe under his rebuke. He owed Philip more than he could comprehend. "I only think you are mistaken."

Philip raised his eyes. "Perhaps I am. But I only meant to remind you that Christ has called you to life, not condemnation."

"Truth. And it does not truly matter which of us is correct. God has seen fit to send me this trial, and I will bear it manfully. If all I have been told is true, there is a good purpose for it." Marcus looked closely at Philip. "I don't suppose you always believe that yourself."

"No, not always." A look of deep pain crossed Philip's countenance. "I struggle with it often. When my father died—"

Philip cut himself short.

Marcus felt a deep thrust. He knew what Philip had suffered. And he knew why he ceased from speaking about his pain. "Do not stop on my account. I know what I have put you through."

Philip shook his head. Marcus saw his eyes glisten. Strangely, his tears seemed more masculine than the emotionless restraint he as a Roman had always strictly observed. Could it be that true men were not afraid to show their pain?

"It is better I do not speak of it, Marcus. A new time has come. I will not fill the bright pathway God has chosen for our lives with my struggles."

A bright new pathway.

The thought stayed with Marcus for the remainder of the night. Could it be his separation from his earthly father was a veiled blessing? Temptations of every depiction abounded in the Virginius domus. Perhaps God *was* with him, shielding him from danger.

Dangers he was too weak to resist.

When morning finally dawned, Marcus came to another decision. Rowland knew of his new faith; now there was another who ought to know.

Delicia.

Fearless though he was, Marcus cringed at the thought of telling her. Delicia was as much absorbed with pleasures and revelry as he had been. What would her response be to discovering her future husband was a Christian?

It was a task to be accomplished as quickly as possible.

Promising to return before nightfall, Marcus bid Daniel farewell and summoned Philip to accompany him.

Marcus's mind was very full as he strode the cobblestoned streets to the domus of Saturius. His heart still ached, and he had little desire for further rebuff. Delicia would not be merciful with him.

And, if by some slim chance she was gracious, he had nothing to offer her in return. It was a chilling prospect.

Father, give me the right words. Help me explain what it is I believe so that she will understand. And, somehow, help her accept my faith for her own. It is the only way there will be peace in our union. Bring her to a saving knowledge of You, and give me favor in her eyes.

The magnificent mansion of Saturius rose up, looming over him. Marcus's steps slowed involuntarily. The domus's scarlet door seemed to beckon him to a pitiless end. He could only image what cruel words Delicia would speak on the other side.

Will you cower from a woman's robe? Be a man! Stand for your Savior.

Marcus squared his broad shoulders, feeling strength ripple through his biceps and tingle in his fingertips.

The time was now.

Lightly, he stepped up the marble steps. He lifted his hand in a firm series of knocks, then, awaited entrance.

The household steward appeared, holding the door close to his body. Cold and menacing, he seemed unwilling for Marcus to enter. "Yes?"

"I am here to see Lady Delicia. Pray present me, Scipio."

The steward's expressionless features did not change. "I am under orders not to admit you, sir."

"Why? I am no stranger to this household."

"Henceforth, Marcus Virginius, you are no more than a foreigner. My master Saturius commands me to say you are never to come here. You are never to see my lady Delicia and are forbidden from all correspondence with her. That is all."

The steward made as if he would close the door. Marcus stepped forward, settling his countenance with a tautness that would cow the most determined slave.

"Not so fast, Scipio. Tell me why."

"Sir, I have many pressing tasks. Pray—"

Marcus's hand closed with angry vehemence around his arm. "Tell me why."

The steward shook off his hand. For one instant, a flicker of disgust replaced his subservient nonchalance. "He who would deny the powers of Rome and scorn a father's commands has no place in the domus of Saturius. It is my master's order and my lady Delicia's wish. Need you further reason?"

"No." Marcus's stern tone subsided. Slowly, he turned away from the steward. Behind him, he heard the door swing shut, the bolt scraping into its lock.

At the bottom of the steps, Philip's countenance was grave. Marcus knew he had heard all. He stepped past him, unable to look him in the eyes. Every detail of his intended humiliation had been witnessed by his own slave. Would his shame never end?

Marcus launched into a quick stride. He had no desire to linger beside the domus of Saturius. It was best he returned to Daniel's home and set his mind on learning a profitable trade.

It was his only choice.

His hearty pace did little to calm his aching heart. Marcus's throat burned. His temples pounded wildly, resounding pain shooting through his forehead. He felt his fingers constrict, pulling his hands into fists.

I am not even given the chance to see her. She has heard the tale from my father, from Saturius, from those who hate me. How can she understand what it is I rest my hope on if she has not heard it from my lips?

Marcus scarcely felt the close presence of the other pedestrians, of their garments brushing against his own. He walked by force of habit, allowing his steps to lead him where they would.

She was to be my wife. Has loyalty amounted to nothing in Rome? If I am a Christian, then my God should be hers. How can she deny her desire to see me?

In his heart, Marcus knew the truth. She did not desire to see him because she did not love him. They had never really loved each other. Their union was meant to be a political one, nothing more.

Delicia lived for pleasure, for wealth. He could offer her neither.

How quickly he had lost his future. From his inheritance to his career to his wife, he had no prospects. It was if God wanted him to rest his entire existence upon Him, trusting fully in His goodness.

An echoing plethora of screams cut Marcus's thoughts short.

Chapter Nineteen

Like the opening of a sea, pedestrians and peddlers alike separated, throwing themselves against the safety of the surrounding walls. Many more dashed into nearby shops and dwellings, slamming the doors against the street.

The rattling sounds of a runaway chariot filled the air. The vehicle itself came unto full view, drawn by a team of agitated horses. They thundered down the street, marking their passing with overturned baskets and destroyed booths.

Marcus paused in his walk. A single glance assured him of the situation.

A patrician of some thirty years was frantically endeavoring to stay the horses' wild dash. Foolishly, he clutched at the reins and shouted unheeded commands, exciting the steeds with his own passionate desperation.

Another man, apparently the rightful driver, was slumped down in the bottom of the chariot. He was clearly insensible, and Marcus could see he would not awaken in time to aid his incompetent master.

Inevitably, the chariot would dash against a stone wall and break apart. One, if not both, of the occupants would be killed.

Marcus braced himself. The chariot thundered nearer, murderous and wild. The horses plunged beside him, their hooves landing with shattering force against the cobblestones. The shock of their tread rolled through the ground, rumbling underneath his feet.

Now. Now!

He threw himself forward. Hands flailing, he caught the reins of the foremost horse. The animal was hot, foaming at the mouth. Flicks of perspiration caught him in the face. His heart rate kicked up a notch, adrenaline pulsing through his veins. If he failed...

For one eternity-like moment, he felt himself dragged along, his sandaled feet scraping the road. He gritted his teeth and clenched the reins tighter. The horse tossed his head, endeavoring to shake him off. His hooves pounded perilously near Marcus's exposed legs.

"Halt!" Firm and clear, Marcus's tone seemed to penetrate the wild instinct governing the steeds. Slowly, gradually, they came to a standstill, tossing their beautiful heads.

Marcus pulled himself erect, maintaining one hand on the bridle. His heart pounded against his chest, his lungs screaming for oxygen. The deed had been swift and almost deadly.

But no harm had come to him.

The patrician leaped from the chariot. Passionately, he shook Marcus's hand, his pallid features flushing with new warmth and relief. "A thousand thanks, my brave young man! By the gods! Your courage shall not go unrewarded."

Marcus struggled to regain his breath. "No reward is required, senator. I was pleased to serve you."

"So you recognize my occupation. That is well. But," and the man looked quizzically at him, "do I not know you? By Bacchus, I swear I have seen you before. What is your name, young man?"

"Marcus, once the son of Rowland Virginius."

The man slapped his thigh, raising his hands in appeal to the gods. "Truth! I remember you. I know Rowland well, though we have not spoken in some months. But how do you say you were once his son? Is he dead?"

"No." Marcus felt the color rise in his cheeks. *What a promising introduction.* "I have been disinherited."

The senator stared at him. He raised his brows, then, broke into a ringing laugh.

Marcus felt his temper burn. What right did this man have to mock him? Had he not saved his life? Shortly, the anger high in his face, he turned away.

The senator's hand immediately found his arm. "No, no, my young friend, do not be so ill-tempered. By the gods, I meant no offence. Come, we will go into a wine-shop together."

"I have no desire to be mocked, senator."

"And you shall not be." The man waved his hand. "By Hercules! I swear I will behave well. You cannot refuse me."

"Then let it be as you say." Marcus forced a measure of courteous pleasantry to his tones. Clearly, the senator was not giving him a choice. "Lead and I shall follow."

The senator nodded shortly. Turning to a bystander, he tossed him a silver coin. "Take that idiot home and throw some water over him." Then, by afterthought, "And see that my chariot is driven home and my team watered. They will need refreshment after that race, by Jupiter!"

Having given his orders, the senator motioned for Marcus to follow him. In turn, Marcus snapped his fingers at Philip. In single file, all three took the few paces to the nearest wine-shop.

Inside, the senator seated himself, motioning for Marcus to join him. They were quickly served a jug of spiced wine. Having swallowed a deep draught from his mug, the senator surveyed Marcus with an open, candid expression.

"As I am certain you know, I am Cleotas Aeneas. And, concerning that wild ride you saved me from, it was entirely the fault of my new driver. The insolent braggart was far from as competent at the reins as he boasted."

"Allow me to express the hope you will secure a better driver before trusting yourself behind those steeds again, Cleotas Aeneas." Marcus's tone was dry. "I doubt I will be present to rescue you again."

"Truth." Cleotas took another sip from his mug. "And you are frank, Virginius. I admire that. Do tell me why Rowland Virginius would disown a dashing, well-favored young man such as you."

"I am a Christian."

Cleotas leaned back, surveying Marcus shrewdly. "A son of Rome and a Christian! A fine state of affairs. A hot-headed fanatic you must have been for Rowland to have disinherited you."

"I think not. My father had merely gained the knowledge I am a Christian when he disowned me."

"Interesting." Cleotas peered into the ruby depths of his mug. "So it was shame and not devotion to your religion that evoked your father's displeasure? Well, there is nothing unusual in that. He was always a proud man. How long have you been a member of this mysterious sect?"

Marcus shifted. "About a week."

"A week." Slow disgust flitted over Cleotas's fine-featured countenance. "And your father did not have the patience to let this frenzy come and go, as all the wild ideas of young men do. A loving father!"

Marcus looked contemplatively at Cleotas. The man did not seem to care that his rescuer was a hated Christian. "Are you unfaithful to the gods of Rome, my lord?"

"No, certainly not." Cleotas waved his hand impatiently. "But I am not such a fanatic of worship that I cannot tolerate the zeal of a new convert. Ah, do not gainsay me. I know your spirit bounds at the chance of experiencing new revelations and mystical ceremonies."

"My apologies, Aeneas, but I must differ. I think you do not take a correct view of Christianity."

"Perhaps so. But I did not say I dislike members of your sect, did I? From what I have seen of your worship, the followers of Christus are hard workers who pay their debts on time. And they are pleasant enough in disposition."

"If there is anything good in us, senator," and Marcus chose his words carefully. He was still so new to this. "It is because our Savior grants us the grace to live our lives according to His will."

Cleotas was silent. When at last he spoke, new seriousness overshadowed his careless demeanor. "I do not pretend to agree with your religion, Virginius. I have studied its teachings and am content to remain a Roman in all things. Still, I like your boldness. You seem a truehearted and resolute citizen."

"I am gratified, my lord."

Cleotas laughed unexpectedly. "Oh, come, Marcus! Lay aside your restraint. I know you think I flatter you, but I meant what I said. And I cannot allow your good talents to be wasted, as Rowland would see them."

Marcus allowed a hint of a smile to play about his mouth. He bent his head ever so slightly. "My lord, you are generous in your compliments. Sitting here with you has indeed been an honor worthy of risking my life for."

"Now you flatter *me*. But, by Hercules, I am not indisposed to receive it. I am not one of those boors who fritters his life away in search of self-improvement. Tell me, where are you lodging?"

Marcus felt amusement welling up within him. This man Cleotas Aeneas was as careless and dashing as any street-side peddler. Charm fairly radiated from everything pertaining to him, from his demeanor to his pleasant countenance. Handsome, richly-attired, and eloquent, it was little wonder he had won such favor in the Senate.

And, beyond the natural elements of a wealthy Roman, Cleotas was fashionable. His fine brown hair was cropped short, while his short beard curled down beneath his jaw-line and chin in the fashion Nero had made popular. He exuded strength and good health, as energetic as any man in his prime could be.

Marcus forced himself to forget his host's charisma and focus on his question. "I am staying with a friend, my lord. A bread-maker."

"That will never do." Cleotas slapped his hand upon the table. "You must stay with me."

"Your offer is generous, my lord. Yet, I promised to return to my friend tonight. I cannot in all politeness break my word."

Cleotas stared at him. "You do not understand me, young Virginius. I did not just mean for tonight. I want you to dwell with me permanently."

Marcus blinked. For an instant, he wondered if Cleotas was mad. Or was it the heat? "I beg your pardon?"

"I see you still do not understand. I will explain." Cleotas leaned forward, again overtaken by seriousness. "Marcus, I have no wife and no son to carry on my name and inherit my estate[5]. You please me well and are exactly the sort of young man I would expect my heir to be. What better reward for saving my life than that you become the inheritor of my wealth?"

Marcus laughed uncomfortably. "Cleotas, I did not save your life for any reward! I should be ashamed to have done so."

"Which is precisely why I admire you, young man. Marcus, if you accept my offer, you will be immediately reinstated to the lifestyle you were accustomed to living. You will live in my home, dwell in my company, and enjoy all the benefits the son of Cleotas Aeneas could have."

Marcus looked searchingly at him. "I will not deny my faith, Cleotas. Surely that would be a problem."

"Not at all. Provided you keep your fanatical views to yourself and do not associate me with them, I have nothing to say about it. Now, what say you?"

Marcus's mind whirled. Surely he was dreaming! It was impossible that he—a disdained outcast—was being offered the position of a son by Cleotas Aeneas himself.

Father, is this Your will? Is this the life You wish me to lead?

Cleotas's hand twitched in impatience. Marcus looked slowly up at him.

"I cannot say your offer does not tempt me, Cleotas. It is generosity in itself. But, I must have time to consider this."

---

[5] Adoption was very common in Rome. Having no male heir was unthinkable. This was especially true in the upper senatorial class.

"Take the night." Cleotas rose to his feet. "Send your slave to my mansion with your answer in the morning. It lies by the *Vicus Jugarius*. He will know the place by the great fountain upon the portico."

"Yes, my lord." Marcus stood. "I promise I will consider your words carefully."

Cleotas laid several silver *denarii* on the table, cutting Marcus's protest short. "We may not meet again, young Virginius. The gods forbid it, but, if the fates are not with me, I wish you to have some reward for your services." Then, with a light salute, "Farewell, Marcus. I will fervently await your answer."

"God be with you, senator." Marcus bent forward, then, signaling to Philip, strode from the wine-shop.

In the open air and humid sunshine, Marcus paused. Reality struck him like a *pilo*, its keen edge sinking into the depths of his heart.

A new life was before him.

Glancing sidelong, Marcus saw Philip's countenance was alive. His blue eyes flashed, excitement sparkling in his pupils. "He *is* watching, Marcus. He has *not* left you destitute!"

"Then you are of the opinion I should accept his offer." Marcus brushed aside his masterly pride. He was ready, even desirous, to speak about personal matters with his slave. Philip's broader experience with things of the faith was certainly a thing to be consulted.

Philip seemed to recognize his own boldness. He quickly melded into subservience. "I cannot advise you, my lord." He paused. "But I can say my heart is for this."

Marcus surveyed him contemplatively. "As is mine." He turned, striking a brisk mannerism. "But I will make no decision until I have prayed. And Daniel must be consulted."

That evening was the longest night of Marcus's life.

Hot and humid, the room he slept in was stifling. Insects hummed beyond the single casement, producing an atmosphere of drowsiness.

In the darkness, Marcus lay on his sleeping mat and stared into the dusky shadows. His eyelids were heavy, but sleep fled from him. He tossed and turned, but movement brought him no relief.

With a sigh, he rose to his feet. Striding cautiously across the dark room, he lit one of the tall oil lamps in the corner. Flickering light spread across the chamber, and he turned back to his mat.

It was then he saw Philip. He had thought his slave was sound asleep on his own mat, but a closer inspection revealed his arms were outstretched and his lips moved noiselessly. Marcus's heart was stirred. He knew Philip was praying. And, somehow, he sensed those petitions were for him.

A pang struck his conscience. He had prayed several times during that evening, but not with the fervor he now saw in Philip.

A lump grew in his throat.

Seconds later, Marcus found himself on his knees beside Philip. He stretched himself out on his face, extending his hands in a wide angle.

The prayer he offered was unlike any petition he had ever offered before. In the temples, he had made bargains, offering a sacrifice in turn for a granted request. Now, he fervently besought God for wisdom; for strength; for His will to be made known.

With the coming of dawn, Marcus had his answer.

He rose to his feet, stretching his aching muscles. Almost simultaneously, Philip arose. A single glance revealed his slave had come to the same answer as himself.

Crossing the room, Marcus seated himself at a humble desk. Dipping his pen in ink, he scratched out his message on a piece of parchment and sealed it with wax and his signet ring.

"Take this to Senator Cleotas Aeneas with my greetings, Philip."

"Shall I wait for his answer?"

"Yes." Marcus paused, seeing inquiry in Philip's eyes. A slow smile played about his lips. "I have decided to accept his offer."

A flashing light illuminated Philip's countenance. Half-smiling, he bowed and left the room.

Marcus leaned back, quietly contemplative. It was assuring to know Philip shared his feelings, however odd it felt to consider a slave's personal feelings. Having considered slaves mere objects for so long, it was difficult to accept the fact Philip was real, a breathing, feeling human being. Somewhere, in the back of the callousness and traditions of Rome, he supposed he had always known slaves were as human as himself. But it had taken Christ's love to awaken him to the fact they were equals.

It was humiliating, in one sense. He and an Iceni slave were equally important. But, then, in the light of all he had done, perhaps it was beautiful. God loved him, a murderer, as much as he loved a faithful slave.

Thank you for loving me. Marcus swallowed against the ache in his throat. It seemed to haunt him so often these days. But, oddly, he didn't care. *Thank you for caring for me, Jesus.*

Two hours passed. Each minute dragged with painful lethargy, overwhelming Marcus with impatience. At last he joined Daniel in the shop, hoping work would relieve his mind.

Fully-assured of his Lord's will, the desire to become Cleotas's son strengthened with each passing moment. He was still overwhelmed by his father's rejection, but his new prospects lifted much of his burden. He would have his career, his high social standing.

And God had not left him destitute.

"Thank you, my Savior." At the bread counter, Marcus murmured the words. "I did not believe You would bring me unscathed from this trial, but Your promises are true. They are true."

Mindlessly, he laid the fresh, crusty loaves in neat stacks. Aiding Daniel made the time slip away faster, but impatience still welled up within him.

Surely, Cleotas had not changed his mind. The possibility was too overwhelming. But, God had brought this new joy into his life.

He could remove it.

Unexpectedly, the door swung wide. Philip stepped into the interior, sunshine streaming in behind him and casting his shadow upon the floor.

Marcus stepped forward, none too patient. "You were gone long, Philip."

"Senator Aeneas took his leisure making his reply, my lord." Philip handed a sealed document to Marcus. "It is here."

Marcus took the parchment and quickly broke the seals. Spreading it out, he quickly scanned the short epistle. "He writes that he is pleased I have accepted his offer. He wants the adoption ceremony to take place as quickly as possible."

Daniel moved from behind the corner, wiping his flour-covered hands on his apron. "Does he say when?"

"Yes; tonight. He has commenced preparations for the banquet and ceremony. He adds he will have many guests present and bids me invite whomever I will."

"He is a prompt man." A hint of a smile covered Daniel's bearded face. "Adonai has truly blessed you, Marcus."

"He has." Marcus folded the parchment, trying to sort through his thoughts. "And I do not deserve it. I cannot begin to understand this strange mercy."

"No mercy is strange when coming from our Savior, Marcus."

"Truth." A fleeting pang struck Marcus's heart, recalling Delicia. Why did he think of her now? He quickly brushed it aside. "And perhaps more of my trials will reveal their true blessing. Who can tell what God has in store?"

Fleeting silence settled over the room.

Marcus looked up at Daniel. "It would please me if you would accept my invitation to the ceremony, Daniel."

Daniel returned to his counter, forming a long loaf. "A former slave and Christian Jew would not be welcome, Marcus. I do not want to mar this event."

"You will not mar it. Jew or Roman, you are my friend. You are welcome."

Daniel smiled slightly, shaking his head. "No, Marcus. It is better you begin this new life in good standing." A kindly, quizzical expression settled over his features. "You will wish to visit the Baths before tonight?"

"You wish to be rid of me." Marcus chuckled good-naturedly. "Yes, I must go. Before I do, though, I must thank you. Your hospitality has been very kind."

"It has been my joy, Marcus."

Marcus hesitated. Everything within him wanted to recompense Daniel for his lodging, but he sensed he would only bring offense. Daniel's kindness was not a thing to be repaid with *denarius*. He decided to say nothing of payment.

"We will not be present at the meetings tonight, but I hope to rejoin them as soon as I possibly can. If the Lords wills it, we will see you soon."

"As you say." Daniel bent slightly, crossing his hands on his breast. "Peace be with you, brothers."

Marcus signaled to Philip. Together, they left the shop, Philip bearing their few possessions.

At the Baths, Marcus completed his usual hygiene routine. Dried and dressed in a white tunic, he stood still as Philip draped the toga around him. Perfumed oils completed his attire, and Marcus led the way from the Baths.

The afternoon was already well into its middle point. The hot sun glistened off of the marble columns of the temples, casting colossal shadows of the gods upon the cobblestoned streets. Smoke rose continually from the Temple of Vesta, mingling with the rising humidity.

A company of *augurs* brushed past Marcus, their heads shielded by tightly-fitting skullcaps. In a small cart, they drew two perfect goats, destined to sacrifice.

Marcus remembered the last time he bought the services of an *augur*. Sharp and pitiless, the sacred knife had slit the animal's belly and revealed perfect innards. The omen had been sure: he, Marcus Virginius, was destined to a powerful career.

It might be true.

Only, it would not be by the will of his namesake, Mars. Now, Marcus knew, there was no fate to decide his fortune. He had something far better: the blessing of One who constantly interceded for him.

The mansion of Aeneas appeared in the near-distance, colossal and beautiful.

Involuntarily, Marcus's steps slowed. He was unafraid, but also uncertain. His future had changed so rapidly in the last few days. Would life as the son of Senator Cleotas Aeneas be the promising one he desired?

Laughter fell clearly on his ears, issuing from the domus. The guests of Cleotas had arrived in good season.

Marcus inhaled deeply. Drawing his toga more firmly about his shoulders, he quickly alighted the steps.

A slave answered his knock. He admitted them, offering a deep bow. "Do I have the honor of receiving my young lord, Marcus Virginius?"

"Yes."

"My master Cleotas awaits you in the library, my lord. Shall I announce you?"

"Yes." Marcus gestured to Philip, who silently took the *pallium* from his shoulders and draped it over his arm. "Take me to him."

Acknowledging his order with a low bow, the slave briskly led the way across the spacious atrium and threw open the doors of the library. "My lord Marcus Virginius Aeneas."

Marcus stood a moment in the doorway, taking in the scene at a glance.

The room was filled with toga-clad men. Nearly half of them bore the purple stripe of a senator's office upon their toga and tunic. Obviously, Cleotas Aeneas had no mean acquaintances among his friends. Perhaps that was how he had settled the adoption so quickly. Normally, the process was long and arduous, particularly as Marcus was unrepresented by his biological father.

Clearly, his position in high places had served Cleotas well.

Cleotas came swiftly across the room, raising his hand in greeting. "Hail, Marcus." Lightly, he grasped Marcus by the shoulders, embracing him.

Marcus returned the gesture. The warmth of Cleotas's greeting pleased him. His adoption was not merely the formality of producing an heir, then. Inwardly, he vowed to maintain the warmth between them. His new relationship with Cleotas would be an affectionate one.

"Greetings, senator."

"*Cleotas*, if you will, Marcus." Cleotas rested his almond-colored eyes on Marcus's face, searching him. "You are ready for this final step in becoming my son?"

"With all my heart, Cleotas."

"Good." The warmth deepened on Cleotas's features, easing them into their usual lightheartedness. "Let us then finish up the business."

Maintaining his arm across Marcus's stalwart shoulders, Cleotas turned to his guests, silencing their murmuring conversation and laughter with a slight uplifting of his hand. Every eye turned to him, expectant.

"My friends, you are gathered here to witness the adoption of this young man as my son and heir. I have already told you how he saved my life and of the affection I now hold for him. For those of you who do not recognize him, I present Marcus Virginius."

Several hearty, murmuring greetings sounded from various points across the library. Marcus lifted his arm in silent acknowledgment, bending his head to their polite nods.

Cleotas again lifted his finger. "You know I despise formality, my friends. For my sake, I know you will acknowledge Marcus as my son and heir, honoring him as you would me. That is all I would say, except," and Cleotas turned lightly to Marcus, "I now present to you my son, the young Marcus Virginius Aeneas!"

An echoing chorus of handclapping and cheers followed Cleotas's unaffected speech. Their acclamation continued as, before them all, Cleotas took an ornate signet ring from his finger and slid it onto Marcus's.

Marcus sensed a thrill as he felt the clasp of the ring around his finger. It symbolized so much. More than his future, his career, it portrayed the generosity of the man who was now his father. He again grasped Cleotas by the shoulders.

"You will never be ashamed of this day, Cleotas. On my oath, I'll never dishonor you or this symbol of your affection."

Cleotas laughed. "That is just what I like so much about you. Always sincere, always grateful. Jove! What a thing it is to have an upright son. The contrast between us will soon be made evident."

He rubbed his forehead ruefully, shook back his head, and again laughed. "But, come! My friends are eager to greet you." He raised his hand over the company, summoning them nearer. They moved forward, grasping Marcus by the shoulders, welcoming him.

Marcus accepted their attentions with easy graciousness. His whole body was warm from their touches, their masculine embraces. Respect for Cleotas was evident in their hearty welcomes, fueling his own estimation of his new father.

The line of well-wishers gradually cleared; the room again became noisy with jesting laughter and conversation.

Of the two men still waiting to greet Marcus, one was a statesman. Grave, placid, and corpulent, Marcus at once recognized him as Lucius Annaeus Seneca, Emperor Nero's personal advisor.

"The gods favor you, young Aeneas. You have made an excellent connection in your new father."

"Your honor me, Seneca." Marcus recalled Rowland reading Seneca's works, delving deep into Hellenistic Stoic philosophies. Like others believing in Stoicism, Seneca considered virtue sufficient for happiness. "It is my great joy to stand before our emperor's advisor."

"The feeling is mutual, my young friend. Our excellent senator is highly honored, and his son must be no less so." Seneca nodded amiably. "The gods grant you success, Aeneas."

He moved away. Marcus turned to greet his final well-wisher. Instant shock rolled through him.

Saturius.

Marcus felt the color washing up in his face. He had not seen Saturius earlier. Odd that his former father-in-law to-be was among the guests.

Saturius approached. He raised his arm, making no motion to embrace Marcus as had the others.

"All hail, Saturius." Marcus made no effort to relax his rigidity. *God forgive me.* He could not yet forget the dishonor Saturius had done him.

"Hail, young Aeneas."

An awkward pause followed. Marcus felt a wave of irritation. Could not Saturius make his greeting and depart?

Saturius cleared his throat. "The gods favor you. Senator Cleotas is a well-respected man."

"Truth. I am grateful to have won his good favor." Would Saturius never go? Marcus felt a well of aching resentment rise in his chest. His dishonor had hurt him more deeply than he cared to admit. True, he did not love Delicia. But he had been prepared to take her as his wife honorably.

Saturius shifted, apparently ill-at-ease. "My daughter was, of course, grieved." He avoided meeting Marcus's eye. "With this change in your circumstances, you are to free to visit her again. Delicia would be pleased–"

"No."

Saturius looked up at him.

Marcus met his eye, firmly quiet. "No, Saturius. We are done, she and I. It is better that she finds a man of similar passions. I am not that man now and never can become him again. Besides," he lowered his voice in emphasis, "you would not want a *foreigner* for your son-in-law."

Saturius stiffened. Marcus knew he understood him. He had not meant to bring up his intended humiliation, but perhaps it was just as well. Saturius now knew where they stood.

Most of the guests were filing from the library towards the banqueting chamber, and Marcus saw Cleotas waiting expectantly for him at the door.

"Good day, Saturius."

Marcus strode across the room towards Cleotas, suppressing the dull ache of resignation in his chest. It was officially over between him and Delicia. Not now by the command of Saturius, but in his own heart.

It was for the best.

"The feast begins, Marcus." Cleotas clapped him heartily on the shoulder. "Take your couch so that we all may eat."

"As you say." A smile curled around Marcus's lips. Swallowing, he freed his mind from everything but the present moment. It was his new life with Cleotas that mattered, not the broken dreams of his past.

In the banquet chamber, Marcus stretched himself out on the low couch at the head table. Cleotas seated himself on the couch nearest to his, and the guests followed suit.

With a clap of Cleotas's hands, the slaves entered the room. The hands of the guests were washed, officially commencing the meal.

231

The murmuring sounds of laughter, masculine voices, and music filled the room. The slaves mingled around them, offering trays of olives, various delicacies, and meats.

Marcus served himself from a platter of roasted peacock. Hunger gnawed at his stomach, eager for the familiar food.

His wine glass stood empty on the table before him. Marcus glanced about. Philip stood alone in a corner, waiting for his master to notice him.

Marcus summoned him nearer. Inwardly, he was grateful to see a familiar face. Philip's service was the only comfort he lacked. No other slave had ever sensed his needs as well. He smiled dryly to himself.

Nor had any other slave provoked him as much or as often.

A soft hand brushed Marcus's shoulder. An instant thrill ran through his body, tingling down his spine. He tensed, momentarily paralyzed.

Glancing to his right, Marcus saw Cleotas grinning openly at him. *What...* He slowly raised his eyes, resting them on a young Greek slave.

The woman was very beautiful. She was dressed according to her race, clad in a violet tunic. A soft cape fell from her shoulders, fastened with ornate brooches. She was slim and shapely, her hair soft and coiled in the attractive Greek fashion. A luring smile parted her scarlet lips.

Marcus felt another thrill run down his spine. Her hand again brushed him.

"Do you need wine, my lord?"

Marcus's heart pounded. He felt himself growing hot and cold by turns. Her question implied more than all appearances.

No. I won't go back to that lifestyle. I cannot.

From the corner of his eye, Marcus saw Cleotas lean forward, keenly intent upon him. Amusement played about his mouth, his eyes holding a smile.

The full reality struck Marcus. Cleotas had studied Christianity. He knew fornication was forbidden to Christians. And he was certainly watching to see his new son's response to temptation.

You are not your own.

"My lord?"

"No, no." Marcus did not dare look at her again. The temptation was too strong. His chest pounding, he raised a steely hand of dismissal. "You may go."

Disappointment was evident in the way the young woman drew herself up. She moved away, her look confused and disdaining.

Marcus refused to follow her with his eyes. He averted his gaze until he was certain she had moved from the room. When he did look up, it was to meet the laughing eyes of Cleotas.

Marcus felt the color tingling in his cheeks. Cleotas's amusement stung. His hand clenched his cup. Apprehensive he would shatter the goblet with the force of his own frustration, he beckoned to Philip. "Fill my glass."

Philip bent over him, pouring out the ruby liquid. Though silent and subservient, he looked sidelong at Marcus. Perception was evident in his face, and Marcus knew he was fully aware of his master's inner struggle.

Marcus waved him back.

On one hand, it irritated him that a slave had seen his moment of weakness. On the other, he was grateful there was one individual present who respected what he was standing for.

Unlike Cleotas.

Still amused, Cleotas leaned forward. "I do not envy you, Marcus. Do not touch, do not look. Are you no longer a man that you do not desire pleasure?"

"God knows I do." Marcus raised his eyes. Groaning discouragement threatened to overcome him. He was so weak, so ready to yield. *God help me.* "But what I want does not matter, Cleotas."

"And does your God allow no exceptions for special occasions such as this?"

"No."

Cleotas leaned back. The smile continued to hover over his mouth, dancing in his eyes. "You are standing by your fanatical beliefs better than I thought."

Marcus fingered an olive. If only Cleotas knew he was still distrusted and considered carnal by his fellow Christians. What would he think of *their* spirituality?

"I am a Christian, Cleotas. And, whether I stand or fall when tempted to sin, I shall always be one."

Cleotas seemed to soften. "Then be one, Marcus. I do not mock your virtue. I merely disagree with it." He raised a portion of roasted dormouse to his mouth. "The meaning of life is pleasure. For myself, I will satisfy as many of my desires as I may before Pluto claims me."

Marcus said nothing. For the first time, the sound of the sambucca and flute grated on his ears. Their music reminded him of many things he wished he could forget; things he knew he would still be tempted with.

On the balcony adjoining his bedchamber, Marcus stood looking out over Rome. Dusk was falling. The sky was a masterful blend of scarlet, gold, and blue hues, melting into a soothing canopy of darkness at the horizon.

Most of the guests had departed, but a few still lingered in the library with Cleotas.

Marcus had excused himself on the grounds of a headache. Cleotas had laughingly accused him of being too long at the wine, but, thankfully, the charge was untrue.

However difficult, he was curtailing his old habits.

His eyes roved over the city, resting on the Temple of Mars. The colossal images of the gods perched on its column-enclosed doors and casements were a striking reminder to his former beliefs. Mars was his namesake, his patron.

Somehow, he sensed that sphere of thinking had not entirely changed. If all went well, he intended to become a soldier. He would be a valiant warrior for Rome. It was the safest profession he could settle on as a Christian. He would be actively employed.

Still, temptation would follow him. He would never be safe from its allures.

A quiet step sounded behind him.

Without turning, Marcus knew who it was. His thoughts formed themselves into soft words. "Pray for me."

"I do so every day, master."

Marcus turned. He felt weary, discouraged. New realization was beginning to sink in. "Cleotas is more tolerant of my faith than my father was. But, I fear he is also more given to pleasures."

"Your father had a family." Philip stepped forward. "I think virtue is best found in men who have children."

Marcus saw hesitance linger on the countenance of Philip. He gestured slightly. "What is it?"

"It was my Lord Cleotas who summoned the young woman to your side."

Marcus was silent a moment. He wasn't surprised. Still, Cleotas was too good-natured to have done it maliciously. "My new father is a kind and generous man, Philip. I'm certain my comfort was the only thought uppermost in his mind."

Philip said nothing, but his expression revealed a contrary opinion.

Marcus felt frustration well up within. And what if Cleotas *had* meant to try him? It was only natural for him to test the validity of his son's claims. A slave like Philip could not begin to understand. His words came out sharply.

"Do you think it was *easy* for me to turn her away? You are still little more than a boy, Philip. What can you know of these things?"

"I know you considered me enough of a man to tempt me with them once."

There was a long moment of silence.

Marcus averted his burning eyes, his hands clenching into hard fists. How dare Philip speak so to him, reminding him? His cocky slave would never remember his place. But, it was still the truth. He *had* tempted Philip with pleasures, even as he himself was tempted that afternoon. If Cleotas's motives had been to test him, it was only just.

He could not bring himself to speak. His pride was sorely wounded, but his conscience would not allow him to rebuke Philip. *He is your brother as much as he is your slave. Don't be angry because he has told you the truth.*

Philip raised his eyes. He seemed suddenly ashamed. "My apologies, Marcus. I…" He paused, apparently faltering to find the right words. "I did not mean to remind you of the past. I only meant that I do know what it is you are tempted with. You are not alone."

Marcus softened. Philip still had a talent for riling him. But, somehow, the meek apology melted his irritation. "I understand, Philip."

Philip seemed to hesitate.

Marcus felt a slight laugh rising in his throat. "You may as well speak freely with me, Philip, now that you've already begun."

Philip looked down. "I sense it will be difficult for you here. I do not disrespect your new father; I only comprehend the temptations you are going to be faced with."

Marcus's gaze drifted once more over the city. "I will be faced with temptation wherever I go, Philip. It is not only here." He shifted his gaze to look fully at him. "But I do understand."

"I will pray for you."

"As I will pray for you." Marcus refused to allow his pride free rein. Slave though he was, Philip was his fellow-believer and the one who had brought him to Christ. He forced himself on. "I-I was wrong a moment ago. You have many temptations also. As surely as you pray for my strength, I will pray for yours."

"I thank you." Philip paused, a hint of a smile deepening around the corners of his mouth. "You are changing, Marcus."

Marcus's mouth twitched. "If you knew how much I wanted to hit you a moment ago, you would not think so."

"I'm grateful you didn't."

Marcus smiled a little, easing his gravity. "I do mean to treat you more as a brother than a slave, Philip. I do not say it will be easy; Romans do not break habits overnight. But, God helping me, I will not put off my obligation to you as the one I owe so much any longer."

"You owe me nothing, Marcus."

Marcus shook his head. "You have suffered much at my hands. Even had you not been the one who brought me to Christ, that fact still remains. It is my resolve you shall never know the sorrows in this new household that you knew in the old."

"That means a great deal to me." Philip looked abruptly away, but Marcus saw that his eyes glistened. His voice was choked. "My father would rejoice to see you dealing so kindly with me."

Marcus felt a familiar ache seized his throat. He looked down, squeezing his strong hands and watching the muscles ripple up his tanned arms. At times, he hated his own strength, knowing what pain he had inflicted.

But, those hands that had shed so much innocent blood were *clean*.

"He will know someday, Philip. He may know now."

"I know, my lord." Philip drew a long breath. Marcus saw the effort he made to smile. "At any rate, he knows I have forgiven you."

Marcus slowly placed his hands on Philip's upper arms, gripping them in the Roman fashion of an embrace. He had done so with Seneca, with dozens of men he did not even know. It was the least he could do for Philip.

"And, that, Philip, means more to me than you could ever know."

Part II

For I am persuaded, that neither death, nor life, nor
angels, nor principalities, nor powers, nor things
present, nor things to come,
Nor height, nor depth, nor any other creature, shall
be able to separate us from the love God, which is in
Christ Jesus our Lord.

~Romans 8:38-39~

Chapter Twenty

66 Anno Domini – Five Years Later

The hot Italian sun glistened off the scarlet and bronze attire of a military tribune. His tanned, handsome countenance shone with perspiration, trickling beneath the crested helmet strapped to his head.

He strode down the *Vicus Jugarius* towards a colossal mansion, bronzed, well-built legs protruding beneath his soldier's tunic. Treading lightly up the steps, he laid a strong hand over the short *gladius* swinging rhythmically at his side.

Inside the cool domus, he exhaled deeply.

"Great Caesars! This heat is enough to madden a man!"

A young man of some nineteen years was seated by the sparkling fountain playing at one end of the pool. He rose to his feet, crossing his hands on his chest in swift salute. "I have refreshments laid out in the library for you, my lord."

"If I survive long enough to partake of them. Help me out of this accursed armor." As he spoke, Marcus unclasped his long cloak and threw it unceremoniously on a marble bench beside the pool.

Philip moved forward. With the deftness of experience, he unstrapped the heavily-decorated breastplate and removed it. Laying it aside, he returned for the plumed helmet.

Clad only in his padded tunic, Marcus stretched his arms out to their full length, bringing them over his wet, close-cropped hair. "*Eia!* I arrived none too soon. You say refreshments are laid out in the library?"

"Yes, my lord. Your father is there also. He has been asking for you."

"I will not keep him waiting." Marcus gestured to his cast-aside armor. "Take those miserable trappings away. You may serve me directly afterward."

Having given his directions, Marcus strode briskly through the atrium to the library. Throwing open the door, he lifted his arm in greeting.

"All hail, noble Cleotas Aeneas, beloved senator and father!"

"Marcus." Cleotas looked up from his scroll with an amused smile. "The gods favor you." Then, with a keen glance, "You are rather warm, I see."

"An excellent observation. But, then, it is the fate of those who choose to *labor* for their occupation. Others, I see, are content to lounge the day away."

Cleotas laughed, tossing away his scroll. "You chose your own profession, Marcus; I chose mine."

"Truth. And I would not exchange mine for any other." Marcus poured out a goblet of honeyed wine and sipped its icy sweetness before continuing. "Still, I admit days such as this make me regret I ever chose the active life of a soldier."

"Be grateful you are a tribune of the Praetorian Guard. Many of your more unfortunate fellows are wasting away in Brittanicus and Jerusalem."

Marcus threw himself down upon a couch. Absently, he removed the silver bands encircling his wrists. "You speak truly, father. But, whether in Rome or Judea, there are still duties to be performed. My voice is hoarse from a counsel with my centurions today."

"And the dungeon below the palace? Did any of your men relieve the guard stationed there today?"

Marcus caught the sudden change in Cleotas's voice. "Possibly. Why do you ask?"

Cleotas motioned to his cast-aside scroll. "Your fellow Christians are being captured and tortured at an alarming rate. It seems Nero is still bent on wringing a confession from one of them."

Marcus was silent. A great fire had ravished Rome two years ago, but its fervent heat and fury were imprinted upon his mind as clearly if it had been yesterday. Fire was no respecter of grandeur, and the Circus Maximus had been among the many colossal structures and homes burnt to the ground.

Emperor Nero has instigated the rumor the Christians had deliberately started the blaze. Marcus felt a wave of indignant fury rush through him at the thought. The Vestal Virgins could not have been more innocent.

It made little difference to those hungry for the blood of Christus-followers.

"Many of them will be sent to the Flavian Amphitheatre, I suppose?"

"Yes." Cleotas turned his eyes upon him with a burning sensation Marcus could fairly feel. "Marcus, are you never afraid you might be next?"

"Anything is possible these days. Still, I am a soldier of Rome. My loyalty to her is unchallenged. I do not think my superiors have ever had any grounds for suspecting me."

"What of the centurions and legionaries under your command?"

"Their place is to obey, not to think, Cleotas. You know that as well as I. And my commands seldom infers of my faith."

Cleotas arose to regain his scroll. Contemplatively, he tapped it into his palm. "Still, you must be cautious, Marcus. Caesar's dispositions are unforeseeable. And he is not afraid to execute those closest to him."

"I do not know that *Caesar* is safe himself, father." Marcus spoke dryly. He again sipped from the cold contents of his goblet, attempting to wash away his darkening mood.

Cleotas looked a moment at him. "I know Nero has little of your respect, my son. But, if danger threatens him, it is your duty to speak of it."

"I agree. But there is nothing to say, excepting vague whisperings and rumors." Marcus paused in contemplation. "And it is not for me to speak poorly of my superiors."

"Then you do not deny these whisperings issue from those in high places?"

"No. But neither will I acknowledge that they do. I will only say Nero may not always possess the popularity of the world—or of his Praetorian Guard."

There was a fleeting moment of silence.

In his heart, Marcus knew Cleotas respected the emperor no more than he himself did. He was a known murderer, a man whose sensual and demonic passions wreaked havoc on all those who opposed his designs.

Some even dared to whisper he was losing his reason.

But it was not for those reasons alone Cleotas disliked him. It had only been last year the divine emperor had forced Seneca to commit suicide for the unreasonable charge of treason. However innocent, Seneca had proudly severed several veins, thus suffering an agonizing death by blood loss. That circumstance had forever altered Cleotas's allegiance to Nero, however little he spoke of it.

Marcus thought it best to lighten the subject. He sat down his goblet, striking a brisk mannerism. "A new cohort arrives in the *Castra Praetoria* tomorrow. The prefect has assigned them to my legion."

Interest lightened Cleotas's eyes, dispelling the dark expression overshadowing their pupils. He leaned forward.

"I suppose you will be on hand to observe their reception?"

"It is my custom, yes." Marcus turned as Philip appeared in the door. "Ah, there you are. Well?"

"Begging your pardon, but are you planning on attending the meeting tonight?"

"Yes. Fetch my cape; I will be with you in a moment." Marcus turned back to Cleotas. "I see I am not to be allowed leisure, father."

Cleotas's eyes had followed Philip's departure from the room, but he now raised them with a slightly impatient expression. "And do you allow a slave to command you, Marcus? Stay at home for once and be comfortable. Jove, the priests of Venus are no more devoted than you!"

Marcus picked up his bands, clasping them around his tanned wrists. "And their dedication is sadly pointless, Cleotas." He stopped abruptly, seeing the look that flitted across his adopted father's face. "My apologies, sir. You know—"

Cleotas waved his hand. "You do not offend me, Marcus. I know your zeal for your God. And you know I have little faith of my own."

Marcus paused beside his father's couch. Instinctively, he knew Cleotas wished he would remain at home. They saw precious little of each other since his appointment as a Praetorian Tribune. But, duty called.

And there were additional, more appealing factors to be considered.

"I will not stay long tonight, Cleotas." Marcus met Cleotas's hand in farewell, gripping his forearm. "I bid you *vale*."

"*Vale*, Marcus."

Marcus turned, exiting the library with swift steps. Even when off duty, it seemed he could never shake the soldier's firm stride.

Nor would he wish to.

He would never worship Rome's gods. He was a Christian, and her eagles would never again reign uppermost in his heart and mind. But, nonetheless, he was proud to be an officer of the greatest military force in the world, a tribune of her most elite company of soldiers. The Praetorian Guard had a reputation as highly-skilled men of war. He was gratified to be a leading member of her prowess.

Philip was dutifully awaiting him in the atrium, his master's scarlet cloak slung over one arm.

Marcus approached, allowing him to throw the garment over his shoulders. Waving off Philip's attempts to do it for him, he clasped the folds around his chest and drew one corner over his arm.

He glanced sidelong at Philip as he made his preparations. Five years ago, when he had first come to the Aeneas household, he had had the ring filed from his slave's neck. To this day, he was grateful he had taken that step. It had done much towards easing their positions into something he could truly call friendship.

Finished, Marcus led the way out into the humid outdoors. The sun was setting against the horizon of Rome's colossal structures, but the air was still thick and heavy. Mosquitoes buzzed around his perspiring face as soon as he stepped out, and he brushed them absently aside.

The well-known trek to the home of Daniel did not take long. Marcus lightly rapped on the door. Beside him, he saw Philip's deep blue eyes scanning the darkening street for any nosy neighbors who might summon the city guard.

The possibility was slim. Marcus was in uniform, and it was unlikely anyone would suspect a soldier of Rome and his slave. Still, caution was of the utmost importance.

Particularly when men such as Nero rule.

The door swung open, allowing the two young men to enter. Marcus led the way, giving his whispered greeting to the doorkeeper. "Peace be with you."

"Peace, brothers."

Philip lingered behind to speak with the doorkeeper. Marcus continued on without him. Standing in the entry of the inner room they met in, his dark eyes scanned the company of believers.

Most had already gathered. Simeon. Daniel. Two or three legionaries from one of his cohorts.

He recognized the soldiers instantly, and they paused in their conversation as his eyes rested on them. They began to rise and salute, but Marcus lifted his hand. Among Christians–particularly at the meetings—there were no titles, no differentiation between male and female, slave or free.

They were all one in Christ.

Behind him, Marcus felt Philip brush his shoulder. It was time for the meeting to begin. His heart pounding ever so slightly, he stepped forward into the room. Finding an empty bench, he seated himself, continuing to scan the dimly-lit room.

She was not there.

Philip sat down beside him, leaving room for one more occupant.

Daniel stood up, clearing his throat. An instant hush fell over the softly murmuring congregation and every eye turned on him.

"Peace, brothers. With your consent, I thought it profitable to begin tonight's meeting with one of the psalms. I will begin with the ninety-first. *He that dwelleth in the secret place of the Most High shall abide under the shadow of the Almighty...*"

Marcus caught his breath. His attention was diverted from the beauty of the psalm, caught by a more alluring subject.

Moriah stood in the doorway. Her entrance was noiseless, but, to Marcus, the pealing of all his legion's trumpets could not have announced her presence more fittingly.

She balanced a basket of bread on her hip, her attention fixed upon Daniel. She waited reverently for him to finish, smiling openly on the cluster of children seated at his feet.

They were the only members she seemed to notice.

Glancing from his peripheral vision, Marcus saw all three legionaries watching her. Obviously, their attention was no more fixed on the psalm than his was. He felt his blood begin to simmer. What he would not give to pull rank on them. But that would be unfair. Attempting to cool down, he reminded himself they had as much right as he to attempt to win Moriah's heart.

As Daniel read on, Marcus let his mind go. Moriah had been a lovely girl when he had first met her. Now, five years later, she was an even more beautiful woman. She was of average height, carrying a trim, shapely form. Her features were more defined, more womanly, but she continued to bear a pure, innocent expression.

She was also entirely unmarried.

Marcus knew Moriah had had her chances at marriage. But she seemed content to wait, waiting for a Christian man of flawless character to sweep her off her feet.

Her evident resolve only deepened Marcus's conviction he could never be good enough to win her. He had remained pure since his conversion, had walked uprightly in all his ways. But he knew she remembered his past.

The psalm complete, Moriah stepped forward to pass out bread and wine for communion. A single goblet was circulated around the room. Marcus sipped of its contents, pausing in silent remembrance of the blood his Savior had shed so he could be clean.

As Moriah brought the bread around, she paused at the bench. Her hazel eyes warmed with a soft smile, and she broke off a piece of the unleavened bread for Philip.

Marcus saw Philip lift his eyes with gentle warmth, saw their hands brush as he took the bread from her hand. Their shared look seemed to linger before she finally turned away and offered the basket to Marcus.

Lifting his eyes, Marcus looked at her, but her gaze was not fixed on him. She seemed impatient for him to help himself so she could move on. Fighting his frustration, he took a piece from the basket, and she moved gracefully away.

Marcus glanced sidelong at Philip. The young man was quiet and subdued, partaking of his communion with all the reverence of one zealous for his faith. He looked the perfect Christian, serene and dutiful.

It was little wonder he found such favor with Moriah.

The passing years had been good to Philip. A young man of some nineteen years, he was respected throughout the Christian community as an exemplar of the faith. His diligence to the meetings was unrivaled, his good works and purity unsurpassed.

And his Christian attributes were far from marred by long-faced homeliness. Good looks were also on his side.

The Britons had not ceased to find admiration in fashionable Rome, and Philip was a true son of his race. His sweeping, close-cut blonde hair, fair skin, and blue eyes attracted attention wherever he went. He was tall, standing an inch or two above Marcus. He trained in the Baths or at the barracks every day, and his sinewy muscles matched, if not surpassed, his master's.

Marcus grimaced dryly. It was good Philip was no longer the rebellious little cur he had once been. Had his fiery temper persisted, there would be no curtailing him now.

But, both fortunately and unfortunately for him, Philip was no longer that same hotheaded Briton. He was still governed by spirited courage, but was also somehow very calm and self-possessed.

The final prayer was pronounced, and Marcus looked up in time to see Philip look across the room at Moriah. She met his eyes with her usual smile, the beautiful color flooding her face.

Marcus averted his eyes.

"In the name of the Jesus our Lord, Amen."

The hot sun beamed down on the perspiring cohort, standing at parade attention. Under the sweltering rays, their polished armor glistened, sparkling with dazzling intensity from the unified mirrors of hundreds of breastplates.

Astride his horse, Marcus surveyed the cohort with narrowed eyes. This new company of legionaries was fresh. According to the *prefect*, the majority of the men had only recently returned from their *probatio*, or, basic training.

Their first few weeks within the Roman army had been good to them. Marcus surveyed their tanned, muscular arms, gripping their *pilums* with taut rigidness. They were well-built, well-disciplined machines.

Throughout the whole cohort, not a muscle moved. The legionaries gazed ahead of them, unseeing, unblinking.

Marcus dismounted, throwing the reins to a slave. His centurions closed in behind him, silently following his tread.

Marcus strode to the head of the company. The centurion of the cohort raised his arm in stiff salute.

"Hail, Aeneas."

"Centurion." Marcus raised his arm in salute. "I welcome you to the *Castra Praetoria*."

"Thank you, tribune."

Marcus gestured to the cohort. "These men have recently returned from their *probatio*. What is their character?"

"They are well-trained and disciplined, tribune. None are sickly, none unruly."

"We will soon see." Marcus turned his eyes on the men. He walked down the first line of legionaries, the centurion and his officers falling in behind and around him. As he walked by them, the legionaries brought their *pilums* stiffly back in silent salute, returning it to its outstretched position as soon as he passed.

Up close, they were even fresher in appearance. Some looked no more than seventeen years old. None were over twenty-five.

Marcus lifted his voice to be clearly heard. "Men, I welcome you to the *Castra Praetoria*. You have officially joined the Praetorian Guard, the highest trained company of soldiers in our army. Do not abuse this privilege. You are here to serve the government, the people of Rome."

Marcus paused, allowing his words to sink in. "You will find this is no pleasure excursion. Your station in Rome is no less arduous than one of a combative nature. You will train, you will *work*."

Silence hovered in the air. Marcus turned on his heel. Taking the reins of his horse, he swung into the saddle. "Centurion, have the men fall out. Dismiss all but the first century. I want to see them drilling in paired combat."

The centurion turned, his shouted commands reverberating barrack walls.

"Century one, fall out! Cohort, to the right, face, march!"

The simultaneous echo of marching feet filled the air. Rhythmically, the cohort exited the training grounds, escorted by the senior centurion. Under the shouted directions of their commander, the remaining century disbursed.

The legionaries laid aside their parade weapons, replacing them with doubly heavy dummy swords and wickerwork shields. Forming into pairs, they began to train, wielding their wooden swords in offensive strikes and counter strikes.

Marcus watched their drills with a keen, experienced eye. The soldiers were young and raw to actual combat, but they had obviously trained arduously during their *probatio*.

Well-rounded, tanned biceps protruded beneath the legionaries' scarlet tunics, glistening with perspiration. Their calf muscles stretched and taut, they practiced thrusting their *gladii* beneath the shields of their opponent.

One particular legionary gradually caught Marcus's eye. At first with casual attention, then with growing interest, he studied his movements.

The legionary was decidedly youthful. Fresh-faced and boyishly good-looking, Marcus deemed him no more than seventeen years of age. Still, he had the vigor of a wildcat.

As he watched, the young legionary thrust his wooden sword up beneath his opponent's wicker shield. The objective was an enemy's stomach or beneath the waist, and it became apparent the plucky young man found his target. With an indiscernible exclamation, the defeated soldier dropped his shield. He reeled back, only half-muffling his groans.

Marcus felt an amused smile lurk around the corners of his mouth. Whoever he was, the young legionary was strong and shrewd. An idea began to play in his mind, and he turned to the centurion below him.

"Centurion, have that stripling brought here."

With a wordless salute, the centurion made a sign to his optio. At a quick stride, the optio weaved his way among the combating men and made a quick gesture to the young legionary.

"You are summoned before the tribune."

Even at the distance between them, Marcus saw the flicker of apprehension that crossed the young legionary's face.

Small wonder.

Marcus knew what it was he dreaded. The faintest possibility of harsh discipline would chill the staunchest heart. Among the ranks of Rome's army, soldiers often feared their commanders more than the enemy.

Flanked by the optio and centurion, the young legionary approached Marcus. Respectfully, his eyes uplifted to Marcus's face, he brought his arm across his chest in salute.

"All hail, tribune."

Marcus met his gaze. Up close, the young man's eyes were a deep green shade, their luster steadfast and honest. He recognized his fighting spirit, his vigorous courage. But there was something else that drew him to the young man, something he could not understand.

"What is your name?"

"Alexander Lucianus, tribune."

"You seem a soldier of worth." Marcus paused. "How long have you been among the ranks of Rome?"

"I enlisted several months ago, during the festival of Mars."

"Then you have made good use of your time. Or have you trained with the gladiators?"

"Only slightly, tribune. Our century received some instruction from a *lanista* once before we were summoned here."

Marcus glanced down at the centurion. "I would see this stripling in further combat, centurion." He returned his gaze to Alexander's forthright countenance, meeting his eyes. "Drill with him yourself."

"Yes, tribune." The centurion raised his sword against his chest in quick salute.

His face tinged by puzzlement, Alexander took the *gladius* handed to him by the optio. Both men picked up their shields, and, with easy nonchalance, the centurion advanced to meet his inferior.

Marcus leaned slightly forward in the saddle. He had recognized worthy soldiers before. He only hoped he was not mistaken this time.

For all Marcus's keen observations, Alexander portrayed no trace of hesitance at facing his own centurion. With a visible inhale, he immediately took the battle stance, standing with his left foot and shield forward. With his right foot turned at the angle of a wrestler, he cut an imposing figure, ready to jab his opponent with the shield and deliver a fatal blow with the *gladius* clenched tightly in his uplifted right hand.

Without warning, the centurion lowered his head in battle stance. Stealthily advancing, he raised his sword and brought it swiftly down.

Alexander was ready for him, and countered the thrust with his shield. He struck a blow of his own before safely circling to evade the swift plunge of the centurion's sword at his unarmored back.

Stooping, thrusting, circling, the two men sparred for several minutes. The others, evoked to interest, ceased their drills to watch.

Marcus felt his admiration for the young legionary growing. His amusement also deepened, seeing that the centurion was growing frustrated. What should have been an easy victory for an experienced officer was quickly becoming an embarrassing challenge.

So far, his intuition in Alexander's abilities was proving accurate.

Impatience registered clearly on the centurion's countenance. With each successful counter-strike of his opponent, his anger mounted visibly. His stance became one of wrathful vengeance, mortified by his delayed victory before the eyes of the century.

Marcus knit his brows disapprovingly, knowing from long experience that no soldier who allowed himself to lose patience could safely govern his battle maneuvers.

He was right.

The centurion brought down his sword with particularly heavy force, his thrust fairly screaming with pent-up frustration.

Alexander caught the thrust with his shield, forcibly throwing his opponent back. The act momentarily disoriented the centurion, destroying his balance and battle composure. In one swift move, Alexander stepped up to deliver the final blow.

The edge of his *gladius* caught the centurion a little to the right of his brow, directly where the crested helmet gave way to leathery skin. Marcus saw the lightness of the blow and respected the self-control Alexander maintained over battle instinct.

Even still, a thin rivulet of blood trickled down the centurion's face. It was quickly coupled with a wave of red-hot anger.

"You numskull! How dare you draw blood on me! I'll–"

Several choice words ended the furious outburst. Choked with rage, the centurion snatched his staff from the hand of his optio. He raised it, clearly intent upon delivering the military discipline of *castigatio*.

"Halt!" Marcus felt a wave of indignation tingle through his body. No centurion would hit a soldier because he chanced to humiliate him. "In the legion under my command, no man will be punished for doing well."

"It is insolence, tribune." The centurion sputtered with anger. He gripped the vine with doubled intensity, an artery bulging in his neck. "He–"

"Silence." Marcus leaned forward in the saddle, his eyes narrowed. "If you have been mortified, it is to my charge, not his." He shifted his gaze to the quiet, open countenance of Alexander. "You have done well, soldier."

Alexander brought his arm against his chest in silent salute. He said nothing, but a visible tinge of gratitude warmed his deep green eyes. Marcus glanced back at the red-faced centurion.

"If he is not already, make him head of his *contubernium*. That is all; dismissed."

The centurion's face contorted. His veins bulging with intensified wrath, he brought his arm up in salute. "Yes, tribune."

Marcus flicked his mount with the reins, spurring the animal into motion. As he rode from the training ground, he glanced back.

Alexander stood watching him go. Marcus could recognize the signs of loyalty in his soldiers as he knew the palm of his own hand.

Its fierceness in the admiring eyes of the young legionary was unmistakable.

Chapter Twenty-One

In the coolness of his quarters, Marcus laid down his pen. Waiting a moment for the ink to dry, he rolled up the scroll and laid it with his other accounts.

The duty of keeping records was his least favorite task as a tribune, but, fortunately, he did not fulfill it alone. His centurions were even busier recording events and proceedings than he was.

Marcus poured himself a glass of cool water. Tipping his head back, he swallowed thirstily, allowing the liquid to trickle down his chin. Satisfied, he wiped his mouth with the back of his hand.

"Great Caesars! At last that is done."

Across the room, Philip briefly looked up. He sat cleaning his master's armor, polishing it to shimmering brightness. "You are on duty tonight, are you not?"

"Yes." Marcus set his cup down within arm's distance. "Why do you ask?"

"I pledged Daniel I would assist him with handing out bread to the poor before night fell. Still, if you need me here, there is time to send him a message."

"No, no, you must go." Marcus paused. A secret fear gnawed at his heart, vexing him. It was a torment he suffered from often of late. As if casually, he again picked up his pen. "Tell me, do you suppose Moriah will be there?"

"I cannot say for sure, my lord, but she generally is. You know her works of charity among the poor are beyond measure."

"Yes." Marcus bit his lip, vexed. Philip's apparent indifference to his question was fairly maddening. He confided nothing of what he actually felt for Moriah. His praise for her was that of any Christian who was renowned for good works.

Philip placed his master's armor and cloak in its assigned place with easy competency. Slinging his own cape over his shoulder, he paused at Marcus's desk.

"Farewell, my lord. I will return in a few hours."

Offering his usual salute, he strode across the room.

Marcus felt his frustration rising. It boiled inside of him, venting itself before he could stop it. "Philip!"

Philip stopped in the doorway. Turning, he stepped a little towards Marcus. "Yes?"

Marcus looked down at his folded hands, squeezing them together. The uncertainty of Philip's feelings for Moriah was killing him. Day after day, it seemed, he watched them together. He saw their unified devotion to Christ, their youthful purity and good works. They were both perfect exemplars of Christianity, upright, strong in the faith.

And what was he?

Yes, he was a Christian, but little else. He was a young man with a scarred past, a past of murder and lust he knew Moriah remembered all too well.

Even beyond all that, he had the instinctive feeling she despised his occupation. Violence was his life. He trained his men with brutal insensitivity, ordered them flogged when they failed to meet the full measure of Roman competency and submission. He oversaw the crucifixion of slaves, he fought, and he *killed*.

Above all, he protected the person of Nero.

Why should he wonder that a sweet spirit like Moriah shunned his company and affections? Could he blame her for lavishing her respect on a man such as Philip?

"Philip, I–"

Marcus could not bring himself to say more. Mingled pride and fear of the truth kept him from it. After all, if Philip did love Moriah, what would it profit him to know? He would not mar Philip's joy, the servant whose prayers had won him to Christ. And he loved both of them too dearly to shatter their happiness and wellbeing.

"Tell Daniel and Moriah I bid them joy in the Lord."

Philip's striking smile flashed across his face. "Of course. I would have done so even if you had not asked." He laughed ever so slightly. "Do not look so grave, Marcus. I know you would like to offer them your greetings yourself, but you will see them soon enough."

Marcus forced a smile to his lips. "You are right, of course." He looked down, continuing to guise his heartache beneath quiet comradeship. "Go—it is growing late. And I would not have the brethren say I kept you from attending to the work of the Lord."

Philip raised his hand, the amused smile still deepened on his handsome countenance. Swiftly, he left the room.

Marcus continued to look down. In sudden frustration, he snatched up his quill pen and snapped it in two, hurling the pieces against the wall. Slowly, his anger expended, he leaned forward on the desk, resting his head in his hands.

The crashing sound of a spear being struck across a buckler quickly aroused him. He sat erect as the guard at his door entered.

"A legionary to see you, tribune."

"Very well." Marcus straightened himself erect, lapsing into the stern commander. "Send him in."

Briskly saluting, the guard left the room. In a matter of seconds, a legionary entered, bringing his arm up against his chest in respectful salute.

"All hail, tribune."

Marcus glanced briefly over him before speaking. *Alexander Lucianus.* The afternoon's work had almost erased the memory of the valiant young stripling from his mind. "Yes?"

"My centurion orders me to report that your command has been fulfilled and to give you this scroll of today's proceedings."

Marcus rose to take the scroll, his eyes flitting briefly over its contents. Still stretching it open, he half-glanced up, again surveying Alexander's youthful face. The deep green eyes that met his in soldierly respect were striking, set against such a forthright, open demeanor.

Again, the feeling crossed him that this was no ordinary legionary.

"My command that you be made head of your *contubernium*? Very well; dismissed."

Alexander wordlessly saluted, his armor reverberating ever so slightly against his metal-banded forearm. Marcus half-turned, then paused, noticing Alexander made no move to go.

"Well? Have you not fulfilled your orders?"

"Yes, tribune, and I crave your pardon. I could not go without first thanking you for your generosity with me today."

"It was no generosity, soldier." Marcus resumed his seat, fixing Alexander with a meaningful gaze. "In my eyes, reward has its place alongside discipline. You chanced to do well; you were rewarded."

He paused a moment. "But I do acknowledge your gratitude. It is becoming in a soldier." He gestured slightly. "Dismissed."

Alexander turned in silent obedience and strode briskly to the door. In its entry, he turned. As if unconsciously, he crossed his hands upon his breast. "Peace be with you."

Marcus's mind seemed to snap. Had his eyes deceived him? The most promising legionary in his new cohort had forgotten the military salute in his presence. But, it was not that—unbelievable as it was—that had captured his attention.

He found himself on his feet, his voice stern and angry. "One moment, soldier."

Alexander stiffened into machine-like rigidity. Despite his warrior stance, the confused apprehension that filled his tanned face was unmistakable. "Yes, tribune?"

Marcus closed the gap between them. If anyone knew how to exercise the powers of a threatening close presence, he did. "What was that sign you just made?"

With a strange rapidity, all color washed from Alexander's face. He stood motionless, erect and rigid, his eyes locked into Marcus's dark ones.

Silence permeated the room.

Marcus took a step nearer, his face mere inches away from the young man's colorless features. His heart beat fast against his chest, pulsing with the overpowering desire to know the truth.

"Answer me."

Alexander's manly throat constricted, swallowing. He looked unblinkingly into Marcus's searching pupils. "It was a sign of my faith, tribune."

Marcus narrowed his eyes. "What *faith*, soldier?"

Again, Alexander seemed unable to speak. He opened his lips, then, closed them, powerless in the ominous presence of his commander.

Marcus refused to soften his stern tones. His heart yearned to speak quietly, to assure Alexander he had nothing to fear. But, he would not. He would not make the way of escape any easier. Alexander was a soldier of Rome. More importantly, he was a soldier of a Higher Power.

He must answer as one.

Give him courage, Lord.

"I have seen that sign many times, boy, and I know-well what it means." Marcus allowed his voice to darken, his features chiseled in austere warning. "Do not play the fool with me. Stand and answer: are you a Christus-follower?"

Alexander raised his head ever so slightly. Unblinkingly, he continued to meet the burning gaze fixed upon him. "I am, tribune."

The tones were not unbecomingly bold, nor fearful. Marcus felt his heart warm. Here was a true soldier. Still, something pricked his heart to continue.

"Do you dare to answer me so? I could at this moment send you to a death by torture. I give you one chance, boy. Recant this idiotic folly, and I will spare you."

Something about the threat seemed to spark new spirit in Alexander. His eyes flashed slightly, tightening his jaw line. "No, my lord."

Marcus violently raised his hand. Alexander stiffened, his chin upraised. Again, his eyes flashed, anticipating the blow. Like a flood, sudden color washed over his face, passion overpowering his quiet respect.

"Strike me, tribune. Flog me, torture me, send me to the arena. I know the things you can do to me. But I will *not* denounce my Jesus."

Slowly, Marcus lowered his hand. His heart was touched as it had not been for many days. Abruptly, his throat constricted, aching.

How little he had known how true his instincts about Alexander really were. He had sensed he was a good soldier.

He now knew Alexander was also a courageous brother.

"I am always pleased to find a man who is not ashamed to own his beliefs, Alexander." Marcus knew the simple quietness of his tones was a bewildering contrast to his former severity. "Well done."

Indescribable shock flooded Alexander's white countenance.

Marcus continued to meet his eyes, crossing his hands upon his chest. "Peace be with you, my brother, in the name of our Savior."

Alexander stood momentarily speechless. Abruptly, the blood washed over his face. He turned away, hiding his face in his hands.

"Great God." Marcus heard his almost unintelligible groan. "And if I had denied You?"

Marcus stepped forward. For once, he had no compulsion against laying aside his military authority. He laid his hand lightly on Alexander's shoulder, compassionate.

"I often test my soldiers, Alexander, but you must know I seldom feel the satisfaction of seeing one pass inspection as well as you have today."

Alexander turned. He straightened into soldierly erectness, but all of his military training could not mask his overwrought feelings. He swallowed, his throat constricting.

"Tribune, I–"

He paused, apparently unable to speak.

Marcus surveyed him with understanding. "Your loss for words is reasonable, legionary. One would not presume to believe I am a Christian. Still, it is the truth."

"I beg sincere pardon of you, my lord tribune." Alexander's eyes sought his, his low voice tense. "You do not test me? You are not trying to take the lives of my brethren?"

Marcus saw the searching appeal in his pupils. Again, he placed his hand on his shoulder. "No. I swear by our Lord and Savior I am who I say I am. But, if you do not believe me now, you soon will. Time will reveal I make no offerings to Jupiter."

Gradually, Alexander's breathing regained a normal rhythm. His eyes momentarily closed. "Praise God."

Marcus let his hand fall, offering it to him. Alexander's gaze drifted up from his metal-banded forearm to his eyes, half-shaking his head.

"No, my tribune, I—"

Marcus stopped him. "Do not be afraid to take my hand, Alexander. I am more than your commander. I am also your brother."

With slow, respectful hesitance, Alexander took his hand.

Marcus grasped his forearm. Looking into Alexander's green eyes, he sensed his obedience was provoked by fear. Contemplatively, he loosed him.

"You are afraid of me. That is right for a soldier of Rome. But, when we are alone, you must remember we are equal in Christ."

"Why did you do it?" Alexander's voice was soft.

"Test you?" Marcus turned away, pouring out a goblet of wine. "I wanted to see what you were made of, if you were as courageous for your faith as you are on the field of combat." He paused. "And I consider my own life too valuable to risk losing it to a so-called Christian who is not willing to die for his beliefs."

Alexander remained silent. He seemed half-desirous to speak, but could not completely forget that he was standing in the presence of his austere commander.

Marcus drew near him, stretching out the goblet. "Drink, Alexander. We will share wine, you and I."

Alexander took the goblet. He brought it to his lips, swallowing.

Marcus took it from him and lifted it to his own mouth. He did the unthinkable by sharing the same goblet with a humble legionary, but it was an act he was more than willing to make for a brother.

Even as You drank of a far deeper cup of suffering for me, Jesus.

The loyalty he had seen earlier in Alexander reappeared in his eyes, warm and honest. In his heart, Marcus knew he had made a friend in this brother.

And, in those volatile times, it was a friendship he would need.

"Just once, Alexander. Can you not down me even once?" Marcus's laughing voice filled the sand pit training arena.

Alexander, stripped to the waist, was shiny with perspiration. He drew a hand across his forehead, breathing heavily. "You mock me, tribune. You have downed me four times already."

"And the statutes of wrestling require only three." From his position on the sidelines, Philip uttered a ringing laugh. "I wonder you dared take on your commander."

"He challenged *me*, my friend." Alexander looked up into Marcus's twinkling eyes. "And I shall not be such a fool as to accept him again."

Marcus laughed. He strode across the sandy pit and picked up a rough towel, patting his face and neck. "I only wanted to ensure my position as an officer had not weakened my muscles, Alexander. It has been some time since I grappled with a hearty young legionary."

"You shall not have much opportunity again unless you command me, my lord."

Marcus chuckled. Lightly, he threw Alexander's tunic across the arena at him. "You should wrestle with Philip someday. If I make you cringe, he will make you beg for mercy."

Alexander rubbed his arms ruefully. "Then may God forbid that day ever comes." He pulled his tunic over his head. "Great Caesars! I do not take defeat well, even at the hands of my tribune."

Philip went to him and good-naturedly helped him don his armor. "You are a strong and honest man, Alexander. Those qualities will take you far, regardless of anything else."

Marcus saw the look that passed between the two young men. During the last few weeks, a deep friendship had developed between Alexander and Philip. Without a doubt, Philip was already becoming an influential mentor, and Alexander made no secret of his respect for him.

But, then, he did not hide his regard and zealous loyalty for Marcus either. When off duty, he often sought his counsel. And, though his position as a legionary made it more difficult for him to lay aside respectful homage, Marcus knew their hearts were knit in friendship.

Marcus pulled his tunic over his broad shoulders. "Come, Philip, do not let your pity for Alexander cause you to forget your duties." He beckoned mirthfully. "Whose servant are you?"

Philip chuckled. He came forward and began to strap the pieces of Marcus's ornate armor onto his broad back and chest. "A thousand apologies, my master. It was the least sign of sympathy I could give my sorrowing brother."

"Enough." Marcus gave Alexander a pointed look of amusement. "He must learn to accept his defeat." Armed, he slung his cape over his shoulders, pulling one end around his arm. "That is all, legionary; dismissed."

Alexander silently saluted and left the arena. Marcus stood watching him go, tightening the silver bands on his forearms.

"He will be a good commander someday."

"Even as he is a fine Christian now." Philip's eyes also followed him. "He went yesterday with Moriah and me to distribute food among the poor. His compassion was very evident."

Marcus turned slowly to face him. "You say he went with you and...and Moriah?"

"Yes."

Marcus felt a pang. No man, least of all one as manly and upright as Alexander, could fail to be attracted to Moriah. And, if she did not already love Philip, Alexander's good looks and winning, forthright character would certainly win her.

His position was only growing more and more hopeless.

Marcus's eyes wandered over the columns encircling the wrestling training arena. Like those formidable pillars, a barrier seemed forever driven between him and Moriah. Perhaps it was meant to be. He could never hope to deserve her.

"I will visit my father this afternoon." Marcus threw down his towel, resisting the urge to expend his frustration by tearing it in two. "See that my horse is saddled, Philip."

He turned away, unable to keep his strong fingers from clenching themselves into fists. A quick hand caught his arm.

"Marcus, what is it?"

Marcus turned slowly, allowing his dark eyes to meet Philip's keen blue ones.

Philip looked searchingly at him, new gravity overshadowing his features. "Your countenance has changed towards me, Marcus. Tell me what it is."

Marcus opened his lips, then, shut them. He half-turned away, unable to tell Philip all that was in his heart.

How can I, Lord? He is upright, virtuous. He would give her up to me if he knew. And I cannot bear to break both of their hearts as mine is.

"If I have done amiss, my lord, then—"

"No, no." Marcus forced a smile to his lips. "There is nothing wrong. You are too sensitive, my Philip."

Philip's eyes were still keen with searching. "I know when my master looks differently upon me."

Marcus laughed, concealing the bitterness threatening to catch his throat. "You imagine it." In the Eastern fashion, he placed an arm around Philip's neck, swiftly embracing him. "Say no more. I will return later."

Turning on his heel, Marcus strode away. He knew without looking that Philip stood watching him go.

How keenly Philip could discern his moods! But, this time, he would not share the pain that shadowed his heart, the bitterness that threatened to separate them. He would overcome it in time. And Philip must not know how he felt.

By the time Marcus had made his preparations to leave the *Castra Praetoria*, his horse was ready saddled.

Taking the reins from the slave who held them, he swung lightly into the saddle. Squeezing his muscular legs into the animal's sides, he cantered from the barracks, receiving polite salutations from the gate-guard as he exited.

The ride into the heart of Rome was a long one, but to Marcus, time flitted away with little acknowledgement. His mind was full, and the milling plebians, patricians, slaves, and peddlers who separated around his mount were one swarming mob to his unseeing eyes.

A beggar limped in front of him, and Marcus drew in rein to allow his pass. The momentary delay brought his mind from his milling thoughts to his weary body. The day had been a long one.

He straightened his shoulders, lifting a hand to his aching neck. Without warning, his eyes fell on a slender form.

Moriah.

The figure was closely covered by a long veil, but Marcus caught a glimpse of her face as she turned. Even if he hadn't, he felt certain he would have recognized her maidenly form, her graceful carriage.

His hands hesitated on the reins. Everything within him screamed out to rush to her, to speak with her. Of course it was out of the question. Masculine pride swelled in his throat. It gripped him in its powerful control, refusing to let him move.

Instead, he watched her.

Moriah moved gracefully among the produce peddlers, filling the basket she balanced on her hip. She was clearly a well-known customer. The peddlers seemed to greet her by name, offering her warm welcome to their stalls.

From his position, Marcus could detect her low, clear voice, her occasional laughter. Oh, great Caesars! What a beautiful woman she was. Her purity was clear, a clear beam of light in the sinful darkness of the noisy, crowded forum.

Without warning, Moriah looked up. By some strange chance, her eyes drifted over the scores of people between them and were lifted to his eyes. They immediately darkened, and a wave of scarlet blood flooded her face.

Marcus felt his own cheeks burn. She had seen him. More than that, she had seen how intently he was gazing upon her.

Embarrassment nearly choked him. The full reality of how he must have looked struck him. How was Moriah to know his thoughts were pure ones and not the lustful desires of any ordinary Roman officer?

Moriah turned resolutely away from him. She seemed unwilling to be further tainted by his presence. With the swiftness of a young roe, she began to mingle with the milling crowd leaving the forum.

Marcus's eyes continued to follow her, his throat aching.

Abruptly, a rich litter passed, born by four stout Gothic slaves and led by another. It momentarily blocked his view, hiding Moriah from sight.

Chapter Twenty-Two

The litter passed ruthlessly through the crowd, the Gothic slaves spurred on by the impatient commands of their master. The milling throngs opened by waves around them. No one, it seemed, was willing to risk the anger of a high-ranking patrician.

A ringing, maidenly cry suddenly echoed above the chaotic noise of the forum.

Marcus's heart took a sudden leap. His eyes scanned the street with tense searching, finding Moriah's slight form in time to see the slave leading the litter shove her unceremoniously from the path. She lost her footing and fell beneath his feet, fruit rolling from her fallen basket along the cobblestones.

A red-haze of fury dimmed Marcus's vision. The uncivilized brutes! How dare a *slave* touch her? Now was no time for inaction.

He spurred his horse forward.

Just before him, the litter abruptly stopped. A patrician leaped out, striking one of the slaves with the flat of the hand.

"Clumsy oaf! Stand back."

Amidst the crowd of curious onlookers, the patrician took Moriah's arm and drew her to her feet. "Great gods, maiden! I beg a thousand apologies. My men are too callous by far. I regret that they," and his wanton eyes passed unashamedly over her fair face, "have handled so fair a woman as you in such an uncivilized manner."

Moriah drew herself up, quickly averting her burning eyes. She pulled slightly away from the young man. "No apology is needed, my lord. I thank you for stopping."

She half-turned away, making it quite apparent she desired to go. The young nobleman only laughed and held her fast.

"Don't be in such a hurry, fair one. Allow me to make recompense for this blunder. A goblet of wine with me, perhaps?"

"I am not thirsty, my lord."

"Not thirsty, eh?" The patrician drew her a little closer. "That is strange coming from one who is more beautiful than the Vestal Virgins. But, perhaps you will allow me to make my apologies in another way. I—"

"No, my lord." Moriah pulled as far from him as his inexorable hands would allow, the hot blood dying her fair face and neck. "No recompense is needed. Please let me go."

Again, the nobleman laughed. "You are too modest. It is not every day the gods allow my litter to pass one as beautiful as you. Come to my home with me—we will settle on a price for," and his hand lightly touched her veil, "this *unfortunate* accident."

"Let me pass." Moriah spoke in a sort of cry. She struggled in his hold, her eyes searching the crowd in agonized appeal. "Let me go!"

The nobleman tightened his grip. "Nonsense, pretty one. Come—"

Enough. Marcus was grateful years of physical training had hardened his fists into balls of steel. One quick step out of the crowd, one swift blow, and the patrician was on the ground, his words cut into a sputtered grasp. Marcus placed himself at Moriah's side, laying his hand over his *gladius*.

"I think *I* am better suited to attend this young woman, you filthy swine."

Choking on his enraged expletives, the nobleman stumbled to his feet. "How dare you! Do you not know—" His words died suddenly on his lips. Slowly, his uplifted hand dropped to his side. "Marcus Virginius."

Stunned recognition flooded Marcus's mind. *Thallus.* He met his sardonic gaze for a long moment before at last breaking the silence.

"It has been many years, Thallus."

"Too many, to be certain." Thallus's cool sarcasm was unmistakable. "So, what are you now? A sweeper of the streets? Or perhaps a priest of your new...*religion?*"

Marcus felt his anger rekindling. By a great effort, he maintained an even tone. "You know very well I am the adopted son of Senator Cleotas Aeneas."

"Ah, yes. Marcus Virginius *Aeneas*." Thallus's narrowed eyes drifted over his armor-plated chest, his helmed head. "You are a legionary?"

"A *tribune*."

"And because you are a Praetorian tribune, you think you can interfere between me and this woman?" The anger in Thallus's voice mounted. "You are a fool, Marcus. What is she to you?"

The heat poured into Marcus's face. What indeed?

Only the woman I love.

The thought send warm blood flooding with burning intensity throughout Marcus's body. His heart pounded. He did not dare look at Moriah. One glance, and he knew she would sense his thoughts.

"Thallus, the maiden is the daughter of a close friend."

"A close friend!" Thallus laughed scornfully. He drew a step nearer Moriah. "Naturally, Marcus. I've seen your ways, your manner of taking your pleasure." His hand lightly brushed the side of Moriah's garment. "You will not beguile me out of my way with this woman, as you have with others."

Marcus's chest constricted. Of course Thallus would remember the past. And he had no qualms against speaking of it before the young woman they both knew was purer in heart and body than an arbutus of Capri.

Fury burned so hot he again saw red.

Through the scarlet mist, he saw Thallus's hand, rising with menacing deliberation against the folds of Moriah's garment. His smirk widened, glancing sidelong in silent challenge at Marcus. His fingers tightened, closing around her arm.

Adrenaline shot through Marcus's body. Seized by enraged strength, his hand closed on Thallus's upper arm. "Take your hands off her."

Thallus's face flamed with angry color. "I warn you, Marcus—"

"No." Marcus leaned close to Thallus, allowing his face to smolder inches away from his glinted eyes. "I warn *you*." He half-drew his *gladius*, ominously permitting his slow deliberation to create his point. "I am a soldier, Thallus. Do not challenge me."

Thallus met his fiery gaze for a full moment before relinquishing his grip on Moriah. Slowly, with a spat onto the dusty street, he backed away.

"So be it, Marcus. Play the *honorable* rescuer if you will. I will not forget. Even," and his blackened face became chillingly repugnant, "as I have forgotten nothing of the past."

Marcus made no reply. His hands fairly itched to throttle Thallus around the throat, but he satisfied himself with merely clenching them into impenetrable fists. Now was no time to quibble about the past.

With another spat, Thallus leaped into his litter. A vexed command set his slaves in motion, and the litter passed swiftly down the street. With his departure, curiosity ceased, and the milling crowd gradually dispersed.

Marcus glanced sidelong at Moriah. She was pale and he could see her hands trembled. Still, she still bore the same quiet, graceful carriage that always distinguished her.

Marcus knelt and began picking up the strewed fruit lying in all directions on the street. Little of it was bruised, and he wordlessly placed the sound produce back in Moriah's basket. Silently, Moriah joined him.

The task complete, Marcus lifted the basket to her arms.

"I thank you, Marcus." Moriah lifted her hazel eyes to his face, her voice simple. "You have dealt very kindly with me."

"It was no kindness, Moriah." Marcus spoke almost sharply. Instantly, he hated himself for it, but his mood was too riled to speak lightly. The intentions of Thallus towards the woman he loved were far too real for pacifism. "Do you think I would stand by and see a sister debauched by that foul oaf?"

Moriah momentarily averted her eyes. When she again raised them, her pupils were soft. She said nothing, but Marcus felt the quiet searching in her gaze.

Abruptly, he turned away. "I will escort you home."

"There is no need, Marcus. I—"

Marcus cut her soft protest short. "Do not argue with me, Moriah. I know the ways of men such as Thallus. He may lurk in waiting for you."

"God will protect me."

A bitter laugh caught Marcus's throat. "As He would have saved you a moment ago, I suppose."

"He did." Indignation sparkled in Moriah's lovely eyes. "Or have you forgotten you came to my rescue?"

"Exactly." Marcus took her arm. He felt grim authority sparked by her tone. Every passing minute, every recollection of Thallus's vile lasciviousness deepened his passionate ill-humor more. "And I will not stop protecting you until I have seen you safely at your father's home."

Moriah opened her lips, then, by some afterthought, shut them in a firm line. Again, averting her eyes, she balanced the basket of fruit more securely on her hip.

Marcus laid a quick restraining hand on the shoulder of a passing boy. "Take my horse to the *Castra Praetoria*, lad." He pressed a *denarius* into his hand. "Say you are sent by the Tribune Marcus Virginius Aeneas, and they will receive you."

The boy made a quick salute and took the reins of the animal. "Yes, master."

Marcus gave him a quick slap on the back in passing. With quiet authority, he gave Moriah's arm a slight pull and led her into the middle of the street.

The walk to the house of Daniel was a very silent one.

Marcus looked down at Moriah once or twice, but her gaze remained fixed straight ahead. Unblinking, soft, bordered by long brown lashes, her eyes refused to acknowledge the man at her side.

Marcus jerked his own head upright and looked forward. He set his chin, blinking. The harsh afternoon light settled on his countenance, revealing the aching pain behind his stern mask.

Was he never to be forgiven?

It is all for nothing, Lord. She will never see me as the man of honor I strive to be. I have fought, I have struggled for nothing!

Instant shame bordered on Marcus's heart. He knew he did not serve the Lord to win a woman's hand. But, oh, how many times he might have had another woman to wife. He was ready to lavish his affection and care upon the woman who would call him her husband, ready to give her every tender consideration.

Only, he knew in his heart he could never love any woman but the one at his side.

At the door of Daniel's shop, Marcus loosed Moriah's arm. She turned, her eyes cool and quiet as they met his.

"I thank you, Marcus. Your concerns were very kind."

"Give thanks to Christ." Marcus's voice was husky. By some impulsion he could not control, he leaned passionately forward and grasped her hand in his own. "Try to forget, Moriah. Forget the past. And, God help you—" his voice faltered, "try to forgive."

He loosed her with painful swiftness. Catching his breath with a ragged sound, he turned away and strode quickly from her.

Anger boiled within him during the entire walk home.

He could not pretend he was not angry, that he was not hurt. By all the Caesars in their succession, surely it was permissible for a tribune to feel pain. Would he never be rid of the torture that *woman* inflicted on him!

Marcus checked his thoughts ever so slightly. Moriah was too gentle to wish to hurt anyone. Still, she had to know in some measure what torment she was bestowing.

I have been pure, Father. Since the day You redeemed me, I have tried to walk worthily. I have confessed my sin before You. What else should I do? Tell me what I must do!

Marcus felt no response to his passion. In some respects, he was not surprised. How could he expect to know God's plan? Its vastness was unsearchable. He could only trust and hope.

His personal chiding did little to cool his temper.

He strode swiftly up the steps to the vestibule. Scarcely waiting for a slave to answer his pounded knock, he swept into the atrium.

Cleotas appeared in the library door. "Ah, Marcus! You are home at last. What kept you?"

"I was detained." Marcus maintained a low voice. "Pardon me."

Cleotas eyed him. Contemplatively, he tapped the end of his scroll into his palm. "We will speak later, Marcus. You are weary. Bathe and rest, and we will talk over refreshments."

With that and the soundness of his wisdom, Cleotas vanished. Marcus knew he sensed his adopted son's irritation. And, as always, Cleotas avoided conflict like the plague.

Yes, he would bathe. He would rest. Perhaps then his good humor would return.

"Philip!"

Philip appeared in the doorway leading to the gardens. With a look of relief washing over his face, he strode forward. "At last! I was beginning to worry about you. You said–"

"I know what I said." Marcus cut him short, his voice sharp. "Have you prepared my bath?"

Philip stood still. "No, my lord. It is your custom to bathe in the public houses."

"Did it never occur to you I might desire one here?" Marcus jerked his cape from his shoulders with angry force. He could feel the heat rising in his face. "Can nothing be done without my commanding it?"

Silence permeated the room.

Marcus felt a tinge. It had been longer than he could remember since he had rebuked Philip. It had been years since he had raised his voice in anger at him.

Philip's eyes drifted downwards. "No, my lord, I did not think of it." His quiet subservience was strikingly humble. "May I be forgiven."

Regret smote Marcus's heart, but he was in no mood for humility. "Don't just stand there like a gawking cub! You know what I desire."

Philip silently bowed. He said nothing, but Marcus saw his wary countenance as he left.

Tired frustration welled up within Marcus. Panged by the quiet whispering of his conscience, he walked slowly to the garden. Wearily, he sank onto a marble bench beside the fountain.

For many minutes, he leaned forward, his head in his hands. It seemed an eternity before the tranquil silence of the garden was at last broken.

"Your bath is prepared, my lord."

Marcus looked up. Philip stood a few paces away from him. His eyes were gravely quiet, and Marcus could feel their searching.

Could he never lose his temper with a slave without guilt?

"Thank you, Philip." Marcus rose as he spoke. He led the way inside, knowing without a glance that Philip followed him. Pain and frustration intensified with his every step. It was as if his own sandaled tread pounded the ache deeper into his heart.

In the atrium, he stopped.

He could go on like this no longer. He was weary of battling the pain, the ceaseless torture of uncertainty that bound him. Now was the time to know the truth. Once and for all.

"Philip." Marcus turned, facing the young man behind him. "I must ask you something."

Philip steadily met his gaze. "Speak on."

"I must know." Marcus struggled to find the right words. "I pray you, what-what are your intentions for marriage?"

"Marriage?"

"Yes."

Philip raised a quizzical brow. "Surely, you have not forgotten a slave cannot legally marry."

Marcus bit his lip. Philip was not making it easy on him. "You know the laws of Rome have nothing to do with this. I would recognize your marriage, even as our brethren would."

Philip laughed slightly. "I thank you for that avowal, my lord. But, even with your consent, there is no denying the fact I must have a woman to wed."

"Precisely." Marcus again felt heat creeping up his neck, around his jaw-line. "So, I beg of you, be candid with me." He felt the words escape him, rushing from his lips. "What are your intentions towards Moriah?"

Philip's amused expression melted into unmistakable confusion. Slowly, a glimmer of understanding filled his face. "You think I am in love with Moriah?"

"In a manner of speaking, well, yes."

Philip's laughter rang out, filling the atrium. "The idea is an absurd one, Marcus! How could I presume to love the woman that you, my lord and master, adore?"

Marcus felt a wave of stunned disbelief. His cheeks begin to burn. "You mean—"

"I mean that there has never been anything between Moriah and me except a mutual desire to seek and save the lost, Marcus. We work well together. She is a virtuous woman, and I do not deny I enjoy her company. But that is all. She understands that as well as I."

Marcus could feel the color rising clear into his forehead. Swiftly, he turned his head away, but he knew his embarrassment was clear. "Have I been so obvious?"

"To me, yes. I cannot answer for anyone else." Philip drew nearer. "I have known your feelings for Moriah for some years, Marcus."

Marcus said nothing for a moment. Relief and pain worked so heavily together he could scarcely command his voice. "Even still,

275

Philip, though your word has made me free, I can never have a chance of winning her."

"I do not see why."

"Have you not seen it?" Marcus turned towards him, allowing the tormented pain he felt to work in his face. "She shuns me, Philip. In five long years, in all that has transpired since my conversion, she has not forgiven me for my past."

"Marcus." Philip's voice grew abruptly firm. "You are a new creature."

"I am a *murderer*."

Philip's eyes blazed, sudden indignation washing in scarlet color over his face and neck. "By God's grace, Marcus! Will you never forget the things which are behind you?"

"And how can I forget?" Angry frustration bordered on Marcus's tone. His heart swelled, gripping his throat. "How, Philip? She will not let me."

"I cannot think Moriah has harbored bitterness against you for all these years."

Exasperation worked in Marcus's face. "You would think well of anyone, Philip. You refuse to see faults as others do. But, by the Caesars! Do not be naïve to the truth. I know, pure and virtuous as she is, Moriah has never accepted me because of the things I did to you."

Slowly, Philip's countenance quieted. "If these things are true, it would be folly indeed for Moriah to reject the hand of the godliest young man I know because of any of my past sufferings."

Marcus's throat constricted. The words echoed in his heart, tightening his chest. He half-turned away, his voice low and choked. "I am not godly, Philip."

"I disagree."

Marcus felt Philip's hand rest on his shoulder. His voice was low and gentle, the same tone he used when speaking of Christ to a nonbeliever or comforting a grieving widow.

"Whatever anyone else thinks of you, Marcus, I know the truth. I see the things you are tempted with, the things you resist for Christ's sake. I know your uprightness. You stand for Christ alone and are not ashamed. And *anyone*, Marcus, whether it be Moriah or one of this world, who does not value these things in you is unworthy of you."

Silence permeated the room for a brief instant.

Marcus swallowed, attempting to smile. He brought his hand over the one upon his shoulder. "You are a faithful friend, Philip. I could desire no better one."

Philip smiled a little, but gravity still hovered over his face. "Have you spoken to Daniel of your feelings?"

"No. I-I cannot."

"Do you think it honorable to hide your intentions?"

Marcus grimaced bitterly. "How like you that is. Always thinking of honor. But, no, I do not suppose it is."

Philip looked steadily at him. Marcus caught his message behind his clear blue eyes, and he again felt a well of agonized desperation.

"You cannot understand what it is I feel through this, Philip. My uncertainty is tortuous, but her blatant refusal would kill me."

"You cannot reap a reward without pain, Marcus. Is that not the motto of a soldier? Surely, giving God the opportunity to bless you is better than shutting the door to His plans."

Marcus stood silent a moment. He let his gaze drift past Philip through the threshold opening into the gardens. Lazily, a refreshing breeze stole softly into the atrium, cooling his heated cheeks.

Philip's words rang of the truth he would not have had the courage to face on his own.

Lord, I want Your will. Have I been impeding Your plan? You know my heart. Give me the strength to know Your desires and fulfill them.

The answer of his Lord's will burned like letters of fire into his mind.

"Bring me a parchment and pens." Marcus spoke quietly, but he lifted his chin with steady resolve. "I will follow your counsel."

A warm light flooded Philip's eyes. He clapped Marcus compassionately on the shoulder before swiftly striding away.

Marcus watched him go. The dull, pulsating pain intensified in his heart. He fiercely shook his head, trying to evade its clutches.

Where was his trust in God?

Slowly, wearily, he felt himself pulled by an unseen power to his knees. Resting his arm on one of the ornate benches beside the pool, he buried his face in his hands. His heart swelled, beseeching his God for the love of the woman he would gladly give his life for.

And, lurking deep within his aching heart, was the petition that her answer would not crush his spirit—and his faith.

Daniel watched Moriah's face with tender searching. Before him, her hazel eyes scanned the parchment held taut in her hands.

Slowly, the scarlet color flooded her face. She lifted her flashing eyes, bringing the parchment down. Tightly, passionately, she gripped it until her knuckles showed white.

"And?" Daniel maintained a quiet voice. "What do you say, Moriah?"

"What is there to say, father?" Moriah's voice was tremulous. "You know I must refuse him."

Astonishment struck Daniel with almost painful intensity. He felt it seep throughout his body, moving him a step forward. "What? Do you know what you are saying?"

"Yes."

"You cannot." Daniel struggled to speak. Already, the thought of relinquishing his beloved adopted daughter to another's man care filled his heart with an aching void of loss. He could not imagine life without her presence, her gentle ministrations. But he would not for a moment see her throw away herself for his sake. "You do not know what you are turning down."

"I *do*, father."

"Marcus is the best and godliest of young men, Moriah. His profession is sound and honorable; the wealth of his inheritance is beyond fathoming. You would lack for nothing."

Moriah lifted her chin. Her hazel eyes sparkled, luminous through the soft mist bordering her lashes. "There would not be honor, Daniel. And that means more to me than all the vain riches this world can offer."

Daniel surveyed her searchingly. "And why no honor? Marcus is an upright, courageous man. You saw his epistle, Moriah–he loves you with all his heart and soul."

"I am sorry for that, as sorry as any woman could be. I never gave him any cause to love me. Indeed, I gave him every reason to know my true feelings."

Daniel felt a slow well of disquiet rise in his heart, troubling him. It was not like Moriah to speak with such strange defensiveness. Her tone was low, but he detected an almost heated ring behind its quiet front.

"I do not understand you, Moriah. Tell me once and for all why you cannot wed Marcus."

Moriah averted her eyes. Her veil framed her face, shadowing the quiet resolution etched inexorably on her countenance. "I will not place my hand in ones stained with blood, father."

Low as her tones were, they struck Daniel's heart like a dagger. Slow disbelief rolled like shock through his body. "Marcus is a godly believer, a new creature in Christ."

"He is also a murderer."

"Moriah." Daniel fought to restrain his pained indignation. "I cannot believe I hear these words from your lips. You reject Marcus because of his past?"

"Is it not reason enough?"

"No." Daniel found himself speaking unnatural severity. Could this truly be his beautiful, godly daughter? Wherever she went, her gracious spirit won new hearts to Christ and provoked others to good works. Bitter unforgiveness did not meld with the Christ-like woman he knew her to be. "Not when Christ has redeemed and forgiven him, as He has for us all."

Moriah's chin trembled. Her eyes filled, pain registering on her features. "Do not judge me, father." Her whisper was tremulous, wounded by his severity. "I do care for Marcus, as a brother. But, please, you cannot ask me to become his wife."

Daniel's heart swelled. Her distress and his own mingled emotions smote him like the blow of a taskmaster, aching in his heart. His hands rested in gentle compassion on her arms. "Moriah, you know I have pledged to never force you to wed a man you cannot respect or love. But I must ask: is this your final word?"

"Yes."

Daniel was silent a moment. His grip intensified upon her arms, loving. "I am grateful I am not going to lose you, daughter." His husky voice faltered ever so slightly. "But God give me grace. I do not know how to tell Marcus."

Moriah said nothing. She stood motionless for a long moment, resting her chin on Daniel's broad shoulder. At length, she pulled away from his caressing hands. Flipping the end of her veil over her shoulder, she smiled through her tears up into his face.

Daniel watched her pick up a basket and disappear into a back room. His heart ached, burning in his throat. For the life of him, he did not understand why peace had deserted his soul.

During the long, sweltering hours of that night, Daniel tossed on his couch. He could not sleep. The aching burden hanging over his heart continued to intensity, almost sickening him.

Prayer brought him little relief. Instead, it only seemed to deepen the strange impression that a mistake had been made.

Many men had asked for Moriah's hand in marriage before. Rejecting them was always a painful task, but it had not tortured him as he was tormented now. He sensed with all his being that something was wrong in this particular case.

Was it because he loved Marcus so? He and Philip were like sons to him. Was it only his own selfish desires that caused him to shrink from breaking the hard truth to Marcus?

Or was there something deeper behind his pain?

Daniel groaned aloud. He could not understand. He knew only that he was bitterly confused and tormented, pressed to agony by the certain feeling he was thwarting God's will.

But Moriah had made her choice. He had long ago pledged to never force her hand in marriage.

And, right or wrong, it was a pledge he could not break.

Chapter Twenty-Three

Alone in his personal record-keeping chamber, Marcus leaned back and stretched his arms behind his head. He closed his dark eyes, allowing his mind to go.

The day had been an especially tiring one.

A legionary had been convicted of committing the same fault three times. Marcus had no choice but to condemn him to death under the sentence of *fustuariaum*. The unlucky legionary was beaten to death in front of the legion by the others in his *conteburnium*, or, squad unit.

Marcus thought back to the execution. As he watched, his mind had been full. Achingly, he had wondered what Moriah's opinion was of a man who condemned other men to a brutal death.

He steeled himself. There were those, even among the brethren, who had to do Rome's dirty work. Lawfully executing a man was one of those tasks.

He brought his hands forward, stretching them out to their full length. Aching from his rigid position, he stood upright. His eyes drifted downwards, focusing on the copy his scribe had made of his letter to Daniel.

His heart burned, aching with the apprehension that constantly overshadowed his chest. The uncertainty of his fate was killing him. Still, the silence was not as difficult to bear as the pain of rejection.

The clash of arms against a buckler startled him. Quickly recovering himself, he drew himself sternly erect as a legionary entered.

"A man to see you, tribune."

"I presume he has a *name*." Marcus made no attempt to hide his sarcasm.

"He calls himself Daniel of Bethlehem-Judah. He claims his business is important."

"Very well; show him in." Marcus felt a well of trepidation tighten his throat and chest. In another moment, he would know if his life would transform into the blissful heaven-on-earth he imagined.

Or if it would not be worth the living.

Daniel entered with quiet courtesy, offering a swift gesture of respect. Marcus nodded curtly at the legionary, and he retired with the traditional salute.

Alone with his guest, Marcus stepped forward to offer him his hand. "All hail, my friend."

"Greetings, Marcus." Daniel took his hand, gripping his lower arm. "I hope I do not disturb you by coming here."

"No, to the contrary." Marcus forced himself to speak lightly. Inwardly, his heart pounded against his chest, tightening his throat. It was ironic that he could face a thousand deaths in combat without fear, but standing in the presence of his own familiar friend chilled his heart with apprehension. "Will you be seated?"

Daniel nodded his thanks. Marcus began to pour out a glass of wine, but Daniel waved his hand.

"No, no, Marcus. My business will not take long."

The moment had come. Marcus forced himself to assume a military countenance, setting his face rigidly. Slowly, he seated himself behind his desk. "I-I suppose you received my letter."

"Yes."

Marcus saw Daniel shift, as if in discomfort. Keenly surveying his honest countenance, he immediately sensed the hard truth. Moriah had rejected him.

And Daniel was unwilling to tell him.

"Speak on, my friend." Marcus's voice was low. "Say what you must."

Daniel looked steadily at him, his eyes gravely quiet. "There is no easy way to frame the truth into words, Marcus. You are my brother and my friend, and I do not deny my heart is sore for you."

"But Moriah has rejected me." Marcus's voice was husky. It was better to say it himself than hear the words from the friend and mentor he respected so well.

"Yes."

Marcus felt a slow wave of pain wash like a rippling fire through his body. Abruptly, he looked away, tightening his fingers until they bit into his palms. The ache crept upward, constricting his throat.

"Why?" He did not recognize the sound of his own husky query. It almost startled him. Soldiers were expected to mask their pain, guising it under stern callousness.

He himself was a soldier of soldiers. He recognized blood as water, demanded rugged strength of himself and others. Scenes of torture and killing were familiar to him, sometimes exercised by his order or at his own hand. Above all, he knew the pains of duty, experienced through the loss of a friend in battle or by condemning one of his own men to the lash or death.

All of those things did not compare with what he felt now.

"I beg you will not ask me that, Marcus."

"I will know." Marcus raised his head, feeling a flash lighten his eyes. "Tell me why, Daniel."

Daniel hesitated. His bearded face was overshadowed with quiet sympathy, every feature revealing the pain of his task. "Marcus, you are our brother. You have been upright, steadfast in the faith. You are well respected. You—"

"I do not care to hear about my virtues. Tell me my fault in this." Marcus made no attempt to take the edge off his interruption. His heart ached bitterly, nearly suffocating him.

God, I did what I thought was Your will. Is this my reward for following Philip's counsel, for seeking the honorable course?

"You have done nothing amiss, my brother. The difficulty does not lie in the present, but in the past."

A moment of silence filled the room before Daniel cleared his throat to continue. "Marcus, the Lord has redeemed and justified you. But some memories linger on; yes, even prejudices. The murder of Beric—"

"That is unjust." The boiling pain and anger rolled through Marcus like a wave. "It was over five years ago, Daniel."

Daniel lowered his eyes. "She has not forgotten."

"I was a zealous son. I was trying to honor my father's wishes and the nation that birthed me." Marcus felt his voice beginning to break, lapsing into choked huskiness. "God knows how I have repented of the things I did, Daniel."

"I know that, Marcus."

Daniel's quietness did nothing to ease Marcus's agonized desperation. He felt as if he were drowning beneath all the pent-up emotions he had harbored for so long. Struggling for the mastery, he tried to curtail his passion, but to no avail.

His throbbing, pulsating heart refused to keep silent.

"You say I am redeemed. Yes, praise be to God, I *am* His child! And I have begged His forgiveness again and again for my sins, for the things I did to Philip and others. Is it not enough that *He* has pardoned me? Or," and his heated voice died to a broken whisper, "is there another judge beside God?"

"Marcus." Daniel arose, his eyes a mirror to Marcus's anguished heartache. Gentleness was evident in his voice, in the hand he laid on Marcus's shoulder. "It is not I who condemn you."

"Does it matter? You speak for her."

"But I do not *agree* with her."

Marcus could not speak. The growing lump in his throat was far too restricting. He blinked rapidly, turning slightly away from Daniel.

The pressure of the hand on his shoulder increased.

"I do not pretend to understand this, Marcus. There is nothing I want more than to see you and her happily wedded. I would go so far as to say I even believe it is the Lord's will that you marry."

"That is no consolation."

"Perhaps not now, but later. My brother, see beyond your pain and try to understand. Our Savior works in mysterious ways."

"Do not blame *God* for her prejudice, Daniel."

"I do not." Daniel paused. "I only seek to give you hope. I have prayed long and arduously concerning this matter, and I do not speak lightly when I say I believe time may heal your heart."

Marcus turned to look at him. "Is that the hope you give me?"

"Not entirely." Daniel's gaze became distant. "I also think it possible a mistake has been made." His hand squeezed Marcus's shoulder. "Give this time. The Lord may soften her heart."

A bitter laugh caught Marcus's throat. "What if she is right? I am unworthy. And I know now what I have suspected for many years. I am also unforgiven."

"*Marcus—*"

"Do not rebuke me." Again, Marcus's husky voice faltered. "Do not tell me I am pardoned when I am not." He paused, biting his lip. Slowly, he stretched out his hand. "You have been kind to tell me in person. I thank you for that."

Daniel took his hand, his eyes overshadowed and troubled. "Perhaps we should talk of this at another time."

"No. Do not broach the subject again."

Daniel hesitated. Slowly, he dropped Marcus's hand and turned to the door. At its threshold, he stopped, facing him. "I feel for you, Marcus. Know that I will pray for you."

"Thank you." Marcus lifted his hand in farewell. He desired to be alone more than anything in the world. "*Vale.*"

The door closed quietly behind Daniel's exit.

Marcus stood motionless a moment. Slowly, he sank into his seat and buried his face in his hands.

His worst fear had come to pass.

The sorrow of rejection by the woman he loved was torturous. But, knowing her reasons, her harbored unforgiveness was a prejudice he could not bear. He had known it was possible, had even expected it. But it did not mean he could stand the burning, wrenching pain of its injustice.

He was alone. Worse, he was unforgiven.

The anguished thought came to him. He had forever separated Philip from the one he loved more than anyone else on earth. Was it not just that he was now separated from the one he had no desire to live without?

"Great God." His groan filled the room. "Will my punishment never end?"

Minutes slipped into hours. Time lost its meaning, its gripping power. The shadows moved austerely across the room, revealing the waning afternoon.

Marcus sat with his face buried in his hands, his elbows almost driven into his writing table. His lips moved constantly, silent in their intensity. Slowly, the tell-tale moisture crept between his tightly-clenched fingers, falling in two or three salty drops to the desktop.

Outside the room, he gradually heard voices. They came nearer, laughing, lighthearted. It was not difficult to discern the tones of Philip and Alexander.

It was too late to hide his emotion. Marcus did not lift his face from his hands. His spirit felt crushed within him.

I am already driven into the dust. What does it matter if a legionary does witness this in me?

The door swung wide, and Marcus sensed Philip and Alexander stepped into the room. Their laughing conversation immediately hushed.

"My lord?" Philip's voice held a ring of keen concern. "Is all well?"

"I'll return later." Alexander was audibly subdued. Marcus heard him leave the room, shutting the door behind his exit. Clearly, the young legionary was too respectful to view his commander's apparent weakness.

Marcus felt a strong hand grip his shoulder. He could sense Philip kneeling beside him, bringing himself to his master's eye level.

"Marcus, what has happened?"

Marcus lifted his head, allowing Philip to see his misty eyes. His voice felt strained, still husky in spite of his two hours of silence. There seemed no way to share the difficult truth.

"Daniel was here."

Grave understanding flitted over Philip's face, tensing the hand he maintained on his master's shoulder. "He brought ill news, then?"

"Yes."

"I do not understand." Philip's voice was low, but Marcus detected an edge of tightness. "Why?"

Marcus's eyes drifted down over Philip's searching, pained countenance to the muscular arm extended in brotherly compassion to his shoulder. A deep, riveted scar creased the skin, mirrored by a second line also stretching across his left arm.

His voice cracked, fighting his brokenness. "You know why, Philip."

Philip's hand dropped slowly from his shoulder. His deep cobalt eyes lowered, his hand absently touching the scars. When his eyes lifted, it was with a fiery blaze Marcus had not seen in many years.

"The only marks that can be seen are ones I *deserved*."

"And the ones you didn't? Her memory of the flogging I gave you, of Beric's death are etched in her heart with blood, Philip."

"Just as our pardon and the *world's* are sealed in blood." Philip spoke passionately, his voice a tremor of indignant anger. "The blood of Jesus Christ our Savior is all that stands."

Marcus said nothing. Weary discouragement hung like a dark cloud over him. He felt oppressed, forsaken. For five years, he had buried the truths about his past.

In a few words, they had resurrected to haunt him.

Philip gripped him by both arms, forcing him to look at him. His indignation spilled over, washing in color over his face. "Marcus, forget. Move forward in Christ, and, by God's grace, *forget!*"

"That comes easily from one who has never harmed anyone."

"Does it?" Philip leaned back on his heels. "I tell you, Marcus, there is much I would undo from my own past if I could. Every time I look at you, I am ashamed to remember the rebellious things I once said and did."

"And you compare that with persecuting the believers?"

"Yes. Sin is sin, Marcus." Philip softened. He leaned forward, quiet, yet passionately earnest. "But I have learned one thing you have not. It is that there is *no* condemnation to them that believe."

Marcus sat silent. He squeezed his fingers tightly together. Slowly, fighting back his true feelings, he forced a slight smile to his lips. "Your concern for me is more than I deserve."

Philip's eyes sought his. "No. It is what brothers ought to feel for one another." He paused. Again, his hand found Marcus's shoulder. "Do not despair. If this is the Lord's will, Moriah will come to see the truth. In the mean time," and a slight smile began to play about his lips, "nothing will separate you from *His* love."

Nothing will separate you.

The words echoed in Marcus's mind. Slowly, like a rising dawn, peace began to envelop him. The darkness of his pain would not vanish, he knew, but he was sustained by a greater strength–a hope that passed all understanding.

Moriah brushed through the milling crowd of shoppers in the market end of the forum. The basket she balanced on her hip was already laden with food, mostly wine and unleavened bread for communion.

Considering communion, she drew a cloth more securely over the food items. Bread and wine were already well-known as Christian food.

Despite outward vigilance, her mind was not truly on her tasks. Her heart ached, pained with the events of the last three weeks.

Daniel had said little to her concerning her rejection of Marcus's proposal, but she felt his disapproval. Not necessarily in her choice, but for her motives. He had delivered a message about the sin of unforgiveness to the brethren only the night before, and she had felt as if every word was directed to her conscience-smitten heart.

She had cried herself to sleep as a result.

Still, she could not bring herself to forget the murder of a man she had respected. Every tear Philip had shed on the day he had first told Daniel of his loss had smitten her tender heart. She had seen his weeping, the bandages that were clearly visible beneath his servant's tunic.

And she had seen enough scourging in barbaric Rome to know what it was Philip had suffered.

You judge a man who didn't know what he was doing. Her conscience screamed out at her. *You harbor bitterness when Philip himself has forgiven the past.*

Moriah felt the tears welling up in her eyes. What was it that kept her from acknowledging Marcus's goodness, his upright virtues? She knew he was respected, that he was a godly man. Why could she not forget his past and honor him for who Christ had made him to be?

Perhaps it was pride.

The ugliness of the word tingled Moriah's cheeks, coloring them in pomegranate red. Surely, pride was not among her faults. Was it not discernment that kept her from marrying Marcus?

A jolting bump into a pedestrian dispelled every thought from her mind. She caught her basket in time to keep the contents from being spilled into the street. Looking up, her eyes met a noxious pair of masculine eyes.

"Great gods!"

Moriah blushed furiously. Her heart almost failed her, recognizing the arrogant carriage and lustful gaze of Thallus.

Her color seemed to amuse him. He laughed gratingly.

"I see you remember me. Great Diana of the Ephesians! We have met again." He leaned close to her, tainting her with his hot breath. "And fortune would have it that the accursed Tribune Virginius Aeneas is nowhere in sight."

Moriah looked wildly about. Everyone was intent on their shopping, too busy to heed the dire predicament of a young woman.

God, save me!

Thallus's hand closed menacingly around her wrist. "We were rudely interrupted at our last meeting. It will not happen again today."

"Let me go." Moriah's breathing was bated and tense. She attempted to snap her wrist from his grip, but his grip tightened.

"Let you go?" Thallus's mocking laughter filled the air. "How cruel you are. I know women such as you. You claim virtue and innocence, but, at heart, you are all the same. I won't let you deny yourself and me."

Moriah's mind whirled. She had not fully appreciated Marcus's valiant assistance three weeks ago. What she would not give now to see him charge through the crowd and pluck her from the fiendish oaf who held her.

"*Let me go.*"

Thallus looked sneeringly at her. "The tribune was not a fool. For the first time in my existence, I will acknowledge him as a man of impeccable taste. I–"

Moriah twisted violently. Thallus stepped close to her, grabbing both of her arms. The basket fell onto the street, spilling the bread and wine onto the cobblestones.

"What have we here?" Thallus touched the food with the tip of his sandaled foot. "Bread and wine." A fiendish expression crossed his face, exploding into anger. "By the gods! A vile Christian!"

Moriah's color vanished into snowy whiteness. "The only person deserving of the term *vile* is you, sir. Unhand me."

A stinging slap fell swiftly across her face.

Moriah stumbled back, the blood tingling in her cheeks. Thallus jerked her closer, enraged disappointment and disgust working in his face.

"Hold your peace! By Jupiter, I might have known. A Christian *sow!*"

"Let me go." Close to tears, Moriah pushed her uplifted wrists against his chest, endeavoring to distance her face from his. "*Please,* let me go."

"No." Thallus ground his teeth. "Oh brave Nemesis! You have at last granted me my revenge. I am beginning to see the truth. Tribune Virginius Aeneas's gallant stand for you was not merely a matter of principle, was it?"

"You have no right—"

"Say no more." Thallus held up his hand. "Your color speaks for you. By all the gods in succession, I swear I will have my revenge. Justice will be served when Marcus finds that his glossy fruit has been plucked."

Moriah's mind whirled, encircled by a terrifying black dizziness. She stumbled, feeling herself pulled tightly into his arms. His hot breath fell like a scorching flame on her neck, his fingers dug ruthlessly into her arms.

God, help me!

Her lungs gasped for air. She felt as if she could not breathe. Slowly, she felt herself going limp, succumbing to his brutal hold.

God, don't let me faint—don't let him take me!

A rolling wave of thunderous applause steadied Moriah's mind. Loudening into an unchecked roar, the handclapping and cheers grew near.

"Make way! Salute your divine emperor, Nero Claudius Caesar Augustus Germanicus!"

A dozen richly-clad slaves came into view, each bearing the Imperial rod of office. The sight of them cleared a wide path through the forum's crowded market place, revealing a royal purple and gold litter.

Its occupant sat carelessly atop his cushions. His pale, dull blue eyes scanned the street below him, careless, yet intent. Corpulent and fleshy, his appearance was loathsome to the few who spurned his vices and grotesque practices.

To most, he was the idol of Rome.

His pale eyes fell upon Thallus. In one fluid motion, he raised his jeweled hand, and the litter stood motionless. "Thallus Quinctia. What does the son Saturius do here with," and his wanton eyes fell on Moriah, "this beauteous woman?"

Thallus raised his arm in swift salute. "I have some acquaintance with this woman, divinity, and halted to speak with her."

"And has she proven worthy of your attention, Son of Saturius?"

"In beauty, yes, Caesar. However, I fear I have discovered a slight difficulty."

"And what is that?"

Thallus cleared his throat, the turn of his eye sending chills down Moriah's spine. "I believe she is one of those fanatical sorcerers called Christians."

Nero's bloated face lapsed from interest into cruel displeasure. "If this is true, you are to be commended, Son of Saturius. The danger from these obstinate Christus-worshippers rises every day."

His cool, colorless eyes rested on Moriah's face. "Tell me, woman, are you a Christian?"

Moriah's heart pounded wildly. The perspiration broke out on her pallid skin, moistening her face. There was no chance of escape.

And she would never deny the truth.

Thallus's grasp tightened, nearly expelling a gasp of pain from her throat. She lifted her eyes to the emperor's face.

"I am, sire."

The calmness of her reply flickered interest in Nero's eyes. He leaned ever so slightly forward. "You are not ignorant, girl. You know how many of your sect have been condemned to their just deaths. Still, the divine Nero," and he glanced around the onlooking crowd with pompous eyes, "is merciful. Come with me into the temple of Venus and offer incense. It will save your life."

"I cannot do that, sire." Moriah heard her own tones tremble. She knew the stories, the terrible sentences of her dearly-beloved brethren. Almost every day, her mind was haunted with gruesome tales of bloodshed and gore.

But there was something else beside her fear, her terror of the arena. A strange inner strength sustained her. Its peaceful whispers calmed her, settling her heart into a more natural cadence.

She was not alone.

Nero raised his brows. "And why not?"

"Jesus Christ is the son of God, the Savior of the world. I have pledged to follow Him. Come what may," and again, Moriah heard her voice shake, "I will not deny Him."

Fuming irritation crossed Nero's face. "By Bacchus, these Christians are all the same! Even their women are as stubborn, insolent sheep, going aimlessly to their own slaughter." A theatrical sigh escaped him. "Still, it pains me to sentence such a beautiful woman as lion's bait."

"Why do so, divinity?" An officer, who had been fixing his lascivious eyes for the past five minutes on Moriah's white face, turned enticingly towards him. "If you will pardon my boldness, idol of Rome, the woman is too beautiful to be wasted on gladiators and leopards. Her beauty is more fitted, shall we say, to *servitude*."

Nero blinked, then, slapped his thigh, throwing back his head in merry amusement. "By Pollux, Gaius! Your ingenuity is worthy of the gods. I could not propose a more satisfactory plan myself."

Thallus's eyes deepened with sinister satisfaction. Humoring Nero by his quizzical expression, he feigned misunderstanding. "Do I understand you correctly, sire? You wish to place this young woman upon the auction block?"

"Naturally, man! Gaius, I place you in charge of the whole business. Take this maid to the palace dungeons and confine her. When a convenient time for her sale comes, see that the bidding begins at no less than seven thousand *denarii*. The money will proceed into my treasury, of course."

The officer bowed. "As you desire, divinity."

Nero reaffixed his nonchalant gaze upon Thallus. "I think the business is settled satisfactorily, do you not?" Then, without waiting for his reply, "I hope to see you at my next banquet, Son of Saturius. *Vale.*"

The jeweled hand was lifted, and the litter passed on. Moriah saw the expression of utmost pleasure Thallus sent after it before turning to fix his cool eyes again on her.

"Divinity is indeed within the emperor."

"Did you ever doubt it?" The officer Gaius's tones were dry. Stepping forward, he grasped Moriah's wrist and drew her towards himself. "Come, pretty one. *Venus* awaits."

Panic began to tingle in Moriah's numbed mind. She was helpless in the merciless power of the officer—and his wanton eyes had not escaped her notice. There was no law, no command that would withhold his lust.

Keep me pure, Father. Somehow, don't let him or any other man harm me.

"Wait." Thallus tossed him a small purse. Moriah saw his keen eyes narrow. Obviously, he too had seen the officer's crafty attentions. "See that she is treated with dignity. Her loveliness must not be filched before the time."

A low chuckle escaped the officer. "Truth, Thallus Quinctia. You strike a fair bargain."

"See that you keep it."

"Have no fear." Gaius cast a laughing glance over his shoulder. "I will expect to see you at the auction."

Moriah felt as if the atmosphere was closing in around her. Numb with shock and disbelief, she submitted to the callous guidance of the officer as he led her beneath the colossal structures of the forum towards the Imperial Palace.

Before its myriad of marble steps, Moriah felt the shadow of an immense statue of Venus fall on her. She half-lifted her eyes, resting them on the goddesses' figure.

An instant shudder rolled over her.

In a single instant, she had been deduced from a free plebian woman to a slave. Her worth was now no more than a common strumpet. Unless a miracle of immense scale occurred, Roman law endowed her master to own her, body and soul.

And, if that master was Thallus, his only god was Venus.

The sea-foam goddess of sensuality, a vision of Thallus offering Venus an offering of roses flitted through her mind. She could almost taste the myrtle-tainted wine, feel the burning shame of slavery in his household. If he should purchase her…

Moriah closed her eyes, washing away the terrifying thought. When she again opened them, she was in the palace dungeon.

The clang of steel sounded in her ears. Echoing like a gong, she felt the cold, mysterious power of helplessness. Her eyes focused to the dim, shadowy lighting, revealing the stone floor and barren walls of her prison.

The shriek of some tortured victim reverberated with frightening unexpectedness, traveling throughout the jail.

Suddenly nauseous, Moriah felt a groaning cry escape her own lips. A dark cloud seemed to settle over her, and she sank to her knees on the hard floor.

Chapter Twenty-Four

"Tribune, there is a legionary wishing to see you."

Dark irritation washed over Marcus's face as he straightened himself. Two of his assembled centurions also glanced up, impatience tightening their already-serious expressions.

"This is the second time you have interrupted me." Marcus's voice was sharp with exasperation. He saw the guard flinch. "Great Caesars, I am of the mind to reduce your rations."

The guard's rigid stance melded into nervousness. "My apologies, tribune. The legionary will not be turned away. He insists the matter is of the utmost importance."

"And who is this brazen idiot who refuses to obey orders?" Marcus caught a glimpse of a tanned countenance just beyond the open door. *Alexander.* "Let the oaf in. I am more than willing to teach him a lesson in observing a little respectful compliance."

The guard turned and gave a sharp order. Alexander entered, saluting.

"Hail, tribune."

Marcus eyed him sternly. He knew nothing short of an emergency would induce such persistence in his respectful young protégée. Still, he would never permit his centurions to know he had befriended a humble legionary from his own legion.

"Your business with me must exact the urgency you claim, soldier. Nothing less will pardon your insolence from a thorough flogging."

Marcus saw Alexander stiffen, though to no surprise. His rank itself would cause even the closest friend to cringe under such a threat.

"The matter is one requiring your private ear, tribune."

Marcus glanced over his centurions. "You are dismissed. Go, all of you."

With silent salutes, the centurions filed out. The guard brought up the rear, closing the door upon his exit.

Marcus seated himself with new casualness on the edge of his writing table. He folded his arms across his chest, gesturing. "Well?"

Alexander maintained a rigid soldierly pose. "By your leave, tribune, I—"

"At ease, Alexander." Marcus interrupted him, slightly impatient. "You know our customs."

"They do not normally involve scourging, my lord tribune."

"Enough." A hint of a smile played about Marcus's mouth. "I spoke lightly."

"And *I* did not." Alexander snapped into a frustrated sense of urgency. "I told the truth when I said the matter was serious."

"As you better always speak the truth with me." Marcus held up his hand, seeing Alexander's sudden crimson color. He casually stood up. "Peace, my brother. I have never seen you so riled."

"There is good cause for it. This involves Moriah."

Marcus grew suddenly rigid. "What do you mean?"

"She was taken today to the Imperial dungeons."

"How? Why?" Marcus closed his hand with abrupt force around Alexander's arm. His heart pulsed, nearly cutting off his air. "Stand and tell me everything."

"We don't know everything. The story is that a patrician stopped her in the forum today, certainly for no good purpose. By some cursed chance, the emperor's litter passed and he stopped to inquire."

"And? Hurry up, man!"

"It is said she was accused of being a Christian. Apparently, she admitted it and was arrested. She—"

Alexander stopped abruptly.

Marcus looked keenly at him. The adrenaline rushed like a sea-gate flood through his body, tightening the force of his grip. "There is more. Go on."

"You are as pale as a spirit already, Marcus. I–"

"Don't talk to me about my looks." Passion tightened Marcus's face. "You will tell me everything. That's an order."

Alexander's green eyes flitted downwards. Subdued by Marcus's tone, he again stiffened into soldierly discipline. "She was not sentenced to the arena. Instead, she is to be sold as a common slave to the highest bidder."

"At what prices?"

"Some say no less than seven thousand *denarii*."

"By the gods!" Marcus checked the pagan exclamation too late. "For one woman? Why such fantastical bidding?"

"Because the money drops neatly into Nero's coffers. Why else? And it may be that he does not believe we poor," and Alexander lowered his tone, "*Christians* can afford such prices."

"Heaven preserve us." Marcus brought his arms behind his head, clasping his hands together. Indignant frustration boiled through him. Beneath it, however, was a pain so strong he could scarcely breathe. "How do you know all this?"

"The brethren have eyes and ears everywhere."

"We do indeed. Praise the Lord not all of us are poor." Marcus paused in contemplation. "No price is too much for Moriah."

Alexander looked oddly at him.

Marcus felt the slow color rise in his cheeks. With the words spoken, he realized too late how tenderly passionate they had sounded. Irritated embarrassment seized him, spilling over into his words. "Why do you look at me that way? Would you have your sister in the faith live a life of shame?"

"You know I would not, Marcus." Alexander's quiet voice was a striking contrast to Marcus's wrath. "I was only unaware that it would be you bidding for her."

"Who else can?"

"No one, I suppose. But are you certain you can pay?"

"Yes, certainly." Marcus turned, meeting Alexander's forthright gaze. The young man's tone both quieted and puzzled him. "Why shouldn't I?"

"They say a high-ranking patrician will certainly bid and claim her, no matter what the cost."

Marcus felt the hairs on his neck bristle. "What patrician?"

"The noble Thallus Quinctia, son of Saturius."

"Thallus Quinctia." Marcus repeated the words in slow disbelief. Slowly, full understanding crept over him. He felt his hand clench into violent fists. "Great Caesars! The infernal swine!"

"Do you know him?"

"Perhaps better than he knows himself. The man is a devil. If he is so closely involved, this whole business was meant as nothing more than an insult against *me*."

"He does have a close hand on it. They say the auction will be held tomorrow night—at his request, of course."

"He'll not be victorious in this pretty scheme." Marcus's hand closed vehemently around his *gladius*. He felt the hot blood rushing through him, controlling him. "I'll purchase Moriah no matter what the price. And, if I fail, I'll kill him in cold blood on his way home from the auction."

Again, Alexander looked with quiet strangeness at him. "You would murder a man?"

"Protecting a woman's honor from a beast like him is no murder."

"I wonder if our elders would say the same."

Marcus knit his brows, somewhat surprised. Alexander had never made the slightest challenge to his will in any regard before. "Do you question me?"

"As my commander, never, my lord tribune."

"And as my friend?"

Alexander studied the patterned floor, his green eyes quietly contemplative. "Perhaps I do. Your wisdom and understanding is far beyond me, and I think you know the esteem I have for you."

300

He paused. "But I cannot help but wonder if you are being guided by the Spirit or your own carnal lust in this matter."

Marcus felt a sudden pang. Slowly, his hand dropped from the hilt of his sword. "You doubt the integrity of my resolve?"

Alexander looked up at him, his honest eyes overshadowed by soldierly contriteness. "I see I have offended you. My apologies, my tribune."

"No." Marcus closed the gap between them, studying Alexander's quiet face. "I wish to understand you fully. What do you mean?"

Alexander seemed strangely unable to look at him. "Your hatred for the man who would defile our sister in the faith is understandable. It is your passion to buy her that I do not understand. Perhaps I wonder what it is you will do with her."

Marcus felt the blood drain from his face.

He could understand the question coming from any other Christian brother, but not Alexander. The full depth of the young man's seeming accusation sank slowly into him, so sharp he could scarcely swallow the sudden smarting lump that rose in his throat.

He could feel the veins in his neck constrict. Despite his best efforts, pain tightened his voice. "I will sign her freedom papers in your presence if that is what you desire. And I swear upon my honor as a believer," and his eyes narrowed, inches away from Alexander's unblinking ones, "I *will* preserve her purity."

Slow apology filled Alexander's face. Contritely, he began to bend in the rare custom of pressing his commander's hand to his lips. "I did not mean to accuse you. Nor would I challenge my own tribune's honor, Marcus. My concern for Moriah—"

"I understand. Do not humble yourself." Marcus forced himself to speak lightly, though the thought of resuming his inexorability as a commander crossed the back of his mind. Punishing this legionary's rashness would be an easy vent to his humiliation.

But it would not be fair.

Alexander had spoken as his friend and brother, and he himself could not deny he deserved some measure of suspicion. He was not really angry at Alexander's boldness as compared to hurt by his mistrust. He felt sensitized, doubtless from Moriah's recent rejection and the stirred-up memories of his past.

Still, he knew Alexander's honest heart well enough to understand his sincerity. Swallowing his pride, he maintained his position as a friend. "I am a man and a military tribune. Your mistrust has its grounds."

Alexander's face relaxed visibly. "You are always more than understanding with me. I am grateful, Marcus."

Marcus's hand rested atop his shoulder. "Say nothing of it." He paused. "When you are relieved of your duties tonight, go to the brethren. Tell them Marcus Virginius Aeneas will do everything within his power to save Moriah. Tell them to pray."

"Yes, sir." Alexander sensed the conclusion of their meeting. Snapping again into his military formality, he brought his arm against his chest. "As you command."

Marcus watched him turn and stride towards the door. He felt drained. A cloud of mixed emotions settled over him, rendering him strangely subdued. Unexpectedly, he heard his own voice.

"Legionary."

Alexander turned. "Sir?"

"Pray for me."

Alexander's eyes softened. Ever so slightly, he nodded. Wordlessly, he exited the room.

Marcus stood motionless a moment. Slowly, feeling overwhelmingly helpless, he began to pace the room.

His heart felt sick within him. The tables had turned so suddenly against him, against the woman he loved more than life. Moriah's perilous predicament was worse than his most vivid nightmare.

Was it possible God would allow her to be forever snatched from him? Or, worse still, heartlessly defiled and shamed?

The thought sent the blood tingling back into his pallid cheeks.

He would save her. No craven, lustful hand would harm her. And, if one did, the owner's life was forfeit. At that moment, he no longer cared about the laws of Rome, Moses, or anyone else.

He would kill the man who tainted her.

God help me. Keep her pure until I can save her.

Drawing himself sternly erect, Marcus strode from the room. Thankfully, the meeting with his centurions had been the last duty of his day. He was free to take his leave.

Out in the dusty courtyard, he blinked under the glare of the late afternoon sun. The heat was intense, worse than usual.

Or was it own enflamed feelings?

A quick glance revealed three or four legionaries standing idle. Marcus swiftly approached them, recognizing their startled apprehension. "Bring me a horse."

"Yes, tribune." Like an echo, all four men saluted and set off at running speeds.

Marcus watched them go. In his current mood, their swift pace had been their wisest choice.

They returned, one of them leading a well-bred mare. Marcus snatched the leather reins from him and swung into the saddle. The legionary nodded at him.

"The gods go with you."

Marcus raised his hand in swift acknowledgment, then, spurred his mount forward. In a quick dash of dust, the mare cantered forward.

The ride through the bustling maze of streets and pedestrians to the mansion of Aeneas was strangely short.

Marcus moved his lips in wordless petition. His very soul was sore, aching with the ceaseless worry hanging over him. Would he be able to rescue Moriah from the heartless jaws of the lion prowling in want of her?

Before his father's mansion, he quickly threw himself from the saddle. Almost running, he strode up the steps and into the welcome relief of the cool atrium.

Philip met him. "Greetings, Marcus."

"And to you, Philip." Marcus made no attempt to hide his hurry. "Is my father in?"

"Yes, in his own apartments. Can I bring you anything? Some wine?"

"Later perhaps. Thank you." Marcus stepped quickly past him. Breaking almost into a jog, he stepped up the stairs to the apartment of Cleotas. Not bothering to knock, he swept into the room.

"All hail, Cleotas."

Loosely clad in a tunic, Cleotas was lying indolently on a couch, an open scroll in his hand. Startled, he half-started up. "By the gods, Marcus!"

"Father, I will be brief." Marcus didn't bother to apologize. There was but one thought in his mind, overflowing into words. "I may need to borrow some money. Have I your permission?"

Cleotas blinked. "How much?"

"Up to eight thousand *denarii* if necessary."

Cleotas's jaw went slack. "Eight thousand *denarii*! Boy, are you mad? By Pollux, what could you possibly need such a sum for?"

Marcus bit his lip. Any explanation he might make was certain to be awkward. He felt Cleotas's eyes rest with suspicion on him.

"Have you been gambling or running up debts in my name, Marcus? Don't hesitate to tell me the worst; I am accustomed to the pranks of young men."

Marcus felt the color rise in his face. "I have been doing no such things, Cleotas. Surely you know me well enough for that."

"Then out with it. What *have* you been up to?"

Marcus hesitated. "To be blunt, I want to purchase a female slave tomorrow night. She goes for a high price."

Cleotas stared at him. Without warning, he laughed aloud, the frown speeding from his features. "Ah, Venus has finally claimed you, Marcus! There—do not color so. I know and understand. So you want a female slave, eh? And a beautiful one? By Bacchus, you shall have her."

Marcus felt the blood sweep through his neck up to his forehead. He had meant to clarify himself, but, instead, he had given the exact opposite impression he had meant to make.

A stammered explanation rose to his lips, nearly choking him. "You have always been generous with me, sir, but I fear you misunderstand me. My intentions—"

Cleotas interrupted him with a swift gesture. "Make no excuses, Marcus. If you want this woman, have her. I care little about your *intentions*. Tell my steward to give you my note for whatever amount you wish. Does that please you?"

"Yes, naturally. But—"

"Then get out of here. I dislike young men who burst without the proper permission into my chambers. Remember that in future, Marcus."

Scarlet-faced and feeling decidedly helpless, Marcus raised his hand in farewell and left the room.

Outside, he leaned against the wall, closing his eyes. His heart pounded fast and hard against his chest, mortified. He would have to explain later. Cleotas must never think he had gone back on his principles.

Still, beyond his embarrassment, new peace enshrouded him

Even if he was outbid with his own gold, he had the note of Cleotas to ensure he would win Moriah's freedom. The match was fairly set between him and Thallus Quinctia.

Dusk had fallen over Rome.

The street corners were lit by blazing torches, dimly lighting the way for the nighttime pedestrians—drunken patricians, beggars, slaves hurrying homewards, and women of ill-repute.

Marcus swung his scarlet cloak across his broad chest and around one arm. He had completed his day's work too late to exchange his military armor and tunic for his toga. Still, he had no fear of his note being rejected at the auction. The name of the Tribune Marcus Virginius Aeneas was not unknown.

He glanced down at the female stola and cape slung over his arm. Slave auctions were generally indecent spectacles at best, and he had no idea how he might find his intended purchase. At one time, he would have thought nothing of it. Now, he breathed a prayer of gratitude.

How much You delivered me from, Father.

Gradually, the increase of fiery torches and the indistinct murmur of male voices signified his approach to the forum. A well-lit auction room appeared on his right, and Marcus turned in.

The auction ring was a bustle of activity. A line of miserable wretches were stationed around the block, awaiting their turn to be sold. The auctioneer himself stood leaning against the accounting table, speaking with the scribe charged with recording the revenue.

The room itself was stifling hot, humid with the mingled heat of dozens of swarming bodies. Greasy plebians, haughty patricians, and soldiers loitered about, awaiting the sale's commencement.

Marcus looked keenly around the ring, searching for Thallus. It was not long before he found him, standing near the block, and chatting freely with a fellow patrician.

He felt his blood begin to wax warm. Somehow, the mere sight of Thallus always aroused twin passions of indignation and contempt in his very soul. He moved forward, intent upon gaining an adjacent place near the block.

As he pushed through the milling buyers, Marcus saw Thallus turn. His cool eyes lifted, meeting Marcus's. His gaze instantly narrowed, a noxious expression stealing over his careless one.

"Almighty Jupiter." Marcus heard his low, spatted curse. "The *mendicos* are in."

Marcus glared stonily at him. He knew Thallus was well-aware of his wealth and status, but the pompous dog still dared to insult him as a beggar. It was a taunt that would not serve him.

Knowing his taunt had been heard, Thallus addressed him a louder key. "Hail, tribune. Are you looking today or buying?"

"Buying." Marcus kept his tones short.

"Male or female?"

"Does it matter?"

"I suppose not." The eyes of Thallus narrowed. "However, assuming from your vast command, I dare say you do not need any further service from *male* attendants."

"Nor do I need your incessant probing." The corners of Marcus's mouth twitched in disgust. "How I spend my money is my own affair."

"Provided you have the money, that is. They say officers drink and gamble without restraint. I, to the contrary, have a well-laden purse."

Marcus glanced contemptuously at him, refusing to answer. His pointed warning was none too inconspicuous. *Boast loudly, Thallus.* Humiliation would be a nice touch to top the success of snatching Moriah away from his claws.

A sudden blow fell on the gong, its reverberated peal silencing the murmuring buyers. Marcus felt his breathing quicken, tightening his chest.

The time was at hand.

Clearly, Thallus had been at pains to see that the auction was conducted to his personal satisfaction. Moriah was the first lot to be sold. Fleetingly, Marcus wondered how much he had paid to ensure he would not be out uncomfortably late.

His throat constricted as Moriah was half-pushed to her position on the block. The flickering light of the oil lamps danced over her, and he felt an immediate pang stab his aching heart.

Beauty was only a shaming curse for a slave.

The auction masters had evidently been at pains to accent her loveliness. Her hair was loose and unveiled, flowing over her bare shoulders. Though attired, her thin garment was boldly revealing—scandalously so for a virtuous, modest woman like Moriah.

A murmur of appreciative whispers swept through the cluster of men. Several uncouth remarks were laughingly shouted out, and Marcus felt the tingle of raging anger sweep up his spine.

Thallus himself had been among the brazen speakers.

Marcus saw Moriah's eyes rest on Thallus, saw her visible shudder. Thallus laughed aloud, his grating chuckle paling Moriah's already ghostly countenance even more. The pleasure he took by her terror was sickeningly clear.

Marcus's fists clenched until the strong fingers bit into the palm. The burning temptation to strangle Thallus were he stood was growing increasingly desirous. Silently, he prayed for resistance.

Heavenly Father! Let this be over quickly.

The auctioneer mounted the block beside Moriah, extending one hand to the crowd, the other closing around her fair white arm.

"Silence, citizens! I have here a fair lady, a talented companion for a noble family! She can sing and play as an entertainer; she can labor in your *domus*. Consider her, gentlemen. She is of child-bearing age, if that suits you."

Marcus had never so despised the sing-song prattle of an auctioneer before. Hearing Moriah's virtues spoken in so flippant a manner fairly maddened him, coloring his bronzed cheeks. What was she? An animal to be traded, a plaything of a man's lust and whim?

God forbid.

Christian charity was quickly failing to be one of his virtues.

The ceaseless whine of the auctioneer's voice continued. "By the command of our divine emperor, the bidding shall start at seven thousand *denarii* for this crowning beauty. Step up, gentleman! Who will start the bidding?"

The finger of Thallus arose. "I take it."

"Excellent! Any higher?"

Marcus glanced sidelong at his opponent. The sneering expression of Thallus's face was enough to launch a violent stream of bids from his lips, but he prudently remained silent.

Several more bids were placed, amounting to seven thousand and five hundred *denarii*. The price was clearly too exorbitant already to go much higher.

The auctioneer rubbed his hands together, surveying his bidders. "Come, gentleman! Have we any higher bids? Surely, this lovely woman is worth more!"

Thallus again raised his finger. "Seven thousand, six hundred *denarii*."

"Ah, hah! Any more?"

Marcus lifted his finger for the first time. "Seven thousand, eight hundred."

"Very good! Any higher?"

Thallus raised his finger. His glaring expression bristled the hairs on Marcus's arm, forming a visible tension between them. "Eight thousand."

Marcus felt a slow smile of amusement curl around the corners of his mouth. He alone could discern the slight ring of desperation that had bordered on Thallus's voice. Little wonder. The bidding was already outrageous.

He took a slight step forward. "Nine thousand."

A murmur swept like a rolling wave through the crowd.

Thallus's expression remained frigid, icy in its mingled disbelief and rage. Several patricians sent curious glances his way. Obviously, it was a well-known fact he intended to buy this lot.

The auctioneer looked from him to Marcus. "The bid is nine thousand *denarii*. Have you any higher bid, my noble friend?"

Thallus opened his mouth, then, shut it. He shook his head, his teeth visibly clenched.

"Sold to the noble tribune for nine thousand *denarii*!"

Marcus felt a chill of relieved satisfaction run through him. He refused to look at Thallus. He knew already that the young nobleman's face was black with enraged mortification. The tension between them could be fairly felt, bristling, weighting the air.

Its snap would not be scenic.

Stepping forward, Marcus laid his own and his father's note on the revenue table. The scribe glanced carelessly over them both, nodding.

"Tribune Marcus Virginius Aeneas. Your name is known and trusted, sir. You may take your new purchase home tonight and a collection will be made on your notes tomorrow."

"Good. Release the woman."

The scribe turned, gesturing carelessly to the guards. "Give her to her master." Then, bristling, "Gently there! This man paid a fortune."

Assuming a respectful carriage, the guards brought Moriah down from the block. White-faced and shaking, she seemed ready to drop. Subservient, she would not look at Marcus, hiding her drawn countenance with her tresses.

Marcus felt a pang of concern. She was clearly exhausted, doubtless overexerted by fear and her tortured shame. Quickly, he tossed a guard a coin.

"Open that room there."

The man obeyed, unbolting the door of a small room used for guarding slaves. Inside, a dozen scantily-clad women sat in shivering apprehension, awaiting their turn to be sold.

Quietly, Marcus led Moriah to the door and laid the modest clothing he had carried with him over her arm. "Go in and put these on, then come out to me."

Moriah's hands quivered as they closed around the clothing. Silently, she disappeared into the dusky abyss of the room.

Marcus waited for her, guardedly blocking the open door. The suspicion that Thallus might attempt to steal back his lost prize was a strong one, and his hand crept over the hilt of his *gladius*.

His keen eyes drifted over the noisy, crowded room. Another auction had begun, and three or four men were avidly bidding for a poor slip of a Greek on the block.

Thallus was nowhere to be seen.

Behind him, he felt a soft presence. Glancing over his shoulder, he saw Moriah, neatly attired and veiled. He beckoned her forward, laying a protecting hand on her cloaked back.

The crowded buyers made way for them, allowing them to pass out of the auctioning room. Outside, with the oil light casting flickering shadows on the cobblestoned street, Marcus cast a keen glance behind them.

No assassin was in sight.

His hand closed over his *gladius*. He would take no chances. God alone knew what murderers Thallus might have thought to hire.

With his free arm, Marcus led Moriah away from the noisy forum. The way was dark and quiet, a striking contrast to the chaos they left behind them. Full moonlight glistened off of Marcus's armor, coupling its light with the blazing torches of occasional pedestrians and at street-side corners.

Beneath his arm, Marcus could feel Moriah trembling. It was obvious he was leading her towards his own domus, away from the childhood home she had had no desire to leave.

Marcus wanted to explain, but he felt strangely unable to speak. His desire had been to take her immediately home, but legal matters made it impossible. Until the papers could be signed and witnessed, Moriah was his slave. She could not return to Daniel without the threat of being branded a runaway or—worse still—being terrorized by Thallus.

No. Marcus steeled himself. Whatever she or anyone else might think of him, he must personally oversee her protection. The fortune he had had just spent would avail little if she were seized as a runaway by Thallus.

And he would be certain to take advantage of any such possibility.

Marcus looked down at her. The moonlight shone full on her face, revealing that her eyes were brimful of soft tears. An instant pang fell on his heart.

She trusted him no more than Thallus.

He struggled with the thought. His throat was aching and dry, his heart too full for speech. After all he had saved her from, she still did not believe he was pure. She did not trust his motives, his intentions towards her.

For one short moment, bitterness welled up in Marcus. What was the purpose of controlling himself, of living an honorable life if she refused to think well of him? Her purity, her very life was in his hands. If she was determined to think ill of him, why should he not filch the fruit he could not pluck?

Instant shame tingled through his body. He could almost hear God's voice, whispering in his ear. *You don't live uprightly to seek men's praise and good opinion, Marcus. You do it for Me. Be worthy, whether you are rewarded or not.*

The mansion of Aeneas appeared, dark and silent. Marcus quickened his stride, the pressure of his arm tightening around Moriah's back as he guided her up the steps.

His increased speed seemed to provoke her first resistance. At the door, she stopped, lifting her white face imploringly to his.

"My lord, I *beg* you—"

"You have nothing to fear, Moriah." Marcus forced himself to speak with quiet command. The sight of her drawn face and tear-filled eyes was quickly becoming too much for him, and he feared he might be persuaded to send her home, despite the overwhelming dangers. Swiftly, he opened the door. "Go in."

Moriah's face crumpled into tears.

Marcus felt her tremor, sensed her inner struggle. He knew she was debating fighting him. He would not give her the chance to run. Whether she knew it or not, it would only be to her own destruction.

Hardening himself, he forced her inside.

Chapter Twenty-Five

Just inside the atrium, Marcus released Moriah's arm. Shaking with fear and exhaustion, she stumbled a few steps away from him.

He opened his lips to speak. The sooner he explained her position and his own decisions for her welfare, the better.

A sudden sound cut his intentions short.

Philip stepped into the dim lighting, crossing his arms upon his chest. "All hail, Marcus. I was uncertain where you had gone. I—" Sudden astonishment flitted across his every feature. "Moriah! Praise God! We have been sorely distressed for you. But why are you here, at this of all hours?"

Marcus bit his lip. He had not told Philip of his intentions, unwilling to attract praise or commendation from the brethren. The issue was a sensitive one, and he had hoped to quietly work out Moriah's freedom without fuss.

Now, however, he realized his mistake.

Slowly, dark fury washed over Philip's face. Marcus had not seen his eyes blaze with such unchecked anger since his conversion to Christianity. The expression in them was tangible, fairly prickling his skin.

A railing accusation could not have revealed Philip's suspicions more clearly.

Marcus felt the blood tingle in his face. For a military tribune, the presence of a boyish flush was growing strangely familiar. He opened his lips, ready to defend himself against the unspoken charge.

"Ah! So you have got her, Marcus!"

Marcus clamped his mouth shut. He turned to see Cleotas stride casually across the atrium. Cleotas paused in critical survey before Moriah, his arms crossed upon his chest. A defined nod titled his chin.

"She is a beauty! I must commend you, Marcus. I see the years of restraint have not taken the edge of your good taste."

Marcus swallowed. "Father, I–"

"Ah, there, do not mind me." Cleotas waved his hand carelessly. "She is your slave, not mine. I know my presence is not desired." His eyes twinkled in a knowing wink. "*Vale*, Marcus."

With the swiftness of his coming, Cleotas was gone.

A long silence fell over the atrium.

Marcus glanced sidelong at Moriah. Her hazel eyes were downcast, maidenly color high in her forehead. His gaze traveled downwards, seeing her tightly clasped hands tremble.

Helplessness overcame him. *God, what have I done these last five years that everyone doubts me now?* It was too late for explanations, too late to avow how entirely guileless his intentions were. Cleotas's misunderstandings had entirely nullified whatever excuse he might give.

"Moriah, please go into the library and wait there."

Wordlessly, Moriah bent and crossed the room, her tread soft.

Her subservience hurt Marcus to see. He had spoken gently, but her understanding of his command was clear: she saw him in the light of the master who owned and controlled her.

With Moriah's exit into the library, Marcus turned from following her movements. He was met by Philip's flashing eyes. Abruptly, the young man turned away from him, contempt livid in his features.

"Stay here." Marcus spoke almost sharply. The misunderstandings had come to their final summit.

"Your pardon." Philip's icy tones could have been carried by the frigid mountain snow. "I would not think of diverting your *pleasure*."

He once again turned to stalk away.

Marcus caught him by the shoulder. "I command you to stay and listen to me. By the Caesars, have you no respect for your master?"

Philip turned so passionately Marcus was nearly startled. He stepped back, soldierly instinct lifting his hand to the sword at his side. His British slave was more than capable of knocking him to the floor if he chose to do so.

"Well you speak of respect, Marcus!" Anger rent Philip's voice. "Where is your respect for the things of the faith? Where is your compassion, your decency? Moriah has suffered unspeakable shame already without this. How dare you—a professor and advocate of our faith—turn your own sister into an object of sport? You mock Christian purity, *everything* we stand for!"

Marcus lifted his hands. "Peace!"

He shook his head, trying to rid himself of the torrent of accusations. The aching well of hurt was too much. First Alexander, then Cleotas, now Philip. They were all one in their poor assumptions of his character.

Huskiness threatened to overcome his voice. He felt weary and broken, suddenly more discouraged than he could ever recall feeling. "Do not chide me, Philip."

Philip's fiery gaze lapsed into stony petulance.

Fighting the impulse to lash out, Marcus swallowed back the welled-up indignation and hurt threatening to overcome his control. He heard the sound of his own strained voice, a poignant plea he had never before made to a slave.

"By God in His heavens, do not accuse me of these things, Philip. I cannot bear it coming from you. I am innocent. *Believe* me, Philip, believe me to be the honorable man I have sought to become these last few years."

Philip's eyes softened. Like the flickering wane of an oil lamp, the flashing sparks in his pupils died to quiet searching. "If I have misjudged you, my master, I will never forgive myself."

"It is a reasonable conclusion." Marcus fought to steady his voice. "But I would not do it, Philip. I purchased Moriah to save her from Thallus, nothing more. Surely, it is better for me to be her master than him."

"Yes." New quietness governed Philip. "If your intentions are as you say, her fate is indeed a fortunate one."

Marcus stepped passionately forward. "I swear I am telling you the truth." His voice cracked, feeling as if he were ripping his own heart from his body. This was by far the most difficult temptation he had endured. "As soon as the arrangements can be made, I will set her free."

Philip stood motionless. Slow sympathy visualized in his face. "Marcus—"

Marcus whirled around. Philip's unexpected compassion; his own aching heart; the tortured knowledge of what he knew Moriah was thinking of him was too much.

He leaned his head on a pillar, his strong right arm half-encircling its smooth exterior. Involuntarily, his free hand tightened into a vehement fist, perspiration gliding through his fingers.

Before his eyes, the dimly-lit atrium grew misty.

"I should have never doubted you." Behind him, Philip's voice was almost husky. He felt a hand rest on his shoulder, gripping him. "You have lived honorably since your conversion. I had no right to accuse you."

Marcus straightened himself. Resentment threatened to command him, but he refused to harbor it. Philip had forgiven far greater wrongs in him; he could forgive this insult to his character.

Still, he sensed that, though he forgave, he might never forget.

"You were not alone, Philip. Whatever my good intentions, I know others doubt me. Still," and Marcus smiled a little bitterly, "perhaps Moriah herself will reveal I have done her no harm."

Silence fell over the atrium.

Marcus cast a glance at the library door. The longer he waited, he knew, the more difficult his temptation would grow. "Go to her, Philip. See that she is made comfortable in the guest chamber. And," his voice again lapsed into huskiness, "assure her of her safety."

"Will you not come with me?"

316

"No-no. I dare not. She cannot abide my presence and—and you know my feelings. Go, quickly."

Philip silently crossed his hands on his chest.

His chest aching, Marcus watched him go. Abruptly, he looked away, blinking. The swelling pain was gradually becoming unbearable. His soul screamed for answers, rising in sudden petition.

Oh, God, somehow work Your perfect plan through this.

In the shadowed library, Moriah stood beside the window. It opened into the garden, ushering the dark, sweet fragrance of rose petals into the room. The odor mingled with the dusty scent of scrolls and ink, partially tranquilizing her.

Nothing, however, could entirely still her fears.

Her heart beat in regular rhythm, echoing against her chest. The last few hours had been one long nightmare, a blur of shame, terrifying faces, and Marcus.

Marcus.

She looked down, clasping her hands. They still shook. Her terror of Thallus had lapsed into the deep, frightening pain of betrayal. Sudden hot tears blurred her vision, and she bit her lip.

Is this your way of showing your love?

It was difficult to swallow the bitterness welling up in her heart. She had refused to marry Marcus; now he purchased her. She would not willingly give him what he wanted; he would use her like all Roman men used their slaves.

She had had her misgivings, but she had never considered him capable of this. Somehow, the shame was worse than if Thallus had taken her for his slave. *My own brother. The man who claimed to love me.*

Moriah suddenly closed her eyes, allowing the salty tears to steal in quiet trickles down her cheeks. *Oh, God.* Her heart cried out, her petition too great for utterance. *Do not let Marcus deal this way with me.*

Touch his heart, his conscience. Keep him from this sin—and me from this shame.

A sudden, quiet step behind her sent the blood rushing from her face. Her heart seemed to stop, leaping into her throat.

Oh, God.

The step drew nearer. It was the well-defined tread of a man. She refused to turn, shaking, waiting. Again, she closed her eyes, agonizingly awaiting the sound of Marcus's voice.

"Moriah."

In a burning rush, she felt the color flood her face. She turned, her relieved exhale almost a cry. "Philip."

The handsome young man stood before, gravely quiet. The faint beams of streaming moonlight rested on his face and body, accenting his muscular strength. It was a powerful strength she had only seen exerted on behalf of the weak, the defenseless.

If anyone could save her, it was he.

"What will he do with me?" The question escaped her, a tremulous whisper.

Philip's grave eyes met hers. "You were not purchased as his slave, Moriah. My master's only intent was to save you from the lust of Thallus." His eyes momentarily fixed themselves on the illuminated patterns of moonlight, streaming on the floor. "You and I have done him a great injustice, my sister."

Moriah stood motionless. "I do not understand." She felt as if she were drowning, a bewildering well of mixed emotions settling slowly around her. Surely, she had not misjudged the intentions of Marcus towards her. "Why did he bring me here if not for his own pleasure?"

"You know the laws, Moriah. It is impossible for him to free you immediately. There are legal documents to be signed, and you cannot be released until you are under no obligation or possibility of false accusation."

"Then he—" Moriah cut herself short, closing her eyes. Slowly, the tears ebbed their way through her lashes, trickling down her face. Burning shame and relief enveloped her, sinking into her heart. Her voice faltered, unbelieving. "He will let me go?"

"Yes."

"It cannot be." Moriah felt a half-smothered sob catch her throat. She turned away, resting her arm and head against the wall. This was not the man she had convinced herself he was. "Why? Why will he let me go?"

Philip's hand rested gently on her heaving shoulder. "Because he loves you. And, more importantly, because he loves his God."

Moriah placed her hand over her mouth, trying to still the sounds of her weeping. Until that moment, she had not realized how greatly she had hated and feared Marcus. Now, her feelings filled her with shame more vivid than the one she had endured on the auction block.

He was noble, upright. And she had despised him more than Thallus himself.

Gradually, her weeping stilled. "Why did he not tell me himself?"

"He knows your feelings against him."

"Then he will not even come near me?"

"At least for tonight, no." Philip's hand dropped from her shoulder. She knew he was torn between brotherly compassion and protocol. Though they were now equals in station, she was the property of his master. "Moriah…"

She looked up at him. He had said her name with the whisper of a breath, something like appeal deep in his tones. And the keenness of his deep blue eyes upon her was an expression she had never before seen from him.

Her breathing grew calm, matching his quiet mien. "Yes?"

"Can you forgive?"

The tears started again in her eyes. She looked down. Softly, her hand found his arm, tracing his scars. "Philip–"

Firmly, his hand grasped hers, holding it away from his arm. "Moriah, don't look at it." His voice softened. "Look only at Jesus.

Look at His sacrifice, the blood He shed for all mankind. *Can you forgive?*"

Moriah's heart swelled. She felt the tears streaming down her face. She could not speak to answer, unable to overcome the knowledge of her own unforgiveness and Marcus's unfathomable goodness.

Philip dropped her hand, resting his own on her shoulders. His passion seemed to step beyond rank and bloodline. His eyes sought hers, intently pleading.

"Moriah, my master is far from perfect. He is only a man. But, Moriah, he is *such* a man. He has been faithful to God and upright in his ways. And no one can say more for anyone than that."

Moriah looked at him. Though overflowing, her eyes refused to blink, to turn away from his fervent gaze. The pressure of Philip's hand increased on her shoulders.

"You know his past, the things he did to me. I will not pretend they did not happen. But, Moriah, he did not know what he was doing. Even in my greatest sufferings, I knew in my heart he did not understand. He was a Roman, acting in obedience to his father and his country's demands. And, Christ be extolled, I forgave him."

Philip's hands dropped. His hand closed around his arm, his eyes flickering with something like deep pain.

"Moriah, I sense you have held what you have seen and heard against Marcus. But you see the scars of a punishment I *deserved*. I was a rebellious slave and he a hardened master. Can you not understand? We were *both* redeemed by the blood of the lamb. Marcus is pure before his God. And if you cannot give him your love," his voice softened into huskiness, "at least do not continue to crush your spirit with bitterness. Inability to love a man as your husband is one matter. Unforgiveness is another."

Moriah could feel his fervor. His breath was warm, his whole body alive with an emotion he rarely portrayed. Somehow, his eyes seemed to bore into her soul, filling her with overwhelming heartbreak.

Oh, God. Her soul screamed out, rising above the whirling multitude of thoughts echoing in her heated brain. *What have I done?*

Marcus unclasped the bands encircling his wrists. His cloak came next, and he laid it absently over his wristbands.

Glancing down, his heart twisted strangely. Even in the dim lighting, the redness of his cape was a scarlet flame, a vivid symbol. On the day he had become a soldier, he had laid aside the white tunic of pure citizenship for the scarlet blood of a warrior. *No wonder she despises me.* Even his clothing was a symbol of blood, suffering.

And the hands that longed to hold hers at the wedding altar were one that had killed.

"Oh, God." Marcus felt the groan rush from his lips. "You called me to the service of a soldier, both in Your service and Rome's. Do not let me hate my own calling because I cannot win her love."

Uttering the words aloud was like a *pugio* in his chest. Marcus looked down, fighting heartache. He could never win her love.

Is her affection your only desire, Marcus?

"No." Marcus breathed the words. "You know it is not, my God. I want Your will first."

Then be content in My time, My plan. There will not be given you any trial you cannot bear.

"Is it wrong to want companionship?" Marcus heard the words escape him in a sort of cry. His soul felt sick within him, his spirit crushed. "Is it wrong to want the love of a godly wife? Do I sin in desiring her? Have I not waited, been faithful to You and to her? Why? *Why?*"

Marcus felt himself pulled downwards. Sinking to his knees, he lifted his hands in mute appeal. Strangely, he felt no answer. He heard only a still, small voice.

Worship Me.

"I will love You, my Lord, my strength." Marcus's voice was broken. "I honor and extol You, my God." His voice faltered. "I will serve You, even if You never give me my heart's desire."

The soft night breeze rustled in, cooling his heated cheeks. Slowly, his misty eyes drifted towards the streaming moonlight, dancing off the polished floor of his balcony. Like that ceaseless, constant light, his heart would go on, ever loving, though never receiving love in return.

He arose, letting the pale glimmers rest on his face. His breathing softened, exhaling into a sighing groan.

"I will always love you, Moriah."

In the lavish guest room, Moriah stood at the open casement. Her eyes were dim, still flooded with soft tears.

The luxurious treatment she had been given had not been her expectations for this night of terror. A female slave had bathed her face and hands in scented water, helping her exchange her clothing for comfortable night apparel. Her couch had been freshly made up, decked with perfumed pillows and woven coverings.

In one corner of the chamber, a single oil lamp burned, casting its glow over the room. Its soft light caressed her skin. She looked down, her shadow a maidenly silhouette against the patterned floor.

The form of a woman.

Her throat tightened. A woman that was still pure before God and man.

Suddenly, she crumpled. Leaning her back against the wall, she pulled her knees into her chest and cried.

Realization of Marcus's goodness was one thing. Coming to grips with her own bitterness and the unjust hatred she had harbored was another. She had not seen it as sin before. Now, she realized it for what it was. In all its dark forms, the ghastly head of the monster *sin* arose in her mind, striking repentance into her heart.

Oh, God. I would not forgive him. I would not see his worth. Is it too late to undo all I have done?

She lifted her head. A thought struck her, vivid as words of fire. Her brimful eyes settled on the lamp burning with such a soft, yet steady flame in the opposite corner of the room.

Was it too late for *Marcus* to forgive?

Chapter Twenty-Six

Marcus waited tentatively for the ink to dry upon his parchment. He glanced up, beckoning. "You may sign it."

Silently, Alexander laid down his goblet of wine and came across the room. Leaning over the table, he signed his name on the scroll and applied his seal.

Marcus took up the parchment, his dark eyes scanning its contents. "Alexander Lucianius, legionary of Rome." He nodded slowly, something like sadness stealing over his clear-cut features. "You are my witness to the freedom I bestow on my slave Moriah, *per testamentum*."

"I am honored you desired my witness." Alexander's green eyes were quiet, but Marcus could see their pupils flicker with respect. "May our everlasting Lord bless you for your honorable dealings with our sister."

"Amen." Marcus's voice was soft. Lifting his hand in wordless farewell, he watched Alexander exit the room at a soldierly stride.

Alone, he sat toying with his signet ring. He had already pressed into the wax, sealing his written documentation of his decision.

Moriah was free.

Somehow let this be for Your glory, Father. His heart was sore. A long night of prayer and supplication had brought little relief to his spirit. *May Your will be accomplished.*

The sound of the opening door aroused his attention. Lifting his eyes, he saw Moriah enter, her garments rustling ever so slightly. Strange how so simple a sound portrayed her grace, her feminine modesty.

"You sent for me, my lord?"

"Yes." Marcus stood up, beckoning her to his side.

Moriah drew near, her eyes discreetly lowered. Beneath her modest veil, she bent as he neared him, crossing her hands upon her breast.

Marcus's heart thudded. Somehow, her charm was only more appealing in such subservient form. Nonetheless, it hurt him to see her womanly spirit chained by degrading servitude.

"No, Moriah." Quick and almost stern, he felt the words escape him at a masterful rush. "I do not require this of you."

Moriah stood erect, her eyes still averted. "You are my lord and master. Surely you expect homage from your slaves."

"Yes, from my slaves and the soldiers under my command." Marcus saw the glowing color illuminating Moriah's cheeks, visible even beneath her half-bent head and loosely falling veil. "But you are no man's slave, Moriah."

She looked up at him. Marcus saw the half-inquiring turn of her eyes, the sudden catch of her breathing.

"I do not understand."

"I believe Philip sufficiently explained it to you last night."

Moriah's eyes again became downcast. "He explained your noble intentions towards me, my lord. But I did not think I could possibly be sent home so quickly."

"As long as it was my gold that purchased you, it is indeed possible." Marcus dropped his eyes to the parchment on the table, fingering its edges. The longer he stood alone in Moriah's presence, the more difficult it was contemplating sending her away. "Here is the legal documentation of your freedom. I have had a copy made for your benefit as you leave."

Moriah seemed unable to speak. She stood still, her hands clasped together.

Marcus's voice cracked. "You are free to depart. I have a litter prepared for your use, and Philip will escort you home to Daniel."

Moriah looked up, revealing the soft mist bordering on her lashes. "Thank you, Marcus." Her voice was a soft whisper. "May God reward you for your kindness towards me."

Marcus gazed down at her. Twin battles of love and passion raged in his heart, threatening to overcome him. The sight of her unashamed tears and simple gratitude was even more moving than her subservience.

His hands twitched. He could smell the soft rosy scent of her garments, the sandalwood of her hair. It was intoxicating him, a rush of adrenaline to his veins.

He had to get her out of his sight.

Give me strength. He was so weak, so ready to yield. Temptation was never stronger than when it was about to be lost.

"You may go."

His voice sounded so unlike his own. He sensed Moriah looking up at him, but he steadfastly averted his eyes, looking above her.

Oh, God, let my mind be stayed on You. Men are so feeble, so carnal. Do not let my heart sin, though my body is pure. Help me.

Moriah again bent, the folds of her veil brushing Marcus's hand. "The God of our fathers be with you."

Like a vision of the night, she was gone. Her presence remained, her scent in Marcus's nostrils. Had she only been a mirage of his weary mind?

Marcus stepped to the door. Clapping his hands, he waited until Philip appeared. Almost refusing to look at it, he handed him the parchment copy of the freedom papers.

"Take this with you to Daniel's. Give it to him with all assurance of Moriah's legal restoration as a citizen of Rome. And, tell him—"Marcus paused, fighting the aching lump in his throat, "tell him I return his daughter to him a chaste virgin."

"Yes, master." Quietly compassionate, Philip half-bent. He straightened himself, and, for only lingering instant, touched Marcus's shoulder.

Then, he was gone, leaving Marcus alone with the burning ache welling up in his chest and the full reality of despondent *aloneness.*

At the Baths, Marcus attempted to forget his trials in the soothing relaxation of the steaming hot water.

The warm scents and comfortable drowsiness did partially tranquilize him, but not even Philip's vigorous massaging could drive into the heart of his pain. He lay motionless on the marble bench, his muscles relaxed and snapped of tension, but his soul sick within him.

There was no escape from the throngs of his suffering.

As he settled his toga more comfortably over his military uniform, he wondered dully if he would ever forget; if life could be endured without the satisfaction of his desires. Was he destined to always walk thus: faithful, trusting, hoping, yet ever alone?

The quietness of the Aeneas domus did little to lighten his spirits. Orderly and tranquil, its very stability was a thorn in the flesh to Marcus's apathetic discontentment.

He moved listlessly into the garden. The sweet, warm scent was only a lingering reminder of the unhappy fate he could not change. By all the Caesars in succession! Why could he not forget; why was *everything* a lingering reminder?

Rise up in faith, Marcus.

Marcus's head jerked erect. Was it any wonder he was so miserable, so lost inside his own feelings and desires? Until he buried his hopes and wishes, surrendering them to the God he loved, he would never be at peace. He was a man, a warrior. More importantly, he was a Christian.

It was time to go forward as one.

"Help me to forget." Marcus slid from the garden bench to his knees, not caring if the slaves or even Cleotas saw him. "Great God in heaven, help me move forward. Do not let bitterness fill my life because I cannot have the one thing I want."

Even as he spoke, Marcus realized the convicting truth. All along, it had been about *his* wants. Even when he had saved Moriah, somewhere, at the back of all his noble, truehearted motives, had been the undeniable desire to keep her pure for himself.

Now, he wanted to devote himself to the motives of true charity. Love was not partial, as he was. It did not save Moriah alone, but was lifted up on behalf of the poor and defenseless brethren everywhere.

Marcus felt a tinge. He did not think himself capable of ever becoming the exemplar of faith and charity Philip and the others were. But, in his own way, he could try.

"No longer, Father. I will not dwell upon myself, but upon others. Help me to rise up in Your strength."

As he spoke, Marcus felt a new peace flood his heart. The pain was there; perhaps it always would be. But he could go on. He would not be a prisoner of circumstances, but a steadfast follower of the One who held him in the palm of His almighty hand.

"Marcus?"

From his knees, Marcus looked up. Philip stood along the *peristyle*, clearly regretful for the interruption.

"Yes?"

"A thousand apologies, but Daniel is in the atrium awaiting you."

Stiffly, Marcus rose to his feet. He grimaced ever so slightly. This was precisely what he had hoped to avoid. The accident of his success in the slave-forum was not a thing he wished to be praised for, particularly coming from the adopted father of the woman he loved.

"See that we are not disturbed." Marcus crossed the *peristyle* into the atrium. His dark eyes scanned the room, finding Daniel at one end.

His sandaled feet swished against the floor, and Daniel turned. Masking his discomfort beneath mannerly casualness, Marcus stepped easily across the floor, extending his hand.

"All hail, my friend."

"Peace in the name of our Lord, Marcus." Daniel gripped his forearm, holding him for a long moment. "And may His blessing rest upon you."

There was a slight moment of silence. Marcus felt at a sudden loss for words, awkwardly uncertain what to say. He cleared his throat, partially calming the discomfort of his nerves.

Great Caesars, but boyish uncertainty was becoming frustratingly characteristic of him. Where was his military boldness, the courage that enabled him to lead thousands of men into combat? It was unsettling how the presence of one particular man could shatter his confidence with the ease of a pottery jar.

Daniel's eyes were warm as he spoke. "Marcus, I will not mask the purpose of my coming. I am here to thank you. No," as Marcus opened his lips to speak, "do not stop me. God was with you; there is no debating that score. But your virtue is also to merit."

"If there is any virtue in me, Daniel," and Marcus's voice was soft, "it is not to my credit. You know that."

"Yes. But even the strongest of believers stumble sometimes, my brother. You have stood strong where many another man might have failed."

Marcus said nothing. Did he dare mention how close he came to losing his control, to filching his desires because he could not win them nobly?

"I cannot repay you, Marcus. All I can give is my thanks and the acknowledgment of the worthy young man you are."

"I did not do it for thanks, Daniel." Marcus felt frustration build within him. Why, he could not tell. All he knew was that he deserved no gratitude, no blessing or praise. *If there was anything noble in my actions, Father, it was You shining through me.* "I did only as the Lord directed me."

Daniel looked keenly at him. "And as your own tender love guided?"

Marcus felt no embarrassment in the query. He would not deny it. His love and life were pledged to Moriah, whether she shared that oath or not. He tilted his chin ever-so slightly, quietly resolute. "Yes."

"Then your love continues? It has not died?"

"I am not a fickle man, Daniel. My feelings for Moriah have only grown stronger, never weaker."

Daniel's searching countenance relaxed visibly. "I felt certain of this, but I had to be certain. Marcus, if you could have the hand and heart of the woman you desire, would you accept them?"

Marcus looked dully at him. Why did Daniel torment him with meaningless questions, with possibilities that could never be? "You know I would. It is my life's deepest hope."

Daniel placed a hand on his shoulder. "Then consider it won."

Marcus stared at him. His heart lurched, nearly choking him. The shock was quickly followed by burning anger. "Do not mock me, Daniel. This is too cruel in you."

"I do not mock you, Marcus. I speak truly."

"But *why?*" Marcus felt contempt livid on his face, in his voice. "Because I preserved her purity? Does that make her my rightful tribute? No, Daniel. It is low of you to offer her to me and my acceptance would only be lower still."

He half-turned away, afraid of his own anger. What did Daniel take him for? A man who took advantage of a woman's misfortune? *Does he think I guarded her virginity out of selfishness alone?*

God forbid he would take any woman to wife under these conditions.

"Is it then a sin to wed the woman who is willing to have you for her husband?"

Low and meaningful, Daniel's words halted Marcus in his stride. He turned, disbelieving his own sanity. Surely, his mind was not beginning to taunt him.

"*What?*"

Daniel stepped a little forward. "Moriah is willing, Marcus."

"I don't understand." Confusion shot through Marcus's mind. What could have possibly changed Moriah's heart towards him?

She hated him, both past and present. *Even my occupation is distasteful to her.*

"Who can understand it? It is a confusing thing when a woman's heart is changed. But, Marcus, I think I know what softened her. You have proven you are not the sort of man she thought you were."

Marcus stood motionless, his feet riveted to the floor. His heart thudded. His chest felt tight, unable to breathe or comprehend the full reality of Daniel's words. *Why?*

He heard himself ask the question aloud. "Why? Last night alone could not have moved her heart."

Daniel looked steadily at him. "And why not? One instance of your nobleness was enough to convince her."

"Then this is some outpouring of her thankfulness, some payment she feels obligated to give me?"

"No. Moriah is not an impetuous woman."

"But does she *love* me?" Marcus's voice cracked. He felt frustrated confusion boiling up within him. He wanted to believe, to trust that Moriah sincerely desired him. But after so much rejection, so much pain? *Lord, she hurt me deeply. Can she really be sincere now?*

One thing was certain: he refused to be rejected again.

"I know she honors you. And she loves you enough to marry you. But I think these are things you ought to ask her yourself." Daniel turned towards the library, his call quiet. "Moriah."

Moriah appeared in the library door.

Marcus felt the blood rise in his cheeks. She had to have heard every word that passed between them. But perhaps it was just as well she knew what he was thinking.

Moriah came softly towards them, a soft blush mantling her cheeks. She did not look at him. Her hazel eyes were downcast, maidenly discreet.

Marcus's heart twisted. That was exactly what he loved about her. She was spirited and courageous, yet, still so modest. It was if her reservation came at the most appropriate times, transforming her from a strong woman into an angelic figure of sweet submission.

Did he dare allow himself to acknowledge how perfect he considered her?

"I will leave you alone." Daniel crossed his hands upon his breast, the tiniest hint of a smile playing about his bearded mouth. "May God guide your hearts."

Silence fell over the atrium with his departure.

Marcus fingered his wristband, studying Moriah. She remained silent, never lifting her eyes.

Was it possible that such an angel would give herself to him?

The thought alone sent the blood tingling throughout his body, warming him through. His heart swelled. The echoing sound of his own voice nearly startled him, realizing the abruptly broken silence.

"Speak, Moriah. Tell me if what Daniel says is true."

Moriah lifted her eyes to his face. "Yes."

Soft and simple, her tones were like an adrenaline rush. Marcus's hands clamped into tight fists, forcing himself to remain stationary. He steeled himself. He must not let momentary exhilaration erase the memories of all he had suffered.

All he feared he might suffer again.

"Why? What has changed your heart, Moriah?"

Before him, Moriah's hazel pupils melted into soft tears. "I was wrong, Marcus." Her whisper was broken. "I refused to think well of you. I thought only of your past, of things you did in ignorance and before Christ."

Marcus felt his heart swell. Whatever else, her apology was sincere. He softened his voice, willing his sympathy to overflow to her. "And you now think differently?"

"Yes. I know," and a tremor caught Moriah's tones, "you are who you claim to be. You are a noble Christian, a man of God."

A man of God. Marcus stood still a moment, allowing the words to sink in. They were ones he had never expected to hear from

Moriah. He felt huskiness overcome his tones, swelling in his throat.

"I don't deserve that you should think so well of me."

"But I *do*, Marcus." Moriah's misty eyes flashed sudden light. "Don't think me fickle and foolish. Last night revealed much. I am ashamed," and her voice lowered, "that it took such a sacrifice on your part for me to see your goodness, but my eyes *have* been opened. And I honor you, Marcus."

"Is honor all you feel for me?" Marcus fixed his eyes with piercing keenness on her. His heart ached, caught between love, joy, and the overwhelming fear Moriah's actions were of gratitude. "I must know, Moriah."

Moriah said nothing.

His pulse pounding, Marcus stepped forward, his hands passionately brushing hers. "Speak your heart. Tell me if you love me. If you don't," his voice cracked, "do not be afraid to tell me."

"I care for you deeply, Marcus." Moriah spoke clearly, her voice steadfast. "I can truly say I love you as something more than a brother." Her eyes lowered. "Whether I love you as passionately as a woman ought to love a husband, I cannot tell. But, if not, I know I will learn to."

She will learn to. Somehow, the admittance did not pain Marcus as he would have thought. She cared for and honored him. When most couples married for politics and connections, what more could he ask? *She cares enough to become my wife. Lord, is this Your will?*

Marcus knew instinctively he had no reason to ask. He had always been assured of God's will in this matter. They were meant to marry, meant to raise a godly seed for Christ.

Slowly, curtailing his eagerness, he closed his hands over hers. They felt soft and warm to his touch. His fingers intertwined themselves with hers. "Then, Moriah, in the name of our Lord and Savior, will you wed me?"

"Yes." Moriah's voice was a breath. Her eyes flitted over his face, beautifully expectant.

Marcus felt a rush of adrenaline unlike anything he had ever experienced before. In a flash, sufferings of the past were forgotten, melted into perfect, joyous exhilaration.

He closed the step between them. The desire to kiss her was strong, but he held himself in check. Doing so was the seal of marriage, ending her virginity. He would wait until a bishop pronounced them one in Christ and she was truly his.

Still, nothing would keep him from expressing his joy.

Releasing her hands, he enfolded her in his strong embrace. She came willingly, resting her head on his shoulder. Marcus laid his head over hers, his grip tightening. Again, his nostrils were filled with her rosy scent, warming him.

Through the seemingly endless well of joy resounding in his mind, he became conscious that his heart was singing. It sang as never before. A thousand choruses rang in his mind, but, somehow, only one phrase stood vivid.

His promises are true! They are true!

His eyes closed, exhaling into her soft tresses. Everything was quickly becoming a blur of emotions, overwhelming his heart and mind. But his heart would go on, going on with singing.

It would never end.

Chapter Twenty-Seven

"In the name of the Father, Spirit, and Jesus Christ our Lord, may you be known as man and wife." Daniel's voice carried over the wide banquet chamber, filling every nook with his joyous tenors.

His milling listeners stood silent. Their countenances were alive, some with quiet joy, others with approval. Overall, the atmosphere was one of satisfaction. From soldier to patrician, they were in one accord of thanksgiving.

Philip, leaning against one of the pillars, felt his throat swell with a sudden aching pain. He stood in clear view of the wedding couple, close enough to see Marcus's fingers squeeze his bride's hand. She lifted her eyes to his, her face caressed with blushes.

Philip swallowed. He felt a bittersweet ache tugging at his heartstrings, washing in a faint mist over his eyes. He blinked, allowing the watery smile to widen over his face. Despite the emotion, his heart was singing.

Thank you, Lord. I praise You for this glorious day.

Daniel's strong voice carried on. "What God has joined together, let no man put asunder. I bless you, my son and daughter, in the name of our Savior. May your union be fruitful, an olive tree around your table. Amen and amen."

A swift explosion of applause echoed through the room.

Philip mingled his handclapping with the others. He blinked again, clearing the foggy mist blurring his vision. As his eyes regained their focus, he saw Marcus bend over Moriah, placing his lips to hers.

The deed was done, the official seal given.

In the year of their Lord, sixty-six *anno domoni*, Tribune Marcus Virginius Aeneas had taken his wife.

Philip saw the lingering love-look shared between them. His heart warmed. Since the day Moriah had pledged to wed Marcus, he had seen a great transformation in her. It was if she had purposed to knit her heart to his.

And love had grown.

As a new dawn. Philip brought his arms up, folding them against his broad chest. His heart continued to swell. The mix of emotions he felt was beyond even his own understanding.

The month following his master's betrothal had been heaven on earth for Marcus. Philip had seldom seen a more joyful, contented man or a more cherished bride-to-be. Marcus had lavished every attention upon Moriah, endowing her with every possible token of his affection.

Even today, her rich wedding attire was a symbol of Marcus's overwhelming care for her comfort and happiness. She wore the traditional white tunic, though had declined the elaborate belt of Hercules. In every possible respect, she and Marcus had desired a Christian wedding.

In light of that desire and with the need for safety, only Christian brethren had been invited to the ceremony. Later, a banquet of high-ranking officials and Praetorian officers would be held to satisfy Cleotas's wishes and Marcus's own public duties.

Philip's eyes rested on Moriah's sparkling face, feeling his heart again grow warm. Moriah looked more beautiful than ever, her countenance alive with radiance. She chatted gracefully with the guests, accepting their well-wishes with blushing charm.

Your ways are not our ways, Lord. He lifted his heart in silent praise. How miraculous it was that it had taken Nero's persecution and the shame of the auction block to bring Moriah to the full-realization of Marcus's noble goodness.

As always, God's plan was vast and mysterious.

He saw Cleotas approach Marcus, folding him in a quick, hearty embrace. Releasing him, he took Moriah by the shoulders and kissed her on both cheeks.

Philip felt a smile tugging at his mouth. He remembered the conversation Cleotas and Marcus had shared about Moriah. Cleotas's angry confusion had been unmistakable.

"Over nine thousand *denarii* for a slave! Marcus, my *son*." Philip recalled the veins bulging in Cleotas's neck, deserted of all his charming good-humor. "If you had wanted a wife, I could have gotten you one for nothing. And a dowry to enhance the deal, by Pollux! But you choose a *slave?*"

"You either can't or won't understand me, Cleotas." Marcus's tense, low voice had bordered on frustration. "I already attempted to explain I did not buy Moriah for my own lustful intents. I purchased her only to preserve her purity from men like Thallus Quinctia." The sarcastic bent of his voice rose into unbreakable resolve. "I've restored her as a Roman citizen. And I will *marry* her."

Cleotas threw his hands in the air. "And to think that when you brought that-that—" a quick warning look from Marcus checked the language on his lips, "*slave* home I had hope for you. I thought you were at last coming to your senses. But by the gods, Marcus! I will never understand you Christians."

"You don't have to. But you did promise not to interfere, father."

"So I did. But—oh, great Jupiter! She spent a single night in this household. You claim she is still chaste. So be it, Marcus! You don't have to wed her. Your goodness will enable her to marry another."

"I am not marrying her for some misled form of duty, Cleotas." Philip recalled Marcus's passionate voice, his almost fierce attempts to explain himself. "I *love* her. And I love her too much to offer her any position lower than that of my wife. Praise God, I'll take her to me with honor: pure, a Roman citizen, and coming to me of her own free will. It's what any true man ought to offer a woman, not merely a Christian."

The conversation had ended abruptly.

From his serving corner, Philip had seen the anger of Cleotas's countenance melt into something deeper than confusion.

It became clear upon his face. Marcus's words had stirred thoughts that had never crossed his mind. It was as if personal responsibility had never before burdened him. Marcus's intentions were for honor. His had never been for more than his pleasure.

After all, what sort of a male, let alone a Roman one, liberated women in such a man's world?

Whether the conversation changed Cleotas's viewpoints about his lifestyle, Philip did not claim to know. He only knew that, behind all his frustration, there was a deep respect for the young man he called his son.

And he endeavored to love Moriah on account.

His mind flitting back to the present moment, Philip saw Moriah's eyes warm at Cleotas's embrace. In spite of his carnal Roman ways, Philip knew she loved him, for Marcus's sake if for no other reason.

Cleotas looked a moment into her lovely eyes. A smile played about his lips, and he winked at Marcus before returning to mingle with his guests.

Philip dropped his arms, taking a half-step forward. He had curtailed the burning to desire to congratulate Marcus long enough.

Almost as quickly, he stopped.

Several legionaries approached Marcus, Alexander among them. As usual, the slave must bide his time.

He leaned back against the pillar. The soldiers took their leisure congratulating Moriah and making polite salutations to their commander. Marcus was cordial, even merry, but his eyes continually roved beyond his congratulators, searching for someone.

Philip instinctively stepped forward, making himself visible. He sensed Marcus was looking for him, perhaps desiring some service.

Marcus's face relaxed. He beckoned slightly.

Politely, Philip made his way around the group of men to Marcus's side. He bowed slightly, expecting a trivial command. But Marcus laid a hand on his shoulder, drawing him closer.

"Stand here."

Philip was tinged by confusion. He looked at Marcus, surprised by his low voice, his almost mysterious command and close presence. This was not like his master. When in company, Marcus was ever the stern Praetorian tribune, the proud Roman patrician. His friendship with his British slave was a private matter, never exposed to the public eye.

Marcus met his inquiring gaze for a long moment before turning away. He raised his hand for silence, his strong voice reverberating through the room. "A moment's peace, good friends. Gather around; I have a few words."

Silence fell over the room.

Philip felt the pressure of Marcus's hand increase, squeezing his shoulder. A strange tingle rushed down his spine. He could sense the eyes of the guests resting upon him, expectancy deep in their faces.

His confusion deepened. *What do they know that I don't?*

From his peripheral vision, he saw Marcus turn towards him. Instinctively, he faced him. Immediately, his eyes were locked into the dark pupils of Marcus's gaze, as so often had been his case.

Marcus's voice was strong when he spoke, but there was a strange huskiness bordering on his voice. Philip saw the apple rise and fall in his throat, his manly neck tightening.

"Friends, I cannot express the joy it has given me to have your presence on such a glorious day. Your happiness and support of our wedding is a thing Moriah and I shall remember always. And, as it is a day of rejoicing, there is yet one event I crave you to witness."

Philip felt his lips move in silent inquiry. *Marcus?*

The corners of Marcus's eyes narrowed with a hint of a smile, but he made no sign of explanation. He faced the guests more fully, the huskiness in his voice growing more evident.

"Many years ago, I purchased a young British captive as my attendant. You see him here beside me. He has served me faithfully, devotedly. The truth be told, I cannot express how tireless his care for my needs has been. Nor can I express how much he has become to me."

Marcus turned, looking fully at him. Philip swallowed against the aching lump forming in his throat, seeing the faint mist gleaming over Marcus's dark eyes. The tingle again swept down his spine.

Lord, I don't deserve this. Marcus knows the person I was before I knew You.

"Philip has been my slave, but I do not hesitate to say I could love no earthly brother, no close companion better than he." Marcus's voice abruptly lowered. Philip saw his swallow, his efforts to control the voice that was wavering. "I have said I cannot find the words to express what it is I feel for him. Rather, I will demonstrate it."

Marcus beckoned slightly. Glancing in the direction of his gesture, Philip saw one of the younger household slaves step forward and hand Marcus a felt cap. Instant recognition ran like a thrill through Philip's mind.

The pileus.

A symbol of freedom, worn by slaves emancipated by their lords.

Philip's heart-rate quickened. *God, I must be mistaken.* He looked from the cap in Marcus's hands up into his dark eyes, attempting to see through the meaning behind his steady gaze. *My lord?*

Marcus's voice again grew strong. "As you are my witnesses, I pronounce my slave Philip *free*. He is a citizen and freedman, with no obligation to me his former master," and his eyes warmed, "except by law of patronage."

A wild chorus of handclapping shook the room.

Philip's mind whirled. His eyes closed, masking the stinging wave of tears that blurred his vision. *Lord, I don't understand.* The aching lump in his throat intensified. *I deserve nothing. I am nothing. Why have You chosen to show me Your love this way?*

His eyes opened, feeling two strong hands grip his arms. He returned Marcus's embrace, fighting the overwhelming flood of emotions. Somewhere deep inside him, he felt a laugh spring to his lips, sob-like.

The unexpectedness of Marcus's gift was too great, too much for him to comprehend. He had never dreamed of freedom. A life beyond slavery was something he had surrendered years ago, relinquishing the bitter sting of servitude to God's perfect will.

The limitless possibilities of full surrender had simply never entered his realm of thinking. He could almost hear Daniel's voice echoing in his mind.

When your will is His, Philip, the sphere of His plan is boundless. It can cross the highest mountain, the greatest impossibility.

Philip felt himself released. Marcus brought the cap up, touching his forehead. The applause loudened.

He was free.

Again, Philip found his vision blurred. It had been many years since tears had found their place in his eyes. Yet, somehow, he would have it no other way.

Before him, Marcus himself was misty-eyed, his smile watery. "The Lord bless and keep you always, my faithful servant." His voice was soft, husky. "May his face shine upon you and give you peace."

Philip started.

The ancient blessing was almost more than he could bear in itself, a holy consecration of his new life and its freedoms. He could not have desired a greater pledge of brotherly love from his master.

His throat constricted. It was not the blessing alone which moved him.

341

Marcus had spoken in the language of the Iceni.

It had been years since he had heard the beautiful language of his forefathers. Instant memories overwhelmed him.

For a moment, the woodsy scent of his green hillsides, the rising smoke of the tribal fires, the misty atmosphere of the isles he had called *home* rose in his mind. His nostrils filled with the scents, his heart with bittersweet recollection.

Marcus's kindness in evoking such memories was almost as great as his gift of freedom.

His hand found Marcus's, gripping it. Emotion became the bursting desire to speak, to again bask in the tongue of his tribesmen.

"I can never thank you as you ought to be, master." His tongue glided over the Iceni words, shaking a little. His speech was almost as polished as if mere days had separated his voice from his language. "I can only praise God for His goodness through you."

"It is enough, Philip." Marcus's misty eyes warmed. "I know your heart." He clapped Philip on the shoulder. "Let us speak no more of this until later. Only, always remember that, wherever God calls you or whatever you must do, you will always have a place here."

Philip nodded. The overwhelming possibilities of his future were only dimly beginning to have their place in his mind, but he recognized the fullness of Marcus's heart beneath his pledge.

Marcus returned to his guests. The laughter and conversation resumed, filling the room with noisy exuberance.

Philip stood still. The words still rang in his mind. He would never tire of their joyous meaning.

I pronounce my slave Philip free. Free.

The atrium was dark. Only the flickering light of a few oil lamps bathed the room, sparkling against the quiet water of the pool.

Philip stepped into the room, his sandaled feet creating a soft slap against the marble floor.

It was late. The guests had finally gone, leaving a welcome haven of peace with their departure. Only the bountiful store of wedding gifts and a somewhat depleted storeroom hinted of their earlier presence.

Marcus and Moriah had made their retreat; Cleotas was slumbering off his wine. With the exception of a household watchman or two, the servants were asleep in their quarters. Only he was awake, left alone to recall the events of the day.

Absently, Philip leaned against a pillar. In his British fashion, he crossed his arms on his chest, contemplative.

His eyes surveyed the patterns on the floor. How well he remembered the ornate designs of the Virginius atrium blending into one swirling color, the agony of the rods tearing his back and distorting his mind. The events of his boyhood seemed so distant, yet, their misery was etched in his mind and heart as if it were yesterday.

You are nothing! Your God is nothing!

The echo of Marcus's anger played in Philip's mind. For a moment, he could almost feel the rods, the inexorable grip of the hands that had pinned him to the floor. He would never forget the racking pain of that flogging.

But, just as quickly, the memory faded, replaced by something he would never forget.

The touch. The voice.

Philip closed his eyes, remembering. In his deepest agony, when he had thought himself ready to die, the presence of Jesus had been with him. And it had returned to comfort him after the death of Beric.

Philip opened his eyes. How many scenes of violence and suffering an atrium such as this one had witnessed. But, unlike the Virginius domus, this household had witnessed scenes of goodness.

The Lord bless you and keep you. There had been a time he would never have believed such words could issue from his master's lips.

Did he choose to do so, Philip knew he could again summon the mist to his eyes. The presence of emotion was still with him, bordering close on his heart. The scenes of the day were fresh, playing over and over in his mind.

Only Christ could have wrought two such miracles—the union of the two friends he loved and his own freedom.

Freedom.

Philip stretched his arms out to their full length, bringing them back again. Strength rippled through his arms, tightening his muscles. He felt like a new a man. The very word *freedom* seemed to course through his veins like adrenaline.

He was a citizen of Rome, a freedman. He was free to marry, to vote, to manage himself as his own master. He had long since ceased to fear corporal discipline, knowing Marcus would never again strike him, but now his safety was legal. No man could subject him to bodily harm.

He was *free.*

The sound of a quiet knock interrupted his thoughts.

Philip started a little. The hour was far too late for honest visitors. He paused, waiting for the sound of the knock to resound. Presently, it came, soft and timid. The sound was almost as if it were a frightened child.

He glanced around the atrium. The slaves were certainly in too deep a slumber to have heard such a diffident knock.

Swiftly, he crossed to the *vestibule.* A slight tinge of hesitance pricked his instincts, but he brushed it aside. The watchmen were within the close vicinity, though he doubted he would need their services. He had forgotten nothing of his savage training in the wild British Isles.

With slow cautiousness, he unbolted the heavy door. He opened it, his eyes adjusting to the midnight darkness.

A silhouetted form captured his immediate attention. The figure was decidedly maidenly, delicate, and wrapped in a long cloak.

"Yes?" Despite the indistinct murmur of activity that could still be heard from the distant forum, Philip almost started at the sound of his own voice. The hour seemed much too late for speech. "How may I assist you?"

"You are Philip of Briton? The servant of the honorable Tribune Marcus Virginius Aeneas?" Soft and clear, the girl's hushed voice was almost musical.

"Yes." Philip looked keenly at her. Clearly, the maiden knew him from someplace, though he could not imagine where. Her tones and bearing were too noble for him to have to have met her on his errands of mercy among the poor. "Do you have business with me?"

"More particularly with your master." The girl drew her cloak more securely around her shapely shoulders. Her eyes were clear and honest, looking steadily into his. "May I enter?"

In answer, Philip held the door open wider. She stepped past him, modestly dropping her gaze.

It was then he noticed how dark her eyes were, fringed by equally dark lashes. He felt a chill of uncertainty. There was something about the turn of her gaze, the steady manner in which her pupils met and commanded his that was strikingly familiar.

In the atrium, she threw back her hood, revealing faintly-curling hair. It was dark, coiled attractively against her head.

Philip closed the door, glancing at her. Her form was slender and shapely, her height slightly taller than the average woman. It was clearly obvious she was Roman born and bred. Everything about her breathed the grace and authority of a patrician, yet, she somehow bore an entirely distinct touch of modesty.

Seeing him look at her, she tilted her chin ever so slightly, her eyes catching his gaze. Her expression spoke little. She seemed open to his curiosity, as if it was not a British slave who stood before her.

"May I pour you a glass of wine?" Philip compelled himself to speak pleasantly, mingling his subservience with compassion. The girl obviously had an important reason for coming at such a late hour to the Aeneas domus. "You must be weary at such an hour."

"I am. Thank you." Spoken softly, the girl's answer was again clear and distinct. Strangely, it was not the clarity of command. She was gracious, even humble.

Philip felt his confusion mounting. No ordinary Roman lady spoke pleasantly to a slave, particularly one receiving her at the dead of night. Everything about her signified friendship, even equality.

The feeling that he had seen her before grew stronger.

He stepped to her side, handing her the goblet. Her eyes mirroring thanks, she lifted the goblet with both hands to her lips, cradling it.

Marcus.

Philip tingled with a running thrill, the thought a startling one. Everything about her was his master, only in feminine form. The dark eyes that commanded him; the bearing; the natural authority. Even her manner of cradling her goblet spoke volumes. There was nothing that did not equal Marcus's comportment and particular ways of doing things.

He stepped closer, the thrill running again through him. "My lady?" His voice grew soft, his eyes running again over every feature of her countenance. "Diantha Virginius?"

She looked up at him. "You recognize me."

"It has been many years." A wave of shock rolled through Philip's body. "You'll forgive me if I say you've grown."

"I was a child." A tinkling laugh escaped her. "And you were a rebellious boy. I will never forget how you tried my brother." Her eyes wandered over him. "But you have not changed much. I have never forgotten you."

"I fear there is little good to remember me by, my lady."

"No." Diantha drew herself up. New earnestness flickered over her face. "There is much I recall about you that is noble."

Philip looked at her. Like Marcus, he could not see through the thoughts behind her dark eyes. Still, there were few options to her words. *Is it possible she respects Christianity?*

Her gaze was steady, holding him. Somewhere, deep inside him, he realized his heart was pounding. In that, there was one difference between her and Marcus. He did not mind the sway she held over him.

He half-shook his head, freeing himself. All of his experience with ministry and service ought to have won his confidence in the presence of a noble lady. Why, then, did he feel so nervous, so boyishly uncertain and awkward?

A cough arose in his throat. "Will you explain what you mean, my lady?"

Diantha drew a little closer. A slow, bittersweet smile touched her lips. "Please, do not call me that, Philip. I am not your lady."

Something about the manner in which she said his name triggered the heat in Philip's cheeks. It crept upwards, deepening his awkward confusion. "I do not understand."

Again, Diantha did not answer his questions. Her eyes drifted downwards. "They say today was my brother's wedding."

Philip made no answer. He struggled to recall that he was free, but to no avail. Captivity had made its mark on him, holding his tongue. A slave did not speak unless he was asked a direct question.

A moment of silence filled the atrium.

Diantha looked up at him. "What sort of a woman has he taken for his wife?" Her voice was soft, as if she feared his answer.

"A woman of the best and godliest character." Philip felt warmth spread through his chest. "Moriah is a jewel beyond compare. Your brother is a blessed man."

"I am grateful to hear it. I feared…" Diantha's voice broke off. She smiled, but Philip saw her chin tremble strangely. "My greatest desire was that Marcus would stand by his principles and choose a wife worthy of him."

Philip considered her. *Stand by his principles.* The words echoed in his mind. What kind of a Roman lady valued principle above power? The preachings of Seneca had been influential in their time, but he doubted the words of the dead continued to impact the youthful. Rome spawned indulgence, self-pleasure. *Why does her disowned brother continue to attract her care?*

He studied the patterned floor. "My lady—" He paused, glancing up at her. The slight flicker of her eyes signified she had not changed her mind about his use of the title, but she said nothing. "I beg your pardon, but I must ask. Why did you come here?"

Before him, her face crumpled into tears.

Philip felt a start, confused and almost hating himself. Swiftly, he stepped forward, touching her shoulder.

"If I have hurt you, I will never forgive myself. Please—" His voice died, at a loss for words. Seeing a woman weep always pained him beyond depiction. A silent prayer formed on his lips for her. *Be with her, Lord.*

"You have done nothing." Diantha shook her head, brushing her hand against her cheek. It came away shiny with moisture. "I have longed to cry all day." Her chin trembled, her words spilling in a tremulous rush from her throat. "My father has disowned me. I was cast from my home only this morning."

The intensity of indignation began to simmer in Philip's chest. He felt a wave of sympathy, understanding what it was she suffered.

His mind flashed back to the past. Though little had been shared with him, he had known how deep a void of hurt Rowland had created in Marcus's heart. The scars of disgrace and pain had been masked, but he often wondered if they had ever healed. In his mind, it didn't seem possible. Marcus had respectfully chosen not to abandon the name of Virginius, but, to all who knew Rowland, the additional surname was a daily reminder that he was not Cleotas's flesh and blood.

It seemed an unthinkable cruelty to inflict the same punishment upon his only daughter.

"Why?" Philip spoke gently, his voice low. He had seen much suffering in his ministry, but the sight of pain never ceased to move him. The circumstances behind her disgrace were nothing; his was a ministry to comfort and uplift the sorrowing.

Diantha inhaled slowly. She appeared comforted by his touch. Blinking, she forced a watery smile to her lips. "I am a Christian."

The unexpectedness of her answer was another vivid shock.

Philip was silent, a torrent of questions flooding his mind. Did she speak honestly? Or was this a malicious trick of Rowland, intended to entrap and harm Marcus and Moriah on the happiest day of their life?

Diantha seemed to sense his mistrust. She drew herself up, and again Philip was surprised by her quiet authority. "Do not be afraid to trust me, Philip. I swear by all we hold sacred I am telling you the truth."

Philip looked quietly at her. In his heart, he was prepared to believe her, but cautiousness was the first rule of wisdom. "Can you prove it?"

Surprise flitted across Diantha's features. Philip sensed she struggled to determine which course to take. It was not every day she was doubted, even resisted by an insolent British slave.

Her voice faltered. "Even Daniel, one of our great elders, believes me."

"So you say." Philip spoke quietly. "Forgive me, but I have seen much treachery. I am certain you understand."

"I do, Philip. You know perhaps more than myself or even Marcus what it is to suffer for Christ." Diantha's eyes never left his. Still full of soft tears, they remained honest, unwavering. "I can give you no proof of my integrity. That is a thing time alone will reveal to you. I can only throw myself on your goodness and trust you to believe in me."

"Diantha." Philip gentled his voice. Inwardly, his heart was warm. Her simplicity was convincing, even appealing. "You are Marcus's sister. It is not for me to believe or not believe you. That is not what I meant by my questions. I mean only that we as believers must be discerning."

He allowed his expression to relax, certain that his eyes already betrayed his trust. "Come, I will show you to a guest chamber. In the morning, you may see your brother and explain why you are here."

Diantha's moist eyes warmed, but she said nothing.

Philip signaled for her to follow him. Swiftly, he led her across the silent, dusky atrium to one of the guest apartments. At its door, he gestured.

"Do you require an attendant, my lady?"

"No, not tonight." Diantha paused. She seemed to be gathering her scattered emotions, recollecting her quiet strength. "You have been most kind."

Philip stood looking down at her. Something about her answer triggered his respect. *What Roman lady denies the services of slaves?* Her gracious authority and simple sweetness was strikingly appealing. In many ways, she seemed more British than Roman.

Powered by something he didn't understand, his voice grew soft. "Goodnight, Diantha."

He turned, half-striding away. A strange feeling encompassed him, confusing him. In ten short minutes, this Roman girl had filled him with feelings he had never before experienced.

Nor did he understand them.

Behind him, her soft voice stopped him in his stride. "Philip."

"Yes?" He turned. Somehow, he was almost glad to do so. Her soft dark eyes met his, immediately holding him.

"You are no longer a slave, are you?"

"No." Philip felt a rush of adrenaline, highlighting his cheeks with color. "My master freed me today." He paused. "How could you tell?"

Diantha smiled. "You have always walked like a warrior. That in itself has not changed. But today you both speak and walk as one with a mission."

"I have always had a mission, Diantha. My calling is to win the lost to Christ." Philip paused, considering his words. "But you are right. Before, as a slave, my work was bound within the restrictions of my master. Now, Christ alone is my authority."

Diantha played with the corners of her cloak. Slowly, her eyes smiled up at him. "Goodnight, Philip." She turned, vanishing into the dark recesses of the guest chamber.

Philip stood motionless. He felt the corners of his mouth curve into a smile. Swiftly, feeling the unexplainable desire to laugh, he hastened up the staircase to his own apartments.

Chapter Twenty-Eight

Marcus enfolded Diantha in his strong embrace, his hands gripping her shoulders. Her face was buried in his shoulder. His head rested atop hers, his cheek pressed against her dark hair.

From his serving corner, Philip felt a smarting lump gather in his throat. He could hear Marcus's husky voice murmuring her name.

"Diantha. Little sister."

Diantha raised her head, her eyes luminous through their tears. "Marcus. Oh, praise God that I have seen you again."

Marcus held her at arm's length. Slowly, he raised his hand, caressing her cheek. "It is a bitter trial that brings us together, my Diantha. But it has its blessings. I wonder if father considered this joyous possibility when he put you from his heart and home."

"I doubt it, Marcus. But let the past be. I am here with you." Diantha paused, her eyes roving in quick survey across Marcus's countenance. "You will let me stay, will you not?"

Marcus laughed. The sound was husky, a rush of pent-up emotion. "What a question! Cleotas will have to be consulted, but I am certain he will readily welcome you. You will again have a home, Diantha."

"Praise God." Diantha's voice choked. Half-shaking her head, she smiled up at him. "I was afraid, Marcus."

"Of what?"

"Of many things." Diantha drew a shaky breath. "Mostly that you would not receive me, that my father's daughter would be scorned. But the years have not changed you, Marcus. Your love has not ceased for me."

Marcus's countenance overshadowed. "Nor has it for any of my family." He hesitated. Slowly, his hands gripped her shoulders. "Tell me, Diantha: how is my father?"

"Rich and still influential. He has not changed, Marcus."

"I feared so." Marcus swallowed, averting his eyes. "I-I have not heard you mention our mother." He looked up. "How is she?"

Diantha's eyes filled afresh. "Dead, Marcus." Her voice was a whisper. "With your disgrace, both of her sons were dead. She pleaded for you with our father for months. He refused her, and-and she died not long after it was said you joined the *Praetorians*."

Philip saw Marcus's hands clench, his face pale with sorrow. "Hatred is a terrible thing. I regret it lowered my father enough to my break my mother's heart."

"It is not your fault, Marcus. You did the right thing."

"Yes." Marcus touched her hair, his mouth hinting a soft smile. "And, now, please Jehovah, the right thing will be done by you. My wife," and he lingered over the words, "will be a friend and guide to you. She is resting from the fatigues of the wedding, but I will have a servant take you to her. For now, you must bathe and freshen yourself."

He turned to a female slave. "See that Lady Diantha has all she requires in the way of attire and service. I will purchase a personal attendant for her, but, until then, you must see that she is properly attended."

"Yes, my lord." The servant girl bowed.

Diantha lifted thankful eyes to Marcus's face. He squeezed her shoulders a final time before lifting his hands in dismissal.

She flitted gracefully away. The graceful sound of her movements met Philip's ears. A strange tingle rushed down his spine. He allowed his eyes to follow her to the door, willing her to look at him.

As if wishing had conveyed an audible appeal, her eyes lifted in his direction. Their gazes met. Her eyes warmed, then, like a breath of fresh air, she was gone. Still, her presence seemed to linger, filling every nook of the room with grace.

Philip averted his eyes. She was a beautiful girl. He was a man; he recognized a beautiful face when he saw one.

But was it right for him to cast his gaze upon her? He was dedicated to the Lord, to the ministry. His years of celibacy had been fruitful ones and, beyond the natural desire to someday marry, he had been content. Why, then, did these strange feelings haunt him? Since yesterday, he had not been able to put Diantha from his mind.

It was then he realized Marcus was gazing intently upon him.

Philip felt the color tinge his lightly tanned cheeks. Had Marcus noted the look Diantha had cast upon him, the turn of his own eyes to follow her? With difficulty, he found his voice.

"May I congratulate you, my lord. I am happy for this newfound joy."

"As I knew you would be, Philip. Truly, it is a faithful saying that our Lord's blessings are new every morning." Marcus paused. "I thank you for welcoming Diantha last night. Your consideration to her in my absence was most kind."

"It was nothing, my lord." Philip laughed slightly, partially easing his discomfort. "It was a pleasure to welcome her. And, were it not, I should have still done it. I am not such a fool as to arouse my master from his wedding chamber in the dead of night."

Marcus chuckled. "Your prudence was wise." He glanced around, searching for something.

Philip discerned his thoughts. With swift subservice, he stepped to a table and poured out a glass of iced wine. Turning, he held the goblet out to Marcus, its gold basin brimful with chilly sweetness.

"My lord."

A strange look crossed Marcus's face. Slowly, he accepted the wine, yet made no move to touch it to his lips. "You no longer need to call me that, Philip."

Philip slowly turned, pouring himself a goblet of wine. Marcus's voice bore a shade of quiet rebuke, but there was something else beyond his reminder. It was as if sadness encompassed him.

354

"Master." He turned, lifting his fingers to silence the quick protest he saw in Marcus's eyes, on his swiftly-opened mouth. Quiet resolve washed over him. "Do not rebuke me, Marcus. In my mind, you will always be my master."

Marcus smiled, but his eyes held the same sadness of his voice. "Christ is your only authority now, Philip. I am your brother and friend only." He paused. "What will you do with your freedom?"

"That all depends on whether or not you intend to send me away, Marcus."

"Send you away?" Marcus laughed, his chin tilting back. "Do not jest with me. You know you have a place alongside me for as long as you desire it."

"I am glad." Philip smiled. His fingers absently traced the pattern of his goblet. His thoughts were many, almost too many to form into speech. Slowly, decision flooded him, weighting his words. "You ask what I will do. You must know that the thought uppermost in my mind is still to be your personal attendant."

Marcus nodded slowly. "I confess that is what I hoped. Your service and comradeship mean much to me. But I must now pay you for your services, Philip. No freedman may labor unrewarded."

"Agreed." Philip set his goblet down. "I will not need much gold for myself, but a little of it goes a long away among the needy." He paused, again forming his thoughts into words. "This brings me to my main desire, Marcus. With my freedom, it has come into my mind to spend more time laboring in the service of Christ. Daniel has often expressed his wish I would join him more often during his ministrations to the poor."

"It is a noble wish." Marcus swallowed a draught from his goblet. His features were contemplative as he set it down. "But you are not required to ask me, Philip. Need I remind you again you are *free?*"

"And need I remind you I still consider you my lord?" Philip felt a smile again hover over his lips. He stretched out his hand, laying it lightly on Marcus's shoulder. "I still seek your consent."

Marcus looked steadily at him. "You have it. I can never forbid you from serving the Lord with your whole heart."

"It is not enough." Passion flooded Philip's heart. His pulse quickened, considering all he might do for the Kingdom. *You have given me freedom to serve You, Lord. Now give me a special grace to fulfill Your commission well.* "Give me your blessing, Marcus."

"I am not worthy." Marcus's voice was low. "My love for Christ pales in comparison to the sacrifices you make every day for His name."

A familiar pang smote Philip's heart. Would Marcus never recognize his own worth? He looked at him. He knew him so well. The dark hair, the almost black eyes that could command and hold him at will. The strong, masterful figure that led hundreds of soldiers with the unceasing courage and sharp mind of an inexorable leader. *How can such a man above all ordinary men think so little of himself?*

"Marcus." Philip took a step nearer. His heart burned. How could he assure Marcus of what he felt, of the respect and admiration he had for him? "Tell me who is worthy?"

Marcus said nothing. His fingers brushed his goblet, his eyes fixed on the ornate table it stood on.

Philip was quiet. Years of experience had taught him when to speak and when to allow Marcus his thoughts. He continued to gaze at him, knowing his eyes spoke volumes.

At last, Marcus looked up. The corners of his mouth twitched, hinting a quiet smile. "Who would have thought it?" Softness bordered on his voice, almost to huskiness. "My nation conquered yours. Our forefathers struggled and killed, my own brother among them. Britain was paid for in blood. And now a British captive goes out among his conquerors to share the light of God."

The Lord hath anointed me to preach good tidings unto the meek; he hath sent me to bind up the brokenhearted, to proclaim liberty to the captives. The words flashed into Philip's mind. He had often heard Daniel repeat them. It was if Jesus Himself had spoken the words in his heart, giving him double assurance. His calling was sure. *To proclaim liberty among the captives.*

He felt the Spirit stirring in his heart, impassioning his words. "It was not Rome who held me captive, Marcus. I can see it now. It was sin, the works of the flesh. I became free in Christ. And, now, my heart is of one mind to share that sweet release with others. For me, the chiefest of sinners, there can be no greater joy."

Marcus smiled, a watery smile that hid some inner emotion. "You have already given so much of your time and energy for this work. I can only praise God your mind is to now give it your all."

"It is, Marcus." Philip felt his passion redouble. "To give beauty for ashes, as He did." His hand gripped Marcus's shoulder. "Now *bless* me, Marcus. Do not let me begin this great task without the sanction I want above all else."

Slowly, Marcus nodded. His averted eyes revealed little, but Philip sensed he was moved. *Beauty for ashes.* His words were being relived even as they spoke. What ashes could be greater than the sins of their pasts? Yet, standing there, Marcus was sending him out to fulfill the work of the gospel.

Philip sank to his knees. Above him, he felt Marcus's strong hands rest on his shoulders, then his head. His eyes closed, his heart beating in steady rhythm against his chest.

Thank you for this great task, Lord. Give me the strength to fulfill it. Give me Your grace.

The sound of Marcus's voice was strong, his husky tenors filling the room. "Philip, my brother, I charge you and strengthen you. Set your face like a flint; be not ashamed of the word of truth. Follow after the things which make for peace and edify your brethren." He paused. "Be strong in the faith. And may the God of all peace stablish your heart and work His will through you."

Silence filled the room. Marcus's hands squeezed Philip's shoulders.

"In the name of Jesus. Amen."

The words echoed in Philip's heart. He repeated them to himself, a silent prayer. *In the name of Jesus.*

Rowland Virginius tasted his wine. It was bitter to his tongue, burning his throat. Muttering an oath, he set it down, hard, on the table.

Behind him, a dark cloaked figure waited in silence.

Breaking off a plump grape from a cluster, Rowland placed it contemplatively in his mouth. "You say she found refuge in the household of Aeneas?"

"Yes, my lord. Judging by appearances, she was very well received."

Rowland ground his teeth. Rage filled him, seeping into every corner of his heart. "Go. Keep a close eye on the household of Aeneas. I want a full report of their activities."

The spy bowed silently. Dark and mysterious, his departing footsteps were soon lost to hearing.

Rowland again ground his teeth.

Reclined on a low couch, Saturius cast him a derisive expression. "What did you expect, Virginius? That Diantha would go to the Vestal Virgins? You were a fool to disown the girl. Casting these miserable Christians to the lions is the only sure way to end the sect."

"I couldn't do that." Rowland turned to him. "Diantha was my only remaining child. I did my duty as a Roman; no one can require more of me."

"Naturally. But is it not rather unfortunate you did not handle the matter at the beginning? You might still consider yourself blessed, surrounded by *both* of your children."

"What do you mean?" Rowland spat the words, feeling the angry heat pour into his face. "I did all that was humanly possible to rid Christianity from my household."

"By killing one British slave?" Saturius's sarcastic chuckle filled the room. He rose, tossing aside the pomegranate he had been plucking with meaningful deliberation. "I think not, Rowland. You spared the one who spawned the lies that infiltrated your family. How could you expect the Christian scourge to die?"

"How easy it is for you to speak of these things now." The veins bulged in Rowland's neck. Great gods, but his head ached, doubtless from yesterday's long evening. To dull his angry grief, he had drunk himself into a heavy stupor and cursed the foul Christians who had beguiled his only daughter. "How could I know the boy would influence Marcus? Almighty Jupiter, Marcus himself flogged the miserable dog."

"Yes." Saturius's tone was gratingly sarcastic. "It may have been then that the wretched Briton worked his spells on your son."

Rowland turned towards him. Frustration rushed down his spine, weary with the whole conversation. "Marcus made his decision. He was a strong young man who knew his own mind—curse him! No one could work magic on him."

"They say these Christians are terrible sorcerers, Rowland. And I knew your son nearly as well as you did. Marcus was indeed strong—a strong, loyal *Roman*. I don't consider it accidental his head was turned."

"What then?" Rowland snapped. His head pulsed and spun more with each passing moment. Must they continue to dwell upon the past, upon the son he no longer claimed? "Do you insist that he was bewitched?"

"I do. No true Christian wins the favor of a powerful man like Cleotas Aeneas. And it goes beyond that. I heard it in the court of Nero himself that the Tribune Marcus Virginius Aeneas is one of the most powerful and promising officers in the entire Praetorian Guard."

"Do you imply that a Christ-follower cannot have a promising career? Speak sense, man!"

"I am." Saturius made a gesture of impatience. "I think it highly improbable for Marcus to have risen to such a rank while being a member of that sect. Indeed, all things considered, I am certain of it. After all, was not this Briton a Druid before he was a Christian? The combination of two such evils must have been supreme."

"Then," Rowland spoke slowly, choosing his words with slow deliberation, "if—and I say *if*—that British scum holds Marcus under his spell, what can be done about it?"

"What should have been done years ago. He must die."

Rowland laughed sardonically. He lifted his goblet again to his lips, ignoring the burning sensation the liquid created in his throat. "That is not so easily done. Do you not remember the boy? His physique was superb. He must be a perfect gladiator by now—valuable to his master."

"He is." Both men turned at the sound of the frigid voice.

Thallus stood in the door, resetting his white toga around his arm. Icy rancor fairly sculpted his face. Brusquely, he stepped between his two elders, wrapping his fingers around the wine pitcher with throttling strength. His hands shook as he lifted his brimming goblet to his lips.

His cool nonchalance irritated Rowland to no end. "What do you mean? You interrupt us, then drink my wine without an explanation?"

"Careful, Rowland." Saturius's voice was sharp. "My son is not as yours was. He is wise, a Roman. He may serve your purpose."

Rowland eyed Thallus. "Can you?"

"Yes."

"How?"

Thallus gritted his teeth. "By killing that dog of a Briton, as my father suggested."

"And why would you do this?"

Thallus stepped closer. Rowland could feel the heat of his breath, his bitter fury. He made no attempt to hide his innermost

360

feelings. His flashing, narrowed eyes were a formidable sign in one so young and strong.

"I claim no love for your son, Rowland Virginius. Candidly, I *hate* him with all that is within me. Were I to advise you, it would be to tell you to leave him to this despicable," and his words became a spat, "*Christianity* he has embraced, to leave him to his own chosen fate! But then I should not have my revenge."

"And what exactly is this *revenge?*" Rowland spoke coldly. Thallus's self-interest was always evident.

"Marcus loves his British slave as a brother. Nothing could hurt him more than to lose him. For all he has done to me, for the years of shame and rivalry, I will kill the one he values above his life!"

For a long moment, perfect silence settled over the room. Thallus's eyes flashed and glittered; Saturius stood by in silent, pleased observation. At last Rowland exhaled, breaking the silence.

"So we are agreed. The slave Philip must die. But it would not seem that you, Thallus, are not in one accord with our purpose." He eyed him, allowing a sarcastic bent to his head. "Do you not believe in slaying this Briton to free Marcus from his spell?"

"Does it matter what I believe?" Thallus made no attempt to hide his scorn. "But, I will answer you plainly, noble Rowland." His words again became a spat, anger rising in every decibel. "I don't think your son is *bewitched.* I think he made his choice, as we all do. He is a Christian. He deserves to die as one. But," and his hand went downwards, brushing aside his toga to reveal a sharp dagger, "I am content to let him live in sorrow instead."

Rowland felt his eyes locked in Thallus's menacing gaze. The young man's passion was strong, a tribute to Rome. He believed in all Rome stood for: power, strength, and the gods above all nations. *Would that I had sired such a son.*

"Go." He heard his own voice, strained by the force of his own desire. "Kill this miserable Christian slave. And Jupiter grant it will free Marcus from this spell and cause Diantha to see the truth."

Thallus's eyes flickered. "I am more concerned with the favor of the gods and Nero."

Again flicking the scabbard of his dagger with menacing alacrity, he began to casually leave the room.

Rowland felt vexation boil up within him, clenching his hands into fists. "Don't pride yourself, Thallus. You know your intents are not for *Rome*." Angry sarcasm again wet his voice. "They are for yourself."

Thallus turned. A slow, sardonic smile played about his lips. "Tell me, Rowland." He paused sarcastically. "What are your intents? Are they for Rome?"

Allowing the weight of his sarcasm to sink in, Thallus turned and strode from the room.

Rowland slowly released his hands, easing them from their cramped fists. Looking down, he saw the fierce print his nails had created in the tender flesh.

No. His intentions were not solely for Rome. They were not only for Marcus and Diantha either. He had long ago calloused his heart towards his children. But, for the shame and disgrace they had brought him, he would have his revenge.

Jupiter aid him, he would have his revenge.

Chapter Twenty-Nine

The room was dusky. The faint, warm glow of oil lamps bathed the occupants in a serene glow, softening their work-weary faces into peace. Like an indistinct whisper, the low murmur of conversation filled the air.

Philip's eyes flitted over each familiar face. Tired, yet tranquil, their beloved countenances reminded him of the words of Paul.

We are troubled on every side, yet not distressed...persecuted, but not forsaken, cast down, but not destroyed.

It was so very true. Most of the assembled people had experienced tribulation for their faith. Nothing was new to Christians: the hatred of family members, the constant fear of discovery, torture, imprisonment, the lash.

Philip's eyes rested on a youth sitting near his feet, a recent convert. The sturdy young believer was a German slave. At the last meeting, he had requested prayer for strength. His master had discovered his faith in Jesus and threatened him with flogging.

How well he understood what the boy was facing.

Philip crouched, brushing his hand over the boy's shoulder. It was time for the meeting to begin, but he felt drawn to speak to the youth while it was on his heart. The boy looked up at him, his blue eyes a mirror of peaceful inquiry.

"How goes it with you, Arswind?"

"Well, Philip."

Philip paused a moment, considering his words. "And your master? Does he continue to oppose your faith?"

Arswind's eyes were steady, meeting his. "Yes. I expect he'll tear me up pretty good tonight." A quiet smile tugged at his mouth. "But I won't give in, Philip. Nothing can make me renounce my Savior."

"I know what you are facing." Philip's hand gripped his shoulder. "I'll pray for you, Arswind." He again paused. "Just be certain you are walking in His strength, not your own. Remember, with Him, you can endure all things."

"I will, Philip."

"Good." Philip squeezed his shoulder a final time, rising to his feet. "Remember to speak with me before you leave tonight. I'll pray for you then."

Arswind nodded. Philip felt a slight lump gather in his throat. How willingly he would take the pain and disgrace for him if he could. The youth was so strong, so determined to be valiant for Jesus.

Be with him, Father. Let this cup of suffering pass from him, if it is Your will.

It was now more than time for the meeting to start. Philip cleared his throat. He stepped into the center of the assembled throng, the warm light falling onto his face. An instant hush fell over the believers.

"My brethren." Philip spoke clearly, raising his voice just loud enough to be heard. He couldn't risk someone overhearing from outside. "In the absence of Daniel, I have been charged to speak to you tonight. I am certain my message will pale in comparison to what you are accustomed to, but it is my hope something in my words will bless you tonight."

He paused, again taking a quick survey of the room. Marcus, Moriah, Alexander, Diantha—the faces of all those dearest to him were quietly intent, their expressions expectant. How blessed he was to possess such faithful friends.

He would never cease to thank God for the beauty of unity, for the unique love which made varying ranks come together. Even at that moment, a powerful tribune sat in humble expectancy before an ex-slave.

"I will say little tonight, my brethren. I give you one thing: a charge." Philip looked around the room. "We are blessed as few have been or ever will be. We have seen God's glory; we have seen the power of His Spirit. We have witnessed the transformation of lives, have heard the broken-spirited sing. In all of history, who has experienced the privileges we have?"

Deep inside, new fervor swelled in his breast. *Give me Your words, Jesus. Make this Your message.* "Some of us have lived and walked with Christ Himself. Future generations will not be able to claim as much. How then can we shrink back? We must press on, sharing the news of the One who has given us so much."

Across the room, Philip saw Diantha lean forward, her beautiful eyes alive. They shone encouragement, warming him. He heard his voice strengthen.

"He is our Good Shepherd; He has laid down His life for His sheep. He has given His all freely. Can we do less? Darkness shall never prevail as long as we are the light He has called us to be. And so my charge is that we stand as men for His name. Many of us have been trained as warriors—let us be warriors for *Him*."

"Amen." The soft whisper circulated, an echo throughout the room.

Philip gestured. "Let us kneel. Hearts are heavy tonight; many of us face peril for our faith. Only through His strength can we resist temptation and heed the Spirit's voice."

The rustle of clothing sounded through the room. Philip smelled the musky scent of alkaline and earth, used by the fullers to clean garments. In the closeness of the environment, a faint whiff of the Indian cologne the soldiers wore could be detected. Its sweet, botanical scent mingled pleasantly with the warmth of the burning oil and odor of close human bodies.

With every believer in a kneeling position, Philip himself knelt. His arm rested around Arswind's shoulders. They would all pray individually, but he wanted the boy to know his thoughts were with him even at that moment.

The pounding of heavy fists on the door shattered the tranquility.

Every head jerked upright. Drawn and tense, the believers shared expressions of sudden panic. Several of the women drew their hands over their mouths, stifling their cries.

Alexander slipped from the room. In a moment, he was back, his face drawn. "It's the city guard."

"Quick! Out the back!" The panicked whisper spread like oil fire throughout the room. Several of the believers stumbled to their feet, snatching their children.

"No!" Marcus leaped to his feet. Stern and authoritative, his quick command stilled the terrified assembly. "Stay here. Keep quiet and be still unless I am arrested. Alexander, Quintus, Julius, come with me."

The three legionaries followed in quick obedience. Marcus led them out, disappearing into the dusky shadows beyond the inner chamber.

With their departure, the atmosphere grew strained.

Philip borrowed from Marcus's authority, giving quiet instructions. "Return to your positions, every one of you. Pray earnestly for God's protection." The contagious fear of the others welled up like a cold dread in his breast, but he forced a comforting tenor to his hushed tones. In Daniel's absence, these were his people, his flock. *They look to me for strength.* "Remember His power, His mercy. No mortal hand can harm us without His sanction."

Again, the believers knelt, some pressing their faces to the floor. Others sat with outstretched hands, their lips moving in silent petition.

Philip's heart thudded. He knew by long experience how to maintain an outward appearance of calm strength, but nothing could curtail what he felt on the inside. Flashing scenes of the arena flitted through his mind. *Great Jehovah, spare these people. Surrender me, if it is Your will, but save them.*

Glancing over the believers, Philip saw that every eye was closed. Noiselessly, he stepped from the room. Relying on the somber shadows, he eased along the wall towards the door.

It was not long until he heard the sound of Marcus's stern, almost angry voice outside. Peering through a crack in the door, he saw the captain of the city guard standing before the irate young tribune.

"Your explanation is pitiful to the last degree, captain. You expect a man of my prowess—a tribune of the Praetorian Guard—to believe you were sent here to arrest some filthy *Christians*?"

The captain appeared flustered. "I am telling you the truth, sir. I—"

"Oh, merciful Pollux!" Marcus gestured angrily, his invective a tingle to Philip's ears. "Why don't you admit you knew this place was used as a dice-house?" He moved nearer, fiercely threatening. "Admit it, captain. Acknowledge you and these miserable excuses you call soldiers wanted a taste of filched wine!"

"Noble tribune, your name is known and revered throughout Rome. I do not insult your suspicions, but I swear by almighty Jupiter I am telling you the truth. You must believe me."

Marcus eyed him, cold sarcasm cocking his brows. "So you say. Then I suppose you will continue to tell me there are Christians in that miserable hut?"

"No, of course not, tribune." The captain stuttered audibly. "Your word is—"

"Yes, my word *is* sufficient. And it better be, you lout. You have offended me beyond forgiveness tonight. My men and I were very comfortably engaged before you and those blundering mice in scarlet uniforms disturbed us."

"Again, you have my apologies." The captain drew his sword up in swift salute. "I will withdraw my men at once."

"Do so." Marcus's irritable snap was accompanied by a swift gesture to his *gladius*. "You might consider yourself fortunate. Had I not the good temper to stop and consider my intruders, I could have split you from head to belt. Those whimpering *serving* girls would have fared little better."

The captain's face tightened, but his good sense provoked no comment. His swift order sliced through the evening air.

"Company, fall in. About face; march out!"

The heavy thud of marching feet reverberated against the grim stone walls. In swift unanimity, the city guard marched out. Offering a wary salute in Marcus's direction, the captain followed them down the alley. The clink of their armor echoed back from the darkness long after they disappeared from sight, a grim reminder of their dangerous mission.

Philip exhaled slowly, the sound strangely loud in the quiet entry. Relief surged through his body. He had not fully realized how nervous he had been. Swiftly, he slipped back into the crowded inner room.

Every eye turned towards him.

"They have gone." Philip raised a quick hand, quieting the resounding exhales of relief. "But we must disperse quickly. They may return."

"Yes." Behind him, Marcus's voice was grim. Obviously, he had reentered the house with stealthy fleetness. "They *will* return. We will slip out by twos and threes to deter suspicion. Philip, you are our elder tonight. You must leave first."

"Marcus." Philip felt a wave of protest, but he forced himself to observe a respectful tone. Indulging in contention would not profit his on-looking brethren. "Surely it is the place of the leader to endure the most danger."

"Don't argue with me." Marcus's voice was sharp. "You have the most to reveal if they caught and tortured you." His tones softened ever so slightly. "I don't imply you would betray us, but even the strongest of men have been known to break under torture. And, in the end, you would survive only to adorn Nero's private arena. You must go. *Now.*"

Philip nodded in mindless submission. *Listen to him.* Marcus certainly knew more about these things than he. "I will go."

"Let me come with you, Philip." Arswind sprang to his feet, his eyes flashing. "I will kill anyone who tries to harm you."

Philip opened his mouth to decline him. Somehow, he could not accept the offer of violence. Could he allow his enemies to be slain when Christ Himself had not fought His tortures?

"Yes, Arswind." Marcus prevented his speaking. Philip could fairly feel the burning heat of his eyes. "Go with him. And," he drew the boy close, his voice a subtle whisper Philip could scarcely hear, "protect Philip as you have said. The Lord will bless your valiance."

"Yes, tribune." Arswind drew a short dagger from beneath his cloak, its razor-sharp edge flashing in the dim light. "Let's go."

Philip followed him, fighting his conscience. He did not allow himself to wonder where Arswind had acquired a dagger. *God grant his master doesn't discover it.* The law required severe punishment or death for the offense of a slave or one of barbaric race bearing arms.

Arswind was both.

Entombed in the dark entry, Arswind opened the door a cautious crack. Philip stood behind him, praying silently. God forgive him if he was taking the cowardly way out. Everything within him screamed to stay until he was certain the others were safe.

A swift, strong hand pushed the door open a little wider.

"We are keeping watch." Alexander's voice was hushed. "Go out through the alley behind the house."

Philip stepped past him. The three legionaries could be mistaken for any loitering soldiers, spending their hard earned wages on a long night of dice and wine. But, for all their indolent demeanors, he knew their keen eyes were alert to any impending danger.

Hugging the shadows, he broke into swift stride. He knew the alley well, even in the darkness. Behind him, he could feel Arswind's hot breath and knew he kept close to his side.

Despite his personal reservations about killing their persecutors, Philip felt a tinge of gratitude. Arswind's loyalty was unquestionable. He knew without a trace of doubt the strong young German would sacrifice his own life to protect him.

The small houses and apartments swept by like a blurred vision. Gradually, the darkness of the poorer district gave way to the lit streets that revealed their approach to the affluent section of the *Vicus Jugarius*. The chaotic noise of the Imperial forum could be clearly sensed, and its dazzling array of lights illuminated the night sky just beyond the domus-lined street.

Closer to the wealthy section of Rome, they were at a lower chance of danger from thieves.

Philip exhaled slowly. The jog had tempered his heartbeats to a steady rhythm. He clenched his fists, then opened them, releasing his pent-up anxiety. His mind flitted back to the small house they had just left.

Had the others been as fortunate as he?

A brush on his shoulder reminded him of the present moment. He felt a smile tugging at his mouth. Even in the danger, he had to accept the touching humor of Arswind. The boy stood so close he doubted the width of a palm could pass between them.

"You will be late arriving home, Arswind. Leave me now—I should have no danger from here."

"No. I am going all the way with you, Philip."

Philip increased his stride. "Your obedience to an older brother in the faith is commendable. The same for your loyalty. But you do not wish to offend your master any more than he is now."

"He is going to flog me no matter what I do, Philip. I might as well end this evening by serving you. Besides," and a slightly roughish smile crept across Arswind's face, "I should not like to face the tribune if I left you."

A chuckle rolled up in Philip's throat. Somewhere behind it, however, was a deep pain. *He is so courageous for You, Lord. Spare him suffering.* "Don't tell me you are afraid of Marcus."

"You could call it that. Alexander has told me of his strength. And I have seen warriors enough to know when a man is sound of mind and courage. Let's say I am prudent enough to avoid his wrath."

Again, Philip chuckled. Arswind reminded him in so many ways of himself as a youth. He could relate to his circumstances. A similar heritage had sired and raised them, a mutual enemy had snatched them away from their homelands. Knowing all this, he could almost smell the tribal fires and feel the cool British breezes on his skin when they were together.

"You are right when you say Marcus is strong and fearless. He is a natural leader and a good commander. But he is also compassionate. All things said, Arswind, I can think of no better example for you than he."

"If there was one," and Arswind's voice was low, "it would be you, Philip."

Philip's steps slowed. What could he say to this eager young convert, this faithful brother? He was frank and loyal, a promising servant of the Kingdom. And his affection touched him deeply.

The Aeneas domus was before them, standing out like a bright beacon of hope against the dark night sky. God had granted them safety. Again, the pang of concern gripped his heart. *Protect the others, mighty Jehovah.*

At the foot of the steps, Philip turned. His hands rested slowly on Arswind's sturdy shoulders. "I am grateful for your service, my brother. Your concern for my protection was kind."

Arswind made no reply. Looking closely at him, Philip saw his throat tighten. His eyes were downcast as he finally spoke.

"I am afraid to return home. I am ashamed to own it, but...but I am."

"Don't be." Philip squeezed his shoulders. "You have a right to dread your lord's anger."

Arswind looked up, his eyes mirrors of fear. "What if I never see you again?"

"You will." An aching lump began to gather in Philip's throat. So many believers were killed. Swiftly, he shook his head. *I cannot dwell on that.* He must strengthen his brother, no matter the terrible dread of uncertainty. "Please God, you will join Diantha and me to distribute food to the poor at the end of the week."

Arswind nodded. Quickly, almost with boyish impulse, he stepped forward and wrapped his arms around Philip.

Quietly, Philip hugged him back. The boy's sandy-colored hair brushed his chin, and he could feel a tremor in his strong young body. For all their mutual bravery, the dangers were too real to take lightly.

Arswind stepped back, releasing Philip. His eyes sought Philip's. "Will you pray for me?"

"Yes." Philip again rested his hands on his shoulders. "You have my prayers for your safety and the Lord's will. And I give you my blessing, Arswind." He clapped him on the arm. "Now, go. Lord willing, I'll see you in a few days."

Arswind's face relaxed. With a flashing smile, he lifted his arm in farewell. "Goodbye, Philip." He broke into a swift jog, and Philip's eyes followed him until he was out of sight.

The night was humid and close. Philip glanced up at the stars. The hour was growing late, but he would have no rest until the others returned.

He went inside. The atrium, as usual, was only faintly aglow. He untied his cloak and threw it lightly over his arm. A marble bench beckoned invitingly, and he stepped nearer. His muscles were weary from a long day of ministering.

A sudden noise caught his attention. Turning, he saw Marcus and the veiled figures of his wife and sister slip into the room.

"Praise God." The words escaped Philip in a low rush. Relief surged through his body. He stepped towards Marcus. "And the others?"

"All safe, to the best of our knowledge." Marcus drew his cloak from his shoulders and handed it to him. "The legionaries and I kept watch until everyone slipped out."

"Have you put your reputation in danger?"

"I think not. The city guard will not suspect my word. At the worst, they may think I was mistaken." Marcus turned towards Moriah. Lifting her veil, he touched her chin. "I praise God you were kept safe."

Their lips met in a long kiss before Marcus released her. "Go to your rest, Moriah." He hesitated. "It is late. Do not burden yourself to wait up for me."

"It will be no burden, Marcus." Moriah's eyes danced with a coy smile, and Philip felt a tinge of amusement at the boyishly flirtatious glance Marcus sent her. She looked at him. "Goodnight, Philip."

"Goodnight, Moriah."

Moriah flitted from the room. Diantha closely followed her, casting a soft glance over her shoulder. Philip caught the turn of her eyes, reading her maidenly hesitance.

A strange thrill rushed down his spine. *She wants me to acknowledge her.* It was now his turn to feel a boyish stir. His tones refused to strengthen, their decibels soft and uncertain. "Goodnight, Diantha."

Her smile flashed like a ray of sunshine at him. "Goodnight, Philip."

In a moment, she was gone. Philip turned back to Marcus, fighting himself to refocus his mind on the present moment.

"Is there anything you need before I retire?"

Marcus did not answer him. His face was grave, hesitant. "Philip..." He looked down. When he finally looked up, his eyes were overshadowed. "I know you feel I have done wrong tonight."

Philip felt a familiar burning flush tingle his neck and face. He had not intended to mention what had happened. If there was anything that he was uncomfortable with, it was rebuking his master.

His silence seemed to irk Marcus. "Why don't you tell me straight out you disapprove?"

"Because I don't know that I altogether do, my lord." Philip drew himself up, meeting Marcus's eye. "I know your heart. You saved us much suffering tonight. For that, we are all grateful, no matter what our personal feelings about the way you chose to deter our enemies." His voice lowered. "And you are not accountable to me, Marcus."

"You are now an elder. Is that not an occasion for desiring your approval?"

"If you consider the approval of a British *captive* important." Philip smiled, attempting to lighten Marcus's gravity. Then, sensing his growing irritation, "You know I am not here to judge you."

Marcus looked away. His eyes settled on a marble bust of Mars, his expression distant. "I am a soldier, Philip. I am trained to fight, to kill, to do whatever possible to save me and mine. I think it was that instinct which governed me tonight."

"And no one could doubt your courage was honorable." Philip brushed aside his personal misgivings. For himself, he did not think he could lie to save himself or anyone else, but his conscience was his own affair. "If you are troubled, it is to God you must speak. My approval is nothing besides His."

Marcus's face relaxed into a weary smile. "You are right, of course. I will seek the Lord's face. You are a great encouragement to me, Philip. Thank you for choosing to uplift, not criticize me." He clapped Philip on the back. "Goodnight, my friend."

"Goodnight." Philip watched his swift departure until he had disappeared into the dusky recesses of the house. At a slower pace, he made his own way up to his small chamber.

Inside, he quietly knelt beside his couch. His mind and heart were very full. Arswind's danger; the salvation of the soldiers who had desired them harm; the protection of his brethren—a thousand

374

requests swirled in his mind. Above them all, however, a single word held him captive.

Diantha.

"Oh, Lord." Philip felt a groan rush from his lips. He buried his face in his hand, running his fingers through his hair. "I want Your will, Jesus. I always have. But, forgive me, I am afraid to know what it is. I want her, Lord."

It was only a partial relief to admit the truth. Philip pressed his forehead. His heart was throbbing. The weight of a thousand anchors seemed to be dragging his spirit down, haunting him with a single question.

What if his desire was not God's will?

Over the last three weeks, he had felt a small seed sprouting blossoms within his heart. He knew he loved Diantha. And he was almost as assured of her affection for him. She was beautiful, spiritual, and gracious. They worked well together, and her heart for the lost was as great as his own.

What was there to hinder their union?

Philip slowly got up from his knees. Not bothering to undress, he stretched himself on his couch. As his eyes adjusted to the darkness, he stared up at the ceiling.

Confusion ran rampant through his mind. *Why can't I hear Your voice, Lord? Is it because I don't want to hear the truth? Am I in rebellion to Your will?* The thought sent a wave of screaming pain through his heart. Surely, there was nothing he was unwilling to give up for his Father.

He turned over on his side. "I give her to You, Jesus. Guide my heart and hers. Let nothing be done outside of Your perfect plan."

Rest in Me, Philip.

Philip exhaled softly. His heart pumped against his chest, slowly settling into a quiet cadence. The Spirit's voice was a comfort, but he struggled with the absence of a clear answer. His eyes closed.

"I will rest in You. I will wait on Your timing and allow you to lead my circumstances."

New peace flooded his heart. Refusing to burden himself with needless questions, Philip's breathing settled into a steady rhythm. Sleep circled, darkening his vision with whirling drowsiness.

Abruptly, his eyes jolted open.

What if God's will involved something beyond his realm of thinking?

Diantha settled the empty basket on her hip. Only a few crumbs reminded them of the crusty loaves they had started out with.

"Daniel's bread is the best in Rome. It is honorable of him to donate it to the Lord's work."

Philip looked down at her. A quiet smile was on her cheeks, satisfied with the work they had accomplished. His heart twisted. She was so beautiful, so filled with the Spirit. Everything within him wanted to claim her for his own.

Her labors of love among the poor of Rome always warmed him. He was accustomed to servitude, but she had been a patrician's daughter. Until Christ had saved her, her hands had never been lifted in labor for anyone, let alone beggars. He never heard her complain, not even today, when a diseased man had retched on the hem of her *stola*.

"Daniel is a wonderful example to us all. He will always be my greatest earthly inspiration." His eyes traveled over her. Her quiet strength was so strikingly unusual. He would never get over the feeling she was more akin to a British woman than a Roman. "Thank you for your assistance today."

Diantha laughed slightly. "I did very little compared to you, Philip. Your energy seems to have no limits."

"I can assure you it does." Philip felt his own laughter roll from his chest. He allowed his eyes to dance at her, sending a blush to her cheeks that tingled his own face. Everything about her presence warmed him, filled him with unsurpassable joy. "Time seems to fly when I have your assistance."

Diantha shifted the basket needlessly on her hip, allowing her veil to half-conceal her face. Still, Philip could see her blush deepen.

"You are too kind. But I must agree. Considering Arswind was not with us, we made remarkable time."

"Yes." Philip felt a worrisome pang. Arswind had not appeared to work with them that morning. Of course, there was nothing at all alarming in that. His master had doubtless refused his permission to leave.

Or, he had been flogged, as he had feared. The thought was a bitter ache, surging through Philip's body. God's protection was not always granted, he knew. But, somehow, he had felt so keenly Arswind would not be harmed.

Surely he is only detained. Arswind is a strong soldier of the cross. God's hand is with him.

Diantha seemed to read his thoughts. Her hand found his arm. "You are worried about Arswind?"

"Yes. I worry about what his lord might have done to him. He was threatened with scourging."

"And you of all the believers know what it is to be flogged for Jesus." Diantha's voice was soft. "But, if Arswind has suffered, you must also know God has a plan. It may be his master will come to know our Savior."

"As Marcus came to know Christ. Your faith is honorable, Diantha." Philip touched her hand, smiling. "Come, it is growing late. We shouldn't be out past dark."

Swiftly, they walked through the cobblestones streets, avoiding the rain-filled wheel ruts. As the shadows deepened, Philip's hand rested on the small of Diantha's back, protecting her with his strong presence. She drew near him, masking the mingled scents of food and smoke by her soft botanical scent.

At the Aeneas domus, they hastened up the steps and into the *vestibule*. A swift voice cut through the silence.

"Where have you been?"

Philip turned. The voice was startling, almost angry in its intensity. From the end of the atrium, Marcus strode towards them. His tanned face was unusually tight, working with color.

"Well? Answer me, Philip."

"We were distributing food to the poor." Philip struggled with the consciousness that he was being treated once again as a slave. "I told you where we would be and what our plans were, Marcus."

"You didn't say you would be out until dusk." Marcus made him a glowering look. His voice was stern, rebuking. "I have been worried. And what of Diantha? The streets are dangerous in daylight, let alone evening."

Philip felt a wave of hot color flood his face. His neck burned, sending a furious tingle down his spine. His hands clenched into fists, anger lashing out into words before he could restrain them.

"I fulfilled my obligation to you. Nothing happened to *Diantha—* you can see that for yourself."

"Yes. Providence is gracious. And what if something had happened? What could you have done for yourself or her? Is your ministry so important you will risk your life and others?"

"*Remind* me who released me to fulfill the work of the Lord!" Philip met Marcus's flashing gaze, his body posturing angrily. He was furious clear through. He had been free long enough to resent Marcus's conduct. "Am I not answerable to Christ? You—"

He cut himself short, suddenly realizing what he was doing. His own fury startled him. It had been years since he had lashed out in carnal anger at Marcus. He shook his head, swallowing back the angry resentment boiling up inside him.

Marcus seemed to soften. He opened his mouth, but Diantha's spirited, indignant voice cut him short.

"What right have you to lecture Philip? He is no child, nor a slave. He has labored tirelessly for Christ today, and, I can assure you, I was perfectly safe with him. He would not have let anything occur to harm me. He is one of our *elders*, Marcus. Have you no shame?"

Marcus stood silent.

Instant regret rolled through Philip. His own temper had provoked Diantha's indignation. He knew under no other circumstance would she openly oppose and rebuke her honored brother.

"No, Diantha." His voice was soft. "Marcus is my lord; I should not have spoken so." He glanced at Marcus, forcing his eyes to drop in subservience. "I apologize, my lord."

Marcus himself dropped his gaze. "It is nothing, Philip. I was…worried." He looked at Diantha, then again at Philip. "Diantha was right–you are no man's slave. Pardon me, Philip."

Philip nodded absently. Glancing sidelong at Diantha, he saw her gazing strangely at Marcus. Her voice became quiet. "What is it, Marcus? Something is wrong."

Marcus did not answer directly.

Philip felt a sudden thrust. *Diantha is right.* A fresh wave of shame crossed him. He had been Marcus's closest companion for years. Surely, he should have discerned the signs of Marcus's strained temper. "Tell us what is wrong, Marcus."

"It involves you, Philip."

Philip looked keenly at him. "How? What has happened?"

"I received certain intelligence this afternoon." The corners of Marcus's mouth were tight, his voice flat and tense. He seemed to be harboring a dark secret, one which he was unwilling to reveal. "Your life is in extreme danger."

"What causes you to say this?"

"I have my knowledge, Philip. Your name is on the lips of every city guard and legionary in the *Castra Praetoria*. Someone in high places wants you dead, and there is no secret made about it."

Philip was silent a moment. "Who?"

"We don't know yet. But," and Marcus's eyes flashed with an expression Philip knew only too well, "God preserve his soul if I find out."

"Marcus." Philip took a warning step forward. God forbid that Marcus would sin on his account. "There is murder in your heart."

"Don't speak to me about *murder*!" Marcus spewed the words from his mouth, his voice dark with anger. "I am no spirit, Philip. I see the things being done to our brethren. Thank God you are not a soldier, that you do not have to sit in Nero's arena and watch those of your faith die. I have seen the blood, the torture! And I will *kill* before I see those things done to you."

There was something in Marcus's manner that struck a sudden chilling chord in Philip's heart. Marcus's eyes flashed, his fists clenched in a terrible *something* that was more than indignation, more than anxiety for his danger. He felt himself grow cold. "How do you know all these things?"

Marcus looked at him. The icy fire in his eyes slowly melted, softening into weariness. "There is no easy way for me to tell you, Philip. Arswind—" He paused, a single husky tenor catching his throat. "Arswind is dead."

Philip heard the low cry of Diantha beside him. A numbing wave of shock rolled over him, sickening him. For a long moment, he stood motionless. His heart and mind felt dead. Slowly, agonizingly, with his inner acceptance of the hard truth, a burning pain seared through his chest.

"How?" The question fell unbidden from his lips, husky. His soul screamed for an answer. "Who told you?"

Marcus looked away from him, but Philip saw his quick blink, the soft glisten in his dark pupils. "I received the detailed information at the *Castra Praetoria*. Arswind was flogged by his master the night we escaped from the soldiers. He was then handed over to Nero's personal torturers within the palace."

"And?" Philip clenched his fists, forcing his mind to sift through its torrent of questions. *Lord, I was so certain. Arswind—why Arswind?*

Inside, he felt his heart tear, as agonizing as if it had been snatched from his body. "Why to the torturers? Why not immediately to the arena?"

Marcus stood silent.

An icy hand clamped around Philip's heart, tingling him through. Marcus's silence was more agonizing than knowing the truth. He stepped forward, passion lending his numb body strength. "Why, Marcus?" His voice shook, threatening to break. "Great God of our fathers, he was flogged! Was it not enough?"

Marcus looked at him, quiet. "His lord saw it as a sign of loyalty to Rome. He saw it as an opportunity to reveal the whereabouts of a Christian elder named *Philip*."

Philip stepped back. He could sense the blood fleeing from his face. Inwardly, his stomach gripped with nausea, hollowing his voice. "And he was tortured...for *my* sake?"

"Yes. It seems Arswind's lord knows something of you and of the price on your head. Praise God," and Marcus's voice shook ever so slightly, "Arswind revealed nothing. And God was gracious. He did not live long enough to adorn the arena."

A whirling cloud of darkness swirled over Philip's vision. When it cleared, he looked down to see his hands shaking uncontrollably. He felt more shaken than he could ever remember being.

Arswind had suffered for *him*.

From his peripheral vision, he saw Diantha sink down against the wall, pulling her knees into her face. Her shoulders shook, quietly weeping.

His strength suddenly failed him. The numbing powers of shock wore away, leaving his body weak. He stumbled, kneeling beside a bench. With his nausea intensifying, he leaned his head on his hand.

"No, Lord." The agonized words spilled from his throat. "Why Arswind? *Why?* I assured him of Your protection. He trusted me. Why this faithful follower?"

Marcus's hand rested on his shoulder, gripping it. "You now know why I was going mad at your delay, Philip. *Think*, my brother. It could have been you." His voice broke. "Do you still judge me for my concern?"

Philip shook his head. His voice refused to speak. Deep inside, brokenness welled up. He had seen dozens of believers perish under the cruelty of their oppressors. But Arswind had been different.

He held such promise, Lord. He was such a strong young believer. Why? Why because of me?

Marcus's hand left his shoulder. His sandaled feet created a soft slap across the atrium floor, and Philip sensed him taking Diantha in his arms. Their clothing rustled in rising, blending into the sounds of their unified tread. It grew fainter, until it left the atrium altogether.

Philip's body shook. Abruptly, his face dropped into his trembling hands. Alone in the echoing, wide atrium, he wept.

Chapter Thirty

Philip tossed on his couch. The room was warm. A gnat buzzed around his face in search of moisture. He swatted at it, his eyes gazing unseeingly at the roof above him.

Your life is in extreme danger.

The words echoed in his mind, haunting him. He was accustomed to danger, to the daily possibility of being arrested and martyred for Jesus. It was something he had surrendered to Christ when he had first accepted salvation.

Why then did the chilling hand of fear clench his heart?

He again rolled over. He felt sick, still wrapped in nausea. The merciless end of Arswind was raw in his soul, a pulsating wound. He blinked against the salty tears, his ache renewed in his throat. And in his heart.

"Oh, God." The groan rushed from his lips. "Your ways are unsearchable. I know Your plan was perfect for Arswind. But why for *my* sake? Why did he die in such agony?"

Only the chirping of crickets met his ears. Philip closed his eyes, fighting the aching pain screaming in his mind and heart. God did not owe him an answer. And, somehow, he sensed he would never know why.

Still, his mind refused to stand still. It roved through the endless plethora of possible answers. Was it possible the boy had died to give him the warning he needed, to bring awareness to his own danger?

He shuddered. *God forbid.* He felt the moisture steal beneath his eyelids, mingling with his perspiration. *Surely that was not Your plan, Lord. Surely You did not allow his death to preserve my life.*

Either way, the danger was real.

Again, the icy hand clamped around Philip's heart. He felt its chilly power spread through his body. The abrupt realization came to him: his perspiration was not from the heat, but from fear.

The fear in itself was torture. Why was he afraid? What terrors had he not already faced that he could not face again? He who had survived captivity, slavery, the lash, and daily peril should not be afraid to trust in the One who had brought him safely through his trials.

A dull sensation crossed him. He had been nervous, even anxious before. But this was a new fear, a chilling power he had never experienced until now. It was strangely consuming, filling every nook of his soul and body.

What was he about to face? What was this terrible unknown he dreaded with such intensity? Was it possible—and his mind halted in contemplation—God was warning him of some impending trial?

A touch lighted on his hand. *Nothing will separate you, Philip.*

Philip's eyes jerked open. His heart pulsed, oxygen severed from his lungs. "What is it, Lord?" His voice cried aloud into the darkness. "What are You preparing me for?"

Be strong and of good courage. Neither fear, nor be afraid.

Philip's heart swelled. Sudden, torrential peace flooded his soul. Like darkness scattered by radiant light, the icy fear sped from his body. Slowly, his lungs settled into a calming rhythm, and he began to breathe again.

Whatever God's plan held for him, he would not be alone.

His eyes closed. Slumber encircled him, shutting out reality and the unknown future. Instead, he dreamt. And, in his dreams, a familiar face smiled with gruff kindness upon him.

"Philip, my son."

It was Beric himself.

He was alive and well. He looked strong, as proud and valiant as he had been as an Iceni chieftain. His countenance shone with unearthly light, his beard neatly full. And Philip felt their arms clasp, their chests meet in a long embrace. The strong touch was one he could never forget.

His eyes jerked open.

It was early morning. The sun was beginning to make its ascent, scattering the mist-like grayness into full light.

It had only been a dream. *Or had it?*

Philip stood up, rubbing his arms. He stepped to the window and looked out. The early sunlight glistened off the colossal buildings on every side of the Aeneas domus, warming his face. Rome was beginning to stir, awakening to the day's labors. The city was beautiful.

And spiritually dead.

So many souls, Lord. Philip's heart ached. Many of those souls were ones who had killed those he loved best. He exhaled slowly, gripping the sides of the casement. The dull pain of loss had not lessened.

Philip relinquished his palms. It was then he realized they tingled. A warm, strange vibration sped down his spine. He had almost forgotten.

The touch. The voice.

How many years had it been since he had first physically felt what he was certain was the presence of Jesus? He often put the sufferings of that day from his mind, but he would never forget what he had experienced.

But why again? Why this charge to be strong and to have courage?

The questions rolled over Philip's mind. He felt confused, possessed of the knowledge that some certain trial loomed in his future. Strangely, the dull consciousness was void of fear. He felt peaceful, more at rest than he could ever remember being.

Adjacent to his room, Marcus's bell rang.

Philip dressed swiftly. Fastening his wristbands as he went, he stepped into Marcus's chamber.

A swift glance revealed Marcus standing at one end of the room, looking out of the window. Moriah was still wrapped in sound slumber, her arm outstretched atop the coverlets.

"You called?" Philip spoke softly. He did not wish to awaken Moriah. She should sleep even if her husband chose such early hours.

Marcus turned. It was then Philip saw his face was drawn and pale. He did not appear to have slept. Weariness enshrouded his features. "Yes." He stepped forward. "I know it is early. I would not have called, but..." He paused. "I felt certain you would be awake."

"Yes." Philip felt the understanding between them. There was little need for words. He stepped to the wardrobe and took out Marcus's military attire. Quietly, he strapped the polished armor in place and went about the usual motions of fixing his tribunal toga.

Marcus's eyes never left him. They followed him continually, searching. Philip did not raise his gaze to meet them. He did not want to see the weariness, the unspoken question he knew burned in his master's mind.

With Marcus fully attired, Philip turned away. He felt a quiet hand rest instantly on his arm, halting him. He turned, lifting his eyes for the first time to meet the dark pupils looking with searching intensity at him.

"You are not blaming yourself for what happened to Arswind?"

"No." Philip considered his words. He searched his heart, sifting through the emotions to the core of his innermost feelings. "It was the Lord's will. I do not say I understand, for I don't." He paused, fighting the growing huskiness in his throat. "But I do trust Him."

Marcus continued to look at him, his gaze a searching question. It was if he could not bring himself to speak the query bordering clearly on the tip of his tongue.

Philip said nothing. His heart was a surreal well of peace. He had never before felt such strange quietness of mind, such calm in the face of the storm he could almost see looming on his horizon. Even the keen anxiety he saw in Marcus was like a passing whisper, something oddly unable to influence his own feelings.

Nothing could shake him.

"Will you go out today?" Marcus's restraint broke at last. His voice was a low rush, like an escape of cold air.

"Yes." Philip paused. Accustomed to subjecting his will to another for so many years, there were times he faltered to take his own lead, to speak with command. Not so today. He kept his gaze quietly steady. "I promised Daniel I would assist him."

"That pledge was made before, in other conditions. There is no wrongdoing in retracting it."

"You are wrong." Philip saw the wave of dark color that rolled like a cloud over Marcus's face. "I am going."

"Because you are too stubborn to realize your own danger?" Marcus's voice rose in frustration. His tension was fairly tangible.

"No. Because I feel the Spirit's leading in this, Marcus. I must go."

Marcus softened. Again, weariness encompassed him. "If you were still my slave, I would force you to stay here."

"No, you would not, Marcus." Philip laid a swift hand on his arm. Marcus's soldierly concealment of emotion did not usually allow the deep concern he saw in him. "I know you would not hinder the Lord's work."

"No." Marcus turned a little away, his voice flat. "At this moment, I feel I would do anything to ensure your safety." He took an ornate bottle from a shelf, tipping a few drops of the contents into his palm. The musky, botanical scent of Indian cologne filled the room. He brought the liquid over the back of his neck, his throat. The force of his movements betrayed his rising tension. "What good can you do for the work of the Lord if you are *killed?*"

"My life is in God's hands."

Marcus turned. Slowly, he closed the gap between them. "And what of Diantha?"

Philip felt the blood rise in his neck, in his cheeks. Just the sound of her name sent the adrenaline coursing through his veins. With difficulty, he restrained his voice to speak quietly. "She will not be going with me today. But her life is also within His will, Marcus."

"That is not what I meant. What will happen to her if you are murdered?" A sudden husky tenor bordered on Marcus's voice. "What will it do to her faith, to her heart?"

Philip could not speak. His heart pumped wildly. *He knows.* He had seen their feelings for each other. Marcus's soft tenors continued to confirm his thoughts.

"I know you love each other."

Philip swallowed. The desire to explain himself was strong, but he scarcely knew what he could say. "I should have spoken of it. Only," his voice caught slightly, "I have not known how. My life has become...one constant prayer."

The corners of Marcus's mouth twitched in an understanding smile. "Yes. I know. There is nothing you can or cannot tell me about the way you feel I will not have already felt myself."

"I have not spoken to her. I would not–without your permission."

"You have it, Philip." Marcus's hands gripped his shoulders. "I could have no greater joy than in having you for my brother."

"If it is the Lord's will." Philip uttered the words softly. The passion of Marcus's demeanor touched him, but he could not evade the mysterious prick warning his heart. *Be strong and of good courage, Philip.*

"And why would it not be?" Marcus's voice became unsteady. "Why should the Lord deny you your happiness?"

"Because His ways are not our ways, Marcus." Philip allowed his eyes to drift past Marcus. His life seemed to rise up before him. Scenes revisited, flashing through his mind. How many times he had learned to trust his God, coming to grips with the fact that His plan was unsearchable. Each time man had meant him harm, Christ had turned it for good. "We cannot know our future. I know only that I have committed my soul to His keeping."

"I am afraid for you."

"But you will not keep me from the Lord's work." Philip felt a smile rise to his lips, so strong he himself could not understand it.

He did not stop to wonder. All he knew was peace. "Believe in Christ with me, Marcus. Believe that *nothing* shall befall me outside of His will."

Silence filled the room.

"Lord, help my unbelief." When Marcus spoke, it was an audible sigh. He again gripped Philip's shoulders. "Go then. And may God guide your path." In the Eastern fashion he occasionally adopted, he placed his arm around Philip's neck and embraced him close.

Philip quietly returned the embrace. Swiftly, he pulled himself away and left the room, the masculine scent of Indian cologne still in his nostrils.

In the atrium, he was met by Diantha.

Her eyes were slightly red, marked by the appearance of tears. She was pale and, like Marcus, did not appear to have slept. Ceremony thrust aside, she drew very close to him, her eyes searching his.

"Are you going out today, Philip?"

Philip touched her hair. It was soft to his fingertips. As always, her scent was warm and botanical. "I must, Diantha."

"You know what they did to Arswind. They will do worse to you."

"If it is the Lord's will."

"And it *will* be." Diantha's eyes filled with tears. "He has allowed so many of our brethren to suffer. Oh, Philip! Think! Think of yourself, of *us*." Her voice became a soft whisper of pleading. "Is your life nothing that you will throw it away?"

Philip's hands rested on her shoulders. His heart twisted, wrung by the sight of her tears. But, somehow, the depth of her words could not slip past the endless voice of peace engulfing him. It whispered his duty in his ears, urging him to go.

"Here or in the streets, I am in His keeping, Diantha. And I am safer in His will than outside of it. You know these things. In your heart, you *know* my calling is certain."

"Yes." Diantha brought her hand over his own, and Philip felt its tremble. "You are called to the ministry. I do not doubt that, Philip. Nor do I discourage you from it." Her eyes filled afresh. "It is only until this danger is past."

"No." Philip took her hand from atop his and pressed it within both of his own. "Danger is never past for us. And I hear the Spirit, Diantha. Come what may, for whatever purpose He has, I know I am to continue my work."

"But you may be mistaken. You–"

"No." Philip touched her lips, stopping her. "I am not. And you must not dissuade me. Do not let that sin rest on your head."

Diantha's head drooped. Her shoulders shook. "I am afraid, Philip. I am not strong as you are." She raised her face to his. The soft tears spilled down her cheeks, falling in noiseless drops on her *stola*. "What if God takes you from me?"

Philip's arms slipped down her shoulders, embracing her. She seemed to melt into his arms. He held her tightly, resting his cheek against her hair. "Let not your heart be troubled, neither let it be afraid." His voice was a gentle whisper. Somehow, no other words would rise to his lips. There was no other promise he could give. His grip tightened. "I love you, Diantha."

A soft whimper escaped her. Burying her face, she cried into his chest. "I love you too, Philip."

"Then keep holding onto that." Philip put her gently from him. "I'll be home tonight."

Softly, he bent down and kissed her cheek. He hated to pull himself away from her, but the call of his mission beckoned. Leaving behind her warmth, her sweet scent, he strode from the atrium into the morning sunshine.

Outside, the humid warmth was intoxicating. Philip lifted his face to the sun, his sandaled feet leading his way by force of habit. The heat settled into his body. Every core of his being felt rejuvenated.

Abrupt darkness dimmed the light.

Philip glanced up. The sun shone full. No clouds littered the sky. Only this strange dark presence chilled the air, cutting off his warmth. He had felt it before. Once before his conversion. And, once, when his spirit had hovered between life and death under the rods.

Each time, God's presence had been near. *As it was last night, Lord. I know, whatever Your plan holds, You will be with me.*

Daniel was waiting for him at their usual street-corner meeting place. Philip extended his hand as he drew close, a slight smile deepening on his mouth.

"Peace be with you."

"And to you, Philip." Daniel drew him into a swift embrace, his beard brushing Philip's cheek. He motioned slightly, casting a glance over his shoulder. One never knew who might be watching. "Come. We will go into the *Subura* district today."

Philip nodded in wordless acknowledgment. He had been to the slum section of Rome many times before. Known for its poverty, crime, and prostitution, the *Subura* was the center of much suffering. There was no better to place to distribute their food, coins, and good news.

As they made their way around fellow pedestrians and through the bustling commerce, Philip could sense Daniel glance at him.

"You are quiet today."

"My mind is full."

"I would imagine so." Daniel was quiet. He continued to glance sidelong at him. "Marcus told me everything. Does it trouble you?"

"That my life is in danger?" Philip drew his cloak more securely around his shoulders. He sidestepped a jutting piece of cobblestone, collecting his thoughts. "No. It did last night, but...not now."

They were nearing the *Subura*. Philip could smell the rotting garbage, the stifled air of the too-close apartments. Against the shadows of a wine-cellar, Daniel stopped to look at him.

"God's peace radiates from you, Philip. Your courage is evident."

"It is not of myself. God has been with me, Daniel." Philip paused. His pulse surged, desiring to tell Daniel all that was within his heart. "I have told no one this, my friend, but you at least must know."

Again, he stopped to sort his thoughts. "I felt that my life was planned. You must have guessed what has been in my heart: that my greatest wish has been to marry Diantha. I wanted to spend my life with her and in the ministry. But now, my heart is different. My life feels as if it is fading. It seems as if God Himself has warned me that my time in His service is growing short."

Daniel was silent.

Philip looked past him, fixing his eyes on the cobblestoned street. "Even now, I feel that a candle has been lit in my heart. But it seems to be sputtering. Do you think I am wrong?"

"Philip." Daniel touched his shoulder, his voice gentle. "Am I your judge? I cannot know what is in your heart." A sudden catch permeated his voice. "But I pray God you are mistaken."

Philip looked at him. How well he knew the bearded face, the compassionate eyes and strong faith of Daniel. "For the sake of those who care for me, so do I."

His throat felt dry, thinking of all Daniel had done for him. Everything within him wanted to lighten the load of worry he saw in his friend's countenance. His steps slowed.

"If I never say it again, Daniel, allow me to say it now. I count you as one of the greatest blessings of my life. Your friendship and all that you've taught me is something I will thank God for until the end of my days."

Daniel's beard held a smile, but Philip saw its waver. His eyes blinked, his voice hollow in its huskiness. "And for all you have been to me, Philip, I thank Adonai."

They walked on in silence.

The alley closed in around them, the light shadowed by the towering apartments on every side. Garbage and filth lying in the street became increasingly difficult to avoid. An overpowering stench rose from the ruts, substantiating it was not rainwater which filled their murky depths.

Children scrambled past them, their shouts of play and quarreling reverberating against the crumbling stonework. Somewhere, a baby screamed in shrill hunger. On nearly every corner, Philip could feel the wanton eyes of harlots.

How they need You, Lord!

"A *denarii*, by the immortal gods!" A beggar's hoarse whisper caught Philip's attention. The man's shrunken hand clutched at his tunic, pulling him downwards.

Philip quietly knelt at his side, resting his hand on the beggar's threadbare rags. The man was covered in boils. Lice and flies crawled over his diseased body and through his oily hair, spreading the filth.

"Here." Philip gently dropped a coin into his dish. "May the one true God, Jesus Christ, give you peace." He paused. "I should like to tell you–"

With haste Philip should not have been able to guess was possible in a diseased man, the beggar scrambled away from him. Clutching his dish to his chest, he disappeared around a corner.

Philip was still a moment. He had been rejected before. But there was something oddly different about this beggar's hasty flight. There had been a look of terror in his eyes. Slowly, he rose to his feet, turning.

An ominous shadow fell over him, blocking the already dim light.

A single beam flashed momentarily against cold steel. His eyes fell, locking onto the dagger. Its sharp edges were designed to kill. A hard hand held it inches away from his chest, steady, inexorable.

Philip followed the path of the blade up its owner's arm. It directed his gaze into the cold eyes of Thallus.

"The legionary Alexander Lucianus is here to see you, tribune."

"Send him in." Marcus stood by a casement. His gaze had been drifting over the training grounds, but the sentry's voice awakened his thoughts to the present moment. Concentrating was difficult today.

His ways are not our ways.

The thought was a haunting one. Marcus's throat tightened. What if God's ways held something beyond even his worst imaginations?

Alexander swept into the room with more haste than military promptness. His salute was equally swift. "Hail, tribune."

"At ease, Alexander." Marcus motioned to a pitcher of wine. Alexander shook his head, and he poured out a single goblet for himself. "What brings you here?"

"Philip, my lord tribune. I am worried about him."

"That makes two of us." Marcus set his goblet down. "He gives no thought for himself. I couldn't keep him at home today."

"Which was exactly my worst fear. Marcus, there is good reason to believe it is one of *your* old enemies who is behind this scheme to murder him."

"How do you know?"

"One of the believers spoke with me today. He is a slave in the domus of Saturius Quinctia. Apparently, he overheard a conversation between Saturius and," Alexander hesitated, "Rowland Virginius."

"My father?" Marcus stiffened. A thousand thoughts whirled in his mind. It would only make sense for Rowland to despise the life of Philip. "What was said?"

"He didn't know everything. Only that Saturius, Rowland, and the son Thallus are in one accord that Philip must die."

Marcus ground his teeth. His hands clenched into angry fists. "I should have known. Thallus, in particular, has sworn to have revenge against me." He paused. "The question is now: what can be done? Philip is blindly averse to any concern for his safety."

"I want to take a *conteburnium* of legionaries and search for him. It may be this new evidence will convince him to go into hiding. Have I your permission?"

"More than that, I'll go with you." Marcus strode across the room, picking up his scarlet cloak. "Assemble a picked force. I want men who will keep their mouths shut if anything is discovered. Use your own discretion."

Philip met Thallus's cold eyes with a steady gaze. Strangely, he felt no pang of fear. Beyond the first lurch of shock, his heart maintained a steady pace. Everything within him breathed a quiet courage, giving him strength.

"What do you want, Thallus?"

"So you remember me." Thallus laughed sardonically. His narrowed eyes were like piercing beams of icy snow. "But why should you forget? Why would a slave forget the patrician he *beat*?"

The dagger rustled against his clothing, threatening. Philip's mind flitted back to the past. Who would have thought his passionate loss of control at the Baths would return to haunt him all these years later?

His voice kept its restraint. "If I remember you, Thallus, it is for the associations you had with my master."

"Yes. Your *master*." Thallus spat the words. "I have forgotten nothing of the wrongs he did me either. Marcus thought he had his sweet victory when you conquered my slave, when he stole that pretty Christian woman from my arms. But he hasn't. Today I will prove it."

Philip's mind whirled. What was it Thallus meant?

The gripping hand of slow understanding chilled his heart. For one moment, his pulse nearly stopped. Then, it surged onward, filling him with the same, calm assurance he had felt for so many hours.

Be strong and of good courage, Philip.

His senses keen to the danger, Philip felt the presence of others behind him. He was surrounded by at least three men. Against the wall several paces away, Daniel's face was ashen.

Thallus twirled his dagger, playing with it. He seemed in no hurry to continue his point, to fulfill whatever promise of victory he meant. His cool self-assurance was ample proof this was not the first time he had held a man at death's door. When he again spoke, his voice was suavely indifferent.

"Is it true you Christians can hold spells over men?"

"No." Philip continued to meet his gaze. The ridiculousness of the question seemed out of place, but he sensed the meaning behind it. "You are mistaken when you call us Christians sorcerers. We do not exercise demonic powers over men, but," and he allowed a touch of resolve in his voice, "we do have the sustaining strength of our Savior."

"Then you didn't cast a spell over Marcus? He was not forced to become a Christus-follower?"

"No. My lord made his own choices."

"I thought as much." Thallus yawned in his face. "A pity. Marcus would have done better to claim some mystical force. His father might have had mercy."

"I did not think Rowland Virginius capable of mercy."

"Now you understand." A muscle twitched in Thallus's cheek. "Would it interest you to know he sent me?"

Philip was silent a moment. Thallus obviously desired to toy with him. "My only interest is in fulfilling the work for which I came. Allow me to pass."

"Allow you to pass! You impudent *fool.*" Thallus's mockery snapped. "Do you think my business here was for a pleasant chat?"

Philip exhaled with slow control, feeling the dagger prick his chest. He felt Thallus's hot breath on his neck, the scent tainted of strong wine. Everything about his ominous close presence insinuated a cruel pleasure.

"Who do you *think* you are?"

A slow smile tugged at Philip's mouth. God brought him opportunity even then. "I am a child of the one true God." His heart surged. *I am well-beloved in Your sight, Father.* "I am a servant of Jesus Christ—"

A swift, stinging blow fell over his face.

"How dare you speak that name?" Thallus's yell echoed furiously through the alley. "Do you think I will stand here and be preached at, you Christian dog?"

Philip bit his lip. No amount of humility could keep the anger from boiling up within him. He was a citizen of Rome. And even when a slave, his own master had not struck him since before his conversion. The warrior in him itched to double his fists. *Turn the other cheek...*

Thallus pressed the dagger again into his ribcage. Philip could feel the force of his wrath. "Whether or not you cast a spell on Marcus, you were the cause of his shame. It was because of you he left the religion of his fathers. And you must pay for that!"

For the first time, Philip felt a prickle of fear. It ran down his spine, and he became conscious of the cold perspiration standing in little beads on his face and neck. So it was Thallus himself who sought his life.

Thallus's gloating expression revealed he sensed his apprehension. "You know my reason for following you into this sewer. That is well." His brows cocked. "But I am a reasonable man. I know you are a skilled wrestler, a warrior. Recant this idiotic Christus-worship."

"For what purpose?"

"I will make you great." Thallus shifted, a gleam in his haughty expression. "Imbecile, your miserable life is within my hands.

Choose to recant your religion and enter my service. Marcus foolishly allowed your talent to wither. I will take it and restore you to your power."

"My power is not within wrestling, Thallus." Philip felt his heart thud, a dim sensation somewhere behind the overpowering calmness settled over him. He understood plainly the intent of the dagger pressed against his chest. Thallus only played with him. He desired the boastful glory of ravaging a Christian's faith before killing him. "My strength is from the One who gave His life for me. And nothing can take that from me, Thallus. Not even you."

Be strong and of good courage, Philip.

The sounds of clashing armor, of a shouted command filled the alley. At its end, Philip saw a blur of scarlet and silver, a rushing entourage of masculine bodies. The startled shout of one of the men was a distant echo, resounding in his brain.

"Master! The Tribune Aeneas!"

A curse dropped from Thallus's lips. He thrust himself forward, his brutal strength powered by haste.

And a searing, agonized pain shot through Philip's chest.

Philip crumpled. He felt the dagger ripped from his body as his knees buckled beneath him, flooding him with pain so intense his vision darkened. He heard his own breathing, ragged. His hand closed over the wound, a strange, warm moisture seeping through his fingers.

"Swine! Dogs!" Somewhere, Marcus's furious voice echoed through the alley. Philip heard the sound of running feet, of the legionaries shouting at the fleeing men. His eyes closed.

"*Philip!* By God's mercy, Philip! Speak to me."

Philip struggled to open his eyes. He sensed Marcus's hand gripping his shoulder, the other pulling his hand away from his wound.

"Father in heaven. Don't take him. Hear me, Father. *Don't* take him!" Marcus's groans raised into an anguished shout. "Find him! I want that man brought to me. I will kill him with my own hands!"

Philip forced his eyes open. His vision cleared, revealing the agonized expression on Marcus's white features. "No, Marcus." His breathing was labored; he could not force the air into his lungs. Somewhere, deep inside, he could feel a mysterious draining. Was it his life's blood? "Forgive, Marcus."

He could not go on. His eyes closed once again.

Nothing will separate you, Philip.

How could peace be so clear in the face of death?

The voice of Daniel resounded in his mind, as it so often did. *There is no greater terror than the fear of death. But, as a Christian, you are learning to die daily. Thus, when the actual time comes for your spirit to leave your body, you will have already gained the victory over its sting.*

Somewhere, there was a bright, glorious sunset. He could see it, touch it. The sun was setting. But the light only grew brighter, a dazzling beacon beyond the looming horizon.

Darkness was becoming dawn.

Chapter Thirty-One

The Aeneas domus was strangely quiet. The slaves performed their duties softly, their voices a hushed whisper. In the great atrium, the slightest sound created a hollow echo, sighing among the marble images of the gods.

In his chamber, Marcus knelt beside his couch. Again and again, he clasped his fingers together. He felt numb, helpless. *Oh, God.* His soul screamed out, a continuous groaning appeal. *Do not take him from us. You have the power. Let him live. I need him, Lord.*

His bleary eyes rested on the others. Alexander. Diantha. Moriah. Daniel. They were all gathered, watching the body of Philip with hushed fervency. He lay motionless, only his ragged breathing signifying he still lived.

The dagger had done its work well. The physicians bore no hope for Philip. Apparently, it was only a matter of time until his wounded heart ceased beating. *But we know you can heal, Father. You have the power.* Jehovah-Rapha, Daniel called Him. The Great Healer.

Beside him, Diantha knelt beside the couch. She struck a disheveled appearance, worn out by weeping. Her hair was tangled and disorderedly, a striking contrast to its usual smooth glossiness. The corners of her beautiful eyes were red and bleary, continually filled with soft moisture. She clasped Philip's still hand in her own, holding it against her tear-wet cheek.

Marcus's heart twisted. His grief was terrible, but what could it be compared with hers? He wrapped a loose arm around her shoulders. He had seen this day more clearly than he had thought. His own words rose up to haunt him.

What of Diantha? What will it do to her faith, to her heart?

And what of his own heart? Could he live without Philip? His faithful attendant, his brother, the devout young leader who had taught him so many lessons?

Philip had been so much to him. God had taken evil and made it good, turning his selfishness and cruelty into a friendship he would rather die than live without. Through Philip, God had proved He could turn slavery into freedom, enmity into friendship, and darkness into light.

Surely, God would not have given him all that only to snatch it away.

Marcus felt a groan escape him. He buried his face in the soft folds of the bed clothes, not caring who saw his grief.

In his pain, he wanted nothing more than to kill Thallus. There was murder in his heart—and he didn't care. It had only been Philip's agonized plea that had kept him from snatching his *gladius* from its sheath and ending Thallus's miserable life. *Blood for blood.* But Philip had asked him to forgive. So he had let the murderer go, numb to everything but the agony of his feelings and Philip's pain.

A muffled groan sounded above him. Marcus lifted his head. The quick spark of hope he felt at seeing Philip stir was quickly replaced by dread. Was it the seal of death that seemed to hover so closely over his white features?

He half-rose, leaning over him. "Philip." His voice was a husky waver. He could not control himself to speak firmly. "My brother."

"Marcus." Philip's tones were cracked, made nearly inaudible by suffering.

Marcus felt a rush of tears, seeing the effort it took for him to speak. *God in heaven.* His heart swelled, nearly forcing another groan from his chest. *Relieve his pain. Only don't take him.* His hand closed over Philip's free one. "We are all with you, Philip."

"Diantha...where is she?"

"I am here, Philip." Her voice a sob, Diantha leaned over Philip.

Philip took her hand from his own and held it. He did not speak, but his look of quiet contentment signified the comfort of her presence.

Marcus looked sidelong, sensing the rustle of Alexander's clothing as he leaned against the couch. The young man's face was streaked with tears, his green eyes brimming with moisture. In the midst of all his turbulent grief, Marcus felt a tinge of respect. Though kneeling beside a tribune of the Praetorian Guard, Alexander was not ashamed to weep for his brother in the faith.

Philip's gaze traveled over each of their countenances. His look was one of simple gratitude, thankful for their presence. Pain settled afresh over his face, and he closed his eyes. When he opened them, it was to rest them upon Marcus.

Marcus's eyes filled with a torrent of hot tears. In that single look, he recognized everything he had been denying. *Great God, please!* His soul groaned, nearly ripping his burning heart from his chest. Philip was nearly home.

"Philip." Fighting to control the sobs welling up in his chest, he leaned over him. "You are not in pain?"

"No, not now." For the first time, Philip's voice was clearly audible. A faint tinge of color warmed his cheeks, then sped away. "It is well, Marcus."

Marcus saw the spatter of his own tears as they fell onto Philip's face. Everything within him longed to embrace his brother, to spill his own strength over onto his fading body.

"Have you forgiven me?" The words escaped him, his voice broken into restrained weeping. "For all I have done to you, have you truly forgiven me?"

"Yes. There...there is no man...on earth I love...better than you, master." Faint though it was, Philip's smile was enough. His hand moved slowly over Diantha's disheveled hair, caressing it. "I-I...have been...blessed."

His hand went still.

Silence enshrouded the room.

Marcus felt numb. Something settled over him, washing him in cold nausea and a pain so intense he couldn't breathe. Was it only his pain or had he truly seen an unearthly light settle over Philip's face, washing it in perfect peace?

Before him, Diantha's head sank onto Philip's motionless chest. Slowly, the sound of her muffled sobs filled his ears, as hollow as an echo from the past.

A hand gripped his shoulder. Dimly, Marcus heard the sound of Daniel's husky voice above him.

"I am the resurrection, and the life: he that believeth in me, though he were dead, yet shall he live." Rent, Daniel's voice broke. "Take our brother into Your arms, Father. We give him to You."

Around him, Marcus heard the weeping of the others.

Deep inside, something began to break. He struggled against the waves of torturing agony beating again and again at his chest, ripping, tearing his throbbing heart into pieces.

Blinded, blurred though his vision was, his moisture-filled eyes refused to tear from Philip's face. Beautifully serene, Marcus knew he saw the countenance of a martyr. Everything in that look was a mirror of how he had lived for the Christ he had died for.

He tightened his grip on the lifeless hand one final time. *Goodbye, brother.* The ache in his throat was quickly becoming unbearable. *He served You faithfully, Father. Receive Him now into glory.*

His fingers relinquished their grip. Dropping his head, Marcus wept.

Chapter Thirty-Two

The plaintive wail of a newborn cut through the air. Its welcome sound eased the tense atmosphere. Marcus exhaled softly, his eyes closing in momentary prayer. *Thank you, Lord.*

He squeezed Moriah's hand, willing his strength to spill over to her. Her face was weary and covered in perspiration, but the expression of relieved joy that washed over her features was unmistakable. The sorrowing labor of the last few hours was over.

From his peripheral vision, Marcus could see the midwife wrapping the little one in warm blankets. His main concern was for Moriah, but the question still escaped him. "The child? Is it all right?"

"He's strong and healthy. You have a son."

Marcus's heart thudded. "A son?" His voice cracked. He could not contain the overwhelming emotion. It flooded him with joy so strong he could scarcely stand it. "I have a son?"

The midwife beamed at him, holding out the little bundle. Slowly, Marcus released Moriah's hand and rose to his feet, aching from his cramped position of so many hours at her side. According to Roman tradition, he must hold the child, signifying he accepted him.

Custom aside, the desire to touch his son was strong. He *wanted* to hold him.

The warm bundle was laid in his arms. The strong scents of blood and medicinal potions were quickly overwhelmed by the sweet odor of new life, striking Marcus's nostrils in an overpowering rush. He looked down into the red little face, made beautiful by the knowledge that the child was his.

My son!

The baby squirmed, a hungry wail escaping his lips. Marcus softly touched his cheek, his fingers brushing the baby's velvety skin. Then, gently, he laid his hand over his tiny head.

"May God Almighty bless and keep you, my son. May He watch over you and give you peace. May you come to the acceptance of Him and grow into a strong warrior of our faith. Amen."

Marcus turned. On the couch, Moriah's eyes were shining at him. He knew her desire to hold her baby was even stronger than his had been. Gently, he laid the baby beside her.

Uttering a soft coo, the child squirmed, then, began to nurse. For several minutes, there was perfect silence as mother and child bonded. Moriah played with its silky hair, murmuring indistinct assertions of love and tenderness that only a mother could.

Marcus looked on. Somehow, even in the midst of such a beautiful moment, his heart twisted. There was someone he would give anything for if he could be with them, witnessing the first moments in his son's life.

Moriah seemed to read his thoughts. She looked up at him, her voice soft. "It is strange to think it has already been a year since we lost him."

"Yes." Marcus resumed his kneeling position at her side. His heart throbbed, as it always did when he thought of Philip. "It-it is difficult not to be bitter, especially now." He forced a smile to his lips, squeezing her hand. "But God knows best. And we have already seen fruit."

"Four souls were saved last week." Moriah looked down at the nursing baby. "One of them is a slave. He heard Philip's story, and now it is said he does not cease witnessing to his master."

"Others have been inspired to do the same." Marcus exhaled slowly. It was hard to live without Philip. For him, it was a daily struggle of learning to adjust to the absence of one who had been so close. "I heard one brother say he has been convicted to give up his all for Jesus, as Philip did. He only recently went abroad to witness to the Greeks in Macedonia."

"So we see," and Moriah's eyes shone behind a soft mist, "that God has ordered all things for good. He is using Philip's testimony to bring hundreds, maybe even thousands into the fold."

Silence fell over the chamber.

Again, Moriah stroked the baby's silky hair. At last, she looked up at Marcus. "What will you name him?"

Marcus was quiet a moment. In his heart, there was but one name for his son. But, behind his personal feelings and the selfish desire to do exactly as he wanted, love for Moriah was uppermost in his thoughts. She should have a part in naming their son.

"There is only one name I could wish, Moriah. But you must have a part in naming him. He is your son also." He kissed her softly. "Whatever you decide."

Moriah smiled. Lifting the baby up, she kissed his soft head. "Then we will name him Philip. I could not think of a more fitting name for the eldest son of Tribune Marcus Virginius Aeneas. We will want our child to be a brave warrior of the cross."

Marcus fought the swelling lump in his throat. It only intensified, bringing the mist to his eyes. "Thanks, dearest," he said, husky. "You have read my heart's desire."

His eyes drifted downwards, taking in every feature of his son. The child was so delicate, so *perfect*. His fingers crept forward, touching the tiny soft ones. With a quick flailing motion, baby Philip grasped onto his father's strong hand and held it.

Emotion rolled over Marcus.

"My son." The desire to weep was strong, but he curtailed it. Everything within him was an aching prayer for his son. "Your namesake is in heaven, but God saw fit to bless us with you in return. I pray you too will be such a witness for Him."

A little while later, Marcus stepped out into the cool gardens.

His cheeks were hot, flushed with the closeness of the room and emotions of seeing his child come into the world. Still, he would have stayed there forever. It was not until the midwife had insisted Moriah needed sleep that he had finally consented to leave her side.

"My lord tribune."

He turned in time to see Alexander stride towards him, making the military salute. The young man extended his hand, warmth clear in his green eyes.

"I wish you a thousand joys, tribune. The Lord's blessing be upon your child."

"Thank you, Alexander." Marcus gripped his hand. Since Philip's death, Alexander had become closer to him than ever. He had not known before what a quiet tower of comfort the young man was. "I am grateful you came."

Alexander seemed to hesitate. "I assume the child and Moriah are asleep?"

"Yes. I would introduce you, but they must rest."

"Agreed." Again, Alexander seemed to linger over his words. His green eyes were strangely diverted. He lapsed into a long, awkward silence.

Marcus looked keenly at him. There was something oddly embarrassed in his manner. Alexander was always open, candid. "Is there something you wish to discuss with me, Alexander?"

"Yes. That is…" Alexander paused. He finally looked up, meeting Marcus's gaze. "There is something I have long desired to speak to you about. I-I think you may already know what about."

Marcus felt a tinge. A bittersweet suspicion of the truth began to settle around his heart. "Continue."

Alexander's green eyes worked with emotion. "Marcus, I love your sister. I think I always have. I don't know when it first began, but…I wish to marry her."

Marcus's mind flew back to the past. *I can have no greater joy than in having you for my brother.* Had it really been a year since he had uttered those words to Philip? His heart swelled, smarting. He had known this day would come, but had not expected the torturous pain of loss it would recall in his heart and mind. Everything within him ached, longing for Philip.

Alexander seemed to read through his silence. "I know I am not the man Philip was." His voice was husky, and he shook his head. "He would have been a far better brother to you. I am nothing compared to him. But, I do love Diantha, Marcus. I—"

"You will be a good husband to her." Marcus stopped him, resting a hand on his shoulder. Alexander's belittling opinion of himself was painful in its unfairness. His throat ached unbearably, but he forced himself to speak. "I loved Philip as perhaps I will never love a friend again, Alexander. But I care deeply for you also. You are a godly man."

"Thank you, tribune." Soft and husky, Alexander's voice warmed. He straightened, making a visible effort to curtail his nervousness. "Then-then I have your consent?"

"If my sister loves you, I cannot refuse." Marcus forced himself to smile. How little he had thought he would be giving Diantha to anyone other than Philip. *Your ways are not our ways, Lord.* But, behind the pain, he knew he was grateful. Jehovah had not left Diantha hopeless.

He stepped to the edge of the garden. Just inside the atrium, he could see Diantha sitting next to the pool. Her fingers were busy, folding tiny tunics for the baby.

Marcus's swelled, seeing the soft smile which parted her scarlet lips. There had been a time when he had never dreamed he would see her smile again. He called softly to her.

"Diantha."

"Yes, Marcus?" Diantha looked up. Her smile widened. "My dear brother, when may I see the child? I am going half-mad, waiting here."

"All in good time, sister." Marcus smiled at her impatience. He beckoned. "First, there is someone else you must see."

Diantha arose, laying aside the baby clothes. She flitted towards him, grace in her every step. Marcus looked at her for a full moment before resting his hands on her shoulders, drawing her against his chest.

"Diantha." He murmured her name, her hair soft against his chin. "Dearest sister, you know how much I love you. And your happiness means more to me than anything."

"As yours does to me, Marcus." Diantha lifted her head, and Marcus caught the turn of her gaze as she looked past him. Her dark eyes warmed and filled simultaneously. She dropped her head onto his shoulder. "Is-is he here for the reason I think?"

"Yes." Marcus pulled her back, tilting her chin. "Diantha, he loves you. I think you've known it for some time. Are you willing?"

Diantha's eyes met his without hesitation. "Yes, Marcus." Her chin trembled and her eyes filled afresh, but she continued. "On that terrible day Philip went home, I never thought I could love again. But, Marcus, I think God brought Alexander into my life to comfort me. He has done much in healing my heart."

"Then you love him?"

"Yes." The pretty color came into Diantha's face. "But there is more to my heart than the love I bear for him. I know it is the will of my Savior that I marry him."

Marcus felt a quiet tug on his heartstrings. He knew she was right. During the last few months, he had seen the blossom of love that had softly sprung up between the valiant young legionary and his sister. In all their pain and loss, Alexander was God's way of comforting them.

He turned, beckoning. For once, he didn't care who saw the mist in his eyes. *Your plan is vast, unsearchable, Lord. And I thank You for it.* Though he doubted he would ever understand why God had taken the friend destined to be his brother, he knew he trusted Him.

And that trust was enough.

Alexander came forward. Marcus smiled at the tender, fervent way he looked at Diantha. Her own gaze was locked into his, blushes sprinkled across her face. He took Alexander's hand and placed Diantha's in it, fighting the emotion welling up within him.

"Alexander, you have her heart. And you have my consent to wed."

A single look into the young couple's faces was enough to ease Marcus's pain into rejoicing. Inhaling deeply, he rested his hand on Alexander's shoulder, causing the young man to momentarily tear his gaze away from Diantha and look at him.

"Legionary."

"My tribune?"

"It has been on my heart to make the necessary adjustments for your promotion." Despite formalities, Marcus could not keep the warmth from his voice. "Of tomorrow, I am approving your transition to centurion of the Praetorian Guards."

"Tribune." Alexander's apparent loss for words was thanks in itself. His laugh hid a deep well of mixed emotions. "I cannot know what to say. I never expected such an honor."

"The time is right." Marcus clapped him on the shoulder. "Congratulations."

"I thank you." Warm and grateful, Alexander's green eyes met his for a full moment before they dropped to the sparkling dark ones beneath him. Diantha's entire countenance shone with pride and love, a wordless tribute to his promotion.

Marcus saw their desire to be alone. Inconspicuously, he slipped from the garden into the atrium. There, he lingered by the fountain.

He looked into the depths of the water. Calm. Tranquil. Always moving, yet encompassed by the strength of the stonework holding it. Could it be its sparkling peace was a mirror to his own heart?

"Yes, Lord." Marcus breathed the words. "You have brought me to peace. Thank you for your sustaining strength."

Behind him, a familiar step echoed through the room. "Marcus."

Marcus turned. Cleotas stepped towards him, his smile warm, wide. It seemed to fill the atrium. He felt the corners of his own lips twitch. His father's joy was contagious.

"I have seen the child." Cleotas nearly wrung his hand off with shaking. "He is beautiful, my son. The gods favor you."

Marcus laughed heartily. It felt good, a rush to his pent-up emotions. "Cletoas, the child and his mother are supposed to be resting." Then, with new huskiness, "But I am glad you have seen him. My Philip will be a tribute to his Lord. And to…his namesake."

The welling mist that sprang unbidden to his eyes was a surprise. But Marcus felt no shame. His gaze drifted back to the calming water, feeling all it represented encompass his very soul. How could grief be so mingled with overwhelming joy, with the peace he could not understand?

"You miss him." Cleotas's voice was low, reverent.

"Yes." Marcus turned to him. "But I would not call him back, father."

Somewhere deep within, a well of praise stirred his heart. He wanted to worship, no matter the loss, the things he didn't understand. Behind it all was the overwhelming knowledge that God was with him.

And, whatever the future held, He would *always* be with him.

Marcus exhaled softly, the bittersweet mist aching in his throat and eyes. The words rushed from his throat, unstoppable. "Cletoas, God used him to teach me and countless others the truth about His love. I know now that *nothing*, neither height, nor depth, nor any other creature shall separate from His love. And I know that is the kind of the love that can turn darkness into a new dawn, stretching farther and brighter than anything we can imagine."

He paused. "So you see, I can let Philip go. His dawn has come. And mine…" The smile deepened, tugging on his lips. "I fear mine is only a glimmer when compared with his. But by Christ's grace, my darkness is gone. And the dawn of our faith is one that will illuminate the world."

Epilogue

Marcus's words were strikingly prophetic. The glorious light of the gospel did illuminate the world. Trials and tribulation continued, but the good news of Christ's abundant salvation traveled across continent and ocean until the world was encompassed with the message of faith and hope.

Two months later, Alexander and Diantha were married. The joyous event was marred, however, by the execution of Paul. The death of the faithful martyr was a crushing blow to the brethren. But, while many wavered under the shock, many more were encouraged in that he had run his race and finished his course with strength.

In the turbulent years that followed, Marcus and Moriah went on to have five children. Raising a family among the political unrest and civil dispute that followed Nero's suicide was difficult, but it is reported that each of them embraced Christianity. While each of their stories are not known, it is certain that the eldest son became a pastor. Philip Virginius Aeneas served faithfully in the catacombs of Rome for many years before he was martyred under Emperor Trajan.

Little is known about the fate of Cleotas. Most say he lived and died a true Roman, loyal to his country's gods. Still, a choice few say he accepted Christ two months before his death. All agree he remained an affluent, popular patrician.

Thallus Quinctia went on to have a successful career and eventually became a chief friend and advisor of the Emperor Domitian. Some say, too, that it was under his diabolic influence that Domitian launched one of the greatest persecutions of the believers in history. Nothing further is known.

Daniel labored among the Christians in Rome for many years. Two years after the fall of the temple in Jerusalem, he returned to his country. There, he served among his own people, preaching the good news and forgiveness of the Savior they had rejected.

Rowland Virginius is reported to have gained exorbitant wealth until his early death in 72 A.D. While the particulars of his death were shrouded in mystery, some say he adopted the Roman idea of honorable suicide. Little is known of his life up until then. Those who knew him claim he lived in bitterness, resenting the Christus-followers who had deprived him of his children.

Philip's memory was never forgotten. His testimony lived on in the hearts of those who had known him and also in those who had not. There were countless individuals who, upon hearing the story of his faithful love for his Savior, surrendered to the Holy Spirit in salvation. Among them was patrician Julius Calussa, master of the young martyr Arswind. He, along with innumerable others, went on to preach the story of sacrifice and redeeming love to a hurting world.

Thus it was that the sting of death was swallowed up in victory, as men, women, and children came to know Christ's wonderful love and forgiveness. Truly, the darkness of sin was wonderfully transformed into the dawn of new hope and eternal salvation.

The End.

Glossary

Throughout this book, you will experience many new words, as well as some Latin and Iceni phrases. Many of them will be italicized. This glossary was designed for your clarification.

Augur - Augurs discerned the future and omens through the intestines of animals and birds. The animals had to be without blemish and were purchased at great expense.

Apodyterium – the changing room at the Baths.

Atrium – the central part of a Roman house, generally decked with fountains, a pool, and statues of the gods.

Avernus – the underworld.

Baths – the public place where the hygiene-conscious Romans bathed, exercised, and enjoyed massages. Games were often played, and the Baths was considered a location for socializing.

Bibliotheca – the library in a Roman home.

Boudica – The queen of the Iceni tribe in ancient Britain. Her rebellion against Rome sparked an uprising that climaxed into the Battle of Watling Street.

Brittania – the Roman name for Britain.

Caldarium – section of the Baths where bathers could enjoy steaming hot water.

Camulodunium, Londinium, and Verulamium – Roman settlements in Britain that were overthrown and pillaged by Queen Boudicca and the Iceni.

Castagatio – the military discipline of a centurion striking a legionary over the back with his grape-vine staff of office.

Castra Praetoria – barracks and training grounds of the Praetorian Guard.

Centurion – Roman officer commanding 80-480 legionaries, known as a *century*. The century was comprised of a *conteburnium* (8 men). Ranked below a tribune.

Cohort – company of soldiers consisting of 480 men, commanded by a centurion.

Crucifixion – a form of execution, in which the unfortunate victim is nailed to a cross. The purpose is to restrict breathing, resulting in the lungs filling with fluid. After many agonizing hours or even days, the victim dies of suffocation.

Culina – kitchen.

Denarii/Denarius – a small silver coin, the most common coin for circulation. The Bible refers to this coin as a day's wages in Matthew 20:2 and John 12:5. It is also referenced in the book of Revelation.

Domus – a wealthy home or mansion of a Roman citizen.

Druids – The pagan cult dominating ancient Britain and many other parts of the world. Their religious practices included human sacrifice and were eventually outlawed by Rome.

Dupondius – a brass coin worth about one-eighth of a *denarius*.

Eagle (*Aquila*) – a prominent standard used in Rome, particularly for the legions. In many senses, it was worshipped.

Elysium – Roman/Greek form of heaven.

Flagellum – a small whip, often containing sharp pieces of glass. The term used to describe this form of beating is *flagellation* or scouring. It was often a prelude to crucifixion. Known as half-death, there was no limit under the law to the amount of times a victim could be struck. Slaves and criminals were often severally disfigured. Trauma, death by blood loss, and shock were all common results. Ritual *flagellation* was also practiced for Roman citizens.

Gladius – a Roman sword. Short and efficient, it was used primarily for stabbing.

Goths – Germans. Many of them were captured during Roman conquests and sold as slaves.

Imperial Forum(*Fora*) – the public square (or, more correctly, *series* of squares) and center of the Roman Republic and Empire. Located near the Roman Forum, it contained shops, temples, monuments, etc.

Judea – the term used to refer to the Roman province of Judea (Biblical Judah), Samaria and Idmea (Biblical Edom).

Lanista – trainer of the gladiators. Often, lanistas also worked with the legionaries.

Legionary – a private in the Roman army.

Mulsum – honeyed wine.

Optio – the officer directly below a centurion. He generally served as his centurion's assistant.

Pallium – a cape worn by Roman men, considered suitable to be worn over the toga.

Patrician – a nobleman.

Peristyle – an area edging the gardens, not unlike our modern patios.

Peristylium – an open courtyard in a Roman home.

Pilum – Roman spear.

Plato – a philosopher in ancient Greece.

Plebians – often referred to by the slang term "plebs", this was the commoner or middle class citizen of Rome. They were often the shopkeepers and laborers; the working class.

Praetorian Guard – the elite section of the Roman army which guarded the person of the emperor. They were considered the highest-trained company of soldiers in the entire army.

Prefect – an official of high rank; commander of the Praetorian Guard.

Probatio – basic training.

Pugio – a dagger.

Rod – an instrument of punishment in Rome, commonly used on slaves. Also the Caesars bore the Imperials Rod(s) called *Fasces*, signifying they had the power to punish whoever they chose. Though this is not commonly known, this symbol is used in many parts of our American government, including in the National Guard Bureau insignia.

Scourging – a form of beating that was considered commonplace in Rome. Brutally savage, it was reserved for criminals and slaves. Certain forms were also used with soldiers.

Stola – a sleeveless dress; a female garment.

Strigil – an instrument used by the Romans to scrape off the olive oil they used in place of soap.

Subura – slum district of Rome.

Suetonius – Gaius Suetonius Paullinus was the Roman commander who crushed the Iceni rebellion. His rigorous activities dealing with the Iceni were ultimately considered too harsh by Emperor Nero, resulting in his replacement.

Toga – a white garment worn by Roman citizens.

Tribune (military) – Roman officer commanding *legions* (5,400 – 16,000 men) comprised of *cohorts* (480 men) which were, in turn, comprised of *centuries* (80 men). Ranked below the *legate*, or, general of Praetorian rank.

Triclinium – the dining room.

Vale – Roman form of saying goodbye.

Vestibule – the entry way.

Vicus Jugarius – street meaning "street of the yoke makers".

Vicus Tuscus – a main street meaning "Tuscus Road".

Pagan Gods Referenced Throughout the Book

Anextiomarus – Druid/British god of protection.

Aphrodite – Greek goddess of love, beauty, protection, pleasure, and procreation. Her Roman equivalent is *Venus*.

Bacchus – the god of revelry, drinking/drunkenness, and pleasure.

Forest Spirits – the Britons worshipped countless gods, but they also revered nature. Trees, rocks, water–virtually everything–was thought to contain spirits.

Hercules – Roman version of the Greek god Hercales, son of Zeus (Roman equivalent *Jupiter*). Hercules was known for his many adventures and was a reproduction god. He was referenced in weddings and was a deity concerned with children and childbirth.

Janus – god of beginnings, transitions, and time. He often was portrayed with two faces, one looking to the future, and one to the past.

Jove /Jupiter – King of the gods. He was also the god of the sky and thunder. His symbols were the sacred eagle and thunderbolts.

Mars – God of war and agriculture. He was second only to Jupiter and Neptune. Not surprisingly, he was the patron god of the army.

Nemesis – Greek god of revenge; a sort of monster.

Neptune – Roman god of freshwater and the sea.

Pluto – ruler of the underworld.

Pollux – twin brother of Castor, he was the divine son of Zeus (Jupiter). To keep him and his brother together, he requests permission for them to become the constellation Gemini. The pair is regarded as the patrons of sailors and will appear as St. Elmo's Fire. Strangely, they are both mortal and divine. They are particularly worshipped as gods of the athlete and helpers of mankind.

Venus – goddess of love, beauty, fertility, prosperity, sensuality. She was the mother of the Roman people. Julius Caesar claimed ancestry with her. Not surprisingly, her worship was a central part of Roman festivals and lifestyles.

Vesta – virgin goddess of the home, hearth, and family. Her presence was signified by the sacred flame, and she was ministered to by a group of women known as the Vestal Virgins. She was a symbol of and protector of Rome.

Names Referring to the One True God

Holy Trinity:

God the Father: Adonai, Jehovah, Jehovah-Rapha.
God the Son: Jesus, Jesus Christ, Christus.
God the Holy Spirit.

All usage of the term *God* refers to Elohim.

www.ingramcontent.com/pod-product-compliance
Lightning Source LLC
Chambersburg PA
CBHW071143020726
47502CB00002B/249